MW00331664

Colours in the Spectrum

Jayant Swamy

FROG BOOKS

First published in India 2013 by Frog Books
An imprint of Leadstart Publishing Pvt Ltd
1 Level, Trade Centre
Bandra Kurla Complex
Bandra (East) Mumbai 400 051 India
Telephone: +91-22-40700804
Fax: +91-22-40700800
Email: info@leadstartcorp.com
www.leadstartcorp.com / www.frogbooks.net

Sales Office:
Unit: 122 / Building B/2
First Floor, Near Wadala RTO
Wadala (East) Mumbai 400 037 India
Phone: +91-22-24046887

US Office:
Axis Corp, 7845 E Oakbrook Circle
Madison, WI 53717 USA

ISBN 978-93-82473-63-3

Book Editor: Surojit Mohan Gupta
Design Editor: Mishta Roy

Typeset in Book Antiqua
Printed at Nikeda Art Printers Pvt Ltd, Mumbai

Price — India: Rs 245; Elsewhere: US $16

Dedicated to Dear Departed
My Beloved Dad Narasimha Swamy

Faith consists in believing when it is beyond the power of reason to believe (Voltaire)

Acknowledgements

The process of writing is a very personal exercise. Empowering yet liberating, at the same time. Writing indeed gives us the freedom to express whatever we want in whichever way we deem fit. Yet we rarely ever write for ourselves. We want our readers to fall in love with our writing; and, we are very wary of outraging their sensibilities. Fortunate am I, that a host of early readers helped me harmonize dichotomies such as these!

Suma Maheshchandra, Kevin Scott, Syed Pasha, Erin Moore, Deborah Thomas, Nandini Sekhar and Raju K H -- THANK YOU all for investing the time and effort to read the earlier drafts. Without your honest feedback, this novel would not have been in the shape it is today!

Special Thanks to Scott Driscoll for reviewing the manuscript and offering valuable guidance.

I am deeply thankful to Swarup Nanda and the Leadstart Publishing team for reposing faith in me and publishing my first novel.

While writing itself is a solitary activity, the process of publishing a book is a confirmed team exercise. I want to thank Surojit Mohan Gupta -- the Editor and Mishta Roy -- the Cover Artist, for elegantly applying their craft and enhancing the appeal of my novel, Hema Muthya -- Graphic and Web Designer, for the website and Barbara Kindness -- Publicist, for marketing and promotion guidance (USA).

I want to raise a special toast to my friends Ashok and Jake and the members of my writing group, who have played significant roles in my journey to become a published author.

Often, the ones we love the most are the ones we forget to acknowledge. I will take this opportunity to express my deep appreciation to my mother Prema, my wife Vidhya, my brother Arun and my nephew Ahan -- for their everlasting patience and never-ending support.

Above all, I am eternally grateful to the supreme guiding force above us, the Almighty, and my Gurus, for bestowing upon me the grace and blessings to make this happen.

Contents

Prelude: An August Night

Three seemingly unrelated incidents. Same day. Same place. The first day of August 1962. St. Xavier Hospital in the heart of the garden city of Bangalore.

It was a rainy night, the whistling winds sounding like wailing banshees. Not unusual for *Shraavan*, the most auspicious month of the Hindu calendar, which had just begun. The waning moon was but a thin strip, barely visible in the starless sky. Amidst the vast expanse of vacant land, the stonewalls of the hospital rose majestically in the dim road light; frequently the lights would go out and plunge the huge stone structure in an eerie darkness.

St. Xavier Hospital was one of the best-maintained hospitals of Bangalore, well known for discipline and hygiene -- two factors ingrained into the system by years and years of British rule. Hospitals, along with convent schools, were indeed the most valuable legacies independent India had inherited from the British who had departed fifteen years earlier after having governed her for centuries and decades before that.

On the top floor of the hospital, a young woman had died during childbirth. Being from an upper-class family, she had done so in the privacy of the special labour ward; her handsome husband sat on the white chair beside the bed, looking at his dead wife, staring at the thin lips that met in a straight line. For a fleeting moment, his eyes looked relieved, even joyous perhaps.

In the quiet confines of the hospital nursery, their cherubic child lay in a white crib with a blue satin sash. Unaware yet sentient, the child was crying his guts out. Karan. That was the name his father was going to choose for him.

In the general labour ward, another young woman from a middle-class family had died during childbirth. Her frail-looking husband's wailing was heartrending as he held the thin brown child lovingly to his chest, completely oblivious of the people teeming around him. The dull blue fluorescent light cast an ominous glow on the spotless white sheet covering the dead body.

The thin brown child, ensconced in the warm arms of his father, slept soundlessly -- blissfully unaware of his mother's death. Arjun. That was the name his mother had chosen for him.

There was commotion of another sort outside the hospital. An ambulance was bringing in the body of a young man in his late twenties, his face disfigured beyond recognition. He had been speeding on his brand-new motorbike in the rain when a lone bus, a rare occurrence at that time of the night, had collided with the bike, smashing it to pieces and killing him instantly. The immobile man was unaware that his young wife, who was at that moment waiting for him to return home, was carrying the seed of his progeny -- their second child who was to be christened Aarti.

Just as the ambulance pulled up at the hospital entrance, the road lights -- out of their own will and volition -- decided to perform yet another switching off act, plunging the scene in darkness and chaos. Cries of outrage could be heard as matches were struck again and again, until the stretcher had been wheeled into the sanitized hospital corridors.

Purpose served, the spent matchboxes were abandoned and strewn on the driveway, as the stretcher continued to be wheeled into the autopsy room for the post-mortem, the doors closing after it anonymously. The motley crowd of strangers who had discharged their civic duty to the dead stranger had dispersed soon after to be absorbed back into the monotony of their routines.

Three seemingly unrelated incidents. Encompassing the eternal cycle from which there is no escape. Birth. Death. Conception.

Birth. The power of the unknown. Signifying promising futures.

Death. The only proof of certainty in this uncertain world. Terminating unknown futures abruptly.

Conception. The precursor to birth.

Everything in this world happens for a reason. Who would think that the three incidents could be intertwined intricately? Karan, Arjun, and Aarti, bound separately to three individual tragedies, will meet, become fast friends; bonds will develop. The magical Five Star Café will bind them. What they will never learn though is that The God Almighty set up these bonds on this fateful day. The first day of August 1962.

Part One

1. Love Is Not Love Until You Give It Away

June 1 1998

Karan picked up the envelope from the centre table and slit it open with a butter knife. He stared at the DNA test results that unequivocally established Dolly's birthright. Until now, there had been a fifty-fifty chance that he was Dolly's biological father -- the uncertainty of the paternity factor had kept Karan's hopes alive. The single piece of paper that lay before him had destroyed that sea of chance, pushing him into an ocean of rueful certainty. So much for statistical probability. When the outcome is known, probability has no meaning. It is either a yes or a no. One or zero. Like it or not, it is black or white.

"I am taking her with me Mr Karan Khanna." Troy had an air of overbearing pompousness. "Have her stuff packed as quickly as you can . . ." Troy remained seated on the leather settee in the living room of Karan's downtown Pasadena townhome.

Karan had long accepted that life was unfair. Did it have to be this unfair? What would life be without Dolly? Karan stared at the child who had rejuvenated his life. Perched on Troy's shoulder, Dolly was laughing away as Troy tickled her. She had no clue of the magnitude of change happening in her life -- her newfound biological father was soon to take her away.

Indeed. The DNA document had ousted Karan from Dolly's life. He was everything except her biological father. He was her soon to be ex-legal guardian. Her mother's ex-paramour. Her stay-at-home nanny until this day, this hour, when her custody was being claimed. Troy, the blue-eyed blond guy who had confidently stormed into Karan's house uninvited only minutes back, engaged in a heated discussion with him and dropped the undeniable proof of his paternity on the centre table, was Dolly's biological father. Indeed.

****

The morning had dawned bright and beautiful. Karan was watching Bollywood's belated version of *Kramer vs. Kramer*, titled *Akele Hum Akele Tum*, on the new DVD player. Dolly was taking a mid-morning nap. "*Tu mera dil tu meri jaan . . . Oh I love you daddy . . . .*" The poignant father-son song from the movie threatened to make his eyes moist when he heard the doorbell ring.

A tall muscular blond haired man with blue eyes was at the door. "Hello bud, good to see you," Troy held out his hand.

Karan motioned him to come in. He felt something was terribly wrong.

Troy settled down on the leather settee. He seemed to be in high spirits. Karan froze the movie with the remote and offered Troy a hot beverage.

"I want my daughter." Troy pushed the curly locks of his blond hair away from his forehead. "You will give her back to me."

"Where were you when Dolly was born? When Sharon was in labour?" Karan settled down on the futon facing Troy. His rage roared as his mind recited Troy's one-liner. *I want my daughter. I want my daughter. I want my daughter. . .*

"I was a jerk," Troy capitulated.

"You never accepted your responsibility. I was the one who took care of Sharon when she was pregnant, even went to Lamaze with her . . . ," Karan expostulated.

"That is why I am here. To make up for my lapses."

"Sharon was *my* girlfriend. *You* betrayed me."

"Dude. Sharon and I both wanted to get laid."

"When I found out that she was pregnant with a child that was not mine, do you even understand what I went through?"

"Don't hold me responsible for her actions. She was the boss of her."

"I was sharing her body with you, never having known it. Every time I had sex with her, I was touching you, tasting you, smelling you."

"Dude, you make it sound like you and I made out through some theory shit." Troy guffawed.

"Theory of transitivity." Karan said condescendingly. "Do you even realize how repulsive the whole situation was?"

"I never as much as smelt your cologne on her." Troy wiggled a finger at Karan.

"And then, you did not want to marry her." Karan's face turned beet red.

Troy shrugged. "So what's your problem man?"

"I was the one who bore the burden of your follies . . . ," Karan choked on his words.

"I didn't ask you to do it." Troy shrugged.

"Then why do you want Dolly back now?" Karan exploded.

Troy's face broke out into a stealthy smile, that of a crooked winner. "It is my right."

"Parenting is not a random affliction you selectively indulge in when you feel like it." Karan was shouting.

"Dolly is my daughter." Troy waved a copy of Dolly's birth

certificate in front of Karan's face.

Karan looked down at the document. Troy Fond. The entry against the box for the father's name stared back at him victoriously.

Dolly was orange. Pain was orange too. I do not want to lose Dolly. "I ask that you leave."

Troy stood up. "Dude, what if I have my lawyer call you?"

Troy was raven black -- as always. "Can you ever give Dolly the same kind of love and commitment as I have?" Karan asked Troy earnestly.

"Cut it, sissy boy."

"You have come here out of guilt. You are not ready for a family." Karan was like a drowning man willing to hold onto the flimsiest straw to save his life.

Karan watched as Troy looked around the living room, at the floor covered with Dolly's toys, at the entertainment centre filled with pictures of Dolly, at the pile of baby clothes stacked on the dining table, his apprehension writ large on his translucent face.

Karan was sure Troy was wondering if it was fair to tear Dolly away from the doting father that Karan was. "What if you cannot take it after six months and want out? What will you do then? Give her up for adoption?" He continued to exploit Troy's transition from aggressive bully to self-doubting Dumbo.

Troy stood staring at Karan like he had never thought long-term.

"Do that now. Let me keep her." Karan pleaded.

At that moment, Karan heard Dolly crying. He rushed into the bedroom to pick her up. Despite his best attempts, Dolly's sobs got louder and louder. Eventually, he had no choice but to bring her into the living room with him. Much against his wishes.

Troy had again made himself comfortable on the leather settee.

For some reason Dolly stopped crying at that exact moment. She kept looking at Troy like she was mesmerized.

Troy extracted a small colourful globe from his pocket and held it out to Dolly.

A flash of dirty red. Karan recognized it as an expensive pendant he had bought for Sharon; it was made of gems and semi-precious stones. Sharon had fancied it at a curio shop when holidaying at Lake Tahoe. To think Sharon had given it away to Troy!

"Coo. Coo." Dolly made a grab for the colourful object in Troy's hand. She held her hands out to Troy as if asking him to carry her. Soon, perched on Troy's shoulder, Dolly was laughing away as Troy tickled her and cuddled her close to his chest.

"I know how to have my way." Troy had dropped an envelope on the centre table.

****

Karan dropped the DNA test document on the table and walked into the bedroom. It was a late spring morning -- the day was hot and sticky. He reached out to switch on the table fan -- the town home did not have air-conditioning -- when he found the silver letters on the white album sitting next to the fan staring at him.

Karan opened the album and looked at the pictures. He had clicked them the previous day -- he had organized a picnic party at Disneyland to celebrate Dolly's first birthday. The *It's a Small World* ride had been her favourite. They had taken the ride three times. The tune was still stuck in Karan's head.

Karan had wanted to make the day memorable and gone on a clicking spree so he could show her the pictures when she grew up. He had wanted to create pleasant memories she would look back on fondly, sometime in the distant future.

Dolly was orange. Pain was orange too. So was pleasure. The dull ache

in his heart evoked by the happy moments he had spent with Dolly was
orange too. Was that pain or pleasure? Pain no doubt.

It had indeed turned out to be a memorable first birthday. Karan
would never forget it as long as he lived. Dolly would never learn
about it as long as he lived. Karan stashed away the picture album
in his safety locker box. No matter what, Dolly would constantly
remain in his thoughts.

Karan packed Dolly's belongings -- her clothes, her crib, her
toys, and the child seat -- he would not keep even a single item
that would remind him of her. Packing over, Karan silently
placed Dolly's belongings in the living room. Troy started to take
out the packed bags and load them in the SUV parked outside
on the street.

Dolly who was crawling all over the carpet cooing
incomprehensible syllables rushed toward Karan. When Karan
picked her up and held her close to his heart, Dolly snuggled up
to him and buried her little head in the folds of his shirt as she
always did. The touch of her soft arms around his neck, the feel
of her sweet baby breath on his neck, the smell of baby shampoo
in her hair . . . Karan closed his eyes to savour the moments for
one last time.

He could remember every significant detail of the 365 days Dolly
had spent with him -- the day she was born, the day she had not
stopped crying, holding her breath for a whole minute and freaking
him out, the day she had said her first word, the day she had cut
her finger and made his heart skip a beat, the day she had started
walking, her uncontrollable laughter the previous day on the *It's a
small world* ride at Disneyland . . . .

The front door clicked again. Troy had come back in to collect
the car seat -- he must have finished loading Dolly's bags in the
SUV.

"Dolly is allergic to orange juice. She hates having a bath.
She will not eat her cereal without her favourite doll, the Barbie

princess. She loves the colour yellow. She has a great imagination; she chatters endlessly . . . . " Karan handed Troy a checklist.

Troy nodded his head uninterestedly and headed out of the door with the car seat. Karan had no choice but to follow him, with Dolly, who was falling asleep, on his shoulder.

"Please feed her at one o'clock next. Her baby food and diet chart are both in the yellow overnight bag. She is a fussy eater . . . ."

Troy revved up the engine of the SUV. The final moment had arrived. Karan strapped Dolly into the car seat.

"Be kind to her. I have never raised my voice against her." Karan's throat was choked. He rushed back inside the house before Troy could drive away, locked himself in the bedroom and reached into his medicine cabinet for Dr Forrester's prescription pills -- long forgotten and unused. Having washed two pills down his gullet with a tall glass of water he lay down on the bed.

I am good at heart, I never wish ill for others. Yet my life is a series of miseries. Why? Because my mind is a battleground? Or the other way round?

The squeals and laughs of the children swimming in the community swimming pool could be heard outside.

His emotional resilience had been his biggest asset; it was becoming his biggest drawback as well. If he had not possessed that quality, would Fate have been compelled to be kinder to him? Gradually Karan drifted off into a soporific slumber induced by the pills.

He is driving along the endless freeway. Days, weeks, months, years, eons. Every time he tries to get off an exit ramp he finds himself promptly back on the freeway. Resigned to his fate, as he is approaching a tunnel, he sees a familiar figure walking toward him -- olive complexion, kind eyes, caring smile. The fine lines of wrinkles on the large forehead are new. Yet they add character to the face that has since aged.

He keeps driving. Stop or swerve? Neither happens. The car seems to have acquired a mind of its own.

The figure walks right into the car through the windshield and drops a box on the car seat.

He opens the box. It is filled with all his favourite possessions, the family heirlooms. The ivory box with gold inlay. The set of six silver hairbrushes. The gold-lined tiger claw dangling from a thin gold chain. The antique pocket watch. The solitaire diamond set in a platinum ring.

How have they all come to be here? Had he not preserved them in a safe deposit locker back at the Bank of Bangalore?

Karan opened his eyes. There was nobody in the room. The sun's rays filtered in through the open slits of the venetian blinds. For a fraction of a second, Karan thought he saw splashes of colour. *Royal indigo. Soothing lavender. Bright purple.*

For the first time since he had come to the US, Karan had the greatest yearning to go back to Bangalore. In the thirteen-and-a-half years he had lived in LA, he had never once returned home -- not even for a holiday -- he had no one to go back home to. In moments of distress, Karan missed his friends. Aarti, Indu, Arjun, Danny. He had no address, no telephone number for any of them -- there was no way he could correspond with them.

Danny. Wait. The figure in the vision handing him the family heirlooms could have been none other than Danny. When Karan had stashed away those things in the Bank of Bangalore, Danny was the only one who had been with him.

The swimming pool was still busy -- he could hear voices.

Hmmm. The hateful words he had hurled at Danny -- that fateful day back in 1984 just before leaving for the US -- reverberated in the depths of Karan's memory. Why oh why had he taken such a derogatory stance?

The spring sun was setting -- the burning orange ball could be seen through the window.

Little Dolly has been taken away. He remembered with a start. How would he spend the rest of his life without her, his little angel? Was it only the previous day that he had organized a picnic party at Disneyland? It seemed like ages ago.

Karan got out of the bed with a jerk. It was exactly a year since Sharon's death -- she had died the day after Dolly was born. Sharon had reposed enormous faith in him that he would look after her daughter, their daughter. Yet how easily he had lost little Dolly! He had failed her too. Why had he capitulated so easily to the domineering Troy? The DNA document of course.

Dolly was orange. Orange. Orange? Why could he not see colour? Karan closed his eyes. Try harder, try harder. He could still not see any colour flash in his mind's eye. Was he bereft of his special gift -- his ability to perceive people in colour, experience emotions with an associated colour? Karan was consumed by an intense wave of panic. Had he been robbed of the only bright spot in his unpleasantly eventful life?

Karan had to get out of the house. He unlocked the bedroom door, picked up his car keys and rushed out toward his car parked on the street. Soon he was zooming on the freeway at break-neck speed. The late spring sun had just set.

Danny had probably loved him deeply. Karan's heart filled with remorse. Karan could not have reciprocated Danny's feelings -- not in the way he wanted.

The traffic on I-5 South was light at that hour; as he approached the tunnel, he had a sense of déjà vu. Had he not been driving along the same freeway in the vision? He almost expected Danny to walk right into the car through the windshield and drop a box on the car seat as he drove down the tunnel.

Ironical. Karan had always given everything he had, to every relationship -- in fact way too much. If only he had found one woman who loved him as much? Indu. Sharon. Sofia. Fauzia. Did he miss anyone? Of course. Daphne. Nita. Nimmi.

Some stray one-night stands. No love for you Karan. Only sex please . . .

The car had reached the end of the tunnel. The city lights twinkled in the near horizon.

Everyone craves that one thing they lack in life. It was cruel that he had been betrayed out of receiving that one thing he yearned for. Unconditional Love.

Karan continued driving until he had reached La Jolla -- a long walk on the beaches in the moonlit night accompanied by the soothing rhythm of the Pacific Ocean would clear his head.

Maybe there was a message in the vision. That he should go back to Bangalore and find a way to redress the grave injustice he had meted out to Danny. That would be his own redemption as well. Maybe he would then meet the perfect woman who would love him as much as he would love her. Maybe more.

2. Silicon City

June 18 1998

Karan shifted his aching butt in the cramped plane seat for the millionth time. Twenty-four-and-a-half hours in the air with a three-hour stopover en route. He could not wait for the journey to end. The flight was full -- was every Indian in Los Angeles travelling to Bangalore?

His mind was in turmoil. His dreams were dead -- none of the women he had fallen in love with had returned his love; Dolly, the little angel he had lovingly parented, had been taken away from him. He was bogged down with frustrations he could not erase, that haunted him interminably and tortured him continually.

The flight attendant was announcing that preparations were on for landing. After thirteen years and more, he was home. Older and wiser. Sans the only gift he had ever possessed -- the ability to perceive people in colour.

The aircraft hit the ground with a cacophonous thud. The dusty smell of the Indian earth drifted in through the open doors.

He could not think of one thing that gave him solace. Would things ever work out for him? He did not know. What did the future hold for him? He was not sure.

Minutes later, Karan was walking through the dilapidated hallways of the airport to join the tail end of the line waiting to clear immigration. People bustled all around him, jostling him as they went. The air was heavy with the commingled smells of their sweat. The three ceiling fans that rotated noisily above did little to freshen the air. He found it suffocating to be surrounded by so many people. Though it only took a few minutes to clear immigration, he felt it was longer.

Karan trudged along to pick up his bags. A rickety conveyor belt rotated slowly, very slowly, making a whirring noise. He watched from a distance as people rushed to grab their luggage, getting in each other's way, nudging others away, disentangling themselves victoriously once they had their trunks and suitcases. He studiously avoided looking at the local touts approaching and offering to haul his bags for him. While he did not mind paying -- a few dollars would have made them happy -- he was scared they would run away with his luggage.

An hour later, Karan was still waiting. The conveyor belt continued to rotate creakily, but its surface was bare. The crowds had disappeared. Karan felt left out. He was the only passenger who had not found his bags.

He was hot under the bright green spring sweater he was wearing. It was close to noon. Rivulets of sweat trickled down his body and soaked the fabric of his undershirt. He felt dizzy and disoriented. To make matters worse, he could sense the beginning of bowel pangs in his underbelly. He looked around in panic. He had to get home soon. With or without his luggage. He did not even want to consider the possibility of using a public toilet at the airport.

At that moment, he saw a thin, dark man in khaki clothes beckoning him from the far end of the room, a local tout no doubt. He had Karan's luggage on a trolley! "Khanna Sir?" he queried.

Karan could not figure out for the life of him how this man had figured out who he was. Even as Karan followed him silently, the khaki-clad man deftly weaved his way through, and Karan could not stop marvelling, when the man waved his hands at the customs officials and they let him pass without a glance at the contents of the trolley.

No sooner did Karan exit the portals of the airport than he was hounded by scores of khaki-clad men. "Taxi Sir. Auto Sir. Two-hundred-and-twenty Rupees. Fixed rate . . . ."

Again, the thin man came to Karan's rescue. He shooed them away, wheeled Karan's luggage to a white Maruti van, loaded them and slid the back door open. Karan hopped in and rattled off his home address. The thin, dark man got into the driver seat, revved the engine.

Karan laid his head on the soft velvet, thankful for the air-conditioned comfort and the dark-tinted glass windows that would shield him from the hot afternoon sun. In his memory, Bangalore had never been this hot before -- the dry dust was irritating Karan's throat and skin.

The driver must have switched on the car radio. "*Pardesi, Pardesi jaana nahin mujhe chod ke* [Outsider please do not go away leaving me behind] . . . ." crooned the latest singing sensation in filmdom.

The white van gambolled along the uneven streets at twenty kilometres an hour, its trajectory impeded by passing buses and trucks, cars and autos, cycles and scooters, motorcycles and mopeds. The metamorphosis amazed Karan. Was this really the same obscure, laid-back garden city, once known as the pensioner's paradise?

M.G. Road, Brigade Road -- nothing was recognizable any more. Malls and business centres had sprouted -- granite and marble, steel and glass, contrasting strongly with the cement and concrete, brick and whitewash. Retail shops thronged the roads; people thronged the shops. Rex, Plaza, Galaxy, Symphony -- the queues outside the movie theatres were long. Even on a hot weekday afternoon. Co-ed crowds and college students dominated -- they were so fashionably dressed. The outcome of India's liberalization of which he had only read, stared him in the face.

The roads were filled with compact cars of different colours -- red, white, pale blue, beige, brown, navy blue, green, metallic blue, red . . . mostly Maruti. The colourless Fiats and Ambassadors he remembered so well seemed almost extinct. Chit Chat, the popular ice cream parlour where he had hung out frequently as a teenager, was gone. In its place stood a tall skyscraper. The roadside vendors remained. As did the beggars. A thin smile veneered Karan's lips -- beggars were respectfully referred to as panhandlers back in the US.

Karan looked at the passing scenery as the van continued its journey. The Cubbon Park -- Bangalore's pride -- the roads lined with red gulmohars, pink cassias, and purple jacarandas peeking amidst profuse greenery; the High Court building in brick red, the Vidhana Soudha in white and gold . . . . Wait a minute -- what was happening? Why were there two buildings? Vidhana Soudha was being replicated. That was awful. Was it not a landmark building, being the seat of the state legislature?

The van sped along Cunningham Road and Queens Road, lined with the big corporate houses -- Hewlett Packard, Texas Instruments, Motorola, Oracle, Siemens -- Bangalore was no longer just a country cousin of the bay area. It was the new Silicon City -- just as the management guru Tom Peters had predicted years back in his book *The Pursuit of Wow!* The van driver had taken a circuitous route to make some extra bucks. Karan smiled to himself.

"*Yeh mera India. I love my India. Yeh duniya. Ek dulhan. Ek maathey ki bindiya. Yeh mera India* [The world is a bride. India is like an adornment on the world's forehead. This is my India] . . . ." A different song blared from the radio. The van circled back toward Cubbon Park, zipped past the Town Hall, whizzed past the Asoka Pillar and entered South Bangalore with its broad boulevards, rose-garden dividers, and parallel side roads, and finally approached the familiar neighbourhood where Karan had grown up.

The road was freshly asphalted and seemed wider than he remembered. Nevertheless, much narrower than what he was used to in the US. There had apparently been a random sprinkling of rain -- the dry dust had turned into damp, sweet-smelling mud. The familiarity of the smell reminded him of his mother -- she had always joked that Bangalore had four seasons -- summer, winter, rainy, and cloudy -- every day.

The neighbourhood had changed some. The once vacant sites now boasted office buildings that housed software firms and finance companies. The slew of petty shops that had stood at the corner of the road had collectively transformed into PARADE, a department store with a revolving glass door and a brand-new Citibank ATM at the entrance. The twin buildings at the opposite corner of the road were brightly painted -- yellow, orange, green -- housing an orphanage, ANAATHA RAKSHAKA.

Karan's old house, the three-storied bungalow, looked forlorn -- the exterior walls colourless, the old-fashioned windows layered with dust, the doors in dire need of polish; in deep contrast with the thriving liveliness of the neighbouring houses -- smart stucco finish, manicured lawns, modern Georgian windows, barking dogs, incessant chatter of playing children, and the affectionate admonition of their irate parents.

No one paid attention to the lone man who got out of the dusty cab. Karan felt depressed. If only his parents, Vikramaditya and Anita, were alive. If only he had been blessed with a brother or sister. Alas, he was an only child. Everyone's envy. No one's pride. Why did that sound familiar? "Neighbour's envy, owner's pride" had been the tag line of a popular commercial of the eighties for Onida TV.

Karan paid off the cab driver handsomely with a few dollars. Maharaj, the old family cook, opened the gate and silently took the luggage inside. Karan had appointed him the caretaker of his bungalow before leaving for the US.

Inside, the stuffed bison and antlered stag heads adorning the drawing room walls, that seemingly fixed their cold unwelcoming stares on him, were worn out. The once-white mosaic floor was a muddy brown. Something familiar was missing. Aah! The carpets. Silk and wool. Kashmiri and Persian. In vivid colours and intricate patterns. Pomegranate red and burgundy. Emerald green and auburn. Ivory white and peach. Maharaj had probably stowed them away to reduce his maintenance activities. Only the tiger skin rug remained -- rendered threadbare though.

The sofas were bedraggled. Only one of the four stools made from sawn-off elephant legs mounted on a brass base remained. The curtains were faded. Their patterns brought back memories of his mother. In the dining room, the once-white refrigerator was spotted with dirty fingerprints and crusted with food stains.

Karan had the strongest urge to roll on the floor and break into tears. Moreover, an even stronger urge to flee, take the next flight back. He rushed into the bathroom instead.

The white-and-blue bathroom tiles were chipped. There was grime underneath his feet. The exhaust fan did not work. His nostrils burned from the strong disinfecting stench of phenyl. A cockroach scurried through the nooks and corners. Karan pressed the flush as hard as he could. Contrary to his expectation water gushed into the toilet bowl with full force.

Three tall stainless steel buckets of steaming hot water awaited him at the other end of the bathroom, for an old-fashioned bath. Karan stripped off his clothes, dropped them in the old cane hamper, and dipped a stainless steel jug in the bucket to pour the water over his head. This was a new bathing experience for him -- even as a kid he had always taken a shower -- now the showerhead was rusty with disuse.

A full hour later when he came out of the bathroom and entered the bedroom he found his suitcase unpacked and his clothes laid out for him. Just like old times.

The room smelled musty from the old air conditioner rattling away noisily. Karan donned a pair of linen lounge pants and vigorously dried his wet hair with the towel he had just unwrapped from his waist. The afternoon sun mildly scorched the delicate layers of his skin through the huge glass windows. He rubbed a stick of Armani deodorant under his armpits, slipped on an old cotton crew neck, and slicked his damp hair back with his fingers.

A piping-hot thali meal awaited him in the dining room. Maharaj, a short plump man in a white butler's uniform, stood by the dining table obsequiously and readily refilled Karan's plate at regular intervals. Aah -- the luxury of life in India. Savouring the flavour of the simple home-cooked meal, Karan soon forgot that only a few minutes earlier, he was contemplating to return to LA.

In the bedroom, the four-poster bed in teak-and-white cedar had been prepared -- even the huge mosquito net canopy was intact. The white sheets and pillows, though old, were fresh and inviting after the arduous, intercontinental journey, the ensuing hot bath, and the culminating home-cooked meal. Maharaj as caretaker had indeed taken great care to make Karan's arrival as comfortable as he could. Almost instantaneously, Karan was snoring away.

****

The next morning dawned bright and cheerful. Ensconced in the comforting contours of his old bed, Karan had slept continually for sixteen hours -- his body seemed determined to eradicate the jetlaggedness in a single stroke.

Karan toured the old house with a loving languor -- a tall glass of steaming filter-coffee in hand. Memories everywhere -- they brought back a dull ache in his heart.

Karan lingered in Anita's music room, shaking off the dust on her array of musical instruments -- the *veena*, the violin, the *sitar*, and a *tanpura*; he stood staring at the garlanded photographs of Vikramaditya and Anita in the *pooja* room, his mind engaged in many a silent prayer; he longingly arranged and rearranged Vikramaditya's belongings in the master bedroom and the library.

Anita had been green. Sometimes white. Vikramaditya, blue. Since his childhood, Karan had possessed the ability to perceive people with an aura of colour. He would experience certain emotions with an associated colour as well, seeing the colour flash, sort of in the mind's eye. He had secretly enjoyed the experience of seeing people and associating his feelings in colour. It had made life more interesting and fun. Alas, the day little Dolly had been taken away from him the gift of colour had also deserted him.

His friends -- what had become of them? Karan went back down the stairs to the dining room, out through the side door and walked about fifty feet in the untended garden, along the short driveway that led to the spare garage, which had been their *adda*.

The Five Star Café -- they had christened it and semi-jokingly attributed magical powers to it. He opened one of the doors -- the notice posted on the inside of the garage door remained.

> This is to notify that the Café has officially closed its doors -- under the current management -- the charter members are dispersing, pursuing their separate ambitions in life You are welcome to take the stars if you promise not to fight over possession of more than one star each. The stars are magical and will bring good luck to the person in possession. While the Café is not inhabited, the peaceful power will be in effect. So, if you are in town and having one of those rough days, you may take advantage. If you desire the Five Star Café can be reopened under new management . . . all ingredients are left behind, at your disposal. It has been a most interesting venture. *Kabhi Alvida Na Kehna* [Never Say Goodbye].

P.S: There will be no new management. The Café will reopen when we all meet here again.

Karan went inside and opened the small windows at the far end of the garage for ventilation. Not much had changed -- the two divans and a side table along the walls, the huge carpet in the centre of the floor, and the open bookcase against the rust wall remained. Most of the books in the bookcase were discoloured. A tiny, black transistor radio lay atop the bookcase. The aquarium that had stood against the green wall was no longer there. The collage that had occupied part of the beige wall had fallen apart . . . the colour had definitely gone out of the Five Star Café.

A lone red confetti star hung from the ceiling -- it was faded. Another faded red confetti star lay on the divan. Indu had carelessly thrown it there years ago.

Karan sat down on the divan and closed his eyes. His heart felt burdened with anguish. His mind was a battlefield of dejection and sadness. He no longer had the strength to feel rage. There was only negativity in his life, only pain. Even if he wanted to forget it, he needed something positive to occupy his mind, something to which he could look forward.

Things going wrong despite one's best efforts and intentions. Should he attribute it to that anonymous yet omniscient entity? Fate. Providence. Destiny. The collective name for Uncontrollables. For circumstances beyond a mere mortal's sphere of influence.

Why did he not feel the peace? Had the Five Star Café lost its magical powers? Karan opened his eyes. The Five Star Café had probably never possessed any magical powers; as carefree teenagers, they had never had any reason for peacelessness.

He ambled around the Café. His old stereo system was still there. It even had a cassette in it. On an impulse, he pressed the

Play button. An ABBA song from the seventies filled the air.

Where is the spring and the summer?

That once was yours and mine?

Where did it go?

I just don't know

But still my love for you will live forever

Hasta manana until we meet again

Don't know where, don't know when

Darling, our love was much too strong to die

We'll find a way to face a new tomorrow

Hasta manana say we'll meet again

Karan felt a soft ache in his heart. Every time they had made love, Indu had insisted on playing an ABBA song in the background. Indu, his first love, where was she? She had vanished from his life abruptly as soon as she had completed her BA. He had never made an effort to locate her, to keep in touch with her, after that.

A small black-and-white photograph on the side table caught his eye -- it was captioned The Famous Five. He picked it up and stared at the band of gawky teenagers huddled together against the backdrop of Xavier Junior College.

Memories flooded his mind. *Indu was pink. Arjun blue. Aarti white. Danny was a different colour every time. Now everyone would be gray. Colourless, rather.*

He desperately needed to connect with his friends. Immediately. What a waste his life had been. He had done absolutely nothing to keep in touch with them. Karan rebuked himself replete with regret.

"I will make sure the Café reopens," he declared for additional effect as he trudged back to the main house and picked up the telephone directory. It was much thicker than he remembered; the numbers were seven-digits long -- they had been only five digits before. Why could he not find any of their names or numbers? Was he missing something? Frustration. Where were they?

Karan glanced at his watch. Gosh! Pacific Time. He turned his watch forward by a half hour. It now showed half past noon. He flipped through the Yellow Pages as slowly as possible one more time. ARJUN RAO. F.R.C.P. Consulting Psychiatrist and Counsellor. St. Xavier Hospital. Hours of Consultation: MONDAY TO FRIDAY: 11:00 A.M. – 2:00 P.M. & 7:00 P.M. – 9:00 P.M. SATURDAY: 10:00 A.M. – 1:00 P.M. The listing stared back at him with reflected glee.

He rushed up the stairs to his bedroom, changed into a pair of jeans, and was soon walking out of the house onto the bustling streets in search of an auto.

Maharaj had been reluctant to let him hail an auto. "Don't go Karan Baba. The auto drivers are full of tantrums and tricks. They can tell you have returned after being abroad. They will take advantage of you." He had pleaded in Hindi. Karan had turned him a deaf ear.

Karan's efforts to flag the train of autos that trolled by were in vain; most of the autos were occupied, and the drivers of the stray autos that were empty refused to drive where Karan wanted to go. Maharaj was right. Bangalore's auto drivers were notorious for their unhelpfulness.

Sticky with sweat, Karan continued to walk in the direction of the main road until he finally found an auto whose driver deigned to drop him off at the desired destination when Karan had waved a few dollars at him. Minutes later, Karan was rushing along stairways and corridors of St. Xavier Hospital, stopping for directions every time he felt overwhelmed by the maze until he arrived at Arjun's office.

The door was closed. Arjun would soon be done, Karan told himself, and settled down in the general reception area, laden with an array of magazines -- *India Today, Business India, Filmfare, Gentleman, GLITZ;* he had not set his eyes on them in years. When the clock struck two and there was still no sign of the door opening, Karan put down the magazine he was reading and approached the receptionist's desk.

Disappointment. Arjun was in New York attending medical conferences. He was expected back soon; when exactly, the receptionist was not sure.

3. Inner Harmony

June 19 1998

"Synaesthesia is a syndrome that afflicts approximately ten people in a million. The term is derived from Greek -- *syn* means together and *aesthesia* means perception. People who experience sensations of colour are called synaesthetes. They can perceive names and even emotions with an associated colour. The trait is believed to be genetic . . . ."

Dr Arjun Rao, the leading psychiatrist from Bangalore, India, was addressing an audience of incumbent interns, at the Radisson Hotel on Lexington Avenue, New York. He was a visiting delegate for a series of conferences organized by the American Psychiatric Association.

"Different people do not necessarily associate the same colours with the same objects. Most perceive alphabets, numbers, names and emotions with an associated colour. Some synaesthetes may feel or taste sounds or hear or taste shapes. The experience though subjective, is very real, attributable to complex feedback mechanisms in the human brain . . . ."

The conference was a daylong event. It was almost ten o'clock at night before Arjun could extricate himself from a questioning intern community eager to absorb and assimilate every word he uttered, whose badgering for information he had smilingly endured through dinner.

"Have you met any synaesthetes in your life?"

"Do you know anyone who has this ability? Does not the estimate of ten in a million seem too high?"

"You said different people associate different colours with the same object. Can the same person associate different colours to the same object at different times?"

"If this is not a psychiatric disorder, why is it in the conference agenda?"

Arjun did not have all the answers. He was a dilettante in the subject, not an expert. Research on synaesthesia was very nascent. It had only recently begun to be recognized as a real condition.

Arjun entered the hotel elevator and pressed the button for the thirty-fourth floor. He was exhausted. Nevertheless, he felt jubilant. Being in the limelight was a high in itself. He had not always been like this. He had been terribly shy before. Karan had played a principal role in Arjun's transformation from a shy teenager to a loquacious youth.

When Arjun returned to his room, several voice messages awaited him, mostly from the receptionist at Bangalore's St. Xavier Hospital. Along with quick updates on a few key patients, she had stated that one particular Karan Khanna had enquired about him.

A thin smile veneered Arjun's lips. Karan had once been Arjun's best friend. They had met on the first day of junior college exactly twenty years back.

Col. Pickering:	I have come from India to meet you.
Higgins:	I was going to India to meet you.
Col. Pickering:	Higgins!
Higgins:	Pickering!

Arjun had vivid memories of their scenes from *My Fair Lady*, the play they had starred in together, where Arjun had played Colonel Pickering to Karan's Henry Higgins. After that, there had been no looking back. Arjun had miraculously overcome his hesitation to speak in public forums. Throughout his days in medical school, he had been accused of suffering from verbal diarrhoea. The man of many words, he had been called. Why did you not become a lawyer, he had been asked.

Arjun heard yet another New York City police siren as he started to undress -- he heard one every five minutes or so -- even late in the night. He walked over to the window and opened the blinds. New York reminded him of Bombay -- the skyscrapers, the busy roads thronging with offices and people, the plethora of restaurants and shops, the crowded trains, the night-lights . . . the city never slept.

Looking out at the brightly lit metropolitan jungle, he wished he had more leisure time to visit all the *Patel points* as the *desi*s called the most common tourist spots -- he had not been able to afford that luxury, courtesy of the busy conference schedule. He had walked past The Empire State Building several times but had not taken the ride to the top. Anyway, it was no longer the highest skyscraper in the world he consoled himself. He had been to Times Square on two consecutive nights. He had no interest in Broadway's plays or musicals.

Work was his passion. While he had been acknowledged as one of India's leading specialists in the treatment of schizophrenia paranoia Arjun had recently become enamoured by the unexplored territories in the realm of synaesthesia. As Arjun flipped through the pages of a medical journal, his thoughts returned to Karan.

They had not been in touch for almost eighteen years -- since they had finished Xavier Junior College. Arjun vaguely remembered hearing that Karan had gone to Los Angeles to do his master's in computer engineering. Karan was probably a hotshot executive in some multinational firm in the US and was in Bangalore on a holiday.

Arjun was scheduled to return to Bangalore soon. He could not wait to meet Karan.

Part Two

4. Natty Nineties: Homecoming

June 24 1998

Day stretched into night and back into day with an unshackled aimlessness. Karan revelled in the newfound nothingness. Unlike in the US, life was no longer tethered to a perpetual time leash.

While pain itself is ephemeral, the pleasant memories in life always cause the most pain. Karan had not been able to stop worrying about Dolly. He was certain that Troy was clueless about being a father.

Wednesday morning. Exactly a week since he had left LA. Karan lolled in bed. The day was excessively hot and the bedroom was the only place in the house where the air conditioner still worked.

Moments of Dolly's life were indelibly etched in his memory -- the day she had said her first word, the day she had started walking, the day she had not stopped crying . . . When he could no longer control his consternation Karan took out his little black book and dialled Troy's number.

Horrific. The number had been disconnected. Disastrous. There was no forwarding number. How was he ever going to find Dolly again? Until then, Karan had secretly harboured the illusion that one day in the not so distant future he would get Dolly back. Illusions are meant for those who are meant to be disillusioned.

The phone had started ringing. Karan picked up the receiver reluctantly.

"The hospital called me. They said it was an emergency. That you were desperate to see me. What can I do for you? I was visiting your country, the land of milk and honey . . . ." On the phone, Arjun was laughing with unadulterated joy.

"All these years I had no clue where you were . . . ." Karan said.

"I finally arrived in Bangalore this morning. My journey from New York to Bangalore was full of delays . . . a passenger taken ill midair over the Atlantic forcing the plane to turn back . . . put on a later flight but missed my connecting flight in London . . . lost a whole day there . . . then the Bangalore flight was re-routed due to rough weather . . . and finally, when I landed my luggage had not arrived . . . ." Arjun would not stop talking.

"Anyways, glad that you are here. . . ." Karan sat up.

Half an hour later Karan and Arjun were hugging each other like long lost brothers on the doorstep of Koshy's, their favourite restaurant near downtown Bangalore. This was the first time they were meeting after leaving Xavier College. Karan was genuinely thrilled to have his friend back in his life.

Arjun continued from where he had left off his phone conversation. "These last few weeks, I was in New York. I tried looking you up but no luck . . . I had no clue where you were. Anyways glad that you are here now . . . Remember our play from the college days? Higgins I have come from India to meet you."

Karan tried to remember the lines from the depths of his slightly dysfunctional memory as he stood staring at the imposing granite building next door -- The British Council Library -- amidst a brilliant blue sky and fluffy white clouds above and sweet smelling damp red soil beneath. "Pickering, I was going to . . . ." His voice was drowned out in the honking noises from the road -- there was a traffic jam on St. Mark's Road.

"You won't believe this. Aarti recently returned from Delhi." Arjun propelled Karan up the steps and through the entrance of Koshy's.

"Aarti! Our fiction-fanatic friend."

"She had probably read every work of fiction ever written. Do you remember how . . . ." Arjun's volley was unabated.

The décor at Koshy's had not changed much over the years -- the same old portraits scattered on the wall, the fluorescent lights, the ceiling fans -- they were all there. Karan even recognized some of the waiters though they had aged visibly. The familiarity was comforting. Only the Sony Trinitron TV monitor in the far corner was new.

Karan and Arjun ordered a pitcher of beer and picked up exactly where they had left off eighteen years back. The restaurant was sparsely populated -- noon was too early for lunch.

****

"Hello!" Their incessant guy-talk had been interrupted by a feminine voice. Crisp and clear. Karan and Arjun looked up.

A slim and fit woman dressed in jeans and an ethnic *kurti* stood at the edge of their table. Her hair was shorn a short shoulder length. Her triangular face was perfectly made up replete with mascara and lip-gloss. Naturally arched eyebrows framed her smiling eyes.

Arjun was the first to get up and give Aarti a quick hug.

It was Karan's turn next. The faint smell of Aarti's perfume was rejuvenating; the lingering touch of her full body was rhapsodizing. It had been a while since he had been with a woman, made love. His longest period of celibacy. Gosh, what was he thinking? She was a friend. He disappointed himself!

Aarti pushed him away with a bemused smile and swept her hair back with her right hand to reveal dangling silver earrings, thin and long. Very modern. Karan watched in awe as Aarti poured herself a tall mug of cold beer and sipped daintily. She wore a silver ring on almost every finger; an expensive jewellery watch adorned her right wrist. Hip. Svelte. She radiated confidence. To think that this was the same girl the boys called *behanji*, a trifle pejoratively, during the Xavier days! Well she had been goofy and sloppy then.

Aarti looked from one man to the other. "Chalk and cheese. That is how I remember you both."

Karan noticed that Aarti could not take her eyes off Arjun. Like his cologne had cast a magical spell on her. Drakkar Noir.

Arjun continued to talk nonstop. His eyes danced every time he spoke, his smile seemed etched permanently in his face. The boyish mop of hair framing his forehead bounced up and down every time he tilted his head to listen or laugh, taking the years away. He was immaculately dressed even in that informal setting -- Dockers khakis, blue polo shirt, sleek leather shoes and Argyle patterned socks. What a transformation! Gone was the skinny, diffident boy who had bumbled idiotically as a teenager.

Though he could still turn heads wherever he went, Karan suddenly became conscious that he no longer took good care of himself. The soiled track pants and gray crew neck needed a cleansing wash. There was a salt-and-pepper stubble on his cheeks. His grubby nails were untrimmed. He was rapidly adding bulk . . . .

"I wonder what happened to Indu, your first love," Arjun ribbed Karan. "Everyone asked me about your affair in those days. You were the talk of the town. And the envy of all the boys . . . ."

"I talked to her a few minutes back." Aarti pulled out a copy of the fashion magazine GLITZ from her bag and held it open to the third page. The small photograph on the top left corner looked vaguely familiar. Regional Editor: Indumati Agarwal.

"I knew she married in high places -- read about it in the Society magazine a few years back. Her husband is a hotshot business tycoon -- the Bombay Peddar Road types . . ." Arjun rattled on.

"Talk of the devil and there she is!" The next moment Aarti was rushing toward a tall rotund woman clad in a black and white dress who had entered Koshy's. Her face was puffed. Her horrid hennaed hair was set in a page cut. Soon both women were hugging and crying.

"*Arrey mera puraana* hero," Indu encircled Karan in a tight hug next.

Karan could detect the smell of vodka on her breath.

"You are as good-looking as ever." Indu rubbed her cheeks against his salt-and-pepper stubble.

Her joie de vivre was dead. Oxymoronic.

"I never thought I would meet you again." Karan extricated himself.

Zindagi pyaar ka geet hain jisse har dil to gaana padega; zindagi gum ka saagar bhi hain [Life is a song of love that every heart has to sing; life is also an ocean of pain] . . . -- a sad song from the 1980's wafted through the stereo system with the grim face of an aged Rajesh Khanna plastered on the television monitor.

They were transported back to another era, when everything had been different; their simple life had not been tainted by the vagaries of the wicked world. Exactly twenty years back when they had all met each other.

5. The Simple Seventies

July 1, 1978. One of those gray and gloomy days typical of Bangalore. Boys and girls barely sixteen years old streamed through the portals of Xavier Junior College, taking their first steps into the annals of the college's history. The awe-inspiring granite building was located off the main road near the historic Asoka Pillar in South Bangalore; it occupied a major part of the half-acre plot on which it was built and was delimited by a strong iron fence painted royal green. The corridors of the college were abuzz with the discordant din of incessant, inconsequential chatter. There was an air of excitement in the almost festive atmosphere.

A small blue Herald car chugged along the damp black roads lined with green trees and pink bougainvillea, stopped bang in front of the gate, and dropped off its chief occupant -- a tall, fair and good-looking boy who having got out of the car, strode majestically through the imposing entrance with long, confident strides, casting cursory glances at the sparse green lawn to his right, continuing along the corridors until he had joined the long line of students awaiting their turn for registration outside a single office window.

A slim, brown boy was standing in the line, looking around chewing his nails. The tall boy flashed a charming smile and held out his hand. "I am Karan Khanna. From Xavier High School." His tone was clipped, his words crisp. The handshake was firm and strong, the palm fair and smooth, the fingers long and artistic.

The brown boy nervously took the hand offered to him. "I am Arjun Rao. From the Mangalore Public School," he muttered with a nervous stutter.

Karan's smartly creased gray wool trousers flared in consonance with current fashion trends, a pale blue shirt with a long pointed collar, the navy blazer, hair set in a neat step cut, neatly trimmed nails, smart leather boots tapered at the toe, everything was in sharp contrast to Arjun's non-descript threads -- brownish bell bottoms that had been in fashion about five years back, a half-sleeved printed polyester shirt, greasy hair badly cut at a local barber shop, brittle and chewed up nails, ragged Bata slippers with patched up soles.

Karan met Arjun's eyes and held the stare. Arjun averted his eyes immediately. There was something honest and vulnerable about the shy and gawky Arjun. Karan felt a surge of protective instinct in his veins. *Arjun was blue.* The colour of success and calmness. It was also Karan's favourite colour.

Karan possessed a God-given gift -- he could perceive people in colour. He did not choose the colour he associated with the person -- it was involuntary. It baffled him sometimes. He did not have the nerve to discuss it with anybody fearing that he may be ridiculed or labelled insane.

Once, only once, he had made the mistake of expressing it. When he was seven or eight years old, he had exclaimed to his mother "Papa is the best blue I have ever seen." His father who had overheard the remark had flared up. Karan had restrained from talking about it ever after.

The registration window was manned by a mean lackadaisical clerk more interested in gossiping with every person who passed his table than in attending to the work on hand. When one or two of the boys urged him to be more attentive, he displayed a temper so nasty that they shut up. Consequently, the long restless line of incumbent students moved slower than at snail's space.

Karan talked incessantly -- he loved the sound of his own voice, had a variegated vocabulary combined with expressive eyes and dramatic gestures, was a veritable repository of interesting trivia and never missed an opportunity to use it. Having a captive if shy listener, who seemed gratified that the smart Karan deigned to make friends with him, helped.

The long trudge to the registrar's window did have its upside. It laid the foundation for the ensuing friendship between Karan and Arjun, who would be inseparable during their two-year stint at Xavier Junior College.

****

Aarti was the first to arrive in class. Her first day at Xavier Junior College. She was intimidated by the huge classroom crammed with wooden benches organized in three sections, each section separated by an aisle. She chose the fifth bench in the far left section. It seemed sufficiently inconspicuous. She leaned against the wall and looked around nervously.

The blackboard was filled with mathematical equations from a previous class. The rickety table in the front of the classroom was layered with white chalk powder. Boys and girls trooped into the classroom. None of them glanced toward her. Every row in every section of the classroom was soon occupied except the fifth row, far left section. Just when Aarti was beginning to accept that she would be its sole occupant, there was a hushed commotion.

A dusky girl clad in a denim midi and a sleeveless blouse, long dark tresses hanging loose, walked into the classroom on six-inch high stiletto heels and headed straight toward the only bench that could seat her, very well aware that all eyes were fixed on her. Indeed, she was a sharp contrast to the other girls -- most of them wore traditional South Indian dresses, cheap trinkets, gaudy baubles, with their hair done up in oily plaits.

She may have been straight out of a *Femina* or *The Eve's Weekly* magazine, thought Aarti, and what a flawless complexion she had!

Aarti felt drab, dressed as she was in a crumpled white, cotton *salwar* suit, hair knotted in a bun at the nape of the neck, huge glasses, no makeup, no jewellery. Aarti panicked as the dusky girl sat down next to her and tapped her on the shoulder.

"I am Indumati Chatterjee. From St. Xavier Girls High School," she said. "Call me Indu. I hate my mother for giving me such a long name."

Aarti adjusted her glasses repeatedly. Her voice was barely louder than a whisper. "I am Aarti. Asoka Public Convent." She smiled shyly, conscious of revealing her teeth, fully fortified with silver wiring.

"You will look so much nicer once those wires come off." Indu smoothed her own long hair. "You should switch to contact lenses."

"You have lovely hair. How do you keep it so silky?" Aarti was a trifle envious.

Indu burst out laughing so loudly that half the class focused their attention on them, making Aarti cower. The lecturer's entry at that very moment saved her from having to deal with any further behavioural dilemmas. Indu and Aarti would become fast friends after that day.

****

Twelve o' clock. Ding-dong. Ding-dong. Ear shattering clangs of a huge swinging pendulum. Xavier Junior College had one of those old-fashioned grandfather clocks from the British era. The entire student mass, held inattentively captive in their classrooms by monotonous lectures for three full hours, swarmed out for the much-awaited lunch break with a sense of liberated abandon.

The college cafeteria was located under a red-and-green striped canvas canopy just behind the college building. Most of the tables under the canopy were overcrowded with boys. The few girls who had dared to come down to the cafeteria were huddled around a single table at a far end.

Karan and Arjun settled into one of the smaller tables outside the canopy, under a small tree adjoining the green fence. Arjun opened his lunch bag and extricated a battered tiffin box. Karan beckoned the cafeteria boy with a click of his forefinger and thumb. "One egg sandwich, vegetable cutlet with ketchup, and by-two coffee."

Even as he placed his order, Karan shamelessly dug a spoon into Arjun's tiffin box and gulped down the home-cooked food. Once his order arrived, Karan passed it on to Arjun and continued to eat from the tiffin box. "Such tasty food. I should come by and thank your mother one of these days." Karan said without looking up.

"I have no mother." Arjun's voice quivered. "She died when I was born."

Arjun was navy blue. Karan continued to lick the spoon with his right hand and draped his left arm around Arjun's shoulder.

"My father is a great cook." Arjun volunteered more information.

"You are lucky to have such a caring father." Karan looked up.

"He owns a small Udupi restaurant on Kalinga Road," Arjun said softly as he bit into the egg sandwich.

Karan polished off Arjun's lunch, closed the tiffin box, and picked up the coffee cup. At that moment, he saw a dusky girl clad in a denim midi and sleeveless top, her long tresses hanging loose, a food-laden tray in her hand, approaching their table.

"What a fantastic figure she has! Even wears high heels and lipstick! My luck is going to turn soon." Karan whispered to Arjun. "And you can make friends with the *behanji*." He pointed to the fair and thin girl with huge glasses, very plain looking, who trailed the trendy girl shyly, clutching her books to her bosom.

"Can we share your table?" The trendy girl beamed a charming smile.

Karan got up and dramatically pulled out a chair for her. The trendy girl introduced herself as Indu and her friend, the plain Jane, as Aarti. *Indu was a peppermint pink.* Karan instantly felt a magnetic attraction for her. *Aarti was white.* Pure and innocent.

The attention of everyone in the cafeteria was now focused on this table -- separate seating for boys and girls was the norm at Xavier Junior College. There was a lot of whispering, most of it envious, at the mixed group that had dared to defy the norm.

Karan and Indu held court, each competing for a fair share of the limelight, both keenly aware and yet somewhat oblivious of the other two at their table and those in the cafeteria. Arjun sipped his coffee silently. Aarti pulled out a novel from her purse to be engrossed in the surrealistic world of Arthur Hailey's *Hotel.*

In the days that followed, the foursome bonded into a cohesive team. That they were all in the same class helped. Danny was a late entrant to Xavier Junior College; within days of his arrival, he had unobtrusively melded with the quartet. College life soon slipped into a regulated monotony.

****

The windy month of July had given way to a rainy August. The cricket season was in full swing -- one-day international matches were becoming increasingly popular. With India poised to win in the semi-final match against Pakistan, Karan and Arjun who had jointly bunked their English class to listen to the cricket commentary were sitting in the cafeteria -- they always chose the same small table under the tree.

When Karan reached his hand out for Arjun's lunch box, as usual, Arjun nodded his head sideward rapidly. Karan grinned mischievously and stood up. "Hear, hear. Friends, Xavierites, and Bangaloreans . . . ." He banged his fist on the thin metallic table three times. Having got the attention of all the boys in the cafeteria, Karan pointed his finger. "He has denied me my lunch today."

The boys jeered. "Punish him! Punish him!"

"With friends like this, who needs enemies?"

There was no response. Indu had chosen that very moment to make her grand entrance. The boys were no longer interested in Karan's drama. Their hungry eyes devoured the contours of Indu's supple body inadequately supported by a floral-pattern midi dress as she swayed her way sexily to the food counter, head held high, long tresses caressing the air that brushed her, consciously oblivious of the gaping gazes encircling her.

"Father and I are fasting today," Arjun explained the reason for not bringing his lunch box.

Arjun was a dull grayish blue. He sounded melancholic.

"That was only a joke." Karan apologized for his earlier behaviour.

"Today is my mother's death anniversary," Arjun added in a low voice.

Karan gave Arjun a friendly pat on the shoulder.

Birth and Death. So intricately linked. Mourning and Celebration.

Suddenly Karan leaned across the table and said conspiratorially, "Happy Birthday, dude. We are cosmic twins!"

Arjun looked puzzled.

"Dumbo. It is my birthday too!"

"Let's celebrate then." Arjun started to shout out to the waiter this time.

"Keep it a secret. I don't want everyone to know . . ." Karan covered Arjun's mouth with his palm. "Or every Tom, Dick, and Harry here will be asking me for a treat."

Arjun pushed Karan's palms away from his mouth. "You are a popular guy."

"In the US, it is the other way round. If it is your birthday, then your friends will treat you." Karan had set his sights on going to the US soon after junior college. He had come to associate US with personal freedom. His impressions were based entirely on what he read about US in papers and magazines. He planned to do his undergraduate in the US if all went well. That was the only way he could get away from the claustrophobic clutches of his overbearing father.

"Guys, clear the table for me." Indu put her food-laden tray -- three slices of cake, a bagful of potato chips, and a bottle of Thumbs Up cola -- down on the table.

Aarti, lost in the world of Arthur Hailey's bestseller, *The Moneychangers*, slipped into the adjacent chair. Aarti never ate any lunch; as the joke went, she devoured words on the pages of best-selling novels. The boys had kept count -- she had finished reading three Arthur Hailey novels -- *Airport, Wheels, Hotel* -- since college started.

"Indu, how do you maintain such a wow figure on a diet like this?" Karan tried to play footsie under the table.

Aarti looked up from her novel. "Genes, I suppose."

"G-E-N-E-S or J-E-A-N-S?" Arjun's comment did not evoke the desired response.

Aarti and Indu rolled their eyes and circled their mouth to say PJ, short for poor joke, and giggled.

Indu swung her silky tresses playfully, so they brushed Karan's lips. "Somebody up there loves me." Her face had the warm glow of arrogance.

Karan ran his fingers through Indu's hair and looked around the cafeteria in an overt bid to soak in the envious glances from the other boys. True, the boys were all gazing at them. But why did some of them look scared? And others smug? Karan heard an angry roar from behind and turned.

Deena Dayal Purushottam Chandrashekhar, a senior lecturer of Xavier Junior College, known as DPC, stood two feet away from their table, his eyes flashing with anger. "Stop it." He wiggled his index finger at Karan and Indu. "This is not a park for romancing." Generous doses of dribble sprayed out of his mouth.

Indu swept her hair away from Karan and extracted a barrette from her purse.

DPC came nearer their table. "Why don't you girls sit at your own table?" His voice grew louder. "You are breaking the rules of this college. I will complain to your parents." Drops of his dribble sprayed them all liberally.

Karan and Indu exchanged meaningful looks. The next moment, Indu was dragging Aarti toward the cafeteria exit. Karan was dragging Arjun likewise. Indu's half-eaten lunch lay abandoned on the table.

"Never again sit together. Boys and girls. See what will happen." DPC continued to shout threateningly at the retreating quartet. "Remember. No breaking the rules." He was probably disappointed that none of them had picked up an argument with him, as he had hoped, robbing him of a valid reason to complain to the principal.

****

The four of them walked out of the cafeteria, through the portals of the college, onto the pavement to congregate in the dilapidated tea stall in the adjacent building. Danny joined them on the way.

Karan ordered chai as they stood huddled on the pavement, under the neem tree, discussing the injustice that had been meted out.

The tea stall was tiny, occupying the cramped space under the staircase of a huge office building so it had no space to seat its customers. Darjeeling tea, ginger tea, cardamom tea, and masala tea -- the array of teas was so variegated and delicious that business thrived anyway -- the tea drinkers were not bothered that they had to stand in the road as they daintily sipped or crudely gulped their tea.

"Will we be suspended?" Aarti sounded scared.

Karan was busy resting his back against the bark of the tree.

"DPC was just letting off steam." Indu stood next to Karan and leaned her back toward the bark of the tree as well. "No wonder the seniors call him Deewana, Paagal, C . . . ."

"Crazy." Karan said hurriedly, cutting Indu out before she uttered the dreaded C- word loudly in public.

"I hear he has seven daughters -- ages varying from seventeen years to seventeen months." Arjun added his bit of gossip, however irrelevant.

"DPC. A perfect MCP -- Male Chauvinist Pig. No respect for girls. You saw the way he shouted at us." Indu made a crude gesture with her hands that Aarti did not comprehend. The boys turned beet red at the vulgarity it symbolized.

"Did we break any rules?" Aarti sounded scared.

"No way. Separate the sexes. How can there be such a rule?" Indu said at the top of her voice.

"It is not a rule. Only a norm at Xavier." Karan assured Aarti.

"Rule? Norm? What is the difference?" Arjun asked.

Arjun, Indu, and Danny looked quizzically at Karan and Aarti.

"Rules are stated in policy guidelines. Norms evolve. They cannot be enforced." The erudite Karan explained.

While Xavier Junior College was academically well reputed, socially, it was conservative to the core. One such purported practice was the stringent segregation of boys and girls. Separate staircases. Separate queues. Separate seating. Traditionally, the benches in the left sections in all classrooms were reserved for the girls. Those in the middle and right sections seated the boys. Girls and boys sharing the same bench was unheard of.

"Dammit. This is one thing I want to change at Xavier's." Karan was soon engaged in plotting the next course of action with his friends. "This afternoon history will be rewritten."

****

The first session after lunch was English literature. On entering the class, in unison, all five of them headed to the fifth row in the middle section and seated themselves on the same bench. Arjun and Aarti, the shy ones, occupied the two opposite ends of the bench. Danny sat next to Aarti, Karan sat next to Danny, and Indu was sandwiched between Karan and Arjun.

There was a hushed silence in the classroom. The other boys and girls looked at them with a mixture of envy and non-comprehension. There were wolf whistles from the boys' arena and muffled giggles from the girls' arena. Karan and Indu continued to chat, ignoring the reaction they were eliciting. Aarti chose to lose herself in the world of *The Moneychangers*. Arjun opened his English text and pretended to read. Danny remained silent as usual.

When Seeta Murthy, the English lecturer, entered the class, the silence was deadening. The students held their breath with anticipation. How would she react? Would she ask them to disband? Would she subject them to one of her tiradic sermons? Or march them off to the principal's office?

Seeta Murthy was the epitome of the adage that appearances are deceptive. A petite, soft-spoken, middle-aged woman dressed in expensive but crumpled saris, her salt-and-pepper hair always in an untidy bun coming undone, she spoke chaste Queen's English. She was ruthless with the students when it came to correcting English grammar, spelling, and punctuation, that too always in public.

Yet, she was liked well enough to command decent attendance in her classes. This was a major achievement, considering that students often regarded the English class a necessary evil that they would soon have no use for when they had achieved their coveted objective of securing a seat in engineering or medicine. Sad but true. The mechanistic model of university education did not place much emphasis on language and communication.

Seeta Murthy settled down at her desk, took out her copy of Shakespeare's *Macbeth*, instructed the class to look at Act II, and then looked around the classroom, scouting for students to read for the principal characters, as was her habit. Her gaze settled on the fifth row in the middle section of the class.

"Aarti will be Lady Macbeth today." She announced before moving on to choose the other principal characters for the reading.

For the next thirty minutes or so, the chosen characters read their lines. Seeta Murthy expostulated in chaste English with a hint of British accent. She was brutal as ever in her comments when the students deviated from the desired pronunciation. With fifteen minutes to go, she closed the book. These last minutes were reserved for discussions on any topic the class chose.

Seeta Murthy held anachronistically liberal views way ahead of her generation and encouraged healthy debate during her classes that went beyond the realm of the limited syllabus. These discussions, a rare forum for students to express their views within the claustrophobic confines of the state-defined education system aimed at taxing their memory rather than helping them develop their thought processes, was one of the reasons for her popularity.

"Xavier Junior College is finally poised on the frontiers of social transformation," she began, "Thanks to a simple yet courageous act by five bold crusaders. Congratulations!" Beaming, she climbed down from the podium and walked toward the fifth bench in the middle section of the classroom. "Young ladies and gentlemen, you have taken the first step in the right direction today." Seeta Murthy started applauding and soon, the rest of the class had joined in.

She dismissed the rest of the class early, with a motivational parting shot. "Going forward, I would like to see more seating that is mixed. You are the new generation. Venture beyond the predefined confines. Embrace broad-mindedness."

Seeta Murthy spent the remaining time chatting with the Famous Five as she now called them. Inadvertently she had invented a new nickname, an obvious reference to the characters created by Enid Blyton, the popular children's author. That day, for the first time since they had all joined college, the five felt as if they had finally met a teacher who was also a friend.

After that day, mixed seating would gradually evolve as the new norm at Xavier Junior College. Most lecturers would learn to become tolerant of the winds of change except the bigoted DPC. The students would continue to talk about the revolutionary incident for weeks thereafter. Karan and Indu would bask in the limelight. Arjun and Aarti would shun it. Danny? Nobody knew how he felt about it.

****

The Five Star Café was conceived that same evening. The late afternoon sun was mild after the wet rainy morning. The five were seated at Chit Chat, an outdoor ice cream parlour on M. G. Road in downtown Bangalore, where they had headed straight after English class, to celebrate Karan and Arjun's birthdays.

They chattered excitedly -- eating out was an event -- reserved for special occasions as these. The boys would not stop gloating over their victory.

For once, Aarti was not engrossed in the world of Arthur Hailey. "Famous Five. I love that nickname. I have read every single Enid Blyton written to date except one."

"I read my first Enid Blyton when I was six," boasted Karan. "*The Blue Story Book.*"

"I could not even read the alphabet until I was seven," retorted Indu.

Their orders arrived. Everyone's undivided attention was soon focused on the ice cream. Chit Chat was Bangalore's best ice cream parlour, well known for its privately patented hand-made ice cream in exotic flavours.

"I owned the complete Enid Blyton collection. It must still be somewhere at home," Karan said, digging into his vanilla ice cream with hot chocolate fudge and nuts.

"There is one book I could never find in any of the libraries. Can I borrow it from you? *The Mystery of . . . ,*" Aarti whispered in Karan's ears. Her lips were green -- from the pistachio ice cream.

"You can't be serious." Karan looked incredulous. Laughing loudly he repeated every word Aarti had just said.

Indu joined Karan in the laughter. "I stopped reading Enid Blyton when I turned ten." She licked the inside of her tutti-frutti ice cream bowl with her tongue.

"I don't like you." Aarti glared at Karan.

Arjun came to Aarti's rescue. "Indu, we all know you stopped reading a long time back."

"I never read any of that mystery and adventure stuff anyway. I only read those short stories where the toys and dolls got into mischief and the fairy doll eloped with the toy soldier. I always imagined them having sex on those escapades." Indu went on undaunted.

The others howled with uncontrolled laughter, even Aarti.

"You were thinking of . . . err . . . err . . . it when you were not even ten?" Arjun hesitated to say the word sex aloud.

"You are always thinking of sex even now." Karan nudged Indu.

"That shows how healthy my attitude is." Indu shrugged superciliously.

"Indu, you have a one-track mind." Karan said.

"It is the right track." Indu pouted her lips at Karan who was dressed in white sneakers, a windcheater in red, blue and white, brushed denim jeans and a black baseball cap. "You are looking very sexy in your imported threads."

Aarti whispered something in Indu's ears. Soon much to the amusement of the other patrons and the embarrassment of Karan and Arjun, Aarti and Indu were singing in non-modulated, high-pitched tones.

Happy birthday to you

Happy birthday to you

Happy birthday dear Karan and Arjun

Happy birthday to you

When they finished, Arjun looked at his friends with shining eyes. "Thank you all. Nobody ever celebrated my birthday before." He was choking.

"There is always a first time." Aarti looked at Arjun kindly.

"In a way you are lucky. I wish my father wasn't having this huge party this evening," Karan said.

"The kind where all the relatives and friends arrive with these big senseless gifts?" Indu commiserated.

"The grown-ups eat greasy food, get drunk and spew venom; the kids get bored, make mischief, and get scolded." Karan ran his tongue over his chocolate-brown lips in a bid to savour the remnant specks of chocolate fudge. "I hate it!"

"Even worse for the teenagers. They neither belong with the grown-ups nor the kids." Indu pulled out a small compact from her purse.

"Try telling my father that I am sixteen." Karan sounded miserable.

"What a tragedy." Indu pulled out her lipstick from the purse.

"Why don't you tell your father to stop throwing these birthday parties?"

"He won't listen." Karan made a wry face.

"Just stay away from the party tonight." Indu looked into the compact mirror as she applied pink lipstick.

"I don't want to hurt him. . . . ." Karan looked sullen.

"What if I gave you a birthday kiss?" Indu looked at Karan challengingly.

Karan stood up, fished his wallet out of his hip pocket, and took out a crisp hundred-rupee note to pay the waiter who had brought them the check.

No sooner did the waiter turn his back on them than Indu grabbed Karan and planted a kiss each on both his cheeks with her pink-painted lips.

The others looked stunned at this public display of affection. Or was that attraction?

Karan slowly rubbed away the lipstick marks on his cheeks. *Indu was fuchsia pink.* By the time, the waiter had brought him the change, Karan announced he would boycott his father's party. He and his friends would have their own parallel party. Things took a different turn from that point onward.

The venue? Karan lived in a posh three-storied bungalow with a well-maintained flower garden and two trees. There was an unused spare garage at one corner of the huge garden, away from the main house, at the end of a short driveway. The garage was spacious -- about twenty feet square; two high windows on one of the walls provided limited ventilation; it was furnished with two old divans and a side table; a thin carpet covered the centre of the garage floor; an open bookcase stood against one of the walls.

Karan covered the small windows with packaging cardboard to minimize the chances of the buzzing activity being detected. He sneaked in finger food and lots of beverages from the main house and fetched the National Panasonic stereo system from his bedroom so they could listen to popular western pop and rock music -- ABBA, Boney M, Pink Floyd -- pretty much the only western bands they had heard of.

Aarti was the first to arrive, with party games for Karan and Arjun as birthday gifts. "It is so calm and peaceful in here!" By the time the others arrived, she had created five glittering stars decorated with red confetti and hung them from the garage ceiling. The Five Star Café. She christened their future *adda*.

Indu gifted a broad blue tie with Eiffel Tower motifs to Karan; she had bought a set of pens for Arjun. Danny brought along two table lamps for the birthday boys. Arjun was the last to arrive, bringing along several snacks from his father's Udupi restaurant as well as unbreakable plates, cups, and spoons. The rest of the evening was a blast.

Long after his friends had left, Karan stayed back in the Five Star Café, reading the book Arjun had gifted him. The solitude was soothing. He went back to the main house only after ascertaining that the last of the guests had driven away.

On seeing Karan, Vikramaditya was livid; he threatened to disown Karan if he did not call up each guest and apologize individually for not attending his own birthday party. At first, Karan had refused, while Anita tried unsuccessfully to arbitrate their argument. In the end, on seeing tears in his mother's eyes, Karan reluctantly conceded.

****

The next morning, a furious Karan drove through the narrow streets of Bangalore in his blue Herald. Why did his father hate him so much? Conflicting thoughts raged through his mind as he changed gears.

Why did he not resemble Vikramaditya? Was Vikramaditya really his father? The way he harassed him, he was more like a stepfather -- were his parents hiding a bitter truth? Anita always insisted that Vikramaditya loved him but was strict for his own good. Bullshit.

Anita never lied. Vikramaditya must be his father. Then was he schizophrenic? It was more like he had a multiple personality disorder. Can't be; he only had one personality and that was vicious. Was he the human incarnate of some evil wizard? Karan shook his head in an effort to ward off this train of thought.

He had unilaterally decided to go to the US for his undergraduate program once he completed the two-year stint at Xavier Junior College. How would Vikramaditya react to that? Maybe he would be pleased. What if he said good riddance to bad rubbish? The thought was unpleasant to Karan.

Did he love his father? He definitely did. He secretly hoped for his approval in all he did. *His father was blue, mostly a dark navy blue, but he had been a pale baby blue occasionally. But never the rich electric blue that Arjun could be.*

Karan's earliest memory was when he was five or six years old. He had read an entire Enid Blyton book cover to cover -- *The Blue Story Book*. Anita had been so proud of him; she had not stopped talking about it. She had promised a visit to his favourite Airlines Hotel, where he could eat vanilla ice cream seated in the car, then play on the swing, the slide, and the small merry-go-round.

On hearing his father's car arrive, Karan had run out excitedly to break the news. Vikramaditya's nonchalance had made Karan's achievement seem trivial.

Anita had kept her promise and taken him to Airlines Hotel -- alone -- since Vikramaditya had other commitments that were more important, she had explained to him -- he was negotiating some business deal at the Cantonment Club. The Airlines Hotel had not been an exciting place to Karan that evening. The ice cream had tasted salty. Probably from the unshed tears. The slide had felt bumpy. He had refused to sit on the swing. "I will fall and die," he had wailed.

Karan excelled in school -- topping his class regularly -- he was inherently intelligent. Vikramaditya never uttered a good word all those times he signed his report card. Once, just once, in the sixth grade, Karan secured third place in the midterm exam. Vikramaditya had frowned and given him a sermon. Karan had borne it silently. It would have been futile to remind his father that despite being down with jaundice and having missed school for a whole month he had done commendably well. He would only have earned another sermon. On the virtues of healthy eating or something like that.

At school, Karan played every sport there was to play. He won several prizes in the annual sports championships. He was often chosen the lead actor in school plays. His artwork was displayed in several exhibitions. Anita was always there at all these events to applaud him. Vikramaditya, never.

When he was in the eighth grade, Karan had entered the finals of an inter-school debating contest. The event was held at the Town Hall, Bangalore's biggest cultural theatre at the time. Karan had repeatedly requested his father to attend.

The day of the debate arrived. Karan was one of the last speakers to go on stage. Only Anita was in the audience. Despite his disappointment, Karan had won the debate.

When they came out of the Town Hall, Karan proudly holding the huge silver cup he had won Vikramaditya sat in the car glaring at them. "You are late. I have been waiting forty minutes. We will be late for the party." They were all scheduled to proceed directly to some distant cousin's birthday party. Karan had the strongest urge to fling the silver cup by the wayside. Once, just once, could his father not have come in and listened to him speak instead of fretting in the car? Once, just once, could he not have glanced at the silver cup and congratulated him?

"I wish you had come in. Our darling son outshone himself today." Anita was good at garbing her disappointment in gentle admonition.

That night Karan searched every nook and corner of the house, ferreted out all the cups and prizes he had ever won in his student life, and arranged them in one of the library bookcases. Where his father would see them. Every day. One day soon, he would applaud Karan.

Two years had gone by. That day had not yet come. Karan continued to win more cups and prizes.

Karan loved dogs. He never missed an opportunity to feed the countless stray dogs that passed through their street sending Anita into a paranoid frenzy that he would become rabid or develop a ghastly infection if he did not stop. She promised to buy Karan a dog for his fifteenth birthday.

"This is the first time he has ever asked us for anything." Karan had overheard Anita pleading his case with Vikramaditya.

"He doesn't need to. We get him everything before even he can ask." Vikramaditya had stood his ground.

"I have never asked you for anything either," Anita had said softly.

"That is different." Vikramaditya had capitulated. "I will get him a dog."

Caesar, the pedigreed black fox terrier arrived a week later. Vikramaditya had extracted his pound of flesh. Caesar was to be tethered to the kennel, always. Karan was allowed to take him out for a walk once a day. Caesar was never ever to come into the house. The day he did, Karan would have to give him up.

Anita thought the terms were reasonable but Karan was disappointed. There would be no fun if he could not have the dog run around the house with him, share his bed at night, feed titbits under the table.

Six months went by. Caesar had become an inseparable part of Karan's existence, partly filling in the vacuum of missing filial love. Anita occasionally allowed Caesar into the house for an hour or two when Vikramaditya was out of town. Otherwise, Karan diligently complied with Vikramaditya's rules. Except once.

Caesar, diagnosed with a benign tumour requiring surgery, had been in unbearable pain and not stopped whimpering. Karan had surreptitiously sneaked Caesar into his room to comfort him. This single act of transgression was soon discovered and the cornucopian cinders of Vikramaditya's fury ignited. "Caesar has to go." Vikramaditya was obdurate.

Karan argued his case on humanitarian grounds -- the circumstances surrounding the single act of noncompliance were excruciating. Anita tried her best to support him.

Vikramaditya ordered the driver to abandon Caesar in the outskirts of the city as far away as possible, from where they lived.

"Don't do this, Papa. Have mercy." Karan wailed, hugging Caesar. "At least send him to the SPCA."

The driver had physically pried Caesar away from Karan even as a helpless Anita and Maharaj had held onto Karan.

The house fell silent. Anita spent the whole night in the *mandir* praying to the array of her Gods for forgiveness. Though she had not said anything, Karan knew that she was deeply perturbed by Vikramaditya's inhumane act of abandoning a sick dog in the wilderness -- she was a staunch believer in the concept of karma.

In the months that followed, Karan had grown up. Literally. He had learned some fundamental truths. That nothing was forever. That to love was to lose. That those who break the rules all the time get away, but those that follow rules are not pardoned on that one occasion they are unable to obey them.

A small black auto whizzed by, cutting ahead of him, screeching to an abrupt halt before him at the traffic light. Karan braked the blue Herald, barely managing to stop.

That was a close miss or he might have ended up denting the car. Anita would have been upset but not shown it. "Freedom comes with responsibility," she would have said. His eyes became misty

and his heart warmed up when he thought about her. *She was white.
Pure. Like her unconditional love.*

****

The Xavier Junior College curriculum comprised six subjects. The
junior university system was memory-based, and there would be a
board-driven annual exam at the end of the academic year in April.
Student identities would be kept anonymous by issuing them a hall
ticket number for the exams; their exam papers would be assigned
anonymously to lecturers across the state for evaluation. There was no
room for continuous internal assessment -- the practice was unheard of.

Under such an infrequent and impersonal grading system,
students usually memorized the entire academic curriculum in the
few weeks preceding the final exam. There was no real pressure
to attend classes. The real objective was to secure a seat in a
professional college -- engineering or medicine -- at the end of the
two years of junior college.

Most students of Xavier Junior College walked, biked, or took
the bus. Karan was one of those avant-garde, upper middle-class
people who owned a moped at the princely age of sixteen. Arjun
rode his bicycle to college. Aarti walked -- she lived only a few
blocks away. Indu and Danny travelled by bus, though Indu had
no dearth of willing escorts who dropped her home on the pillion
of their motorbikes.

When the five went out together, they either all walked or rode
the bus, depending on the distance of their destination. Karan
would occasionally bring his blue Herald car and drive around
with his friends, much to the envy of the other students.

Group norms evolved. The five decided what classes they
would attend and which ones they would bunk, based on their
collective affinity or dislike for the concerned lecturer and their
career choices.

Karan wanted to pursue engineering, preferably in the US.

Arjun was not too fond of maths and physics; by elimination, he had decided to pursue medicine. Using the converse logic, Danny, who had a pathological aversion to biology, had decided to pursue engineering. The girls had less pressure and more options. Aarti had not yet made up her mind what she would do in life. Indu's career choices changed with time.

They all attended English classes. Seeta Murthy remained their favourite lecturer, no doubt. None of the five cared to attend the elective language class since they did not like to be separated -- Aarti and Arjun had chosen Sanskrit, Danny had opted for Hindi, Karan and Indu had signed up for French.

They boycotted Maths class taught by a rookie lecturer in his early twenties who possessed neither an aptitude for maths nor the capability of keeping his class enthralled. Karan who was a whiz in maths -- he had studied a more advanced syllabus during high school -- promised to tutor his friends during exam time.

They loved to attend Chemistry lectures. Raaj Saxena was sound on his concepts, possessed excellent communication skills, and was a repository of trivia that some of the class loved to lap up. His classes came as a whiff of fresh air amidst the humdrum education system. In an era where India was shut off from the world economy by government policy, his trivial pursuits were one of the few sources of general information.

Maya Devi, a senior lecturer, only years away from retirement, taught Physics. She ruled the class with an iron hand, expecting pin-drop silence in her classes, tolerating no late comings, and religiously monitoring a self-imposed attendance threshold of eighty percent from each student. She was notorious for disallowing students with lower attendance records from taking their final exams. The five attended her classes out of fear rather than interest.

Arjun was the only one who attended Biology since he was the only one who needed good grades in the subject to meet the basic criteria for his medical entrance exams. The others boycotted the class. In return for his infraction, Arjun offered to use a carbon paper while taking notes in class and hand over the carbon copy to Karan after each class. The photocopier was not yet ubiquitous and Xeroxing charges, as they called it, were prohibitively expensive for most students.

Most of the classes they bunked were conveniently scheduled on Thursday and Friday mornings. Viewing reruns of older English movies on morning shows became their substitute activity for Thursdays. *McKenna's Gold, The Guns of Navarone, The Towering Inferno, The Poseidon Adventure, Tora Tora Tora* -- they watched all the action movies of the seventies.

Friday mornings, they hung out at the South Bangalore shopping complex, the closest thing to a strip mall in those days. On those Fridays that a new Hindi movie with superstar Amitabh Bachchan in the lead was released, they managed to watch the movie first day, first show. *Amar Akbar Anthony. Parvarish. Don. Muqaddar ka Sikandar. Trishul.* The list of movies was long. They owed this opportunity to the labours of Karan's Gurkha who would stand in the advance booking lines days before the scheduled Friday and buy them tickets.

Saturday mornings were usually spent at the British Council Library -- one of their favourite haunts. They all came in at nine in the morning, browsed the library, spent a few hours reading their favourite genres, checked out the books they chose to borrow, and left around noon.

Aarti, the most voracious reader of the lot, read English literature, that one day of the week, in lieu of her favourite pulp fiction. She loved Somerset Maugham, Thomas Hardy, even Charles Dickens. She made no bones of her dislike for Jane Austen. "Her protagonists are the epitome of middle-class values. Marriage is their sole raison d'être. They disappoint me."

"You are such a paradox." Karan said.

"Man, why do you use such big words?" Arjun opened the *Oxford English Dictionary.*

"Still waters run deep." Indu was fiercely appreciative of Aarti.

"I agree. And empty vessels make more noise." Arjun responded reflexively.

"People living in glass houses should not throw stones." Indu retorted.

"Birds of a feather flock together." Karan had the last word, sending Arjun and Indu rushing off in opposite directions.

Karan loved P. G. Wodehouse and Arthur Conan Doyle's Sherlock Holmes series. Occasionally, he deigned to include other authors -- J. D. Salinger's timeless adolescent classic *A Catcher in the Rye*, A. J. Cronin's famous trilogy -- *The Citadel, Judas Tree, The Keys of the Kingdom*, and Harper Lee's *To Kill a Mockingbird*.

Danny usually headed for science fiction -- Isaac Asimov and Douglas Adams, even Kafka and Fritjof Capra though these authors may have gone beyond his understanding -- never really getting engrossed in anything, always content to be there with the others.

Arjun hungrily devoured the contents of his favourite comics -- *Asterix, Tin Tin*, and *Archie* -- and browsed through magazines like *The Illustrated Weekly* and *Reader's Digest*. Indu flirted with anything in pants and flipped through the pages of film and fashion magazines in between.

****

They had Saturday lunch together at one of their houses -- mostly Aarti's, Karan's, or Arjun's.

Aarti lived with her mother Anupama and elder sister Bhavna in a typical middle-class locality with whitewashed houses clustered closely together on narrow, tree-lined roads bustling with people. Anupama worked as a teacher at a local school. Dressed in simple cotton saris, her long hair in a braid, Anupama who was in her thirties, could easily have passed off as Aarti's elder sister. Bhavna would rarely be home.

Aarti's old-fashioned house had a huge living room adjacent to the kitchen, popularly referred to as the hall, which was their lunch venue -- the house did not have a separate dining room. The hall had the most beautiful red oxide floor that was maintained spotlessly clean and gleamed glossily in the afternoon sunlight.

Anupama served the most delicious South Indian food. The main course was either spicy *bisi bele bath* or crisp *masala dosa*s or *idli vada sambar*. Always, she served the staple recipe of the Mysorean household -- curd rice with pickles. She would hand out huge, stainless steel plates filled with food, accompanied by tall stainless steel tumblers filled with water. The five would perch themselves on the comfortable pouffes and *moda*s strewn across the hall and eat the food with their fingers, except Karan who always requested a spoon.

The others never tired of mercilessly teasing him for it. They called him *Lord Wellesley* after one of the British rulers. Not that the ribbing had any effect on Karan. "A leopard never changes its spots," Aarti had once remarked.

Karan's family comprised his businessman father, Vikramaditya, who was so busy that none of them had met him in almost six months and his smart and friendly mother, Anita. Karan's posh three-storied bungalow had six bedrooms and six bathrooms distributed across the top two floors. The living room, the dining room, the kitchen with a pantry, the *pooja* room, and the formal sitting room with a powder room, were situated on the ground floor.

For a family of three, they had a huge staff of servants -- a cook they addressed as Maharaj, a gardener they called *maali*, a driver they called *bhai*, a security guard addressed as gurkha, and two maid servants or *bai*s who did all the menial chores around the house.

Lunch at Karan's was served by Maharaj around a glass-topped dining table in restaurant style, complete with napkins, bone china, and silver cutlery; it was personally supervised by Anita. The three-course North Indian meal started with fresh lime, tomato soup, and cucumber salad, followed by *aloo paratha*s or *roomali roti* with several types of vegetable gravy and *pulao* rice, ending with *kheer* and *lassi*.

Arjun and his father lived in a small, dilapidated house located in one corner of a huge plot. Lunch at Arjun's was always a surprise -- never in the traditional mould, with the wildest combinations and the most innovative recipe improvisations. Arjun's father was a great cook -- as Karan had discovered early on at college. He was a weak-looking man in his forties though he looked much older. He spoke very little and smiled too much.

On meeting him the first time, Karan had told Arjun. "He is the most unassuming, down-to-earth father I have met in my entire life."

Arjun looked sad. "He is more like a brother to me. Except when he is down with bronchitis, which is most of the time. I feel like he is the son, and I am the father."

"Child is the father of man." Karan put a protective arm around Arjun's shoulders. "You don't know how lucky you are, my friend."

"Are you scared of your father?" Arjun asked him.

"Let me tell you a secret. I think my father hates me," Karan said in hushed tones.

"You are such a *drame-baaz*. How can your own father hate you?" Arjun sounded incredulous.

The girls had barged in at that moment. "Your father is a carbon copy of you." Aarti told Arjun.

"You mean Arjun is a carbon copy of his father." Karan corrected her immediately.

Food at Arjun's was abundant, dishes stacked on a table with everyone free to serve themselves whatever they wanted and eat it in whatever manner they liked. The liberty that went with the absence of a woman in the kitchen was notably noticeable.

Lunch at Indu's happened just once during the whole year, on the Saturday following Durga Pooja Day during the ten-day Dusshera festival.

At the outset, Indu had explained. "Sorry guys. On one hand, my mother is a terrible cook. On the other hand, she just won't get along with any cook. Most of them leave us in a week or two. The crux of the matter is, we never know where our next meal will come from. Under these circumstances, it happens whenever it happens."

Indu's father was loud and authoritative, yet very friendly. He wanted to know the family history, career aspirations, likes and dislikes of each one of them. He would ask a question and make sure each one of them answered it. What was amazing was that he remembered exactly what each one had said and referenced it during the course of lunch.

"I am very uncomfortable answering private questions in public," Arjun whispered to Karan in annoyance.

"It feels like a group interview," Karan commiserated.

Indu overheard the conversation. Confrontational to the core, she sternly told her father to stop being inquisitive. The others were amused when he actually stopped grilling them.

Karan remarked to Arjun, "They are so alike, peas in a pod."

Indu's mother, dressed in a Calcutta sari worn the Bengali way with a thick strip of *sindoor* in the parting of her hair, as if to complement her husband's overbearing nature, rarely opened her mouth. She conversed intermittently in Bengali, mostly with Indu. She personally served them the mouth-watering Bengali food -- rice and fish curry, *mishti doi*, *rosogollas*.

The boys had enjoyed the meal immensely. The smell of fish had made Aarti nauseous -- she was vegetarian. Aarti had taken great care not to show it lest she hurt the feelings of Indu's mother.

Indu shamelessly let the cat out of the bag the next day. "I threw a tantrum and refused to attend Durga Pooja if I could not invite my friends for lunch. Mother pleaded with Shekhar Dada, her cousin, to let his wife come and cook that lunch for us."

Karan, Arjun, and Aarti were not sure how to react on hearing this. Karan had diplomatically changed the topic.

Lunch at Danny's never happened. Danny spoke very little about his family. Danny had remained an enigma -- he always hung out with them -- always remained aloof -- almost as if he had deliberately erected an invisible barrier around him. Given his sweet and complacent nature, the others did not have the heart to question him. They went out of their way to make him feel included at their homes. On his part, almost as if to make up for it, Danny always brought food -- either sweets or savouries, no matter where they had lunch.

****

Saturday evenings were synonymous with carousing on M. G. Road -- Bangalore's equivalent of the metro downtown. The five would walk the length of M. G. Road a few times, running into classmates, chatting with them on the pavement, hang out at restaurants or ice cream parlours eating cake and ice cream. Koshy's was their favourite restaurant. Lakeview and Chit Chat were their favourite ice cream parlours. Topkapi and Canopy, the more expensive restaurants, were reserved for dinner on special occasions.

It was on these outings that they watched many of the newer English movies at one of three theatres -- Rex, Plaza, or Galaxy. *Star Wars. Saturday Night Fever. Grease. Superman. Close Encounters of the Third Kind.* They enjoyed the action in the films immensely; they rarely followed much of the dialogues because of the unfamiliar western accents.

Except for Karan who expressed displeasure. "I wish more Hollywood movies were released in India. I mean the ones with good dialogues and drama. Our *janta* only wants to see action-packed blockbusters. And even those are released like six months or a year after they have been released in the US."

The rest of their free time, the five friends spent in the Five Star Café, their own collective space, which had gradually acquired an identity of its own. Aarti had generously donated a part of her book collection to fill up the bookcase; she had provided some brightly coloured cushions for the divans. Indu had brought in a small table fan. Danny had contributed a small transistor radio and several games and puzzles; Karan and Arjun had donated the two matching lamps Danny had gifted them on their birthday.

They listened to Hindi film songs on the radio, read books from Aarti's collection, browsed through magazines from the local library, and played all kinds of indoor games -- *Bingo*, cards, carrom, chess, *Monopoly*, *Scrabble*, even *Ludo*. Arjun never failed to bring along snacks from his father's Udupi restaurant; Anita invariably sent over more food and beverages.

During the Christmas holidays, the Café experienced further transformation. Each of the three walls had been painted a different colour -- rust, green, beige. The bookcase had been placed against the rust wall. An entire day had been spent covering a part of the beige wall with collage art using cartoons, glossy magazine cutouts, pictures of favourite cricketers and movie heroines, art that Karan had created as a boy, a poem written by Aarti . . . .

Karan had placed his small aquarium of colourful fish next to the divan against the green wall. The aquarium had a fish of every conceivable colour. Karan faithfully fed them fish food twice a day. He had secretly named the fish based on their colours -- Arjun, Aarti, Danny, Indu, Anita, Vikramaditya, Maharaj, Mrs Pinto his teacher from kindergarten, Seeta Murthy. They were all there.

****

Amongst the idyllic bliss, they did not notice the academic year slip away. It was soon March. One of the hottest months of the year. Annual exams were scheduled for April.

While the five had spent the entire year having fun, for the most part, they were conscientious middle-class students with career ambitions based on their academic credentials. In the first week of March, caught up in the throes of exam fever, they all opened their books, some of them for the first time since the academic year had begun, and chalked out their study schedules. In those two months, they would study around the clock.

There was not much impetus for distraction. There was no television. Pubs had not yet made their appearance. Nor had discotheques. The only breaks they took were to tune to the radio, to the popular *Vividh Bharati* station that beamed Hindi film songs nonstop.

The exams happened in some predetermined university sequence, and not all their subjects were scheduled on consecutive days. The last exam was maths, which comprised five sections: trigonometry, algebra, geometry, calculus, and modern maths. Except for Karan, none of the others was confident of their maths skills; they were doing calculus and trigonometry for the first time. Karan took upon himself the mantle of their coach, promising to bring his four friends up to speed before D-day.

The Five Star Café acquired a classroom setting for this purpose. Karan propped a small, square blackboard against the beige wall and arranged a table and chair for himself next to it. The others sat on the carpet or the divans, facing him, so they could take instructions, work the assignments he gave them, and take his guidance when they had questions.

It was the morning of the maths exam. They gathered in the Five Star Café for one last round of coaching tips. Karan was on his own trip -- he took the role of a coach very seriously. "Take deep breaths. No last minute cramming. Study the list of formulae. Keep calm and you will do well . . . ."

"Maths is a learned skill for us," Aarti told Karan as she browsed through her list of formulae and highlighted the difficult ones. "You grasp it intuitively."

"Profound observation. I can score 90% with no effort. A marginal increase of even 5% in my score requires double the effort. By the law of diminishing returns, the effort is not worth it." Karan theorized.

"Too complicated, cut the funda." Danny screamed.

"Lazy bones. Admit it." Indu flung her eraser at Karan.

"Laziness? No way. Karan was explaining the difference between hard work and intelligence."

Aarti looked up from her formulae. "If Karan ever bursts from the weight of his own ego . . . ," She looked at Arjun " . . . you will be guilty of abetting his vanity."

Indu immediately exchanged a high five with Aarti.

"Abetting. Big word. I need *Oxford* for sure." Arjun rushed to the bookcase mockingly.

"Hey, if I've got it, why can't I flaunt it?" Karan threw small pieces of chalk at the girls, which they cleverly dodged.

"Some flaunt what they don't have." Arjun baited Indu. "They fake it." He added, winking at Karan.

Indu did not bat an eyelid. "Kiddo, it takes guts to flaunt what you fake. Admit it. You don't have the *dum*."

"*Dum maaro dum. Mit jaaye gum Bolo subah shaam Hare Krishna Hare Ram* . . ." Arjun started singing the popular hippie song in a falsetto voice and put a piece of chalk to his lips like a mock cigarette. Soon, the others except Karan joined him swaying and chanting "Hare Krishna" in chorus. They needed an outlet to dissipate their nervousness.

Karan banged the wooden duster on the table several times and addressed his friends in his sternest voice. "Remember we all have an exam at two o'clock." On being ignored, he caught hold of Arjun and clamped his mouth shut with his palm, which gradually extinguished the pandemonium.

At half past noon, Karan drove his friends to college in the blue Herald car. They all rode in silence, experiencing the proverbial butterflies in their stomachs. None except Karan had been able to eat lunch. Indu and Arjun, who usually bickered for the front seat, had sought refuge in the back seat.

****

Aarti sat in the front seat next to Karan, biting her nails and admiring his good-looking profile through the corner of her eyes. The electric blue T-shirt contrasted with his fair skin, making his upper arms look even fairer -- they were so fair and smooth that Aarti had an irresistible urge to reach out and caress them. His hairy forearms brushed her thigh occasionally as he changed gears, sending mild shivers down her spine. His fingers on the steering wheel were so long and artistic, the nails neatly clipped, they made Aarti conscious of her chewed ones. She could feel the power of his strong hairy thighs as they strained the thin material of his off-white pants.

When the car stopped in the parking lot of the college, she had struggled with the door; he was quick to lean against her and open the door. The whiff of his Old Spice cologne awakened her nostrils and transported her into a trance. For the first time in the months she had known him, Aarti looked at Karan with new eyes; he was attractiveness personified. She did not want the magic of this mesmerizing moment to end.

Disembarking from the car, Aarti felt even sloppier in her cotton *salwar kameez*, old *kolhapuri* slippers, and untidy chignon; she cast an envious glance at the svelte Indu, smart in a peach-coloured summer dress and tan wedge heels, long shiny tresses falling straight to her waist, her lips and nails painted peach.

The next few hours were intense. When the clock struck five signalling that the maths exam was finally over, collective sighs and squeals could be heard across the exam halls and in the corridors. Happy days were here again.

"Phew. I maxed it." Karan announced, as he held the car door open while his friends got into the car.

"Me too." Danny shared a high five with Karan before getting into the back seat.

"I feel so empty, so drained." Aarti usurped the front seat of Karan's car before Indu or Arjun staked a claim.

"I should score around seventy or so. That would be twice what

I have ever scored in school." Arjun rolled down the car window.

Aarti and Indu refused to discuss their performance with the boys.

Soon every road song they knew was being sung. *Zindagi ek safar hai suhana, yahaan kal kya ho kisne jaana* [Life is a journey. Who knows what will happen here tomorrow] . . . *Rote hue aate hai sab, hasta hua to jaayega, yeh Muqaddar ka Sikandar* [Everyone comes here crying, the one who laughs goes ahead in life] . . . *Musafir hoon yaaron na ghar hai na thikana* [I am a traveller friends, I have no house, no shelter] . . . .

For once, Danny seemed less restrained -- halfway through the song the voices of the others would trail off -- none of them really knew the lyrics -- only Danny would keep singing.

****

It was a few minutes past seven when the blue Herald car carrying the five arrived at Karan's house. Karan had invited his friends for dinner at the Cantonment Club where his father was a member.

Vikramaditya who was standing at the entrance to the house, glared at Karan. "You are late. I have been waiting since seven o' clock. When will you learn to be more responsible?"

Karan made a feeble excuse and introduced his friends. Vikramaditya nodded cryptically. Karan went in to quickly freshen up and change his clothes, earning another reprimand from his strict father.

When she left home that morning Aarti had no intention of going to the Cantonment Club with the others. "I have to take my mother to the doctor. Even I have a migraine." She had given vague excuses.

None of it had worked. Arjun and Danny had threatened to call it off if she did not join them. Indu had labelled her anti-social.

Karan had escalated the matter to his mother just before leaving for the exam. When Anita had personally requested her to join them, Aarti had reluctantly relented.

They all bundled into the family's big Ambassador car this time, to go to the Cantonment Club -- Karan sandwiched between his parents in the front seat, the other four sitting silently huddled in the back. They were all in awe of Karan's disciplinarian father. Karan and Anita tried to lighten the atmosphere by making polite conversation but soon gave up; all they got were monosyllabic responses from Indu and none from the others. The forty-minute car ride seemed interminable.

The Cantonment Club, one of the legacies of the bygone British era, was located amidst a multi-acre lush green golf course on the tree-lined Garden Park Avenue in old Bangalore. When Vikramaditya stopped the car in the huge porch, a uniformed valet came running toward them with a salute, and opened the car door. Outside of the car, Vikramaditya nodded to Anita, perfunctorily looked in the direction of his son's friends, mumbled what sounded like "Have a good time," and walked away to the bar.

Anita and Karan herded them toward the club's dining room. The décor was faintly Victorian -- from the carved wooden tables to the huge glass chandeliers to the rose-patterned china. Uniformed waiters were taking orders.

Now that his father was not around, Karan resumed the role of the captain of the ship. "Should I order gin and lime cordial for you?" he asked Anita as soon as they were seated around the huge dining table.

Aarti looked around the club in bewilderment. Bangalore's limited glitterati moved around them with consummate ease -- a few cricketers, a couple of local film stars, an upcoming liquor baron and his bevy of girlfriends, a retired film star with his nubile young muse, and the rest, local businessmen and their wives. Several women came by and talked to Anita and Karan. One or two looked vaguely in Indu's direction and nodded their heads. None of them bothered to glance at the others.

Aarti fidgeted uncomfortably; their fashionable dresses, matching jewellery, perfect makeup and stylish hairdos made her even more conscious of her modest middle-class ensemble. She was dressed in her Sunday best, as her sister Bhavna had called it, a pale-green polyester *salwar* suit paired with a floral-patterned *dupatta*; she had piled up her hair in a top knot and borrowed a pair of clogs from Bhavna in a bid to look glamorous, praying all the time she would not topple over every time she walked.

The uniformed waiters were bringing in the appetizers -- *masala papads*, roasted peanuts, French fries with tomato sauce, fresh grape juice for the boys, pineapple juice for the girls and fresh lime juice for Anita.

Noted cricketer E. A. S. Prasanna walked in and sat down at the adjacent table.

"Go introduce yourself to Mr Prasanna." Karan almost pushed Arjun off his chair. Arjun was an ardent cricket fan like every other Indian boy his age. "I want to instil some confidence in Arjun. He is so meek." Karan whispered to Aarti.

Aarti watched with mild amusement as Arjun hesitantly approached Prasanna's table. Prasanna got up, smiled warmly at Arjun, patted him on his shoulder, and autographed the thin paper napkin Arjun shyly held out to him.

"Did you tell him you knew the statistics of his entire career like the back of your hand?" Karan asked Arjun as soon as he was back.

"Gavaskar is my favourite cricketer. He is so good-looking." Typical comments from Indu.

"I got nervous." Arjun was breathless. He carefully folded the paper napkin into a neat square and fit it into his shirt pocket. He looked at Karan and Anita with gratitude and made a speech. Almost. "You made my dream come true. Ever since I was eight years old I wanted to meet him -- my hero, one of the best bowlers of all time . . . ."

His speech was cut short with the arrival of the main course -- puffed *puris*, spicy potato curry, *dahi vadas*. Things got more exciting from there -- an announcement was made by the club management -- *Yaadon Ki Baarat*, a peppy musical movie starring the ultra-modern Zeenat Aman as the heroine -- would be screened in the club's mini theatre.

Arjun, Aarti, Indu and Danny looked at one another with glee. This was a new experience. Something that came closest to television perhaps? In the face of an appetite for the idiot box they had only heard of but never seen until then, the small sixteen-millimetre screen or the black-and-white projector did not seem like deterrent factors.

There was a minor commotion when the dessert arrived -- large slices of freshly made cassata ice cream. "Pìece de resistance." Aarti whispered to Arjun sitting next to her.

For once, Arjun did not mock her for using a big word or refer to needing the dictionary.

Watching a guitar-strumming Zeenat Aman lip sync to the hit song "*Chura liya hain tumne jo dil ko* [You have stolen my heart] . . ." Aarti was inwardly glad she had come along. She could not stop stealing glances at Karan. Unable to forget the intoxicating effect of Karan's nearness in the car that afternoon, keen to sit next to him during the movie screening, she had waited patiently until the others had seated themselves and then pulled a chair next to him.

Karan did not as much as look in her direction. Not even once. His attention was riveted on the screen except when Indu, seated on his other side, would bend over in the dark to whisper in his ears, and he would smile affectionately at her. Aarti found herself going hot with jealous rage -- it seemed to her that Indu was kissing Karan in the dark.

****

That night, as she lay in bed restlessly and sleep evaded her, Aarti was confused and angry with herself for the surge of emotions

Karan had evoked in her. When she finally drifted off to sleep, she had a weird dream.

Aarti rings the doorbell of Indu's house. The door swings open miraculously, and she walks up the stairs. The radio blares an old Hindi song. "*Dost dost na raha. Pyaar pyaar na raha* [Neither friendship nor love remains] . . .

When she reaches the landing, she hears voices and laughter. Aarti walks in the direction of Indu's bedroom. The door is ajar. Aarti takes one step inward and stops. The room is semi-dark; Aarti sees an image in the dressing table mirror on the wall nearest to the door. Karan and Indu are lying on the four-poster bed, the thin white bedspread covering them silhouetting the nakedness of their bodies underneath. Indu's head is on Karan's chest; his fingers are playing with her body.

Aarti turns around and starts running down the stairs. Karan comes out of the room and starts screaming. "Lay off. Now, that you know the truth . . . ." Aarti keeps running down the stairs endlessly until she tumbles and falls . . . .

"Don't do this to me. Don't do this to me." Aarti woke up screaming. She felt all sticky and uncomfortable. Did she have a chum? Cannot be. It was too soon for that. Sliding her fingers underneath the coarse material of her panties, she was horrified to discover she was wet.

Was there a message in the dream? She looked at the clock. It was half-past five in the morning. Superstition had it that an early morning dream would not come true. She felt wide-awake. She was thankful not to be seeing Karan during the holidays.

Aarti, Bhavna, and Anupama would be taking their annual trip to the idyllic town of Mysore to visit her grandparents and cousins. They would stay for a month or so, with the joint family there, in an old-fashioned house situated near the Mysore Palace. Aarti always looked forward to it -- this was the only vacation she had known.

During the summer holidays, Aarti tried to purge all feelings for

Karan. It is a stupid infatuation, she told herself -- he was so smart, good-looking, brimming with confidence while she was such a plain Jane -- he would not be attracted to her. She did not want to lose his friendship by harbouring feelings that were unattainable. She did not want to get hurt. She resolved never to fall in love again, until she met a man who would fall in love with her first.

****

During the same summer holidays Karan, Arjun and Danny hung out together all the time. Arjun had desired to transcend the drudgery of his middle-class existence. Karan was Arjun's hero, a role model he could emulate. Danny was the unobtrusive team player.

They played cricket all morning with Karan's friends from school. In the afternoon, they listened to the latest western music numbers in the Five Star Café. ABBA's "Super Trooper." Boney M.'s "Rivers of Babylon." Disco song "Funky town." They had discovered a new band they liked. The Bee Gees. In the evenings, they drove around town in Karan's blue Herald.

"How did you get a driver's license? You are not eighteen yet." Arjun was curious.

"A resourceful driver, a corrupt system, greedy touts." Karan laughed dismissively. "I have not even seen the interiors of the RTO or wherever it is they issue driving licenses."

"You mean you lied about your age?" Arjun said.

"Baffled your hero could stoop so low!" Danny observed.

Karan had offered to teach them both to drive. He enjoyed being the know-it-all leader.

Within two weeks, Danny and Arjun had mastered the art of driving. Arjun's face would puff up with pride every time he sat in the driver's seat of Karan's blue Herald car and manually change the floor-shift gears. "My father has never owned a car. I never thought I would drive a car before I even turn seventeen."

Karan and Danny were also responsible for Arjun's dress sense undergoing a gradual transformation during the summer holidays. One afternoon, as they were lazing in the Five Star Café listening to the radio -- a cricket commentary of an uneventful five-day test match between India and Pakistan -- they were so bored -- Karan and Danny decided to have some fun at Arjun's expense. They often made fun of Arjun's oil-plastered hair with its old-fashioned upswept peak while Arjun marvelled at Karan's well shampooed and blow-dried hair -- he said it looked like a wig.

Karan and Danny dragged a squeamish Arjun into the main house and then to the bathroom sink, made him remove his shirt and vest, washed his oily hair with a peacock blue liquid -- Clinic shampoo, rubbed his head with a Turkish towel, and blow-dried his hair with a Vidal Sassoon hair dryer.

One look in the bathroom mirror and Arjun would not stop admiring himself. He would comb his hair in different ways, preened at the way it gleamed, caressed it with his fingers, and then muss it up purposely to start all over again.

"Enough. Narcissism is my prerogative. Not yours." An exasperated Karan tried pulling him away from the mirror.

"By Jove, such big, big words. I don't understand narci-sissy whatever prior-getit." Arjun would not budge.

"Here keep this bottle of shampoo." Karan had finally succeeded in weaning Arjun away from the mirror.

The next day, Karan had accompanied Arjun to the local barber on his next visit and given directions to the barber on how he should style Arjun's hair. The barber, while cursing under his breath, had not dared incur the wrath of the authoritative teenager. In place of the oily, upswept peak of hair, Arjun started sporting a thick mop with a right part that covered his large forehead and made him look his age.

"Get rid of that scraggly beard and sparse moustache. Start shaving every day." Karan suggested to Arjun next. Karan himself was clean-shaven -- unlike other boys his age who left their pubescent moustaches untended.

Arjun was horrified -- he did not dare shave off his moustache. Instead, he negotiated with Karan that he would trim his moustache and shave his beard regularly.

Arjun had scrimped and scrounged his paltry pocket money and managed to save the princely sum of one thousand rupees. He was tired of the colourless terry cot pants and dully-patterned polyester shirts he owned, outdated in style. He wanted to buy new clothes and looked to his buddies for help.

Karan was clueless. He bought his jeans at the only men's boutique Bangalore boasted of, got his formal pants tailored at an expensive showroom in downtown Bangalore, and bought only ready-made shirts that were prohibitively expensive. When his dad went abroad on business trips, he usually brought back T-shirts, jackets, and sneakers for Karan. Arjun could not afford any of these with his small savings.

Danny suggested the next best thing -- a modern tailor in the South Bangalore mall whose cuts and styles were literally a cut above the rest. Under Danny and Karan's supervision, Arjun acquired a new wardrobe within his modest budget -- full-sleeved shirts in checks or stripes and straight-legged corduroy pants in the coming fashion of the 1980s. Karan presented him with a pair of brand-new sneakers -- a local brand called North Star that had just appeared on the Indian market.

Only one step remained to complete Arjun's transformation. The most radical change required was also the most invisible.

The day they collected Arjun's clothes from the tailor, on seeing a hosiery store in the mall, Karan had stopped Arjun. "Boy, after all this, you will need new underwear." Karan wrinkled his nose and added, "Your striped *chaddis* . . . Yikes!"

"You have no business peeking at my underwear." Arjun's face was red with embarrassment.

"Can't help it. The *nada* from your underwear hangs out every time you stand next to me to pee." Karan was in the mood to rile him.

"Nobody else can see them, nobody will know." Arjun argued. He had exhausted his budget.

"You know it. That is the point." Karan argued back. "I know it, which is beside the point."

Arjun looked at the hosiery store. A huge ad stared down at him from the opposite wall -- a muscular man clad only in VIP Frenchie underwear was holding a good-looking model on his left arm while he warded off a lecherous villain with his outstretched right hand.

"If wearing miniscule briefs is the secret of confidence, so be it." Arjun grumbled mockingly and grudgingly conceded to go in.

"I don't know my size. I have never bought ready-made underwear before." He whispered to Karan.

Karan cackled with laughter. "Size matters."

Arjun's face had turned even redder with embarrassment. Amidst all the horsing, Arjun bought a set of ribbed cotton briefs. Karan had loaned him the money.

When college reopened, a sartorially-transformed Arjun would enter the portals of Xavier Junior College with a more confident swagger than he had when he arrived the year before.

6. Natty Nineties: Nostalgia

June 24 1998

The television monitor showed superstar Shahrukh Khan and super model Malaika Arora gyrating on the top of a moving train to the rhythm of "*Chaiyya chaiyya chaiyya . . .* " Modern Hindi films songs were preppy.

The four friends had lost all concept of time as they sat talking at the Koshy's restaurant. Unknown to them Koshy's had become crowded. Every table had been taken -- businessmen, journalists, college students, office goers, theatre folks -- they were all there, making deals, having fun or just satiating their hunger. The waiter had brought their orders.

"We have to find Danny." Karan mopped the rivulets of sweat pouring down his face with the sleeve of his T shirt.

The air-conditioner had stopped working. Bangalore was notorious for unscheduled power cuts during summer months.

"Despite hanging out with him so closely, we hardly knew him." Arjun sunk his teeth into the succulent butter chicken.

Karan attacked the aromatic rice and prawn curry with vigour. "Delicious. Tastes exactly as it used to taste then."

"He was friendly and pleasant, never disagreed with anyone," Aarti said. "Yet there was an aura of inapproachability around him."

During the course of a slow lunch, Karan briefed his friends on his failed efforts to locate Danny. The past few days, he had scoured

Bangalore's local directory with a fine-toothed comb for Danny's number. The negative outcome of his endeavour had not come as a total surprise. He had not the faintest idea where Danny had lived. He did not know the name of Danny's father. They had all known him as Danny. Period. Was it his real first name or a nickname?

Arjun turned to Aarti. "I thought Danny used to be your confidant."

"I used to reach out to him -- whenever I needed a shoulder to cry on," Aarti dug into her bloated purse.

"Que sera sera. Whatever will be will be." Indu gave a hollow laugh.

"The last time I talked to Danny was five or six years back," Aarti said.

"The Famous Five may have been reduced to Famous Four." Indu sounded cryptic.

"Danny sounded melancholic." Aarti pulled out a tattered telephone diary from her purse.

"Danny maybe a dead dodo." Indu said.

"What the hell does that mean?" Karan barked at her. Almost.

"Danny can't be dead. Not at thirty-five." Aarti stated emphatically.

"How are your friends? The Famous Five. Is that not what I called you? I may be the harbinger of bad news . . . ." Indu imitated their old teacher Seeta Murthy's clipped British accent.

"You ran into Seeta Murthy and she said that?" Karan was incredulous.

"No way. She can't have remembered Danny. Not after all these years. She must have taught thousands of students at Xavier's over the years." Arjun said.

"After meeting you, I am fairly certain he used to be part of your group. Danny. A distinctly unusual name. If I am not mistaken, I remember hearing recently that Danny may have died under mysterious circumstances." Indu continued to imitate Seeta Murthy's clipped British accent.

"Stop it." Arjun shook Indu gently. "She may have been mistaken."

Koshy's had gone quiet -- the lunch crowds had retreated; the television had been given a brief hiatus.

What if Danny was dead? Volcanoes erupted in Karan's mind. He would never be able to ask Danny for forgiveness then.

"Hope this is not outdated." Arjun called directory assistance from his cell phone and gave them the telephone number that Aarti had provided. He was rewarded with a corresponding address as well as the new telephone number at that address.

"I was kidding about Danny." Indu put her nail file away. "I did run into Seeta Murthy though."

Arjun dialled the new telephone number. The news was neither good nor bad; it was disappointing. A retired brigadier and his wife now lived at that address. They had bought the house a few years back from the sons of the previous owner, who had passed away. The brigadier surmised that Danny had probably been a tenant of the previous owner.

"We can't give up." Arjun looked at his friends.

"Can you help?" Aarti looked at Indu.

"Let me check with my reporters." Indu said.

Where oh where was Danny? The one missing link to their combined past. What had happened to him?

During the second year of college, Danny had played a pivotal role in each of their lives. The enigma had turned into a revelation. Considering how close they had been during those two years why had they not kept in touch or met as a group for eighteen long years? Unfathomable. Unpardonable.

7. Simple Seventies Again

During their second year at Xavier Junior college, the five became rather disbanded, meeting only occasionally. The Saturday routine of the past year had died a natural death. Infrequently, they would make plans to be together and meet for coffee or ice cream before their individual pursuits pulled them away in different directions. Concerted effort was needed even to spend time together at the Five Star Café.

Arjun and Danny were focused on their future career choices and earnestly began to prepare for the exams right at the outset -- getting admission to an engineering college or medical college was competitive. There were several thousand applicants for the few hundred seats available, and larger number of girls had started vying for the courses. Aarti had not made any decisions regarding her career; she seemed to prefer the fictitious worlds of Arthur Hailey and Sidney Sheldon to the real world of growing up pains.

Karan had secretly taken the Scholastic Aptitude Test and obtained scores in the ninety-ninth percentile.

"How can you hide this from your parents?" Arjun expressed shock.

"I don't care much about my father. I do not want to hurt my mother. I will tell them soon." Karan choked on his words.

Karan had also acquired a new pursuit -- signing up for all the cultural festivals in which the college participated. "My oratory skills and charming persona are grossly under-utilized." He told Arjun and Danny when they met in the café one evening. "I will lose them if I don't take drastic action."

"Lamarck's theory of use and disuse." Arjun quipped.

"If you use them anymore than you already do, it will amount to abuse." Danny's retort had them in splits including Karan.

"The trophy closet is only half full. I need more cups and prizes. The day it is full -- my father will praise me." Karan confided.

Arjun and Danny looked at each other and rolled their eyes.

"You were born with the proverbial silver spoon." Danny said.

"Never mind." Karan tried to convince his friends to participate in the debating events with him. "It will boost your confidence."

"I rarely have strong opinions on any subject." Arjun declined. Danny just shrugged.

****

Indu was no longer pink; she was scarlet. Karan worried she would get into trouble. She rarely attended classes, choosing to ride around with boys on their motorbikes.

"Guys, such *bakras*, they make notes for me, give me proxy when I bunk, do my assignments." Indu was leaning against Karan's blue Herald car in the college parking lot. "They give me a ride to any place I ask, so they can brag they slept with me."

"Watch your mouth." At a time when the number of male students in the college was three times that of the female students and most girls were too shy to talk to the boys, Indu's sporting nature had made her the most popular girl in Xavier Junior College. She had no dearth of male admirers and willing escorts, several of them older students who went gallivanting around town with her.

"The truth is, they are so scared, they wet their pants if my fingers so much as brush across their thigh."

"Crass. Crude."

"Cock-teaser, isn't that what they call me?" She giggled loudly.

"Are you hell-bent on scandalizing me?" Karan looked around with embarrassment.

"Why can't I say the word when the guys use it to describe me all the time?

"Nobody dare say such things about you . . . ." The rest of Karan's sentence was drowned in the noise of the Royal Enfield Bullet that zoomed in and stopped in front of them.

"Bye." Indu hopped onto the pillion.

"Dammit!" Karan flailed his arm and kicked at the dust raised by the departing motorbike.

****

When Indu discovered Karan was invariably selected to represent Xavier Junior College at all inter-college events, she followed suit.

Participating in a panel discussion on family planning, the hottest topic of the times, Indu argued that population explosion in India could be controlled by surreptitiously imparting radium pellets to all men below the poverty line to render them infertile.

In the wake of the first test tube baby being born, at an inter-class debate, Indu adopted the stance that all artificial means of insemination should be banned in India. "Our country can't feed the babies being born through the normal process. Why in the world do we need test tube babies?"

Much to her chagrin, she was eliminated in the first round on both occasions.

"Your views are too radical." Karan pointed out. "The lecturers in charge of the selection are conservative."

"*Darpok kahin ke, gaand may dum nahin hain* [Cowards, they have no fire in their ass]." Indu, with her slang-filled candour, made Karan blush.

Yet, on the next occasion, slyly heeding his advice, she took a more conventional stance. The subject was euthanasia. "Man should not play God. Mercy killing is an oxymoron." Indu argued. "Aarti helped me find words like oxymoron and made me memorize the meaning." She whispered to Karan when the results were announced. Indu made it to runner up, though Karan was the clear winner, despite taking the more modern view that terminally ill patients should be given the right to choose to die.

"I have proved my point." She declared. "No more debates for me."

****

The Xavier Junior College Theatre Festival was scheduled for November. Seeta Murthy was set to direct an adaptation of *My Fair Lady*, the classic based on George Bernard Shaw's *Pygmalion*. Karan was her clear choice for the lead role of Henry Higgins.

"Why don't you play Colonel Pickering?" Karan approached Arjun.

"I can't act." Arjun hesitated.

"Listen to me." For three days and nights, Karan coached Arjun for the part, making him work meticulously on his diction.

"A supporting role is a safe bet." Arjun conceded.

When Karan organized an in-camera presentation for Seeta Murthy, not surprisingly, Arjun was selected to play the role.

Very few girls auditioned for the role of Eliza Doolittle. Most girls lacked either the confidence or parental support or both to venture into co-ed activities. Things got further complicated when, soon after auditioning for the part, the girl playing Eliza Doolittle got engaged and announced that her future in-laws did not want her to act on stage. The fate of the play was in jeopardy. Karan and Arjun spent an entire day cajoling Indu to play the role.

Come September and the rehearsals started in right earnest. So did the ongoing quarrels between stoic Karan and volatile Indu -- two individuals with strong personalities.

On the first day, Seeta Murthy announced that she had one typed copy of the script and requested that the lead actors make handwritten copies for their parts.

"Can you write using carbon paper and give me the copy?" Indu fluttered her eyelashes at Karan.

"I am not one of your admirers." Karan quipped. "Why can't you write?"

"I have to take care of my mother -- she is sick." Indu whined.

"Arjun is making a carbon copy for me." Karan exchanged a scheming grin with Arjun.

"Arjun is such a clown -- he is sucking up to you for getting him that role." Indu stalked off.

They continued to fight every day during the rehearsals. Seeta Murthy had abundant faith in Karan's suggestions and absolutely none in any of Indu's improvisations, which only aggravated Indu's exasperation. Indu picked some reason to find fault with Karan.

Arjun watched the brewing conflict from the periphery and desisted from interfering. "Like poles repel." He succinctly summed it up to Aarti and Danny.

****

The play was finally staged at the Town Hall -- an old imposing auditorium from the Victorian era -- a popular venue for professional drama troupes and theatre artistes. It was centrally located and had the capacity to seat two thousand -- all seats were occupied by the student population of Xavier College and their family.

Indu, as Eliza Doolittle, the heroine of *My Fair Lady*, looked alluring in the ballroom scene, dressed in a long, white organza dress with white lace gloves and silver slippers, a bejewelled tiara adorning her top knot. Her dazzling looks overshadowed the fact that she was a pathetic actor. One of her songs proved a big hit with the college students.

"Just you wait Henry Higgins just you wait.

You'll be sorry but your tears will be too late.

You'll be broke and I'll have money

Will I help you don't be funny . . . "

"I don't need to act, just vent my anger at you." Indu had told Karan behind the scenes, just before they returned to the stage for that act.

"The world may treat you as a lady, but you will always be a crass, ignorant flower girl to me." Karan had used a line of his own dialogue from the previous act.

Karan earned a standing ovation for his sterling performance as Professor Henry Higgins. His diction was impeccable, dialogue delivery forceful, and demeanour majestic. Only Anita was in the audience. He abstained from making any antagonistic remarks about Vikramaditya's absence.

Arjun's performance went unnoticed. "At least your stage fright is gone." Karan consoled him.

****

The show had ended. It was half-past eleven. Most of the students had gone home. Indu was smoking her last cigarette of the day. Karan and Indu were standing on the huge steps of the Town Hall. The cool breeze was energizing.

"Stop smoking." Karan gazed at the stars in the sky. "Cigarette begets cancer."

"What's it to you?" Indu shrugged unheedingly.

Karan closed his eyes. All he could see was her face. *She was a fluorescent pink.* "You look gorgeous today."

"Thank you, Professor." Indu stubbed out her cigarette. "Will you drop me home?"

They drove in silence in the blue Herald car. The dusky beauty next to him, still dressed in her organza dress, with her musky odour that was commingled with eau de cologne, cigarette smoke, and whatever cosmetics she had used, set Karan's teenage hormones raging. He kept glancing sideways at her bare arms that brushed against his thigh occasionally. Default or by design?

When they had finally arrived at Indu's house, Karan got out of the car and rushed to the other side to hold the car door open.

"Chivalry is your middle name." Alighting from the car, Indu grabbed him, pressed her body against his and kissed him passionately on his luscious coral lips, her tongue entering his mouth and working wonders within, her supple breasts against his chest as her hands cupped his cheeks. "Good night."

Unknowingly, Karan had embarked on an interminable journey that night. He lay in bed tossing and turning. He rubbed his burning cheeks on the soft pillow. He stripped off his pajamas and wrapped himself in a cool white sheet. He repeatedly thrust his excited organ into the resilient contours of the mattress until he climaxed, calling out her name as loud as he dared. An hour later, the cycle started all over again. Again and again until he was completely dry inside and sticky outside and night turned into dawn.

****

The next day, Karan and Arjun bunked their maths class and walked around aimlessly near the Asoka Pillar in the hot afternoon sun.

Karan kept staring at the Asoka Pillar -- the four lions guarding each of the four directions and the wheel at the centre that symbolized peace and harmony.

"Infatuation?" Arjun asked. "I saw you driving off with Indu after the play."

"The only way to get rid of temptation is to yield to it." Karan quoted Oscar Wilde.

"Are you going to have. . . I mean err . . . err . . . sleep with her?"

"If she will. What do I have to lose?"

"Your virginity," Arjun was learning to carry on quick repartee.

"I've already lost it."

They were both silent for a while as they continued to walk.

"Who was it?"

"I'll tell you later." Karan was keen to end the conversation.

"You are so lucky. Girls fall for your looks."

"Who cares about the other girls? Wish me luck with Indu."

****

Karan had lied to Arjun. What was happening between him and Indu was too private to be shared, even with his best friend.

Like they say, be careful what you wish, for it may soon come true! The next evening Karan had again offered to drop Indu home after college. She invited him in this time. The house was shrouded in darkness. Her parents were out for the evening.

Karan had kissed the nape of her neck; Indu had given herself to him with unconditional abandon, the same way as he had fantasized many times. She had melted in his arms, dragged him over to her bedroom. In the semi-darkness, she had fumbled with her clothes and then his; she had parted her legs, guiding him through her expertly.

An ABBA song played in the background.

"Honey, honey—how you thrill me, aha, honey honey honey, honey—nearly kill me, aha, honey honey I'd heard about you before I wanted to know some more and now I know what they mean you're a love machine oh, you make me dizzy . . . ."

"My first . . . ," she groaned. He did not question the veracity of her claim. Nor did he venture to call the bluff. What he did not know would not hurt him. . . he shuddered in ecstasy as he ejaculated. The sky had not exploded. A million stars had not danced before his eyes. He had not floated away on a magic cloud. Nor had he heard a million violins playing. He felt sweaty. A little tired. All he wanted to do was to go home and have a bath.

When it was all over, he had retreated and dressed hastily, too shy to look Indu in the eye . . . .

At the door, clad in a pink satin robe, Indu laughed brazenly, "Once is not enough."

During the weeks succeeding their first tryst, Karan and Indu made love every day. Sex is one of the simplest pleasures God has bestowed on humanity. When you get none, you crave for some. When you get some, you crave for some more. When you get more, it is never enough. It becomes a habit.

After the first time, Karan was worried to death. What if Indu became pregnant? He had been unable to rack up the courage to buy a condom though he had made three trips to three different drugstores far, far away from his home or college. At the first drugstore, he had waited for the store to be empty of customers so he could go up and ask. After half an hour, he had not succeeded. More and more people seemed to be coming to the store. The pharmacist had looked at him suspiciously. He had slinked away to the next store and so on, returning home unsuccessfully.

The next day Indu had solved his problem. Karan had found a strip of birth control pills under her pillow when they made love. "I can't afford to get pregnant. My mother will kill me." Indu said, making Karan marvel at her confidence and courage. *She was magenta pink.*

****

Academically, the second year posed its own challenges for Arjun. Physics was being taught by the Dean himself, who was trying to pioneer a futuristic culture of active class participation and continuous internal assessment at the college. He had made it mandatory that every student submit an original term paper on a topic set by him. Arjun and Danny, by a quirk of fate, had both ended up with the same dissertation topic -- Einstein's theory of relativity.

Arjun was not particularly fond of physics. He did not know how to go about doing the assignment and sought Danny's help. Danny, who excelled in physics, had completed his assignment after extensive library research and copious notes and generously loaned it to Arjun, to give him an idea about what to do.

A week later, the dean summoned Danny and Arjun to his chamber and launched a diatribe on professional ethics. "I did not expect this from you. I am trying to prepare you guys for a higher education, for life beyond this college. That is the main reason for giving you this assignment. However, what do I get? A word-for-word copy." He held out two identical copies of the assignment. "One of you is a cheat."

Arjun began trembling. He had copied Danny's term paper word for word. Danny was trying to catch his eye, but Arjun was too panicked to do such an honest deed as owning up.

"You will both take an impromptu written test on the term paper topic so I can tell which of you copied. You may lose a year if I decide to forbid you from taking the final exam." The dean, who was in punitive mode, directed Danny and Arjun to write the test in separate corners of his office, as he supervised them in person.

At the end of an hour, Arjun's paper was filled with a shaky cursive writing. Danny's paper contained a single paragraph.

Pardon me Professor. My fault. I had so many things on my plate that in a weak moment I adopted the path of least resistance. If you will grant me 24 hours, I will submit a brand new term paper based on original research.

It was obvious that the dean was astounded by Danny's courage. He let them off after subjecting them to a long reprimanding sermon on the correlation between effort and outcome.

"I am disturbed at your dishonesty, your cowardice." Danny went into a rant mode as soon as the two had reached the secluded parking lot.

Arjun's eyes shone with unshed tears in gratitude; Danny had risked being labelled a cheat to save Arjun from being suspended.

"I wish I had your guts. My father would have died of humiliation had the Dean not allowed me to take the final exam." Arjun was shame-faced. The wind was blowing his hair all over his face. The collar of his black-and-white windcheater was beating against his ears.

Danny calmed down. "Asking for help is not a bad thing. Cheating is."

A tête-à-tête followed, by the end of which Arjun vowed never to repeat the *faux pas*.

Danny was noble. Arjun would never forget the valuable life lesson Danny taught him that day.

****

Aarti's sister, Bhavna, announced her plans to get married to Harshavardhan, the scion of a top business family from Bombay, who had proposed to her.

"What does she see in him?" Aarti grumbled to her mother as they stood at the foot of their small driveway long after Bhavna had zoomed off to a movie on the pillion of Harshavardhan's motorbike. Despite Harshavardhan's suave demeanour and posh grooming, something was missing -- he was self-centred and egotistic, like all men to whom success comes easily, too easily in life.

The evening sun had set. The chirping of birds returning home was subsiding. The city lights had come on. "She is so good-looking while he . . ." Aarti trailed off. At twenty-six, his cheeks hollow and his hair thinning, Harshavardhan did appear a generation older than Bhavna who was seventeen going on eighteen.

"Bhavna and I have had a heart-to-heart talk, sweetheart. She thinks she will be happy." Anupama walked back toward the house.

Aarti followed. "What if she made the wrong choice?" Aarti closed the front door behind them once they were inside the house.

"She has made her decision, she has to stick to it." Anupama switched on the living room lights.

The finality of the response struck a different chord in Aarti's heart. "You mean she can never divorce him?"

"One should not walk into a marriage expecting it to end," Anupama lighted some incense sticks in a bid to ward off the humming mosquitoes.

"How suffocating."

"She will have to make it work."

Aarti picked up her beloved novel -- Sidney Sheldon's drama on marital perfidy *The Other Side of Midnight*. "I feel scared for her."

"Bhavna knows what she is doing."

"I don't want her to get married and go away."

"We should trust her." Anupama walked toward the kitchen to cook dinner.

"I am going to miss her." Aarti burst into tears.

****

The next day, Aarti confided her misgivings to Danny when they were both seated at the Xavier Junior College cafeteria. Danny had gradually become Aarti's confidant during the second year. Danny listened intently -- he had just completed filling out the application forms for his engineering college entrance exam.

"Don't you want to do engineering?" Danny veered the discussion in a totally different direction.

Aarti had been putting off making a decision on her career choices. "I don't want to deal with maths anymore," she replied.

"How about chemical engineering or metallurgy? No heavy-duty maths there." He persisted.

"No Danny. I don't want to be an engineer." Her answer was firm.

"What about medicine?" Danny was not in the mood to give up.

"Too much hard work. I cannot bear the sight of blood." Aarti burst out laughing. "I am not cut out to be a selfless doctor."

"Do you know what you want to be?" Danny stuffed the forms into a brown envelope.

"Me. Myself. Aarti." She toyed with the bookmark in her beloved novel.

"That is profound. Do you know what you want to do?"

She nodded her head from side to side vigorously. Perfect for a drifter like herself, she reasoned.

"If you don't know where you are going, how do you know when you get there?" Danny was a trifle philosophic.

For a rare moment, Aarti let her guard down. "I don't know

what I want to do. I am scared."

"Go after your dreams. Do whatever your heart tells you."

The statement had opened floodgates in her mind. She would not be a discontented doormat housewife. She would have her own career. Of that, she was sure; as sure as a young girl of seventeen can be of her future. She loved teaching; but it was not a lucrative career. Plus, the education system was so controlled -- everything was dictated by the state -- the curriculum, the examination system, evaluation -- there was not much fun in doling out lectures to bored students. She dreamt of designing her own courses, her own assessment methods and exams. But where would she offer these courses? And, what did she want to teach? Good questions. She would cross those bridges when she came to them. She was good at that. Procrastinator par excellence.

The grandfather clock started striking. One, two, three . . . . Aarti was grateful to Danny for being a patient listener. Seven, eight, nine . . . . She could no longer be in denial. It was time she began thinking about her future. Ten. They both got up to go to class.

****

January 1, 1980. Karan and Indu ushered in the New Year together. Indu had accompanied Karan and his parents to the Cantonment Club, and they had danced the night away to the tune of ABBA's "Happy New Year."

Come February, Karan was awarded the Rotary Club's award for best orator of the year for winning the most number of inter-collegiate debates that season. *My Fair Lady* was staged at Bangalore's inter-collegiate drama festival. Karan was voted the best male actor in a lead role.

With the Rotary award, Karan's popularity had grown manifold. A thin line separates confidence from arrogance. Had Karan made the crossover? In the perception of the college students at large, he had; his friends maintained he was the same person.

While Karan had won the best actor award, Indu did not even earn a nomination. This chagrined her so much that it resulted in the first hiatus of their active sex life -- she picked up a fight with Karan for the flimsiest of reasons and broke up with him.

Around the same time, on the eve of Holi, the Hindu festival of colours, Indu was invited to a dirty party, as it was popularly known those days. Indu had been to a few such parties before -- they were mostly held in the house of a friend of a friend whose parents were out -- starting at nine in the night and ending well after midnight in time before the parents returned home. Booze flowed, everyone danced, and the lucky few made out wherever they found a place.

The Holi party was different. It was to be held in a men's hostel in the satellite town of Kalinga just outside Bangalore. Pot was in. Packets of white powder and curved bongs. Soon everyone was on a spirited high.

Euphoria. Levitation. Indu did not want to come down to earth. Her date, a tall, dark and handsome man in his mid-twenties, was nibbling her cold ears, pinching her erect nipples through the sheer blouse, caressing her flat abdomen. In full public view. Indu was laughing loudly. Karan would never have approved of this. The proverbial wet blanket. Lucky they had broken up.

Nazia Hassan's super hit disco number "*Aap jaisa koi mere zindagi mein aaye baat ban jaaye* [If someone like you comes into my life then my life is made] . . ." blared in the background.

Her date's hands soon travelled southward. His breathing became heavier, his tongue pried open her lips and explored the crevices of her wet mouth. Indu did not want the rhythm of the thrust of his tongue to stop. Newton's law of inertia. A body at rest or in motion at constant speed will continue to remain at rest or move at the same speed until an external force is applied . . . .

. . . Indu felt her body hit the ground with a jolt as if she had been thrown out of a slow-moving car. She smiled languidly. She was in marijuana heaven. She waited for the rhythmic thrust of the tongue to begin again. She moaned for a while. Nothing happened. Her mouth was dry. Damn! What was taking him so long? She opened her eyes slowly.

It was afternoon. The sun was scorching hot. The grass pricked her bare thighs. Indu was alone in the middle of some kind of field. Dry grass. Bushes. Mud. Rocks. A puddle. She could not see any civilization for miles around. Not even a cow. Nor a dog. She blinked and brought her wrist near her face. Where was her watch? The expensive Swiss one that she wore only to parties. And the rings she wore on her fingers? All gone. She reached out for her purse. What purse? Fuck. That is where she had stashed the marijuana.

She got up and walked around, to find the nearest road. Thorns pricked the soles of her bare feet. No! They had not even spared her slippers. Every single expletive she knew floated through her mind. Had she been raped? She had submitted herself willingly to the dark man who had been her date. That would not count as rape. It was the marijuana that they had been after.

After two hours of waiting, Indu finally saw a rickety red bus coming down the dusty road. It was filled with labourers and coolies. The driver stopped on seeing a city girl in a skimpy red and black dress waving at him. Indu gave him her most beatific smile and explained she had been robbed. The leering driver dropped her off to her destination without demanding a payment; her smooth legs and bare arms must have provided him a visually appetizing feast.

Indu stood behind a tree near their college. She could not tell Karan what had happened, that was out of the question. Arjun and Aarti would not know how to help her. Danny was her best bet. Indu waited until she spotted him walking toward the college and beckoned him.

"I was on my way to the college, waiting at the bus stop in the morning. A dark middle-aged woman -- she was chewing *paan* --

kept looking at me shadily. I think she drugged me with chloroform and made off with my purse and jewellery. My mother will forbid me to go out of the house if she finds out." She put her head on his shoulders and began to cry.

Danny hailed them an auto and instructed the driver to take them to the Bank of Bangalore. At the bank, Danny handed Indu a bundle of notes -- mostly tens and fives -- money he had withdrawn out of his savings account.

Indu's face stayed glum. *I am such a good actress. So glad Danny bought into my story. So what if I was not nominated for that stupid award. The judges were partial.* "Don't tell Karan." She extracted a promise from Danny.

Indu replaced her ears studs with the money. She bought a few fake rings to replace the real ones she had lost. Her mother would never know the difference. She would admit to losing the Swiss watch.

Indu had not bothered to return the money to Danny later. He had not asked either. He was indeed a good guy.

****

Bhavna's wedding ceremony was held at a traditional marriage hall in the busiest part of Bangalore -- the City Market. When Karan, dressed in a Lucknow *kurta* pyjama had arrived at the venue with Arjun, the traditional rites were in full swing. The marriage hall -- the *kalyan mantap* as it is popularly called -- was bursting at the seams with people, people and more people. Spotting a slim, fair girl with a longish face framed by straight silky hair that fell to her shoulders, it looked oddly familiar from the silhouette -- a new, pretty one, Karan thought. *She is white!*

The girl turned and greeted Karan and Arjun with a dazzling smile. She was dressed in a pastel-pink brocade sari and a matching sleeveless blouse that showed off her fair and lovely arms. Thin gold hoops adorned her ears, elegantly thin glass bangles clinked on her arms, adding an ethnically classy charm. Her lips and nails were painted pale pink; a huge *bindi* drawn with the same pink lipstick glistened on her forehead. Her palms were adorned with an intricate *mehndi* pattern.

Aarti paraded Karan around the *kalyan mantap*, introducing him to all her relatives and friends. "You know what everyone is thinking?" She whispered in Karan's ears. "That we make a ravishing couple; the handsome North Indian boy and the pretty South Indian girl."

"Wow! Our own Dharmendra-Hema Malini jodi." A familiar voice, followed by a low whistle.

Karan and Aarti turned to see Indu walking toward them, dressed in a sheer chiffon sari worn several inches below the navel and paired with a halter neck blouse with a plunging neckline. A shining golden cross nestled precariously at the top of her open cleavage -- waiting to draw embarrassed criticism from the conservatives in the crowd around them.

Did he detect a surge of jealousy beneath her honey-coated voice? *Indu was a hot shocking pink.*

****

The *kalyan mantap* was overcrowded -- there must have easily been over a thousand people in a place meant for a few hundred. Arjun sat quietly in a corner on a cold steel chair. The smoke from the traditional *havan*, the sacred fire around which the rites were being performed, hurt his eyes. He looked around, hoping to spot a familiar face, since Karan had deserted him for Aarti. Danny was not there, he had discretely kept out of the whole rigmarole.

Arjun had deliberately dressed down; he hated social occasions as these with the same passion Indian women loved participating in them. Women bustled around everywhere excitedly, dressed in bright saris, decked in garish gold ornaments. Why did not someone find a way of confiscating all the gold sported by Indian women? Would that not raise the national income, the GDP or whatever the newspapers called it? Those damned economists, calling India a poor country.

The men, in sharp contrast, appeared sedentary and lacklustre, dressed in the traditional white *dhoti* ensemble. Apparently, they had taken a day off at work to attend the wedding. And God knows how many countless weddings they attended in a year. Why could not the factories and offices impose a ban on taking a day off to attend such weddings? Would that not improve productivity? And help boost the national income?

Children ran around everywhere -- screaming, crying, laughing, fighting, and teasing. Should they not be at school? They lacked the discipline -- the parents were to blame -- for making them miss school every other day to attend some wedding or the other. In a few years, the same parents would be chastising their children for performing poorly in their exams.

The trumpet music reached a crescendo and the traditional drums resonated in unison; some significant wedding rite was being performed. People were scurrying around enthusiastically. Aarti, Indu and Karan were making their way toward him.

"What happened to your social skills?" Indu's voice was loud. "Oops! I forgot you have none."

"Don't blame him. He has never attended a wedding before." Karan put a protective arm across Arjun's shoulder.

"Arjun, you are really the eighth wonder of the world." Indu's voice was even louder.

"Food is the best thing about a wedding." Playing the gracious hostess, Aarti led them toward the dining room in the basement.

The smoky dining room was filled with rows and rows of people seated cross-legged on bright cotton carpets, open banana leaves spread out before them, in lieu of plates. A band of cooks, clad in wet towels, sweat glistening on their bare chests, walked around with steel buckets containing piping hot delicacies and served each seated individual one after the other -- a whole array of vegetable curries and steamed rice, *bisi bele bath* -- the rice and lentil dish with carrots and peas, cashews and beans, garnished with grated coconut and dripping ghee, complemented by golden brown potato chips, vermicelli *kheer* flavoured with saffron and raisins, the inevitable curd rice garnished with green chillies, to be eaten with spicy onion *pakoras*.

Karan, Arjun, and Indu found adjacent spots in a corner of the room and hungrily attacked the food served on their banana leaf, oblivious of the burning glances the conservative men and women around them cast in their direction. Indu had committed a cardinal sin -- she was sitting in the men's half of the dining room. Sexes separate. Here too. It was a traditional wedding after all. Yet it did not deter lecherous old men from casting lascivious glances at her, their lustful eyes engaged in unapologetically lewd mental intercourse with her luscious body displayed through the sheer chiffon.

"I want to claw their throats." Indu whispered to Arjun seated next to her, holding forth her long painted nails as she slurped on the piping hot *rasam* and the oily *papad*s.

Arjun gorged on the flaky crepe-like *chiroti*s coated with powdered sugar and mixed with steaming badam milk. "They taste exactly like the French crepes my father makes."

****

The wedding reception, hosted by the father of the groom, was held at the posh High Grounds Hotel, the same evening. The reception hall was airy and spacious; there were no rituals to attend to, the atmosphere was more relaxed and party-like.

Aarti was dressed in an ensemble of blue and silver -- silk *ghagra-choli* dress in copper-sulphate blue with intricate silver motifs, turquoise jewellery set in silver, perfectly made up face highlighted by blue eye shadow, modern hairdo embellished by a small silver trinket at the parting of her hair.

Karan turned up in a navy blazer, charcoal gray trousers and a light blue shirt. He sported the broad blue tie with red Eiffel Tower motifs that Indu had gifted him for his birthday, and a new hairstyle. That afternoon, the fashion-conscious Karan had gotten rid of his step cut. "So passé. Janta has started sporting it."

Arjun had more company in the form of Danny, both smartly dressed in black trousers, white shirt and pointed boots. Indu flitted around in a svelte velvet evening gown and flirted with all the good-looking young men.

A music concert by the local sitar maestro Raja Ram Rao was one of the highlights of the evening. The presence of several high-profile guests was another attraction -- Waheeda Rehman, the retired movie star who had made Bangalore her home; Karnataka's stalwart cricketers -- Gundappa Viswanath and Googly Chandrashekar; national badminton champion Prakash Padukone; upcoming Kannada actors Anant Nag and Shankar Nag; a few local CEOs; a smattering of foreigners. Karan's parents had been invited to the wedding. Anita graced the occasion briefly; Vikramaditya was out of the country.

Dinner was served buffet style at tables covered with spotless white tablecloths. Smartly-uniformed waiters marched around serving cocktails and hors d'oeuvres to the guests. The menu was a blend of South Indian and North Indian cuisine -- Kashmiri *pulao*, *naan*, *malai kofta*, *dahi vada* and *puri-saagu*; with carrot *halwa*, *gulab jamoon* and an array of ice creams for dessert; and filtered coffee.

Like all good things, the wonderful evening came to an end. When it was time for *Bidaai* -- the traditional farewell ceremony -- Bhavna would drive away with Harshavardhan soon after that, to celebrate her wedding night in the bridal suite -- Aarti howled unabashedly, oblivious of the copious tears staining her silver *dupatta*. The crying seemed contagious; in a matter of seconds the entire mass of womenfolk at the wedding reception started sniffing as they wiped their eyes with the corner of their expensive saris.

Karan watched with uncomfortable amusement. Indu was

crying too. The bold and brazen Indu in tears? Indeed a first. Did it prove she too had a heart? *She was a pale baby pink.*

Crying over, Indu asked Karan to drop her home, finally ending the cold war she had initiated against him. When they arrived at her house, she invited him in and they had hungrily made love to the beats of ABBA.

Mamma mia, here I go again
my, my, how can I resist you
Mamma mia, does it show again
my, my, just how much I've missed you
yes, I've been broken-hearted
blue since the day we parted
why, why did I ever let you go
Mamma mia, even if I say
bye, bye, leave me now or never
Mamma mia, it's a game we play
bye, bye doesn't mean forever Mamma mia.

****

How things change. Their bonds with Xavier Junior College were officially terminated once their exam results were announced. Each would follow a different career and go their separate ways.

Karan was waiting to hear from the US universities to which he had applied for their undergraduate programs in computer science. Arjun was leaving for Manipal to do his bachelor degree in medicine -- five full years followed by a year-and-a-half of residency. Aarti would pursue a Bachelor of Science degree in Mysore -- her mother had been promoted as the head mistress of the high school there. Indu was moving back to Calcutta with her parents soon, changing the course of her academics from Science to Arts, which would give her even more time to goof around with the Bengali boys. Danny was the only one who would continue to live in Bangalore -- he hoped to gain admission to the Bangalore College of Engineering.

June 30, 1980. Exactly two years since they had all met. Last day at the Five Star Café. The late summer day was bright and sunny. Karan was working on a small project using poster paper and a dark-blue marker. Indu and Aarti kept hugging each other and howling shamelessly.

"*Chalte Chalte Mere Yeh Geet Yaad Rakhna . . . Kabhi Alvida Na Kehna, Kabhi Alvida Na Kehna . . . Rote Hanste Bas Hi Yu Tum . . . Gun Gunaate Rehna* [As you move on, store this song of mine in your memory . . . Never say good bye . . . Crying or laughing keep humming this song . . . Never say good bye] . . . ." Arjun and Danny played the popular song continuously.

They had all spent the last few days together. The most mundane activity had acquired a new meaning -- for one last time. Coffee at Koshy's, ice creams at Chit Chat, browsing books at the British Council Library, buying audio cassettes at the new HMV store, watching their last Hollywood movie together at the Plaza cinema -- the medical thriller *Coma* . . . . Rest of the time was spent lazing around The Five Star Café -- snacking, drinking chai, poring over old comics, playing *Scrabble* and *Bingo*, indulging in endless bouts of *Antakshari* -- the song based game where each party sings a song beginning with the last letter of the song sung by the opposing party. . . .

The lilting song ended. Aarti and Indu were giggling and making plans to meet during the next holidays. Karan affixed the poster on the inner side of the garage door with Danny's assistance.

This is to notify that the Café has officially closed its doors -- under the current management -- the charter members are dispersing, pursuing their separate ambitions in life. You are welcome to take the stars if you promise not to fight over possession of more than one star each The stars are magical and will bring good luck to the person in possession. While the Café is not inhabited, the peaceful power will be in effect. So, if you are in town and having one of those rough days, you may take advantage. If you desire the Five Star Café can be reopened under new management . . . all ingredients are left behind, at your disposal. It has been a most interesting venture. Kabhi Alvida Na Kehna.

Aarti had borrowed a tube of red lipstick from Indu and added her two lines on the poster.

There will be no new management. The Café will reopen when we all meet here again!

Karan removed four shining red confetti stars hanging from the ceiling and handed them each one. Indu carelessly threw her star on the divan. Danny and Arjun pocketed theirs; Aarti stashed her star carefully in her purse.

"Absence makes the hearts grow fonder." Aarti and Indu hugged the boys one last time and left together. Danny retreated from the Café without looking back. Karan and Arjun stared at each other in steely silence.

Poised to enter a completely new life, they were scared, gripped with an unknown fear of the future, the pervasive uncertainty loomed large threateningly. Boys do not cry. A subconscious indoctrination or a social taboo? A mental block perhaps, that crying would assault their burgeoning masculinity.

"I don't want to cry." Arjun would not stop crying.

Karan put his arms across and held Arjun tight. The reassuring touch was soothing, engulfing them in a sea of unsaid and unresolved feelings, transcending them to a higher plane of intimacy and cementing their bond of friendship in ways words never can.

Long after Arjun had left, Karan sat in the Five Star Café staring at the lone star dangling from the ceiling. *Arjun was the most pleasant shade of blue he had ever experienced.* Karan wished he could have told that to Arjun.

8. Natty Nineties: Togetherness

June 26 1998

Friday evening. The trees in the garden swirled in tandem with the late evening breeze. The pink-orange twilight rendered the dull walls of the Five Star Café deceptively radiant. Aarti had invited herself along with Indu and Arjun over to Karan's place.

Maharaj had opened the windows, placed an assortment of beer and wine bottles and an array of finger food on the side table; he poured them the wine of their choice and returned to the main house.

"Why does life get to so complicated?" Karan sipped his Chardonnay.

"When we are teenagers we are always worried about what other people think about us. In our twenties, we do not care a damn what people think about us. In our thirties we realize the truth -- everybody is so busy thinking about themselves nobody ever has the time to think about others." Arjun philosophized.

"I can't believe it. After all these years our *Bingo* game is still here!" Aarti peered at the contents of the open bookcase.

"I wish we had never grown up." Karan said.

Time stood still. Things were still the same. Time had passed. Things had changed . . . .

Arjun would not stop talking. Karan listened intently. Aarti laughed and joked. Indu remained silent, her stare vacant, her manner disinterested. Her intermittent falsetto laugh sounded hollow. Arjun and Indu did not have a single argument -- not even a difference of opinion. Aarti and Indu no longer giggled. Arjun ribbed Aarti. She agreed to everything he said. Karan watched on amused.

"What a pity that the collage art is gone. It would have been fun to . . . ." Aarti could not stop prancing around. She was visibly excited.

It had gradually grown dark inside the Five Star Café. Karan switched on the lamps. Warm light flooded the café.

"Feel the peace." Aarti extracted a faded red confetti star from her purse, stood on the square carpet in the centre of the café and closed her eyes. "Om. Om. Om."

The other three sat reclined on the divan amusedly watching her.

Om. Om. Om. The walls reverberated the chant. Followed by absolute silence. Aarti remained standing, eyes closed, fingers clutching the red star.

Minutes elapsed. Karan envied Aarti; he had never once felt such peace in the Five Star Café. His eyes silently searched for the little black transistor radio that had belonged to Danny; there it was on the top shelf of the bookcase. Karan reached out with his long hands without getting up; the little black object slipped and fell on the concrete floor with a thud.

The silence had been broken. Aarti opened her eyes. She first hung her star from the ceiling, next to Karan's star; then she picked up Indu's star which lay on the divan and hung that from the ceiling as well.

Digging into his trouser pocket, Arjun extracted a fourth red star and handed it to Aarti. Four faded red stars now hung from the ceiling of the garage.

"Only Danny's star is missing." Aarti clutched a cushion to her bosom. "Once we find Danny we can officially declare the Five Star Café open."

"I have asked one of my reporters to track him down. Promise." Indu gave Aarti a sisterly hug.

Maharaj came back with wine and food refills. The cool breeze had turned cold.

"You are very silent." Arjun turned to Karan. "When we were in college we found it difficult to get our words in when you did the talking."

"You had the kind of life we all envied." Aarti patted Karan's arm.

"An aristocratic father. A doting mother. The gifted son destined to go high places. What went wrong?" Arjun asked.

Arjun and Aarti kept looking at each other. Karan could only guess what they were thinking. Poor Karan had no one in the big bad world.

Until then, Karan had not told another soul about the deadly details surrounding that fateful day . . . the day on which something had died within him.

9. Hate Is The Other Side Of Love

June 30, 1980. *Kabhi Alvida Na Kehna*. Karan could not get the farewell song out of his system -- it was like a stuck record playing within the precincts of his mind. When a forlorn Karan entered the main house, Vikramaditya was in the midst of his elaborate high tea ritual. Maharaj bustled around Vikramaditya refilling his plate with fresh pastries and samosas, making endless cups of chai for him and occasionally lighting his extinguished pipe. Anita had gone to the Ramakrishna Ashram for a spiritual discourse.

Karan loaded a plate with food from the dining table and curled up on the dining room couch with a film magazine in hand. He found it suffocating to be in the same room as his obnoxious father; but Anita did not allow him to take food out of the dining room. He loved his mother too much to disobey her. The icy silence between father and son was unbearable.

"What have you decided?" Vikramaditya inquired abruptly.

Karan pretended to be engrossed in the intimate details and enticing pictures of the film world. His SAT scores were excellent. He had applied to a wide range of Universities in the US. Carnegie Mellon University, Pittsburgh. University of Michigan, Ann Arbor. University of California, Berkeley. University of Washington, Seattle. Much against the wishes of Vikramaditya.

"What did you decide?" Vikramaditya roared.

Karan did not look up from the magazine. "You know very well what I want to do . . . ."

"I will not send you to the US. You are too young to be on your own in an alien country. You will join the Bangalore College of Engineering . . . ."

"What an autocrat." Karan muttered under his breath.

"You will join the Bangalore College of Engineering." Vikramaditya glared at Karan and walked out.

It was his career, his future. How could someone else unilaterally run his life for him, even if he were his father? What happened to democracy and right of expression?

Karan got up and wandered around the house. A few months back, he had discovered huge trunks in the closet of one of the unused rooms on the second floor. The trunks had strong locks on them. Intrigued, he had asked Anita what was in there. Her reply had been evasive. Very unlike her usual self.

Should he really leave home, Bangalore, India? Karan's mind vacillated. He hated solitude. Vikramaditya's flashing eyes and knitted brows came before him. He heard the whiplash tongue berate him, admonish his every act, every behaviour, every word. *Vikramaditya was dull steely blue.* He needed to teach his father a lesson. Maybe separation would help him win his father's approval.

As if drawn by a magnetic force, Karan climbed the stairs to the second floor and entered the mystery room, as he had named it. The room was spotlessly clean. He opened the closet door and dragged the trunks out. Would the contents of the trunks explain why his father hated him so much?

He ran down to the garage and returned with a tool kit. Soon, he had the first trunk open. It was filled with women's clothes -- dresses and outfits, skirts and gowns, trousers and shorts, sweaters and blouses, hats and scarves, slippers and shoes, coats and lingerie, in every conceivable colour. All imported. From England, France, Italy. The styles were no longer in fashion. Probably the sixties or even the fifties.

To whom did they belong? Not Anita, definitely -- she dressed only in saris. They would not have fit her anyway -- these belonged to someone who was much taller than the five-foot-nothing Anita.

When he had the other trunks open, Karan was even more stunned. He found guns and rifles of varying sizes, several bowling balls, a golf set, a saddle and bridle, swimming outfits and diving gear, even a parachute. Karan took them all out one by one, held them lovingly in his hands, caressed them intimately with his palms, and stared at them with open admiration.

Karan had a passion for the wild. He was an amateur horse rider. He had been reading about shooting ranges and bowling alleys in the US and planning to visit them for fun once he was there. He wanted to do bungee jumping and scuba diving as well. Funny, neither Vikramaditya nor Anita shared any interest in those activities. Vikramaditya was not an outdoor person. Forget hunting as a sport, he had never held a gun in his hand.

"Rain drops on roses and whiskers on kittens . . . these are a few of my favourite things . . ." Karan hummed the old *Sound of Music* song. Why did he feel in harmony with the contents of the trunks? He had a mission to accomplish before leaving. He had to uncover the secret of the trunks and discover the truth: why did his father hate him so much?

****

August 1 1980. Karan's eighteenth birthday. When Karan came down for breakfast, Vikramaditya was engrossed in the *Deccan Herald*, the Bangalorean's favourite newspaper, between eating his toast and gulping his tea. *Vikramaditya was a pleasant shade of sky blue.* He looked less uptight than Karan could ever remember. The fine lines on his forehead and around his eyes added character to his natural good looks. Time had been kind to him.

Anita rushed to hug Karan singing Happy Birthday. Vikramaditya did not deign to wish Karan.

At Anita's behest, Karan touched his father's feet with his right hand and raised his hand to his forehead.

Vikramaditya did not bother to bless him. "You can have the white Ambassador car from today. I have bought a new Fiat -- Premier Padmini." He did not look up from the newspaper.

Anita placed a bowl of carrot *halwa* on the dining table. Karan sat down and tasted it.

"What have you decided?" Vikramaditya asked him.

"I don't want the Ambassador," Karan said.

"I only want the best for you." Vikramaditya threw the newspaper across toward Karan.

"I am perfectly happy using the blue Herald," Karan said with his mouth full.

"You will join the Bangalore College of Engineering." Vikramaditya stood up. "Today."

"You can't bribe me." Karan put the spoon down. While he had gained admission to the local college of engineering, it was only a standby -- in the extreme contingency that none of his US admissions came through.

"Don't make me angry."

"The very sight of me is enough for that." Karan pushed the bowl of carrot *halwa* away.

"It is my responsibility to lead you in life."

"Lead me in my life or lead my life for me?"

"I will not pay for your education if you insist on a US college." Vikramaditya visibly trembled with rage.

"In that case . . . ," Karan caught sight of Anita's pleading eyes and stopped. He knew that Anita hated to be in the middle of these father-son skirmishes, as she called them. While Vikramaditya was her strength, he himself was her weakness. Karan loved her too much to exploit that weakness.

Karan slipped away to seek refuge in his haven, the second floor room with the trunks, whose locks had been picked. Immediately he felt better. He rummaged through their contents again. He re-examined each item lovingly, wiped them clean, put them back. He arranged and rearranged them back in the trunks.

Amidst the clothes, a white album with gold trim caught his eye. It contained photographs of an attractive woman -- playing polo, swimming in the sea, flying a private airplane. He recognized the clothes in the pictures -- they were in the trunk. The woman was tall -- five foot six or seven maybe -- and very slim, with high cheekbones, a chiselled chin, and thin pink lips that met in a straight line. It was almost like looking at his own mirror image. Except he would have to be in drag.

Karan was gripped by an unknown fear. What if the woman in the photograph were his mother? No. Can't be. Anita was his mother.

Karan rushed down stairs down to the living room on the ground floor. Anita was stretched out on the recliner sofa her eyes closed. She was humming a mild classical tune. Her lilting voice calmed his frayed nerves.

"Ma, what do the second floor trunks contain?"

Anita's response was desultory.

"Who do they belong to?"

Anita did not respond.

"Why are they always locked?" Karan would not quit trying.

Anita got up from the sofa and went toward the kitchen to give instructions to Maharaj.

Anita was a pallid white. She was hiding something.

Karan ran up the stairs and locked himself in his bedroom. He was anxious -- he had not heard back from the US universities about his admission. Days had passed since he had sent his applications. Then weeks. Now months. He delved into the folders containing the admission paperwork; the deadline to notify the applicants had passed. The admission results were due in the mail any day now.

Playing the waiting game was difficult. Karan decided to contact the universities directly. One by one. It took forever to get through on the telephone. Then, just as he would start stating his case, the line would be cut. Or, the connection would be so feeble he would barely make out what was being said. He managed to contact three universities. Bad news. None of them had accepted him. He could try for the Spring term. Or next Fall.

A series of rejections. For the first time in his life. This was so disappointing. Who needed a birthday like this to remember all his life?

Karan trudged toward his parents' bedroom. The door was closed. He heard low voices -- like Vikramaditya and Anita were discussing a grave matter. Karan slowly retraced his steps without knocking on the door.

If only he had known what was hidden in his father's heart, things may have turned out different!

****

"Honey, soften your stance." Anita draped a brightly patterned silk sari that accentuated her pale rosy skin and delicate porcelain looks. *"Karan's insistence to go abroad is an act of rebellion."*

"Karan has taken after Lila. He has the same thoughts; he even uses the same words." Vikramaditya was seated at the spacious desk situated in the niche adjacent to the dressing table.

"In all these years, you have never held him in your arms, never spoken any kind words to him, and never wanted to know what is on his mind." Anita brushed her long hair.

"Karan is the spitting image of Lila. Every time he looks at me, I shudder. He has the same piercing eyes." Vikramaditya took a respite from the leather folder and the copious office files he was reviewing.

"Karan is an innocent boy."

"Those lips, thin and pink that meet in a straight line, you know why I never let Karan kiss me even when he was a kid?" Vikramaditya ran his tongue along his own lips -- as if he could still taste the repugnance from Lila's kisses. Memories of Lila conjured up venomous spite in his mind. Her death had not liberated him. She continued to haunt him. His face contorted in anger.

"Honey, hate is the other side of love. The opposite of love is indifference." Anita smeared powdered vermilion in the parting of her hair, standing in front of the dressing table mirror.

Vikramaditya looked at his wife quizzically as if to say, "Stop talking in riddles."

"You have been fooling yourself that you hate Karan. You don't want to accept that what you feel is love." Anita tied her salt-and-pepper hair into a tidy chignon.

"He loves sports. He plays every game there is. Just like Lila. When I hear him preparing for those debates he sounds exactly like her . . . ." Vikramaditya placed the files in his leather briefcase.

"You have let Lila control your life," Anita said softly.

"I cannot forget those horrid years I spent with Lila." He wished there was an easy way to purge his bitterness.

Anita came over to his desk. "If you forgive, you can forget."

Vikramaditya looked at her with admiration. Anita had been a great mother to Karan. She had more than made up for the affection he was withholding. He had a lesson to learn from her. She had succeeded in getting the best out of what life had given her.

Anita had worked as his personal secretary for several years. Into her late twenties, she had been a confirmed single girl, shouldering the burden *of chronically ailing parents. Anita was hard-working and efficient, pleasant and patient. He had known she was secretly in love with him. A year after Lila's death, he had proposed to her. She had consented to marry him, a widower with a ready-made son. She had not borne a child of her own. She had showered Karan with so much love that he had never guessed that she was not his biological mother.*

"Karan just asked me about those trunks." Anita cupped Vikramaditya's chin lightly with the palm of her hand and stroked his tousled hair gently.

Vikramaditya did not respond. Opening those trunks was akin to opening the proverbial Pandora's box. Lila had always dressed like an Englishwoman. He should have discarded them a long time back. He had preserved them out of some residual respect for Lila -- after all, she was the real owner of the fortune he had inherited.

"May be we should tell him the truth. He is entitled to know his roots." Anita was in resolution mode as she adjusted the pleats of her sari one last time.

Vikramaditya was reluctant to acquiesce. Soon after marriage, he had decided that Karan should not know that Anita was not his biological mother. Anita had agreed -- she dreaded that Karan would perceive her as the archetypal wicked stepmother if he knew the truth.

Anita collected the car keys and picked up her purse. She was going to the Ramakrishna Ashram for the evening discourse.

Vikramaditya continued to sit at his desk and stare out of the window long after Anita had left the house. The swaying lace curtains brought in intermittent whiffs of the cool air through the open windows.

How Lila had tortured him in the five years of their tempestuous marriage! Lila had been contemptuous of his small town upbringing. That his parents were farmers firmly rooted in their middle-class existence. Hick. She had taunted him. Lila loved parties. Ballroom dancing. The waltz. She sneered at his discomfort in her high society settings, insulted him constantly. Had she ever liked anything about him? The wild sex, definitely. His good looks, perhaps.

In all those years of their marriage, she was never faithful to him.

In body or in mind. She flaunted her sexual dalliances with a vicious wilfulness aimed solely at humiliating him. Lila cheated on him all the time. With several men. Some Englishmen. Her father's friends. Her friend's husbands. His friends' friends.

Why had she even married him? Just so, her father would not cut her out of the inheritance. She was an only child. Her father was a very wealthy man. She would have inherited all his businesses and estates when he died. Alas, she had died giving birth to Karan. And he, Vikramaditya, had inherited her father's fortune.

Was Karan his son? His intuition said yes. Only Lila knew the truth. So what if he wasn't? That was not the reason why he treated him the way he did. Vikramaditya remained sitting at his desk preoccupied. He hated Lila. He loved Karan. He hated Karan because he reminded him of Lila in every which way. Maybe Anita was right. Hate was the other side of love. Anita had not talked in riddles.

Pattering footsteps interrupted his train of thought. Maharaj brought him the day's mail in a small cane hamper. Vikramaditya sorted through the thick bundle, stuffing several official-looking envelopes in his overblown briefcase, placing Anita's letters on the dressing table, tossing the stack of free pamphlets into the wastepaper basket.

There were four international envelopes at the bottom of the basket. Letters from the universities that Karan was expecting. Vikramaditya opened the top three envelopes one by one and read the responses. Carnegie Mellon, University of Michigan, and University of California had sent letters of regret.

Anita was right. Love and hate were two sides of the same coin. He had given Karan material comforts, taken care of his needs, but denied him the love that filled his heart. Life was too short to hang onto such negativity. He had to let it go. What was the essence of his life? His happiness lay in the happiness of the people he loved. Thank God for the regret letters. He did not want Karan to go away. He needed to learn to shower his love on his son.

Vikramaditya slit the fourth envelope with the paper knife. The

University of Washington, Seattle, had accepted Karan for their undergraduate program in computer science.

He had no choice. Vikramaditya stuffed the acceptance letter back in the envelope and walked over to his clothes cupboard.

****

"I have decided to join the Bangalore College of Engineering." A subdued Karan announced meekly at the breakfast table the next morning, looking expectantly at his father -- this should please him -- maybe he would finally get a hug.

"It is time you realized your follies." Vikramaditya did not look up from the newspaper he was reading.

Anita placed a breakfast tray in front of Karan. Thin slices of Niligiris milk bread spread with thick layers of Amul butter. A white-and-yellow double-egg omelette. A cup of hot drinking chocolate.

"Bhai Saab, give the Ambassador car keys to Karan." Vikramaditya hollered to the driver as he got up to go.

Vikramaditya was cobalt blue. Approving at last? Once Vikramaditya had left the dining room, Karan looked up at Anita, his eyes brimming with unshed tears. "None of my US admissions came through."

"Look at it this way *beta*; I get to spend four more years with you." Anita was at her conciliatory best.

Karan's tears had surged past their invisible barrier by now. "Never leave me, Ma."

Anita tousled his hair. "Something tells me you will go there for your Masters."

****

A week passed by. Then another. Yet another.

Karan was listless; he tried to get over his disappointment, reconcile to the fact that he was not going abroad. He wished he could talk to Arjun. Or Aarti. It was more than a month since they had moved away. It seemed like ages, another era. He had no clue how to get in touch with them. Neither of them possessed Graham Bell's wonderful invention -- the telephone.

Time hung heavy on his hands. Locking himself in his room and introspecting had become a habit.

His body craved for Indu. For the uninhibited sex she had provided him. She was away in Calcutta. Of all the times! She had not bothered to leave him a number or an address. Did she even think of him? Was he in love with her? What name should he give the yearning he felt for her physical presence?

His hands went to work vigorously. As his body reached a crescendo, a guttural scream escaped his throat. Even as he ejaculated, he was caught in the throes of a ribbon of sobs. The tears flowed freely. He tried wiping his face with his sticky fingers. He licked the tears off his cheeks. He stuffed his sticky fingers in his mouth. He moved his hands southward. The obnoxious mingling of the diverse bodily secretions was weirdly comforting. He closed his eyes.

The room was dark when he opened his eyes. Was it morning yet? Why wasn't there light? It was only seven o'clock. Why did he need to get up so soon? And do what? Back to sleep. Gosh, he needed to piss. Why didn't he have a hard on? Had he become impotent? From all that excessive masturbation? That contradicted Lamarck's theory of use and disuse. Shouldn't it be the other way? Whatever. This was abuse.

Inside the blue-tiled bathroom, he stood staring at the clear stream of urine hitting the toilet bowl. That felt good. He then stood under the hot shower for as long as he could remember.

Crying can be therapeutic. Healing. He felt unburdened. Boys don't cry. Why shouldn't they? When it would make them feel so much better? And healthier? Whoever made those societal rules? Morons. Why should crying be the woman's prerogative? It was a biological activity. Like laughing. Coughing. Taking a crap. Having an orgasm. Sneezing.

He felt lonely. He longed for Arjun. For Aarti. Their kindness. Their soothing words. Their understanding nods. A reassuring squeeze of the hand. His body ached for Indu -- her flaming touch.

He decided to go out; by then he had realized it was really evening. He walked to his father's bedroom and looked through the small bar. Vikramaditya had wonderful taste in liquor. Maybe he should have a drink . . . he was over the legal age now. That is when he had the brain wave. A night out with Nita. She hung out at the Cantonment Club every evening.

Karan opened the cupboard door. He would borrow one of his father's shirts. The electric blue Louis Philippe. And a trendy watch. The Omega. His father would scream. Karan would scream back. No. He would ignore him and walk away. Better still, he would smile back.

Karan was rummaging for the Omega watch when a stuffed brown envelope caught his eye. From: *UNIVERSITY OF WASHINGTON, SEATTLE.* He opened it hurriedly. His letter of admission. Did he still have time? No luck -- the last day to register had passed.

He had waited forever for this. All his life maybe. Gosh! On his birthday, he had called the other three universities but left this one out assuming he would get the same answer. "Sorry sir, but . . . ," Karan looked at the date stamp. The letter had arrived on his birthday -- one day before he had announced his decision to join the Bangalore College of Engineering. His father had hid it from him, to have his way, to lead his life for him.

His father really hated him. Anita had been wrong. Very wrong. How could a father ruin his own son's future? How could he have done this? Stealth. Of the highest order.

Karan slowly walked out of his father's bedroom, entering the adjoining library. He stood in front of the bookcase that housed all his cups and prizes, looked at them lovingly, reading the inscription on each one of them. They would have to go. He no longer needed to seek his father's approval.

Karan opened the glass door, took out all the cups and prizes, and dumped them into a cardboard carton and labelled it "Garbage." The servants would take the carton away when they came in to clean the library room the next day.

What should he do now? Rebellion? Rage? Revenge?

Vikramaditya was dark blue – the colour of defeat.

No. Confrontation. Confidence. Composure.

****

"I hate deceit. Lies." Karan threw the brown envelope in front of Vikramaditya.

It was the hour before dinner. Reclining on his favourite couch in the living room, Vikramaditya was sipping brandy and smoking his pipe as he leafed through magazines, mostly business. Anita was listening to the radio -- Hindustani classical music even as her fingers were busy knitting -- one of her many pastimes.

Vikramaditya remained silent.

"You have betrayed my trust." Karan looked his father straight in the eye.

Anita dropped her knitting on the carpet. Her eyes were turning red with the tears she was trying to hold back.

"I cannot stay here any longer." Karan stalked up the stairs even as he sensed an aghast Anita rushing after him, tears streaming down her eyes.

Was she Vikramaditya's partner in this crime? *Anita was meadow green*. Probably not. Only a victim of his machinations. Karan's mind was too befuddled to think clearly.

By the time, Karan had reached the second floor Anita had caught up with him. Vikramaditya had followed Anita up the stairs too, taking two steps at a time.

"*Abhi isi waqt*. I am walking out of this house right now." Karan stood at the doorway of the mystery room looking at his parents. "Before that, you owe me an explanation."

He entered the room, opened the closet door, took out one of the trunks, pulled out the contents, and started strewing them around the room. Skirts. Trousers. Sweaters. "Tell me the truth. This is my mother's room." Karan was shooting from the hip. He knew not what the truth was.

Vikramaditya who had just then entered the room stopped in his tracks for a flinching second. *He was a pale baby blue*. His momentary reaction was enough for Karan to know he had hit bull's eye. He flung open another trunk and pulled out the parachute.

Anita was leaning against the wall closest to the door, her eyes closed. Praying.

"You are not my father. My parents, whoever they are, left you all their money." Karan continued to ransack the trunks. Golf clubs. Bowling balls. A rifle. The gun. Everything was now out in the open.

"That is not true." Vikramaditya seemed to have regained his equanimity.

"You are not my father." Karan kicked the empty trunk sending it flying across to the other end of the room.

"Not true," Vikramaditya whispered feebly.

"You are not my father." Karan rummaged through the mess looking for the white album.

Anita remained a mute spectator to the burgeoning altercation;

the enormous self-control she was exercising to refrain from intervention was exemplary.

"I have proof." Karan held up a photograph in Vikramaditya's face -- the woman with the thin pink lips meeting in a straight line -- a carbon copy of Karan.

Anita spoke for the first time. "Karan, all these things belong to your real mother, Lila."

Karan's mind was a combat zone of a multitude of emotions. Anita doted on him. He loved her so dearly. How could she not be his mother? How could this paragon of maternal affection not be his real mother? He felt betrayed by God, by destiny, by life. By Vikramaditya.

"Lila died giving birth to you." Anita's eyes were closed. She was leaning against the wall. The agony of this revelation was visibly unendurable.

"I *am* your father," Vikramaditya said with a profound sense of dignity.

"You are lying. For your convenience. Just like you did about my university admission . . . ." Karan looked around the room and grabbed the gun.

"That gun has not been used in years. You can't do anything with it."

Karan pointed the gun at himself. "Tell me the truth or . . . ." Vikramaditya made a grab for the gun. Karan lunged toward Vikramaditya with rage, missed him, and fell down. The gun hit the ground a few feet away from him. He reached for it. So did Vikramaditya. Despite his best efforts to hold the gun out of Vikramaditya's reach, Karan was losing. Vikramaditya was stronger.

In the scuffle that followed, the gun went off.

****

The shot echoed through the huge house, followed by a piercing scream. Both men turned. Anita's white silk sari was splattered with blood. She lay prone on the floor. She was dead. In a matter of seconds. In a freak accident.

"I have killed the only woman I ever loved. The oasis of my life. The goddess of this house." Vikramaditya was mumbling.

Karan froze. He was responsible for Anita's death. He was a murderer, a sinner. How could he have done this? Killed the one person he loved most?

"She was right. I have let a stupid grudge come in the way of showing my love." Vikramaditya held Karan in his arms and hugged him tightly to his heart. "Believe me, *beta*, I *am* your father. I lied about your admission only because I did not want you to go away so soon."

This was the first time in his life his father had hugged him. Karan prayed it not be the last time. He had waited all his life for this moment. Not under such circumstances though. *His father was the most brilliant shade of blue he had ever seen.*

Karan's tears would not stop. He felt protected for the first time in his life. He had always looked up to his father. Spine of steel. Pillar of strength. Rock of Gibraltar. Except when he was smouldering -- Volcanoes of Italy. Vikramaditya's shirt was soaking wet as Karan rubbed his head against his chest.

"Call the police. Report that I have accidentally killed your mother -- I was cleaning the gun and a shot went off." Vikramaditya extricated himself from Karan and wiped the gun clean of all fingerprints. "Let me call Mr Iyengar. A lawyer should be around when I make my statement."

Karan was rudely jolted out of his stupor. This was a cruel game of fate. He could not lose his father. Not now, when he had just found him. There was no decision to make. Karan knew what he would do. His father could never disapprove of him. Ever. "I have been a bad boy, Papa. I am sorry to have hurt you. Please don't leave me, Papa."

"Forgive me my boy. For everything. If only I had been there for you, shown you my love . . . "

Soon, sirens were heard. The servants had congregated in the back yard, trepidation writ large across their faces. Police constables appeared on the scene.

Karan rushed toward them. "I accidentally killed my mother. I was cleaning the gun when a shot went off." He held out his wrists. "Arrest me."

"No, don't believe him," screamed Vikramaditya, holding out the gun. "Check the fingerprints. They are mine."

"My father is in shock. He is lying to protect me." Karan spoke to the police with a peculiarly inexplicable serenity on his face, his voice studiedly mellow.

"My son is utterly noble and honest. Way too mature for his age. He is lying to protect me . . ."

Lawyer Iyengar arrived at that very moment with the district commissioner of police. Vikramaditya confabulated with them for a few minutes. The district commissioner of police immediately took control of the situation. Their family physician, Dr Ganapati, miraculously arrived on the scene soon after.

Several things happened in quick succession. Mr Iyengar was speaking to the district commissioner of police. Dr Ganapati was injecting Karan with a sedative even as he was finding new ways to protest. The police were asking Vikramaditya for his statement. One police officer was taking the handcuffs out. Another one was filing the statement away. Dr Ganapati was monitoring Karan who was falling into a soporific daze.

A series of gunshots had gone off, sending several reverberations resonating across the house.

Before passing out Karan barely grasped what Vikramaditya's mind and soul were trying to communicate.

****

"Hate is the other side of love." Anita's words reverberated through Vikramaditya's mind. Clichéd, as it had seemed when she had mouthed it, Anita had been right. He loved his son desperately. Why had he been so stupid to be controlled by an old grudge? What had he achieved? If he had let bygones be bygones, Karan would have got the love he so richly deserved. If only he had been there for him, shown his love, taken him out to the park, praised him when he topped his class, appreciated him when he won those prizes . . . Vikramaditya's mind was a repository of reproach.

What would happen now? This innocent boy did not deserve to have his life ruined for a lie . . . He was young, on the threshold of a promising future, his whole life before him. He had to protect Karan. At all costs.

Vikramaditya exhaled deeply. His sorrow was too deep for the tears to flow. He still had the gun in his hand. He had never held a gun before. He prayed fervently that the next few shots would be as effective as the first. With one difference. The first was an accident. These would be intentional.

"God, may this be my redemption. I do not want to go to jail. Nor do I want my son to take the blame – he has his entire life ahead of him. Please protect my son, God . . . Anita, we have shared every trial and tribulation. And triumph. Remember our marriage vows? We will always be together. Here I come." His soul was bleeding. "Last and least. Lila you win. As always."

10. Natty Nineties: If Only

June 26 1998

Time they say is the best healer. Sad, but not true. With time, pain becomes you and you become pain. One forgets what life was without the pain.

"*Aanewala kal ek sapna hain. Guzra hua kal bas apna hain. Hum guzre kal mein rahte hain. Yaadon ke sab jugnu jungle mein rahte hain* [Tomorrow is a dream. Only yesterday is ours. We live in the past. We live in the jungle of memories.]" The song emanating from the collective television transmissions of the houses in the neighbourhood was soulfully philosophical. The door to the Five Star Café remained ajar, revealing the silhouette of four friends in silent commiseration of the shared snippets from Karan's past. Silence indeed expresses compassion more effectively than words.

Indu was the first to leave -- she was a regular hotshot in the cocktail party circuit. The St. Xavier Hospital had paged Arjun -- one of his patients was coming in for emergency care. Aarti planned to get together for dinner with her sister Bhavna and brother-in-law Harshavardhan, now the parents of three teenagers. Everyone had commitments of their own.

Karan switched off the lights and locked the door of the Five Star Café. His heart wept for the vast expanse of love and affection that remained unexpressed between father and son. Walking down the narrow path through the garden shrouded in darkness Karan wished he could come home to a loved one, someone, anyone.

When Maharaj opened the door of the main house, Karan did not go in. He wandered back instead, entered the Five Star Café, lay down on the divan and closed his eyes. Memories of another day continued to haunt him.

To live in the hearts of those you leave is not to die. He remembered a line from some pulp fiction he had once read. By that yardstick, Vikramaditya and Anita were eternal. If only God could bring them back for a single day and give him the opportunity to spend it with them -- what a miracle that would be?

11. Ivory and Ebony

Dr Ganapati had kept Karan under mild sedation for two weeks after the debacled death of Vikramaditya and Anita. The house staff tended to him as distant relatives poured in to visit him. The official story that had been publicized by lawyer Iyengar was that Vikramaditya had been cleaning the gun when it went off killing him and Anita, who was also in the room.

Karan's mind was a veritable battleground. Of images and smells and sounds and tastes.

Anita's screams. The white sari with the huge maps of blood. The salty taste of his own tears. The prickling wetness of his father's face. The prick of the doctor's needle plunging into his hip.

The five gunshots in quick succession, their multiple echoes resonating forever on the empty second floor. The smell of gunpowder. Vikramaditya's serene face -- the nostrils plugged with cotton wool, the blue immobile body.

The sounds of silence. The vacuum within. The blackness around.

The thronging crowds. Their continual chatter. Eulogies for the departed souls. Sympathy for the solitary surviving soul. Commiseration with each other. Barbs and venom for everyone else.

The white-clad priests. Smoke in their eyes. The smoking butt of the double-barrelled gun. The holy fire in the *havan*. The incessant chants of the Gayatri mantra. "*Om Bhoor bhuvasuvaha tatsa viturvarenyam. Bhargoho devasya deemahi. Diyoyonah prachodayaat.*"

The brown copper pots filled with ashes.

The fragrance of incense. The pungency of gunpowder.

Anita's tear stained face, a fleeting memento of the agony within. Anita's ever smiling face, the eternal memento of the ecstasy that once was that would never be.

The cool soothing touch of her cold fingers on his burning forehead. The hot scorching flames of her maternal care that engulfed his troubled mind. Cold hands. Warm hearts.

Daadima, Vikramaditya's aunt, arrived from Punjab to take care of Karan. Without Anita and Vikramaditya, the home was just a house. Daadima took over the kitchen. Her sole aim in life was to cook rich Punjabi food. Except for Maharaj, she dismissed all the other servants. Maharaj tended to every possible chore around the house.

Vikramaditya's business partner bought out their share of the business and Lawyer Iyengar helped Karan invest the money in a trust fund. Karan retained the Premier Padmini, the new white Fiat that Vikramaditya had bought days before his death. The blue Herald and the family Ambassador were both sold off with the assistance of Lawyer Iyengar.

****

Something within Karan had died with the death of his parents. Memories haunted him. Nightmares kept him awake at night.

Karan's energies were expended on one obsession. What if he was not Vikramaditya's son? If he had some unknown genes? It bothered him that he bore little or no resemblance to Vikramaditya.

Yet, Anita had always told him how father and son were so alike -- both fanatically meticulous about maintaining the car; they loved the same foods, hated the exact same vegetables; the irritating habit of checking and re-checking the locks several times before leaving the house. Most important -- when they argued -- they were dispassionately logical, incapable of seeing the other person's point of view; even their voices sounded similar, many people had confused one for the other over the phone.

Karan dug through the contents of Lila's trunks several times over in the hope of finding some evidence, any evidence, that he was Vikramaditya's son. He ransacked every closet and cupboard in the house in a bid to find the proof of his parentage.

Maternity is a matter of fact; paternity is a matter of opinion -- he was reminded of one of his public speaking contests from the Xavier days. Only a DNA test could have confirmed his paternity. That opportunity had been lost forever.

When Karan could bear his agony no longer, he ventured to quiz Daadima, who might have been privy to some family secret. For once Karan was glad for the existence of this single soul that played the role of a surrogate parent, no matter how peripheral.

"*Puttar, yeh nahin ho sakta ki tum mere pote nahin ho* [Child, it is not possible that you are not Vikramaditya's son]," Daadima replied unhesitatingly. "*Chalo saboot hum dikha denge* [Let us go, I will show you proof]."

****

The same evening a reluctant Karan accompanied Daadima to a cottage-style house on Steeple Street, near Bangalore Cantonment. The nameplate read *ASTRO ALEXANDER. ASTROLOGER AND CRYSTAL BALL READER.*

Vikramaditya and Anita had never been to an astrologer, palmist, or tarot card reader. Neither of them had ever wanted to know their future. Anita always used to say "Life is like a book -- you don't need to know until you turn the page what is in store."

Nevertheless, a compelling force propelled a curious Karan up the narrow pathway through the half-open Georgian door of the quaint little cottage, right behind Daadima. The narrow lobby was dark; the single window was covered with thick black drapes imprinted with bright orange pumpkins. The narrow lobby widened into an open hall. A single green lamp perched on a fake marble table cast an eerie glow.

A fat, middle-aged Anglo-Indian man sat at the far end of the hall, gazing into a bright crystal ball. He signalled them to close the door behind them. The walls were painted a bright Andhra blue. The ceiling was painted black and adorned with silver confetti stars and a round white ceramic lampshade that resembled the full moon. The smell of incense emanated from the inner precincts. An antique HMV record player from the fifties played an old prayer song. "All things bold and beautiful, the good God made them all . . . All things wise and wonderful the good God . . . ."

"You are sad. A cloud of darkness surrounds you. You are being sucked of your energy. You come here to seek your past." Astro Alexander looked directly into Karan's eyes as he spoke.

Karan found himself nodding his head in reverent acquiescence. Was he being hypnotized?

Astro Alexander held up a card that indicated his services and rates; Daadima paid him the handsome sum of two hundred rupees. Unquestioningly. She then squatted on the floor.

"Your mother died giving birth to you. Her name was Lily, Lola, Laila . . . ." Astro Alexander gazed into the crystal ball.

"Lila," Karan said as the cuckoo clock on the opposite wall started striking.

"On a rainy night. The month of August. A private ward. A stone-walled hospital. Oh My God! The hospital is near here!" Alexander squealed.

"I was born at the St. Xavier Hospital," Karan added helpfully.

"A mere detail. I see your father staring at your dead mother's face. He was relieved when she died." Astro Alexander fiddled with the green lamp to make the light brighter.

Alexander rotated the crystal ball and watched it silently for a whole minute.

"You resemble Lila. I can see her riding a horse. Swimming in her swimming pool. My God! Shooting bullets from a revolver!"

Karan's mind was busily recollecting the contents of the closet he had stumbled upon on his eighteenth birthday.

"She was an only child. Her father was a very wealthy man. She inherited all his businesses and estates when he died. She was very aristocratic. She dressed like an English woman. She loved parties. Ballroom dancing. The waltz."

The crystal ball was shaking vigorously. Alexander kept shaking his head violently until it stopped, then looked at Karan kindly. "Sorry to say this to you. She did not love your father. She made fun of him all the time. Because he was poor."

"Why did she marry him then?" Karan had sometimes wondered the truth about his hidden past.

"To obey her own father. Or he would have cut her off from his will," Alexander replied. "Lila cheated on your father. All the time. With several men. Even some Englishmen. Her father's friends. Her friend's husbands. Your father's friends." His voice was now a hushed whisper.

Karan's face was very tense. What was he going to say next? Was he not Vikramaditya's son then?

"Your father was pure of heart." Alexander lit a red candle and stared at the molten wax, mumbling and fingering his rosary.

Apocalypse time. Karan was biting his nails, shuffling his feet. He wanted to know the truth. What if it were bitter?

Alexander poured some holy water from a jug into the palm of his hand and threw it at Karan's face with full force, making him choke audibly from astonished shock.

Crazy! How had he started believing in this bullshit? Karan agonized over the wet patch caused by the squirted water on the front of his white shirt.

"Lila knew in her heart your father was a good man. She let him perform the duty of a husband. She wanted her children to be good and pure. Like him. And so are you." Alexander proclaimed.

Was he relieved? Karan's reaction to the whole charade remained sceptical.

"We end for the day." Astro Alexander adjusted the sash of his velvet housecoat and stood up.

"*Main tumhare tarah padi likhe nahin hoon. Par mera dil jaanta hain, hamara rishta khoon ka hain* [I am not educated like you. But my heart knows that our relation is that of blood]." Daadima whispered to Karan.

By the time Karan and Daadima reached the Georgian door and opened it, Alexander had switched off the green lamp, plunging his house in darkness.

Karan and Daadima stepped out. The night was scary -- pitch black darkness and unnerving silence. The roads were even more deserted.

During the course of the next few days, Karan was pleasantly surprised that the erstwhile unceasing conflict of his parentage had abandoned him. *Vikramaditya the Dead was Copper Sulphate Blue.* Vikramaditya was indeed his father; there were no two ways about it.

****

November 1980. Karan joined the Bangalore College of Engineering, where his admission was still open.

The Bangalore College of Engineering was located on the outskirts of South Bangalore, away from the hustle and bustle. The well-maintained campus, boasting of lush lawns, contained separate granite buildings for different departments, a full-fledged library, modern facilities for student activities, and even a delicatessen. Accommodation for students coming from other cities and states was provided in a multi-winged hostel located adjacent to the campus.

Friendship is like love. It is a product of chemistry. If two people hit it off, they become friends. Else, not all the effort in the world can make it happen. Karan did not make any new friends at College. Most of his classmates stereotyped Karan as snobbish. Others labelled him plain reserved. Either way few made an effort to reach out to him. Danny, his one link from the past, who was in the same class, was his only friend.

Freshmen at college had to contend with the ubiquitous syndrome -- Ragging. Karan was caught for ragging three times in quick succession.

The first time was easy. The seniors asked them to play dumb charades. The loser removed his accessories or loosened his shirt buttons. The whole charade lasted half an hour. No limits were crossed.

The second session was a little disturbing. There was a quiz of lewd questions. How often do you masturbate? What is your penis size when erect? What is the bra size of your girlfriend? Graphic responses were mandated. Boys that refused to answer, out of fear or shame, were made to stand on one leg -- for a whole hour under senior supervision. Karan was one of them. Things went a step further when the boys were asked to pair up and mime the sex act complete with foreplay as the seniors jeered and roared with laughter. Thankfully, no nudity or undressing was involved since the whole charade had taken place in a classroom.

The third session had taken a more dangerous turn. The seniors had rounded up over twenty freshmen and made them crawl on all fours to the boys' hostel located at the end of a dirt road a mile away from the campus.

The hostel had four wings, organized to form the four lateral sides of a cuboid; each wing had three floors. The hostel mess was located in one corner of the rectangle formed by the four wings; the remaining central area of the rectangle was open -- it was used for a variety of outdoor sports. The seniors made the boys march up to the third floor terrace of the west wing.

A dark guy wearing a bright red *lungi* doubled up above his knees, his dark hairy chest bare, sat on his haunches smoking a cigarette. He was surrounded by a gang of ten or twelve seniors. Most of them were clad in thin cotton pajamas or a *lungi* carelessly tied around their waist, their torsos bare. All smoked cigarettes and were laughing loudly. They made the freshmen chant "*Jai Ho Velu anna*" a hundred times, as the dark guy blew smoke rings at them.

Velu, obviously some kind of a leader that none dare disobey, for reasons only known to him, had singled out Karan for special treatment, as he called it. Grinning leeringly, exposing bright yellow teeth long enough to be fangs, he ordered the other freshmen to kneel down on the rough cement floor and watch.

"Smoke." Velu thrust his cigarette into Karan's hand.

"I am allergic." Karan pursed his lips.

Velu pried open Karan's mouth with his grubby fingers and stuffed in the lighted cigarette. Karan started to choke on the smoke. Velu held the cigarette in Karan's mouth for a full minute.

"Next." Velu looked at his cronies.

One of the seniors handed a ruler to Karan. "Lift it up and measure his dick." The senior pointed a finger toward Velu's *lungi*.

The other seniors roared with laughter. The freshmen looked uncomfortable.

Karan refused outright.

"Look at his lips, rosy red," the seniors jeered. "Pretty boy. Show us your toy." They surrounded him from all directions.

Karan tried to dash toward the head of the stairs.

"Catch him if you can. Catch him if you can. Pretty boy. Rosy lips. Running away without measuring my dick." Velu roared with laughter.

The surrounding seniors dragged him back to the centre of the terrace.

It was getting dark. The kneeling freshmen whimpered from pain.

Velu pinned Karan by his cuffs. The other seniors started to paw him, unbuttoning his shirt, unzipping his fly, planting wet kisses on his bare shoulders, arms, nipples. When Velu loosened his grip on Karan's cuffs and grabbed the seat of his pants to yank them off, a petrified Karan started running toward the parapet wall of the terrace, despite being countered by the mass of senior boys dragging him back.

One of the freshmen began to cry, evoking profuse laughter from the predatory perpetrators. One of the seniors stuck a pacifier in the crying boy's mouth and started dragging him around.

Karan used this moment of distraction to reach the parapet wall. Without a second thought, he put one leg across the parapet even as the seniors tried to pull him back. He closed his eyes and put the second leg across, saying a short prayer in his mind. If this was the way for him to go, so be it. They had gone too far. It would teach the rogues a lesson. They would be convicted for murder and save several freshmen from the ignominy of being ragged.

Karan waited to hear the thud as he hit the hard ground. He felt nothing underneath his feet. Was he not dead yet? Crap! What if he had just maimed his leg or worse, paralyzed for life?

When Karan opened his eyes, several pairs of anxious eyes peered back down at him. He was lying prone on the terrace floor. The seniors had pulled him back, instead of letting him fall.

"You shall not tell anyone." Velu had brought his face close to Karan.

Karan held his breath. Raw onion and garlic. Uncooked chicken. Cheap whiskey. Velu smelled like a shit house.

"If you do, you are dead meat." Velu had vamoosed from the scene with his cronies.

Karan slowly zipped up his pants and put on his shirt, too shame-faced to look at the other freshmen. None of them made any move to help him.

Holding his shoes in his hand, Karan ran all the way back to the college, not stopping until he had reached the parking lot, collapsing at the door of his car, his clothes disarrayed, hair dishevelled, his feet bare.

****

Dusk had set in. "I was shit scared," Karan and Danny were seated inside Karan's Fiat. Karan had just finished narrating what happened to him a while back. "I felt so disgraced, I wanted to die," Karan confessed.

"Promise me -- that you will not take any drastic steps. No quitting the course," Danny said.

Danny was ivory. The colour of unadulterated friendship?

"We have to report this to the principal." Danny got out of the car. Karan walked the length of the corridor from the parking lot to the principal's office with Danny.

The principal was a tall and bulky man immaculately dressed in a brown suit and red tie sitting behind a huge desk piled with stacks of papers and files, in his stone-walled office adorned with photographs of eminent scientists and scholars -- Albert Einstein, Sir C. V. Raman, Srinivas Ramanujam.

"A slur on human dignity. Just look at this." Holding out Karan's hand mapped with nail marks toward the Principal, Danny launched on his anti-ragging tirade. "Most freshmen are too scared to complain."

"Boys will be boys." The principal made light of the situation.

"Sir, you have to ban ragging with immediate effect," appealed Danny.

"This is part and parcel of college life. The same seniors who ragged you will become your best friends later." The principal pulled over a stack of papers from a file to peruse.

"Ragging can be a crushing blow to individual self-respect . . . ."

"You are overreacting." The Principal did not look up from his stack of papers.

The principal was a bright sunflower yellow. His lack of sympathy was not a surprise. Karan placed a steadying hand on Danny's shoulder.

"It is not fair to encourage such practices," Danny's voice was getting louder.

"I don't have to be fair all the time."

"Barbaric. Degenerate."

The principal rang the bell on his table. His secretary appeared.

"Good bye boys. I am late for dinner." The principal picked up his briefcase.

The secretary thrust a blank sheet of paper toward Danny. "Write down your complaint. The principal will review it later."

"We will submit it tomorrow." Danny picked up the sheet of paper.

Danny and Karan walked out of the principal's office. Danny kicked at a flower pot until it broke. He stamped on the scattered soil.

"Velu has threatened me. I don't want him to know we complained." Karan said.

Danny shaped the blank sheet into a paper rocket and let it fly.

"Fucker. Our principal is worthless."

****

Things remained quiet for a few days. So quiet that Karan felt apprehensive. Then it happened.

Karan and Danny were driving toward the college in Karan's car. When they were about a mile away from the campus on a narrow road with a marshy swamp on one side and the hostel building on the other and dotted arbitrarily with huts, tenements, and random petty shops, the Fiat started to hiss and wobble, forcing Karan to stop the car. Three of the tires had gone flat. Karan cursed aloud. The road was strewn with nails.

Suddenly they were surrounded by Velu and his cronies. Some of the shop-owners and their lounging customers looked at them. None came running. Very unlike them.

Karan looked at Danny helplessly. Danny signalled him to remain calm. Karan emulated Danny's behaviour closely, trying to put on an air of false servility.

It did not take much effort for Velu and his cronies to force both Karan and Danny to march toward the hostel. They were taken to the mess located in one corner of the central area that was flanked by the four wings of the hostel. Inside the mess, the walls were almost black from smoke. The dining room portion, with its rows and rows of cold iron tables and chairs, was deserted. The suffocating smell of kerosene emanated from the adjoining kitchen where lunch was being cooked.

Velu gave them both an empty glass bottle each and ordered that they urinate into it in full public view. Danny refused outright. With dignity. Karan followed suit.

Minutes went ticking by. Velu's threats did not work. The other seniors fell silent one by one. Something in Danny's demeanour was indeed intimidating. His quiet refusal did not leave them much room for bullying.

"How dare you disobey me? Don't you know the power of Velu Anna?" Velu was suddenly screaming at the top of his voice. He picked up an empty bottle himself, lifted his *lungi* up and urinated into it in front of them. Karan and Danny looked away; the seniors watched them hawk-like, like they were ready to thwart any attempt to escape. When the bottle was full Velu held it out toward Karan and Danny and ordered them to drink it.

Once again they refused. Velu screamed louder and louder as he gripped Karan. One of Velu's cronies fell upon Karan and tried to pry his lips open.

One of the cooks who had come out of the kitchen on hearing the commotion and been a mute spectator until then, pulled off Velu's *lungi* and started running in the direction of the pantry, which was at the opposite end of the dining room.

Butt naked and vulnerable, Velu had no choice but to let off his hold on Karan and concentrate his efforts on regaining his *lungi*.

Acting in a flash, Danny grabbed the glass bottle from Velu and smashed the top off it to use it as a weapon. Holding it in his defence, he started backing toward the telephone, dragging Karan with him.

The cook had hurled Velu's *lungi* inside the pantry. As soon as Velu went in to retrieve it, the cook bolted and locked the pantry door from outside, pocketing the huge iron key and standing guard, looking menacingly at Velu's cronies.

Danny continued to hold the broken bottle in one hand as he made a telephone call to the principal's office. Sensing trouble, Velu's cronies started slipping away from there one by one.

When the principal arrived, only Karan, Danny, and the cook remained. Velu could be heard screaming curses and abuses at them all.

The principal issued a circular the same afternoon warning students about crossing the limits of decency in the course of ragging.

Karan and Danny were disappointed. They had hoped him to ban ragging. The only silver lining -- Karan and Danny were not caught for ragging after that day -- they had most likely been declared pariahs in senior circles.

****

Karan found it a drag to attend more than one or two classes a day. He was no longer motivated to participate in the debates and cultural events he had once so loved. His grades in the first semester exams were decent but not exemplary. He studied his textbooks only on the eve of the exams.

During the second semester on finding out that Danny was in trouble with one of the courses -- Advanced Quantitative Techniques -- the cryptic concepts were way beyond Danny's comprehensive capabilities, Karan offered to coach him. For a few days, the two held coaching sessions everywhere -- at Karan's house, in the college library, at Koshy's.

When the mid-term results were announced, Danny had topped the class; Karan's score was much lower.

"I could not have done this without Karan's help. I would have flunked." Danny vociferously appreciated Karan amongst their peers.

Danny was yellow, a colour that Karan abhorred. Danny's high score was an act of treachery. Karan stopped talking to Danny after that day. He no longer offered to drop Danny in his car. When Danny came and sat next to him in class, he got up and sought another seat, oblivious of the other students who watched the drama with open amusement.

Danny continued to make friendly overtures, inviting Karan to join him at his table in the deli during lunch. Karan dumped his food tray in the garbage bin and walked out, uncaring of the student community howling with laughter.

Around the same time Karan's social life veered in a new direction -- Indu had returned to Bangalore.

"Living with my parents was suffocating," Indu told Karan, referring to her life in Calcutta. "They are always in the clutches of relatives who disapprove of everything I do or say."

Indu was soon enrolled in a premier girls' college in old Bangalore for her second year BA. Indu's flat became the perfect haven for their rendezvous; they spent long sinuous afternoons there making love. Sensuous. Passionate. Obsessive. Ecstatic. *Indu was scarlet -- the colour of unbridled lust.* Karan became acutely Indu-dependent.

Karan sometimes believed he was in love with Indu. Other times, he would swear to himself she was a mere outlet for his physical urges. He could not discuss his relationship with anyone; least of all Indu herself. They were on two separate planes; he loved to intellectualize, analyze his feelings, and hypothesize every situation; Indu found this weird. She probably meant esoteric, the word being outside the realm of her addled vocabulary.

Indu partied wildly through the night. Men and boys picked her up, dropped her back. Was she cheating on him? She claimed no one else would sleep with her, since everyone knew that she and Karan were a couple. Karan chose to remain suspended in the hazy threshold zone between trust and mistrust.

Karan often conjectured at the dichotomy of biology and society. Biologically, teenage years were high testosterone years for the boys. Yet Indian society expected boys to remain celibate until marriage. No wonder the college was full of frustrated youths whose academic productivity suffered. If only they could get laid, they would probably do much better in their studies. For this to happen, where were the girls? The girl-to-boy ratio on campus was rising no doubt, but society dictated that girls guard their virginity for the man they would eventually marry one day in the not so distant future.

Even if some girls agreed to put out, where would they do it?

Most middle-class boys and girls lived with their parents. They either walked to college or rode the bus. Few had parents who owned a car and fewer were allowed to drive.

Some of the boys had met their future marriage partners on campus. Their relationships would remain platonic until they graduated, found jobs, and got married. Obtaining parental permission to get married to the girl of their choice would be a whole story unto itself.

Parents had their own separate priorities for choosing spousal partners for their offspring. Family name. Caste. Religion. Language. Dowry. But they were always the last ones to learn about their children's clandestine romances. The more aggressive boys may defy their parents in the future, and, at the risk of estranging them, marry the girl of their choice. Others would simply comply with their parents' wishes and let their love die a natural death. Unrequited. Unsung. Unspoken. Forgotten.

What the boys want is sex. They delude themselves they are in love. They end up getting married. Karan analyzed. They think sex equals love equals marriage. Theory of transitivity. What happens once they are married and the yearning for sex wears off? They lose interest in each other, become fat and ugly, spend the rest of their lives frustrated, fighting with each other. Facts of life.

****

The next two years went by in quick succession. Danny and Karan remained distant during this time. Circumstances coaxed them to come closer during their final year of engineering.

Karan had become a confirmed loner. He lived alone in the big house save for Maharaj -- Daadima had returned to Punjab. He spent a large part of the day lolling around in bed watching television. When Bangalore had finally been added to the television network Karan had acquired a brand new Onida colour TV. He had no plans for life after college.

Somewhere along the way, his relationship with Indu had settled into a dull monotony. They felt jaded -- almost like a married couple. It was only a matter of time before the inevitable happened.

One day Indu vamoosed from Karan's life.

Karan had sensed this all along. Yet when it actually happened it seemed like the end of the world. He needed a kind soul who could offer him solace. He immediately thought of Danny. He knew not where Danny lived; and Danny did not have a telephone. Karan felt helpless.

Karan could not fall asleep. He lay on his back on the large canopy bed in the cold confines of his blue bedroom, dressed in an old pair of shorts and a tank top, watching a late night movie on the Doordarshan channel. Raj Kapoor's *Mera Naam Joker*, the story of a circus clown who makes other people laugh, while hiding his own sorrows -- none of the women he falls in love with, reciprocate his feelings.

As the Joker on screen sang *Jaane kahan gaye woh din rehte hain tere yaad mein* [I do not know where those days have gone, I continue to live with memories of you]. . . . Karan empathized so much with the pathos that he was wallowing in self-pity by the dollops; by the time the movie ended, he was so exhausted that no more tears would come.

****

The next morning all hell had broken loose on the college campus. It was ragging season at college -- the latest freshmen batch had arrived a few days back. Manish, one of the first year boys who lived in the hostel had been discovered dead in his room.

The police arrived on the scene and started a questioning spree. Separately, Karan and Danny were both part of the crowds thronging the hostel. The hostel boys were discussing the deceased.

"Velu and his cronies are responsible for this. They are nowhere in sight."

"They used to brutalize Manish mercilessly. Because he belongs to upper caste."

"They have been around forever. Perpetual seniors." Sniggers. "They keep failing their exams every year."

"What did they do to Manish?"

"The usual. And then more. They took away his money, his music system, even his books."

"Is that why he committed suicide?"

"He was trying to leave the hostel with his suitcase when Velu and his cronies caught him. They were afraid Manish would go to the police. He comes from a rich family."

"They stripped him naked, shaved him . . ."

". . . down there." Hushes.

"Inserted hot candles up his asshole." Shudders.

"They pissed on him. As he squirmed. In public."

"Why didn't anyone complain?"

"Several boys heard him screaming but were shit scared to come out and help . . ."

"Complaining won't have helped. Velu has influence."

"His dad is a politician. Even the Principal is scared to antagonize them."

"It seems Velu even shagged on him." Sounds of disgust. "And Velu's friends kept shouting Ragging-Shagging."

As Karan watched, Danny introduced himself to the Inspector of Police and gave him a lengthy narration. With animated fervour.

From there, the events took a rapid turn. Taking cue from Danny, several freshmen and previously abused sophomores blurted out the outrageous acts they were subjected to; several seniors who detested Velu and his gang also gave their statements. In the midst of all this, Manish's lawyer uncle arrived.

Karan and Danny looked at each other. *Danny was a rich peacock blue -- a mixture of peace and protection.* Karan's eyes brimmed with silent gratitude. *Three years back, if not for you, there might have been a dead body -- me.* How could he have been so mean as to stop talking to Danny? Had he seen the wrong colour? Definitely. *In retrospect, Danny could not have been yellow that day two years back.*

The police managed to arrested Velu and his cronies the same night, pulling them out of bed. The Principal issued an official circular banning ragging and making it a punishable offence. He even summoned Karan and Danny to his office and apologized to them for not heeding their words three years back. Their courage had been vindicated. Finally. At the cost of a freshman's life.

****

July 31 1983. Late into the night, Danny and Karan sat drinking at Deep Purple, the brand new pub in downtown Bangalore. The décor was classy, the crowd up market; there was even a piano bar in the lounge.

"Yesterday, I dozed off after we had sex," Karan wiped a tear off his eye. "When I woke up, the room was dark. I switched on the lamp. I found a Post-it note stuck to the lamp. *Good-bye. I am leaving for Bombay. Lock the door before you leave. The owner will take care of the rest.*" Karan recounted. The afternoon sun streaming its rays on their faces, he and Indu had had slow languorous sex -- which was usual; several times in one afternoon -- that was unusual. Now he knew why -- it had been Indu's parting gift.

"Men's hearts are made of glass. Tough on the exterior, very easy to break, crack, shatter to smithereens." Karan expostulated. "Women's hearts are made of elastic. Flexible. Resilient. Why did I not realize this simple truth?"

Danny listened, expressing his solidarity through his silence, occasionally nodding his head vigorously.

"When I read the note I was like what the fuck . . . I rushed out of the bedroom, not a stitch of clothing on me . . . I must have looked like Archimedes. Except I did not know the opposite of *Eureka*. That would have been the most appropriate thing to say."

Karan summoned the waiter to order another pitcher of Kingfisher beer. Danny was still sipping his first mug.

"When we started out I swore to myself our relationship was purely physical. I don't know when exactly this emotional involvement started. Being in love is difficult. I can't live with her. I can't live without her." Karan was down the glorious path of self-realization.

"Did she not feel the same way?"

"No emotional conflicts for her," replied Karan. "I was not her boyfriend. Just someone she fucked."

Danny focused his attention on draining his first mug of beer.

"I missed the signs. This was her way of ending the relationship. Bloodlessly."

Karan had been busy with his engineering exams. Indu had gone away for three days. Mysteriously. Her cousin's wedding she had told him. She had wanted to borrow his mother's jewellery. Karan had bought her a few trinkets instead -- he would not part with Anita's belongings. Ever. Indu had then borrowed an expensive leather suitcase from Karan.

During the three days she was gone, Karan had taken care of several chores for her. He had stood in line at her college to pay her exam fee. "I hate those long lines. I get restless." She had told him before she left, volunteering him to do the chore for her.

He had to water her plants every day. "I know you can never say no to me." Indu had signed him on for the task before she left.

On the second day, Karan had finished the chore and was about to leave her flat, when he had almost been accosted by her landlord. Indu had not paid the rent ever since her roommate had moved out.

Karan was rendered an unwitting target to the threats the landlord had brought for Indu. He had ended up writing a check to cover three months' rent, to pacify the landlord.

Stealth. Karan had not even known Indu's roommate had moved out.

After Indu's return Karan had discovered the counterfoil of an air ticket to Bombay, while the wedding was supposed to have happened in a small town not far from Bangalore. Indu shrugged it off as belonging to one of her cousins.

"Now I understand. That is when she interviewed for the job in Bombay," Karan said, draining his mug.

Danny kept looking at the clock above the cash counter. The pub was half empty by now.

"Once the openness is gone, a relationship is over." Karan declared. In a rare moment of shared intimacy, he added. "When we lay spent in bed she once said, if pleasure is a sin, then to sin is a pleasure . . ."

Danny looked at the clock one more time and then at the pianist.

". . . Profoundly profane or profanely profound? Was my reaction."

The clock struck twelve. July had given way to August. Karan had turned twenty-one. The pianist played the Happy Birthday song for Karan. Danny clinked his beer mug with Karan's and presented him a birthday card.

The pub was closing. It was raining outside. Karan's car was parked on the road. Karan rubbed his prickly cheeks on Danny's neck as they walked in the middle of M.G. Road in the middle of the night, letting the tears flow. Incessantly. "I have no one in the whole world. I dread the solitary existence that awaits me."

"Why don't you try to locate her?" Danny asked.

"This morning I tried calling Indu's parents in Calcutta -- so I can get her Bombay number. Damn Bangalore telephones. I managed to get through once. Her mother was saying something but I could not hear clearly." Karan could not bring himself to tell him the rest of the story.

Disappointed, he had banged the receiver down with such force that several envelopes fell down from the telephone table -- Maharaj usually placed all mail on that table. There was an envelope from the Jubilee Nursing Home that Indu's erstwhile landlord had been kind enough to forward. Karan perused the contents of the envelope. It contained a bill, some medical reports and a brief letter from a Doctor Rosario. Medical Termination of Pregnancy. Stealth yet again -- Indu had told him it was food poisoning.

It had to be his child. Intuition. There was a soft ache in his heart for the child that would never be born. He had no one who loved him. No one to shower his love. Having his own child would have given a new direction to his loveless life. If Indu had not robbed him of the opportunity to do that. Without giving him a chance.

It was unfair. The child could not have been created without his involvement; it had been destroyed without his knowledge. Whoever said it was a fair world we lived in? Women had way too much power when it came to motherhood. Despite all their complaints. The pain of child bearing. The responsibility. The hardships to bring a child into the world. It was a façade. To make men believe that women were underprivileged and overburdened.

ADDRESSEE NO LONGER LIVES HERE -- Karan had written on the envelope and instructed Maharaj to mail it back to the Jubilee Nursing Home.

Karan opened the door of his car. "I have to find a new girlfriend."

After that day Karan and Danny spent more and more time together with each other. In the college library. In the delicatessen on campus. Hanging out at the pubs of Bangalore. Karan frequently indulging in what he called, desultory rambling; the quiet and attentive Danny a perfect foil for the endeavour. The protector and the protected. The sensible and the sensitive. Truly the odd couple.

****

June 6 1984. Karan and Danny were seated on the sixth floor open-air terrace of The Garden Pub on M.G. Road under a red-and-white chequered canopy. It was a month or two before their final semester exams at the Bangalore College of Engineering. Karan's GRE results had been announced and he was applying to US universities for a master's program in computer science.

Danny kept looking at his watch every few seconds as if he was nervous. His mug of Kingfisher beer was untouched.

Danny was a fluorescent mauve. Karan could not fathom why Danny was so restless. After all these years, Karan often felt he hardly knew him. Danny rarely talked about himself. Or his family. Soon they would be going their separate ways.

The sun had almost set. The city lights had started to come on. The cool breeze brought in a mélange of mixed aromas. There were only a handful of people in the pub -- it was a weeknight. The small black-and-white TV beamed the evening news.

"Nearly 300 people have been killed as Indian military troops stormed the Golden Temple in Amritsar, held by Sikh militants. The militants have suffered heavy casualties owing to the sophisticated weaponry used in the army's attack -- machine guns, anti-tank missiles and rocket launchers . . . ."

"I have something to tell you," Danny said abruptly.

" . . . Operation Blue Star, as it is being called, is the culmination of the growing tension between Prime Minister Indira Gandhi and Sikh militants led by Sant Jarnail Singh Bhindranwale . . .," Tejinder Singh, the TV reporter continued to read the evening news.

"Karan. I admire you. Immensely. I adore you. Profusely. I worship you. Fervently. I love you. With all my heart." Danny kept staring at the red-and-white chequered tablecloth.

Karan looked at him incredulously. It sounded so rehearsed. Like he had been practicing to say it. The garish neon light illuminated Danny's solemn face. *Danny was deep purple – the colour of passion.* "You are not drunk are you?" Karan beckoned the uniformed waiter. "I am famished."

"*Kaash.*" Danny's voice was low.

"It is a phase. You will get over it." Karan quoted some vague Freudism he had read somewhere. "Chicken cutlets and grilled sandwiches." He quickly gave their orders to the uniformed waiter so he would go away.

Danny kept staring into Karan's eyes.

"My feelings for you have always been normal." Karan continued to clarify. He found Danny's silent stare disconcerting. "That of a friend. Nothing more. Nothing less." Karan's discomfort teetered at the end of its tether.

More people were entering the pub. The air was getting heavy with cigarette smoke. The crowds were getting boisterous.

Karan had no idea what was happening in Danny's mind. He picked up the pitcher and drained it down his own throat. He was agitated. How had this happened?

The waiter brought their orders and placed them on the table.

"Danny, what's wrong with you? Please say you did not mean what you said . . . ." Karan's voice was low and conciliatory.

Danny continued to stare at Karan speechlessly.

Danny was royal indigo. Speckled with gold. Rich. Decadent. "Stop looking at me that way." Karan's voice was louder than he had intended.

The raucous laughter at the neighbouring tables died down abruptly. The other patrons looked curiously in their direction.

Karan shuffled his legs under the table and inadvertently brushed against Danny's outstretched legs under them. "You perverted bastard." Karan exploded, inserting an ulterior motive to an innocuous happening, which was not even Danny's fault.

On TV, Tejinder Singh continued to report the evening news. "The opposition parties have castigated the Prime Minister Indira Gandhi for desecrating the Sikh place of worship. Public opinion across the country is predicting her imminent downfall . . . ."

Karan suddenly got up and rushed out of the restaurant without looking back. Going down the six flights of stairs in anger, the shameful words he had uttered reverberated in Karan's mind.

He felt a peculiar sympathy for Danny as he got into his Fiat. Sympathy is debasing. Like class difference. Like caste difference. Like economic status difference. Trying to assert the relative superiority of the sympathizer over the sympathized. Should it not be the other way round?

****

Karan drove the Fiat toward Nita's house. After Indu had departed from his life, he had replaced her with Nita, the daughter of a family friend. On the rebound, Nita had pointed out. Karan knew Nita had always been attracted to him. Nita loved to go for long romantic walks in the moonlit night, the cool evening breeze blowing through their hair. Sex was not a staple diet of their relationship. It was sporadic. Only on the rare occasion Nita deigned to admit she needed it.

Karan was thankful that night turned out to be one of those rare occasions. He wanted to expurgate the unpleasantness that lingered in his mind -- his own shoddy behaviour at the pub.

Karan stopped interacting with Danny after that day. He avoided going to the classes they had in common. He did not as much as look in his direction if their paths ever crossed by chance. Out of sight, out of mind; that way he will get over me, Karan rationalized.

The final semester exams were finally over. Karan would soon be westward bound -- he had an acceptance from California State University. His dream for many years was finally coming true.

The night before his scheduled departure, Karan could not fall asleep. He knew not when he would ever come back to Bangalore. Maybe never. He had no family, no friends, anyway.

Danny was pale violet -- the colour of compassion. The harsh and hurtful words he had hurled at Danny in the pub haunted Karan from the depths of his mind. How could he have been so mean? Why had he taken such a derogatory stance? It was not Danny's fault. Karan felt like scum; a dreg of society. He had to seek Danny's forgiveness. He would find Danny's house and meet him in person. He had less than twenty-four hours to do it.

Good intentions. A simple thing. If only one knows what a tomorrow has in store for them.

October 31 1984. Indira Gandhi, the first woman Prime Minister of India was shot dead by two of her bodyguards at nine o' clock in the morning. She received sixteen bullets at close range in the chest and abdomen. Payback for having ordered the Indian troops to storm the Golden Temple of Amritsar in a bid to capture terrorists -- her assassination was reportedly the terminating aftermath of Operation Blue Star that she had ordered five months back. Outbreaks of religious violence broke out across India. Accompanied by rioting and massacre. Thousands of people lost their lives. Security was tightened. The Indian army was on high alert. Gatherings of four or more people were banned across the nation.

Karan could not leave the house for days, right until the day he left for the US, as soon as normalcy was restored to a turbulent nation. Would he bear the burden of guilt of an unsolicited apology for the rest of his life?

12. Natty Nineties: Beckoning

June 26 1998

The onset of a jet-lagged slumber had ensconced Karan in the throes of tiredness as he lay on the divan in the darkened Five Star Café.

Come to me son. Baritone voice. Melancholic yet Macabre. Karan sat up with a jolt and switched on the lamp. There was no one there. His mind was playing games with him.

Karan went back to the main house. The cold drilling gaze of the stuffed bison and antlers adorning the walls of the living room bore into him. He called out to Maharaj, ordering him to dismount them and store them away and started to go up the stairs. On an impulse, instead of going into his bedroom on the first floor, he continued to climb the stairs all the way up to the second floor.

Come to me son. He heard the voice again. Mellifluous yet malevolent. In the distant horizon, he could see the face of a slim and tall woman with thin pink lips that met in a straight line beckon him. Lila.

Karan approached the room where he had discovered the mysterious belongings that fateful afternoon before his eighteenth birthday and opened the door. It was dark except for the sliver of moonlight shining in through the window panes. The closet door was open. Lila, dressed in a silver taffeta ball gown, stood in the empty closet, her arms outstretched.

Was Lila ruining his life with her wanderlust? Karan tumbled into the closet.

What if Lila's soul had entered his body at the time of his birth -- the time of her death as well? Had she continued her dalliances through him, making him go from woman to woman, seeking sex -- while he deluded himself he was looking for true love?

When Karan opened his eyes, he was lying on the cold mosaic floor at the foot of the closet. The room was swathed in darkness -- the waning moon was hidden behind a cloud. The closet door was closed. Lila was gone.

13. Love Was Not Put In Your Heart To Stay There

When we are young, we have stars in our eyes. We have dreams. We romanticize the unattainable. Once the dream is attained, everything seems dreary. Once we are There, we realize there is no There. There is now Here. Disillusionment follows. Life is drudgery. Yet it is important to dream.

November 1984. Karan started the master's program in MIS at the California State University Long Beach, near Los Angeles. He lived on the 300-acre campus with its minimalist architecture and naturalistic landscapes, in one of the international house residence halls. Initially his life was restricted to the campus. He spent long hours at the university library. He worked as a research assistant on a university project for the US Department of Education where his primary responsibilities comprised running advanced analytics and computing predictive metrics for literacy.

Karan fit into the US way of life effortlessly. He watched football and baseball on television with his American roommates, became an avid fan of the Los Angeles Lakers, the undaunted basketball champions and successfully tried his hand at skiing on the snow-covered mountain slopes at nearby ski resorts.

During the spring term, Karan met Nimmi, a graduate student doing her masters in organizational psychology. Nimmi liked to be around him. "Every girl goes through a phase when she wants to be surrounded by masculine energy." She told him. "The nearness is satiating in itself."

Karan craved for a respite from his ceaseless solitude. *Nimmi was pale yellow. Inconspicuous in the background. Unpleasant in the forefront.* They were cohabiting in a studio apartment off the campus by the time the spring term ended. Karan took care of rent and living expenses. Nimmi told him she could not afford to pay for anything. Her father's business back in Delhi was operating under heavy debts and losses and she considered it beneath her dignity to take up a job.

Karan found life with Nimmi uneventful. She let him be. They never had a single fight during the months of their togetherness. They partied in the clubs and bars of West Hollywood Friday and Saturday nights. They spent many a weekend bumming at the beaches -- Laguna, Malibu, and Redondo.

June 1986. Karan completed his master's program summa cum laude. Nimmi quit the university, conveniently succumbing to her parents' wishes to get married -- an arranged match -- with a moneyed non-resident Indian whose family was intent on finding him a good Indian girl with home values. Nimmi fit the bill or so they all thought. It was another matter that Nimmi's grade point average had been pathetically low the past two terms -- the university had put her on probation and given her a warning.

Karan's feelings were mixed. Relief. He was not ready for marriage yet. Thank God, she had not persuaded him. Rejection. Was he not good enough to be her husband? He had been a devoted boyfriend and a loyal lover. What did she see in that NRI except the money? Karan did not attend Nimmi's wedding.

Karan went back to playing sports -- his first passion -- with a vengeance. Cricket with the *desi*s. Baseball with the whites. Golf by himself. Several tennis tournaments.

In the course of the next few weeks, Karan had got an offer from COX Corporation, a reputed food and beverage company, and joined the teeming thousands of immigrant students embarking on careers in computer programming. He moved to Burbank, renting an apartment that was a short commute from his work place.

****

Karan remained girlfriend-less for the next few years. He partied almost every weekend -- frequenting discos and bars, campus parties and *desi* shows, clubs, and restaurants. There were a few one-night stands with women he fancied; several stray affairs with girls he found attractive; they all died a natural death within days, nothing was serious. Until he met Sofia. At California's best beach resort; and was seduced, instantly.

"Sexy. I love your butt." Sofia playfully pretended to grab his ass. A multi-coloured sarong was wrapped over her gold lamé bikini that exposed a figure to die for.

It was late evening. The beach was deserted. The summer sun was yet to set. Karan was dressed in a pair of white Calvin Klein clam-diggers and a multicoloured Hawaiian shirt. The granular sand was prickly beneath the softness of his soles.

Sofia pushed Karan onto the sand, lay down on top of him, and unbuttoned his shirt. "I love the hair." She ran her fingers on his hairy chest. Her sarong fluttered in the warm beach breeze. "Why didn't I meet you sooner?"

Sofia was royal green speckled with gold. Regal. Majestic. A wild cat. Pixie-faced with high cheekbones. Blond hair. Blue-green almond shaped eyes -- definitely some Oriental genes there.

"I was saving myself for you." Karan quickly gave in to the pleasures of the flesh as he stared at the vast expanse of the darkening blue sky illuminated by the blazing ball of the setting sun.

"As you save so you spend." Sofia unzipped his fly. Nifty fingers. Creative tongue. Hot flesh. Karan was soon traversing in outer space.

Six days later, Karan moved in with her. Until then, he sent her a bouquet of six red roses every day. She owned a posh house in Beverly Hills -- she was a rich heiress -- the estranged daughter of a famous Hollywood director who had committed suicide recently. She would not allow Karan to share living expenses -- the concept was alien to her.

Sofia lavished him with expensive gifts. A brand-new bottle-green BMW Z4 Coupe. Exclusive membership to the Beverly Hills Sports Club frequented by movie stars. Shopping on the famed Rodeo Drive -- where the rich and famous did their shopping -- whenever she was in the mood for it. Versace jeans. Armani sweaters. Gucci shoes. Cartier watches. Golf clubs with KK etched on them.

Sofia was an inveterate gambler. Whenever bored, they drove up to Las Vegas -- Gamble Ville -- and stayed at the MGM Grand Hotel. Sofia gambled away at the casino with Karan in tow. When she was losing, she would declare, "Let me win once, just once, and I will stop." Once she had won, she would state, "Now that I am winning, let me win some more -- I will stop when . . . ." Eventually they would be forced to return to Los Angeles -- Karan had a job to preserve. He refused to quit his job though Sofia had suggested it several times.

Sofia was aquamarine. Speckled with silver. The most pleasing colour he had ever seen. He had come to believe that in her, he had found the consummate woman who would love him. Bear him a child. Give him a family that would put an end to his solitary existence.

Karan had been honest with Sofia about his past peccadilloes. "You are a serial-monogamist." She had slotted him into her chosen stereotype. "I am a multitasking polygamist. Don't expect me to be faithful." She had replied.

Karan refused to take her seriously. Until reality did a check on him. After six months of exciting togetherness.

****

Karan was at the men's salon of the Hilton Hotel in downtown Los Angeles, getting himself one of those fancy haircuts, a mushroom cut. The barber, who had unburdened only half of his relationship woes was persuading Karan to get burgundy highlights in his hair. That is when Karan saw her.

She was rushing toward the elevator, closely followed by a tall young stud with a gorgeously-sculpted body that was developed by gym rigor or steroids. *Sofia was parrot green.* Soon, they were both riding up in the elevator -- one of those fancy transparent ones. Karan could see that the stud could not keep his hands off Sofia. The elevator stopped at the eighth floor -- the highest it would go.

Fight or flight? Karan took a deep breath. He wanted to find out the truth. It was now his turn to unburden to the barber, who was blow-drying his hair.

The barber sympathized with Karan's plight -- his own boyfriend was always cheating on him. He volunteered to introduce Karan to the lobby manager. Minutes later, Karan was in possession of a room key -- the lobby manager had empathized with Karan's predicament -- his own wife had cheated on him.

It was just like her, to do whatever she did, openly. Karan felt a stilted admiration, as he rode the fancy elevator to the eighth floor. Why was he suspecting her of cheating on him? He had known her for months. She would not cheat on him. There might be a logical explanation. His intuition did not have to be always right.

Karan swiped the card on the door of the eighth floor bedroom and entered quietly. The room was dimly lit. The stud lay on the bed, his long legs sticking out. Sofia was mounted on him, moaning gutturally, her body jerking up and down. Her hair was swaying all across her back. The stud was laughing with pleasure as she slapped and scratched him.

Sofia stopped galloping momentarily. Her instinct may have

registered the presence of a third person in the room. She got off the stud, ran into the bathroom and closed the door.

"Couldn't you have waited a little longer?" The stud looked up lazily as he continued to fondle himself. "No way can I stop now."

Karan's mind was blank. His body was numb. He could hear the sound of the shower running in the bathroom.

The panting stud continued to stroke himself to a jerky climax. Once spent, the stud rolled off the bed, got into his jeans, and extended his sticky hand to Karan. "Hey. I wish we had met under better circumstances, but who cares."

Karan did not accept the extended hand.

The stud started to put on his dirty white sneakers. "You must be the husband or the boyfriend. I can't help it if pretty gals throw themselves at me. I have to take care of my hormones." He let himself out of the room.

Karan collapsed on the couch devastated. How could she do this to him? He was a skilful lover, Sofia had told him herself several times. "I feel sorry for all those women who have never had an orgasm. They have never experienced ecstasy. Obviously, their men are to blame. Sex is not a perfunctory favour they are doing themselves . . . I am sooo glad to have you Karan." Yet, why did she sleep with other men?

Sofia had come out of the bathroom, spruced and dressed in the white Turkish bathrobe provided by the hotel. "It was one of those urges. Nothing serious."

Karan stormed out of the hotel room in disgust.

****

Sofia was jade green. Royal and romantic. Karan continued to go steady with Sofia despite her act of hyper-impudence for the sole reason that she may one day be the mother of his child, the treacherous act notwithstanding. He seemed to be in perennial denial, his deepest fears obfuscated by the consolation that her infidel act was but an arbitrary aberration.

A few weeks later Sofia dumped Karan. His crime? He had dared to point out that she could show a little more respect -- she had been bitching more than usual about her mother.

Sofia had looked at him with stunned surprise. "No one ever tells me what to do. Or what not to." She threw him out of her house that very minute. In the middle of the night.

Karan had tried to reason with her. Silence was her weapon. Deadly and effective. Karan had no ammunition that could stand up to it. Luckily, he had not yet vacated his old apartment.

The next night, Karan parked his BMW Z4 in her driveway and rang the doorbell incessantly. He knew Sofia was inside -- the lights were on, in the living room and her bedroom. There was no response. He rang the bell again and again and again. So intently was he concentrating on this repetitive action that he did not hear the siren of the approaching police car. Or see the flashing red and blue lights.

"Sofia, give me another chance." He was still screaming when the police officer had got out of his car and aimed a gun at him.

"Get back in your car." The police officer instructed Karan to drive his car to the Beverly Hills police station and followed him closely, his car lights flashing.

Sofia had complained to the police that Karan was stalking her. It took Karan all of two hours to extricate himself out of the sticky situation. He had to provide evidence that Sofia had been seeing him out of her own free will and volition -- he showed the myriad cards she had given him with her every gift. He had carried them for a very different purpose -- to remind Sofia of her feelings for him. It helped that the police officer was deeply interested in cricket and had discovered in the course of interrogation that Karan played the game.

While the police officer was convinced that their affair had been consensual, he had not forgotten to warn Karan never to stalk Sofia again. Hell hath no fury like a woman scorned. The police officer had quoted Shakespeare!

Karan was badly shaken by the incident. He had not expected Sofia to be so brutal. That same night all the clothes and gifts Sofia had bought him were delivered to his apartment by a FedEx representative. Sofia never asked Karan to return the BMW she had bought him. *Sofia was still the most brilliant emerald green Karan had ever encountered.* Rich and generous. Something was terribly wrong. Amongst all the women he had been intimate with, Sofia's colour aura was the most gorgeous. Yet their relationship was not meant to be.

****

Time just passes us by. What a cliché. In the five or so years that Karan had worked for the COX Corporation, there had been no career -- only a series of jobs. Was the colour of his skin to blame, in a country ruled and dominated by the Caucasian male? Or was it just how corporate America functioned? He was not sure. Probably the trickledown effect of the Bush-Iraq war, he rationalized. The year was 1991. The US economy was in the throes of one of the worst recessions ever at the time. Jobs were hard to come by. At least he was not laid off during the economic downturn -- for which he was thankful.

In the meantime, winds of change were blowing in his motherland. When India, which had a adopted a protectionist economic policy and chosen to remain isolated from the flattening global economy until then, had been on the verge of bankruptcy -- depleted foreign exchange reserves and a huge balance of payment deficit -- the Finance Minister Man Mohan Singh had not only abolished all trade restrictions but allowed direct foreign investment with immediate effect -- a path breaking decision that would make India a world economic power in the coming decade.

Living in the US had taught Karan to trust people. During his early years, he had been pleasantly surprised that people trusted other people, which was in sharp contrast to the general belief in India -- that people could not be trusted. Karan had his own theory of why the general belief was the opposite in the two countries. India was roughly one-third the geographic size of the US but with three times the population. Which meant, in India, almost ten people were competing for the same resources that an average person enjoyed in the US. It was no surprise that trust levels were so low there.

Christmas Eve. It was six weeks since his break up with Sofia. He had been invited to a dinner party in West Hollywood. Karan parked his BMW in one of those self-regulated parking lots, where, to pay for parking, he had to insert dollar bills into a numbered box through a narrow slit.

A brown PT Cruiser was the only other car in the parking lot. Its owner was at the pay box depositing cash. She was taking forever. It was a dark moonless night. The parking lot was badly lit. Karan could not determine what was taking her so long. He went nearer. He realized that she was paying for parking slot 8.

"Wrong one. My car is parked in 8." Karan said impatiently turning up the collar of his fleece jacket to protect his face from the winter wind that was threatening to chap the skin of his unprotected face and lips.

The girl looked up. For a moment, Karan thought it was Sofia. Except this girl had dark hair. Waist length. And olive skin.

"Am I not parked in 8?" She was using her car key to push the bills through the slit in the box.

"No. You are parked in 9, but you just paid for 8." He shrugged inwardly, is she dumb?

She moved back and looked at him. Dark limpid eyes. Sad. Almond-shaped.

"Since you have paid for my parking, I can pay for yours." Karan paid a few dollar bills for parking slot 9.

She thanked him profusely. "What a tragedy that would have been." She walked away.

Karan walked over to the restaurant. He did not enjoy the party. The crowd was too rambunctious, the music too loud, the food stale. Karan hastily bid good-bye and returned to the parking lot.

He started the car, drove out of the parking lot, toward the freeway entrance. It was raining lightly. He switched on the wiper -- a plastic envelope was stuck to the wiper. Must be one of those restaurant advertisements. For New Year Eve. He stopped the car and retrieved it.

It was a parking violation ticket for twenty dollars. The damned girl had conned him -- she had made him pay for her parking -- she had probably been pushing scraps of paper into his fee deposit box. He had to teach her a lesson. He turned his car back toward the parking lot so he could write down the registration number of the PT Cruiser -- it was gone.

Karan suddenly found the whole incident very funny. To think that the girl had fabricated such an elaborate scene for a mere four dollar parking fee -- she must be badly broke.

****

A few days later Karan was dropping off one of the interns on his team, at the airport. The intern was going back to Detroit with three pieces of check-in luggage, but did not want to pay the airline fee of forty dollars for the extra piece of baggage. The intern kept looking at Karan as though he had the power to make this financial responsibility go away.

The airlines clerk made an offer the intern could not resist. "Pay me ten dollars. Cash. I will check it in." Karan thought there was something vaguely familiar about her. The gait. The gestures. He could not put his finger on what it was.

The intern paid up; all three pieces of luggage were checked in.

The weather conditions were bad. The intern begged Karan to stay until the flight took off -- just in case a ride back home was needed; the intern did not have money for cab fare.

Karan reluctantly sat down in an uncomfortable yellow airport chair, head down, eyes closed, his palm on his forehead. A few minutes later, he felt a nudge. The airlines clerk stood before them. "If the flight does not take off, come see me. I will return your money. A deal is a deal," she said.

Karan was awestruck by this paradox. Honesty amidst corruption? The flight finally took off a hour later that night. It was not until he was driving home that the pieces fell in place. The airlines clerk was the con girl from the parking lot. Sad eyes. Long hair. She must be really reeling in the throes of penury. Conning people at the parking lot for four dollars. Offering baggage favours for ten. What next? He would soon find out.

A few days later Karan was browsing through the Burbank Best Buy -- Apple had just halved the price of all its computers -- when he saw the con girl again. She was haggling with the counter clerk to return a fax machine purchased thirty-one days back. She claimed it was unused, though it was obviously otherwise.

The returns clerk did not relent. The fax machine blocking her line of sight, the hassled girl turned around, and bumped into Karan. She showed no sign of having met him before. Yet she was unburdening her woes to Karan. She had bought the fax machine to send out resumes. Having finally found a job as a teller with the Bank of America, she no longer needed it. She had planned to splurge the money on a dress. Her name was Fauzia.

She was up to her tricks again, Karan could not help thinking.

Fauzia looked perennially lugubrious. For no reason. *She was brown. Earthy. Insipid. Chocolate only when she smiled.* Karan hated brown; but he loved chocolate almost as much as he loved sex. Karan dated Fauzia for several weeks -- she continued to remind him of Sofia.

****

In the aftermath of the Bush-Iraq war the US economy was ravaged. Recovery from the recession was sluggish. Fauzia was laid off from work. Her roommates threw her out; they did not believe she could afford her share of the rent anymore. Fauzia moved in with Karan.

A few days later when Fauzia and Karan were browsing the aisles of Wal-Mart, a bulky man with a ruddy face clad in a brown Pathan-suit pounced on them. He was accompanied by a fat figure in a black burkha.

"*Saali.*" He held Fauzia by her long hair and slapped her cheeks. "What have you done?"

Karan started to intervene, but the burning look on Fauzia's reddened face froze him. "Lay off."

"*Khandaan ko badnaam kar diya* [You are the black sheep of the family]." The man banged his own forehead with his palm.

Even as other shoppers stopped in their tracks in horror, and the store manager started to walk toward them for God knows what, Fauzia fell into the man's arms and soon both were sobbing in contented unison.

"*Abba jaan*, I will never disobey you ever again." Fauzia turned on the faucets of her tear glands full blast.

"Allah is punishing you for your sins," the man howled even louder, beckoning the burkha clad woman to join in the communal crying.

The other shoppers turned away, hovering around to observe the drama discretely from a distance. The manager remained a mute spectator, waiting patiently to escort them politely out of her store in case they went back to slapping. The three of them cried their hearts out. When they showed no signs of stopping, Karan slinked home by himself.

Fauzia left Karan's apartment and his life the same night. Forever. She was going back to her parents -- it was the most natural thing in the world. They had come down from Vancouver, Canada, in search of her, when news had reached their ears through relatives that she was living with a man outside marriage. A non-Muslim at that. As she bid him a cheerful goodbye, Karan could not help noticing how she had changed colours. *She was now beige. Benign. Harmless.*

Karan once again faced the disconcerting prospect of melancholic solitude.

****

In a bid to break the monotony of his uneventful life, Karan booked himself on the Caribbean cruise and was soon caught in a torrid affair on board the ship with a married woman. Right under her husband's nose. *Daphne was peach. Pleasant.* No commitments. Only fun. Take things as they come.

On the last day of the cruise, Daphne made a peculiar request. "Aujourd'hui mon mari veut nous joindre [Today my husband wants to join us]."

They were seated under a parasol near the swimming pool.

"Qu'est-ce que vous dites? Il nous a découvert? [What are you saying? Has he found out about us]?" Karan was sweating. He had no idea how to deal with an irate husband.

Daphne giggled. "N'alarmez pas. Je l'ai dit. Et, il veut que nous nous amusons [Do not worry. I have told him about us. And, he wants to join in the fun]."

"Pas comprends [I don't understand]," Karan's mind was unable to entrench itself within the realms of comprehension.

"Il aime . . . comme on dit . . . le ménage-a-trois [He likes . . . as we say in French . . . threesomes]," Daphne entwined her arms around Karan.

She was peach. Unpleasant. Karan excused himself hastily. The next few hours were a tremendous torment. He was sure Daphne and her husband had both slept with multiple partners. Both probably swung both ways. What were the chances Daphne had not given him AIDS? Sixty-six percent? Fifty? What if he were already infected? He ended up staying in his room for the remaining time of the cruise, fearful of running into the Du Ponts.

Back in LA, he confessed his crime to his Family Physician and was recommended a blood test for HIV to assuage his anguish; with a follow-up test sixty days later -- the average gestation period of the virus in the bloodstream -- to be sure he was negative. He was also given a health manual on safe sex, which he had learned by heart before he left the doctor's office.

****

Fall of 1994. Karan had completed ten long years of life in the US. In the dawn of the democratic Clinton era when the US economy was slowly recovering from the ravages of one of the worst recessions in history, Karan launched a vigorous hunt for a managerial job that would save him from the tragedy of remaining a programmer for the rest of his working life -- and eventually secured an entry-level project management position with Zyatt, a prominent hotel chain. That is where he met Sharon.

Zyatt was on an acquisition spree, greedily gobbling up smaller and medium-sized hotels. Karan was assigned to attend several presentations made by the big six consulting firms looking to help Zyatt seal its merger and acquisition deals.

At one such presentation, Karan was seated at the far end of the boardroom on the thirteenth floor of the corporate office in downtown Los Angeles, looking out of the window at the neighbouring buildings -- skyscrapers in steel and glass. The quality of the consultants' presentation was technologically outstanding -- Power Point slides with colour graphics, Excel spreadsheets with pivot tables, overhead projectors connected to laptop computers and laser pointers. Yet Karan had the nagging feeling that something was amiss.

Karan had randomly looked to his left. Long legs. Dark-brown hair speckled with gold and honey. Sharon was femininely voluptuous without qualifying as plump. She oozed sensuality from every pore of her ivory body. He had never seen her before. She was probably from one of the other departments. *She was red. Deep vermilion. Energizing.* Alarm bells were ringing in his mind.

"The numbers look funky." Karan leaned over and whispered to her. "I am not the financial expert though."

"Are you sure?" Her dark brown mascara-lined eyes looked back into his.

Karan was soon explaining to her where the anomaly was. "1:18. The share-exchange ratio is way too high. It should be more like 1:13.5." He had no idea how he knew all this. Something had probably rubbed off from the years spent programming for financial software.

"Con job?" She was looking into his eyes again, her quizzical expression now mingled with admiration.

"A big piece of the share valuation, that whole subsidiary chunk, is being double-counted." Karan elaborated, pointing at the dazzling three-dimensional bar chart the consultant was displaying on the screen. "The more I explain, the more I am convinced I am right."

The consultant finished discussing the implications of the bar chart. Millions of dollars. He challenged the audience -- the crème de la crème of the hotel conglomerate's management team -- drawn from several departments -- if they had any questions before moving forward to outline the next steps.

Sharon's ivory hand had shot up. "The share-exchange ratio is way too high. There's no way that it can be 1:18. I believe it should be 1:13.5." Sharon's tone was firm.

Karan let out an involuntary gasp; gaped at her unabashed act of plagiarism; griped inwardly at his own lassitude.

Sharon had the audience eating out of her hand, as she explained and re-explained where the anomaly was. "That whole subsidiary chunk is being double-counted," she concluded.

Karan marvelled at the clarity with which she had put across the observation he had only minutes ago painfully explained to her. He was certain that she did not understand it at all. Yet what a great job she was doing of packaging it and parroting it in front of the management.

Pandemonium broke out since a 1:13.5 ratio would have meant higher cash outflows for the conniving conglomerate if the deal went through. In the end, the consultants who had believed they were on the verge of sealing the deal, did not get the assignment. The whole merger deal was off.

Karan entered the elevator on the thirteenth floor and hit the lobby button. Why had *he* not said it? Lack of confidence? Just bad luck. The elevator rattled and rattled. Oh my gosh! This thing was going to crash. Or was it stuck? He would look like a fool if he got trapped in it.

After what seemed like an eternity, the rattling stopped. Karan looked at his watch. Only forty-five seconds. The elevator door opened. He was still on the thirteenth floor.

Karan ran out into the hallway. The long-stemmed chandeliers were swinging. People were running down the staircase. He joined the exodus not knowing what was happening until he tuned in to the buzz of conversation. He had been in the middle of an earthquake. Richter scale 6.8 magnitude. They should not be running. Shouldn't they be dropping down to the floor and staying there?

When he got out of the building, there stood Sharon. Tantalizing. He described to her what he had just experienced. Animatedly.

"Was there a puddle in the elevator when you got out?" She furtively looked at his fly.

Karan's face turned a beet red. "Congratulations." He hastily changed the subject. "On your stellar performance this afternoon."

****

In the days that followed, Sharon Stanley was promoted to Director of New Businesses for saving the conglomerate millions of dollars and a possible class-action lawsuit as well in the distant future. She landed a plum assignment -- an amalgamation deal to consolidate four smaller hotels. By design or default, Karan was a prominent member of the cross-functional team she formed to execute the assignment.

Sharon gave Karan a free hand during the initial phase of the assignment. "You have a trillion ideas. You are so resilient," she praised him.

Once he had completed all the groundwork and it was time for the big presentation to the steering committee, Sharon sang a different tune. "Can we change that? Would you please redo this for me?"

When Karan had spent several nights redoing spreadsheets and Power Point slides to suit her whimsical specifications, "You are not assertive." Sharon had declared.

They were both sitting in her office, conducting a dry run of the presentation. Karan punched away at a complicated Excel spreadsheet, his back to the window. Sharon was enjoying a grande Starbucks latte. Soft music wafted through the central stereo system. It was a gorgeously sunny day in Los Angeles.

"I saw several advantages in doing it the way you suggested." Karan did not look up from his laptop. He was reminded of Maharaj, his old cook who would often mutter "*Kaam bhi karo, thappad bhi khaao* [The one who does the work also gets beaten]" to himself when someone found fault with his cooking.

"You should learn to push back." Sharon tossed the empty Starbucks cup in the garbage bin.

"There is not necessarily one best approach." Karan was on the defensive.

"Pooch thinks you are low on self-respect." Sharon's attention was diverted by the pile of faxes that had arrived during the night.

Karan stopped working, stretching back in the revolving chair and staring at the ceiling. Pooch, his boss, was very tight with Sharon. As Sharon had once commented, Pooch was the whitest of white guys in the company. He had grown up with the staunch belief that all white men and only white men were equal. That men of colour should try twice as hard to prove they are half as good.

Pooch praised Karan when he wanted his work done and off-loaded Karan's knowledge so he could use it for his own benefit, marketing it to the top management as his own. Pooch rarely invited Karan to his meetings. In the rare meeting he was invited to, Karan was royally ignored. Pooch addressed all his comments only to the white guys, snubbing Karan in mid-sentence. His tone was always harsher when he addressed Karan -- bordering on the derogatory at times.

Karan looked across at Sharon. She was done sifting through the faxes and was back to reviewing the Power Point presentation.

"Okay. Retain the original version then." Karan got up.

"What a loser!" He heard Sharon say as he walked out of her office with his laptop.

The same evening Sharon had sweet-talked Karan into changing it all back exactly the way she wanted it. *She was a rich ruby red.*

The nature of their work as the project progressed threw them both together constantly. Driving. Meetings. Presentations. Lunch. Dinner. Wherever they went, he held doors open for Sharon, rushed to get her coat, let her walk two steps ahead of him, did not let her pay when they were not on an expense account . . . Sharon loved it. He belonged to that rare category of men who epitomized chivalry, she told him.

When Karan moved out of his Burbank apartment and rented a townhome in posh Pasadena downtown, Sharon moved in with him. "It is convenient and saves me the commute to work."

Sharon was a dirty translucent red. "Anyways, you sleep with me every night. Why do you need your own place?" He had concurred.

"My parents will freak out." Sharon grinned devilishly.

Karan knew that she had a penchant for doing the exact opposite of whatever her parents, older generation Christians settled in the Bible Belt, would have approved.

Karan slipped into the rut of letting Sharon trample all over him. Love? Fear? A bit of both perhaps. He did not want to lose her. He pictured her as the mother of his child-to-be.

****

It had been a wonderful summer. Karan had been awarded the best-golfer-of-the-season title at the local Golf Club. He was planning to buy a house next spring. Sitting at the table set for two at Maggiano's Little Italy -- Sharon's favourite restaurant -- Karan lovingly fingered the diamond ring nested in the pocket of his seersucker coat. Should he ask her before dinner or after? Should he pop the question and then slip the ring or the other way round? Should he stand up and give her a bow or remain seated and smile casually?

When Sharon finally arrived she looked pensive. She had kept him waiting longer than usual. She did not bother to apologize, which was not unusual. She had cut her dark hair short recently and tinted it copper. Much against Karan's wishes. Her high cheekbones looked flushed.

She carelessly brushed aside the bouquet of red roses he had placed on the table to a corner and sat down. *Sharon was crimson.* She looked good enough to eat, in her short dress in rust and pale pink.

Karan signalled to the waiter to bring the champagne.

She took a sip from the champagne flute. "I am pregnant."

"Whoo hoo! That is such a wonderful wedding gift!" Karan pulled out the engagement ring from his jacket pocket and signalled the waiting waiters. The band started playing a slow romantic tune as he knelt before her and made a grab for her fingers. "Will you marry me?" Karan was the epitome of earnestness.

The group of noisy middle-aged women at the adjacent table had stopped eating and watched them out of the corner of their eye, giggling. The conversation in the surrounding parts of the restaurant subsided. Karan and Sharon were the cynosure of all eyes, amidst the serenading music.

Sharon pulled her hand away brusquely. "You are not the father," she shushed.

The serenading music continued. Karan remained kneeling, holding the ring midair.

"It's so like you to assume responsibility for everything that happens around you." There was unspent anger behind the camouflaged hiss.

Karan continued to hold out the engagement ring. Fourteen blue diamonds shone brilliantly, emanating every conceivable hue of colour in the spectrum -- Anita's heirloom ear studs had been dismounted from their traditional gold casing and set in the platinum engagement ring.

"That doesn't change anything. I still want to marry you."

The giggling women wiped away imaginary tears from their eyes, their lips arched in plastic smiles. Like the reaction was expected of them.

Sharon sat in the straight-backed chair, legs crossed, head held high, staring back directly into Karan's eyes that were level with hers. The gleaming diamonds had not even merited a sideward glance from her.

"It takes two to tango." She was curt.

Sharon had turned an oily maroon. Karan slowly put the ring back in the case, stood up, eased himself into his chair, and picked up his drink.

First Indu. Now Sharon. One had slinked away silently. The other was throwing her infidelity in his face. Why was he the one to get hurt? Always?

The music had stopped. Embarrassed patrons who may have guessed the outcome went back to their respective worlds, avoiding eye contact with them.

Neither Karan nor Sharon spoke. Sitting in silence, the sounds around them became unbearable -- the low drone of continual chatter from neighbouring tables, the clank of knives and forks, and the clickety-click of the waiters' boots as they bustled from table to table.

The TV monitor was beaming the latest episode of the Jerry Seinfeld show. Jerry and Elaine were waiting in line for soup.

"Don't you want to know who the father is?" Sharon broke the silence.

No soup for you. The soup Nazi screamed at Elaine on the TV monitor. No love for you. The line echoed in Karan's mind.

"I am seeing Troy." Sharon volunteered.

Troy was Sharon's personal trainer -- a muscular six-footer with baby blue eyes and curly blond hair. Karan remembered running into Troy at the gym, several times. *Troy was raven. Stark, raven black.*

The first time, Troy had been on the treadmill next to him and introduced himself. Karan had run into him in the exercise room next. Troy had looked right through him as if Karan did not exist. Then, Karan did not see him for weeks and forgot about him.

One day, in the locker room, a dripping Troy clad in a clinging wet Speedo had materialized before him. "Dude, care to join me for a swim? Race you." He had thumped Karan on his bare shoulder.

"I can't . . . I mean I don't know how to swim." Karan admitted, grinning sheepishly. He had always wanted to go swimming. Anita who had been afraid of water had never allowed Karan to learn swimming.

"Busted. Gonna learn?" Troy shook water off his buff body.

"Wanna coach?" Karan threw back the challenge.

The lessons lasted a few days. Troy started to cold shoulder him again -- he was so predictably unpredictable.

"Go ahead call me whatever names you want. Whore, nympho, f*** c***. That does not change anything." Sharon clinked her wine glass.

How much more convoluted could this get? She had been spending the nights with him and sleeping with Troy during the day. Gosh. And Troy had been swimming with him some evenings.

"Troy is wild." Sharon closed her eyes.

"To think that every time I had sex with you, I was touching him, tasting him, smelling him." Karan crinkled his nose.

"He ignites a peculiar passion in me." Sharon's eyes remained closed.

Was she crunching her thighs together? *Sharon was red. Blood red. Nauseating. No. just bloody. Deliberately insensitive.*

"What makes you so sure Troy is the father?"

"Woman's intuition."

"*I* could be the father." Karan was tenacious.

"*You* are not." Sharon sneered emphatically, collected her jacket and purse, and hurried out of the restaurant without a further glance in his direction.

Karan put his head into his hands.

Ego: I always feel betrayed at the end.

Superego: You give too much of yourself to every relationship. That is the root cause of all your problems.

Id: Born giver. Born loser.

Super ego: Not all people, even your dear ones, how much ever they love you, can reciprocate the depth and intensity of your emotions.

Ego: I am starved for love.

Superego: Only an innocent child, pure of mind and heart can give you the kind of love you crave.

Ego: That unborn child is being taken away from me.

Id: Born giver. Born loser.

Superego: You only have control over the love you feel for others and the way you express it. You have no control over the intensity and depth of another person's love or the way they choose to express it or its significance.

Id: Born giver. Born loser.

Karan sat drinking late into the night. The restaurant was deserted; there was none to watch the rather shameful act of a dejected man turning on his lachrymose glands full throttle. He lovingly fingered the diamond ring nested in his coat pocket one last time. If he ever proposed again, it would not be with this ring of blue diamonds. The diamonds had belonged to Anita and would continue to belong to her.

****

The next day Karan sauntered in to work early and rode the elevator to the thirteenth floor. The hallway was deserted. He sat at his desk, switched on his computer, and entered the initial password. The system did not recognize it. He checked if the caps lock was on and re-entered the password. No luck. The password could not have expired -- he had changed it only three days back. Maybe there was a keyboard error. He re-entered the password yet another time -- slowly, very slowly, and counted the number of bullets that showed up -- no luck.

Karan was dialling the phone to call MIS -- they may have reset his password -- when he saw the pink Post-it. "See me first thing in the morning. — Pooch."

Dave Pooch, Karan's boss and Director of Information Technology, and Shawn Dingram, Director of Human Resources, awaited Karan's arrival in Pooch's office. They subjected Karan to a rigorous inquiry, almost an inquisition, as he sat on the edge of the chair facing the two of them. Sharon had filed a complaint against him -- sexual harassment.

"Sharon and I have been seeing each other for some time. Yesterday I proposed to marry her."

"That is not how she sees it." Pooch was obviously enjoying this. He had always hated Karan. "She had complained before. Twice. In case you have forgotten, I gave you a warning each time."

"The affair was consensual." Karan said. "And there were no warnings."

"Whatever happened was not consensual." Dingram waved a four-page document at Karan. "Unwelcome advances. Her complaint says it all. With all the gory details. Dates. Places. Comments. Quotes."

"What do you want to do?" Pooch cut to the chase.

"I have done nothing wrong." Karan's reply was brutally honest.

Dingram was reading out the charges from Sharon's complaint. It was concocted to say the least. A total pack of lies. It made Karan out to be some kind of a perverted predator. Sexual innuendos. Unwarranted physical contact. Acute and persistent.

Karan was aghast. "There is always another side to every story." His reply was feeble this time.

Pooch and Dingram were unwilling to listen. "You have two options. Either you quit or we will let you go." They said in unison.

Karan looked out of the window -- at the tall steel and glass monuments all around. He had loved Sharon with all his heart. He did not want it to end like this. For no fault of his. "Why don't we get Sharon here? If she will . . . ," Karan looked at Pooch and Dingram pleadingly.

"Sharon is on vacation." Pooch cut him off.

"She will not come back to work until you are out." Dingram got up from his chair and paced the small office.

"Sharon is a very valuable resource," said Pooch.

"Remember how she saved us millions of dollars."

Karan remained silent. He was the one who had told her about the share ratio and made her valuable.

"If you don't want to turn in your resignation, let us know." Pooch said with an air of finality.

"I will be glad to file a complaint with the Equal Employment Opportunity Commission," Dingram added.

Sharon had won. She knew how to abuse his gullibility. Pooch and Dingram had conspired with Sharon. *They were both the colour of mud.* How could a single, fragile individual like him take them on? They were backed by the power and clout of the organization. No matter what he said, he would be hurt. Karan tendered his resignation. No more bitterness for him.

****

Experience had taught Karan one important lesson. Life does not come to a standstill just because the person you care for no longer reciprocates. Experience had not taught him another lesson. Not to risk everything on one endeavour. Especially when he was in a relationship. Times like these made him aghast at the magnitude of his solitary existence. There was not one soul, friend or family to whom he could turn for solace.

Did he have a lacuna in his personality that prevented him from having fulfilling relationships? Why did he end up being exploited in every relationship? Was that the price he paid for being genuine? For refusing to wear a mask in his close relationships?

Last resort. Karan decided to see a therapist. He did not want to remain embittered for the rest of his life. He called up the health insurance company. A customer service representative asked him his date of birth and zip code and gave him three choices. All within a radius of three miles. Julia Chenille. Adam Forrester. William Teller.

Karan needed a man's point of view. Julia would be more sympathetic to Sharon. Adam or William? William Teller's secretary sounded bright and chirpy. However, when she started to say, "With thirty years of experience behind him, you can rest assured Dr Teller . . . ," he put the phone down. He needed a therapist nearer his age.

The next day Karan was in Dr Forrester's first-floor office. There was no secretary. Nor a TV. Nor a telephone. Karan sank his slim posterior into the plush confines of a velvet couch and faced Dr Forrester who was a little older than Karan had expected, with a serious but kind face. He found the experience of unburdening strangely relieving. Purgatory. A little embarrassing at times. Dr Forrester had a way of ferreting out fossiled secrets from the depths of Karan's heart.

Karan: "What is it about me? Nobody loves me. I cannot maintain a single relationship. I do whatever it takes to make it work, but it does not work for me. How could I have kept Sharon happy? What could I have done so she did not have to look elsewhere? There must be something missing. Or this would not happen. Again and again."

Dr Forrester: "Don't be so hard on yourself."

Karan: "The same thing happened with Indu. When I was studying engineering. I never put the ball in the other person's court. I never call them on their accountability. I am too willing . . . Forget the women. I could not even win the approval of my own father. No matter what I did."

Dr Forrester: "You are not responsible for everything that happens around you."

That struck a chord. Sharon had used the exact same expression the day she had refused his proposal.

Dr Forrester: "You have to move on. Sometimes it is more difficult to let it go than to hang in there."

In the course of the next few weeks, Dr Forrester knew more about Karan than Karan had ever known about himself.

****

Once something happens, no matter what, unpleasant memories remain. If you forgive, you will forget. Conventional wisdom. Some things are difficult to forget. Even if you forgive.

One evening when Karan got back from his weekly session with Dr Forrester, he had four voice mails -- all from Sharon. "SOS. I need you." She sounded frantic. The same message each time.

Gal what gall! After everything she had done to him! Did she really think he was some kind of a puppet on a string that she could manipulate? Of course she did. Because he had let her do it. Let her go to hell. He deleted each of the messages. *Sharon was a bright fire engine red.* Karan was soon dialling her number -- he wanted to make sure her child was safe. He still hoped against hope that he was the father.

Sharon answered on the first ring -- as if she were waiting for his call. As if she knew he was definitely going to call her. She was indeed an expert in exploiting his goodness. She knew very well that Karan never said no to anyone who had ever asked him for help.

The next day he met her at a quaint Italian café in Pasadena for a late lunch. Sharon ordered capellini pasta with foccacia bread and a tall glass of lemonade. Karan ordered a traditional risotto dish and Riesling. There was no music or champagne this time. Sharon looked radiant. Her pregnancy was showing. She talked like nothing had ever gone wrong between them.

Troy had thrown Sharon out of their apartment the previous night. Their relationship would not have worked in the long term. Troy had the nerve to call her anal. He was the sloppiest boor she had ever seen -- food scraps always piled up on the living room carpet; stained, unwashed dishes that had to be thrown away every few days; beer bottles adorning every conceivable nook and cranny in the apartment. He hated grocery shopping and believed he should not do what he hated. Sharon had failed miserably in making him partake in the chores.

"I am not your mother," She had yelled.

"I have never known her, whoever she was," Troy had laughed. "You cannot be her, you are too young."

His laundry went unwashed for weeks; to make it worse he used up her clean towels and piled them up too. She even caught a bad infection because of this.

He went without underwear for days. "Soon you will be borrowing *my* underwear." Stinging sarcasm from Sharon.

"I would. If they were white and coarse instead of pink and flimsy," Troy was unfazed. "Gotcha." He had rolled with laughter.

Karan listened. Living together is all about developing interdependence. A state that is a healthy mélange of dependence and independence. That is what Dr Forrester would have said. Karan said nothing -- Sharon would not understand.

Sharon loved to have the TV on full blast every minute she was home -- watching her favourite programs. She would not give Troy the remote; she would not let him watch sports -- football was such

a barbaric game anyway. She loved to zoom off in Troy's new SUV
-- she did not think it necessary to take his permission; he could
always use her car instead. She never understood why he made
such a big racket about TV, sports and cars.

They both loved partying. Always with her friends. Never his
-- they were uncouth. And no, he could no longer have a boy's
night out. How could he even think of leaving her alone when she
was pregnant? She was entitled to make the rules. She made more
money. She worked dog hours at the office. Much longer than him.

Two very strong personalities, Karan analyzed. Each wanted
control over the other. Neither wanted to be controlled. He was
turning into Dr Forrester.

"I am glad I dumped him," Sharon's tone was untainted by
regret.

With the baby due in a few months' time Sharon needed help.
Her parents did not approve of her unwed mother-to-be status. Her
mother called Sharon's unborn child a product of sin. "What will
everybody say?" She whined every time Sharon called her.

This attitude only made Sharon resolve to rebel stronger. As
always. "I am going to have the baby. I want someone who will
love me unconditionally." She had told her mother.

"How would she ever understand that? She already has me. She
is so out of sync with times." She told Karan.

Sharon was a warm coral red. Karan desperately wanted to be the
father of Sharon's child. Sharon moved back into Karan's townhome
in downtown Pasadena.

****

Karan and Sharon fell back into the familiar pattern. Karan
started a new job as a business analyst for a music recording and
production company near San Diego. He spent a lot of his time
helping Sharon. He even went to Lamaze classes with her. He

accompanied her to all her doctor appointments. During one such appointment, the doctors detected an aggravation of a pre-existing heart condition; severe complications with Sharon's labour were forecast.

Sharon was forced to go on a long sabbatical from work much against her wishes. She stayed at home and cooked elaborate Mediterranean meals three days a week and did little else. Karan did every other conceivable chore there was to do around the house. Once, just once, she offered to do the laundry. With disastrous results. Karan's favourite J. Crew sweater was ripped into shreds. His white underwear garnered streaks of blue and pink. His black cashmere sweater shrunk to half its size. Sharon never ever did his laundry after that. Or her own.

Time hung heavy on her hands. She became progressively bilious. A compulsive control freak. A pathological faultfinder. For the most innocuous reasons. He was the man. It was all his fault that she was forced to stay at home. That he would never get pregnant and never know her pain. That it rained in LA in the middle of summer. That the sky was still blue and the grass green when her moods were gray. That the new episodes of *The Days of Our Lives* did not take the turns she had predicted.

Karan felt like he was perpetually walking on eggshells. If he invited her out for a movie or to the mall, he was inconsiderate, rubbing it in that she had nothing better to do. If he went by himself, he was selfish, gallivanting all over town while she was cooped up in that cubbyhole he called home.

Several times Karan threatened to leave -- he knew not how else to handle her double-bind theories. It only made matters worse. Copious tears. Gut-wrenching self-pity topped off by laments of a death wish. He would apologize not knowing how else to end it and promise never to hurt her.

That was her objective. Once it was achieved, the cycle would start all over. She never once thought it appropriate to apologize. Or admit she was wrong.

One night when Karan walked away from the scene without apologizing, Sharon had stormed out of the apartment in a rage, driving away in his BMW convertible before he could stop her. Minutes later he received a call from the police. She had crashed his car on the I-5 freeway, given Karan's address and phone number to the police, and begged them to drop her back.

Sharon had refused to take any responsibility for the accident -- though she had been speeding twenty miles above the speed limit -- and that too in the wrong lane. It was indeed a miracle that she was not hurt. Karan had to trash the green BMW. Why was he always at the receiving end?

Sharon was such a fleshy red. He wanted to call off their relationship. She had no right to ruin his life. They were not married or any such thing. How could he ask her to leave when she was bearing a child? His work became his escape. Deadlines were his refuge. The bathroom was his haven. Karan did not feel comfortable going back to Dr Forrester whom he had abandoned as soon as Sharon had come back into his life.

There were all kinds of support groups and non-profit organizations for women in abusive relationships. Victims of domestic violence. None for men. Men were either not being abused or did not recognize they were abused. Or, maybe they just did not want to admit it and sully their macho image.

Desisting decision making is itself a decision. On one hand, we expose ourselves to the vagaries of external forces, the machinations of other people. On the other hand, we absolve ourselves of the responsibility for what happens to us. By attributing it to that much-abused monster. Fate.

Sharon was hospitalized during the last few weeks of her pregnancy and maintained under mild sedation. Her delicate heart condition had turned serious.

Karan was not allowed to see her except during visiting hours. A part of him felt guilty. Another part was grateful he had a valid reason not to be with her all the time. *She was the colour of dirty blood.*

****

May 31 1997. Karan, back from work after the long horrendous commute, sat in the living room of his Pasadena townhome looking out of the window at the children swimming in the community swimming pool. He could hear them squealing and laughing. It was a lovely spring evening. The spring sun would soon be setting.

He felt an inexplicable sense of elation, almost euphoric. *Colour orange everywhere.* Karan was levitating when he got a call from the hospital. Sharon had delivered. Karan was soon holding little Dolly to his heart. *Dolly was orange. Dawn was orange. So was twilight. Hope was orange too. Burning bright.* Dolly was cosmically united with him. So what if she might not be his biological daughter? Maybe she was.

Karan was not allowed to see Sharon who was still in the ICU. Every time he closed his eyes all he saw was a swirl of blood with pieces of floating flesh. *A very dirty red.* Karan spent a torturous night sitting in an uncomfortable chair under the harsh fluorescent lights of the austere hospital waiting room.

The last time he had met her, a day or two back, she had been softer than usual, holding on to his hand with a steel grip, unwillingly letting it go when the visiting hour had ended. Her parting remark had been unusual. "I know that come what may, you will take care of my newborn baby, you never say no. Come to think of it, you have never ever said no to me for anything."

In the wee hours of the morning, Karan was summoned to an emergency meeting with Sharon's doctor. Sharon would never see her daughter, nor experience the joys of motherhood, the thrill of holding her new born to her heart. She had succumbed to the call of death from the aggravated heart condition.

Karan stared at the doctor. Her parting remark had proved ominous. Had Sharon somehow known death was riding toward her? He would never know. Her body had not fought its end. Mind had not won over matter. "I am sorry. We did our best." The doctor's pager beeped signalling his speedy exit.

****

Everything changes by the minute. Walking out of the hospital Karan was reminded of his university days in the eighties.

He would pass old Mrs Davis's house every day when he returned home from class. She was always out on her patio between four and five in the evening and never let him sneak by without a chat. She was a lonely woman pushing ninety who craved human company, a soul to whom she could speak. How he hated having to escape her! He hated even more to be held captive by her ceaseless chatter.

One day he had won a half marathon. That day he ran home eager to share his triumph. With her. That day Mrs Davis was not there. It was understandable. Winter was just setting in. She would not come onto the patio until spring. He would tell her the good news on the first day of spring. He would be nicer to her next year, he promised himself.

Come spring and he did not see her for a whole week. Something was amiss, he felt a foreboding. He learned, from the local dry cleaner, that Mrs Davis had died in her sleep on the last day of winter, and her son had held a quiet funeral that excluded all neighbours.

Yes, nothing was forever. Except strokes of bad luck perhaps. Not really, this too would pass. Karan consoled himself as he found a pay phone and geared his courage to call Sharon's parents.

On hearing of Sharon's death, her parents arrived in LA. Sharon's mother was delirious with grief; her father remained impassive. They silently arranged for a quiet funeral the same day and a private memorial service the day after. They subtly hinted that they were incapable of shouldering any responsibility toward Dolly, offering to set her up for adoption.

Every time Karan thought of the baby, his heart was torn with love. It was unbelievable. She was his daughter -- even if Sharon had insisted otherwise. He refused to part with Dolly. Sharon's parents did not have the familiarity to coerce him one way or the other. His stance may have been unfathomable to them. They displayed a marked preference to return unencumbered to the comforting confines of their own cloistered world, uncluttered by such contradictions. They had succeeded in disowning Dolly without having inherited her, negating Dolly's existence even before it was established.

****

Karan felt like Silas Marner. Dolly became the focal point of his existence. The first three months, he went on paternity leave. The doctor's clinic trained him to feed, bathe, comfort, and take care of a newborn baby single-handedly in every which way.

The sunny days of spring were followed by hotter days of summer. Dolly was too young for day care. The thought of having to tear himself away from her every day was not palatable. Karan changed jobs internally within the music company, opting for a lower paying data analyst job that gave him the luxury of working from home.

Summer gave way to shorter days of fall. Come October, it was time to turn the clock back by an hour. Karan joined Single Parents, a peer-support group for adults raising a kid alone, which started functioning as the extended family he did not possess. A single mom in the group invited Karan and Dolly to her parents' place in Palm Springs for Thanksgiving dinner. Several members threw parties during the holiday season. Single Parents ushered in the New Year together at a club near Long Beach. After that, the dark, dank days of winter went by at their own slow pace.

Finally, it was spring again -- time to turn the clock forward for daylight savings. The days were getting longer with the approaching equinox until it was Dolly's first birthday. Karan organized a picnic party at Disneyland with the Single Parents group. Even though Dolly was too young to go on most of the rides -- many of the other children were -- and how they loved it.

The next morning Troy had arrived at his doorstep, produced the DNA results that had unequivocally established Dolly's birthright and whisked her away from Karan.

Part Three

14. Natty Nineties: Fun City

June 27 1998

Karan, Arjun, and Aarti spent a great deal of time together over the weekend. Indu had bailed out. She was busy with her assignments at *GLITZ*, or so she had claimed. Arjun drove them around Bangalore in his bright red Maruti Esteem.

Pain is truth; truth is pain. Karan was preoccupied with his thoughts. His life was a series of obsessions. He was always the lover, besotted with the current object of his affection. Yet all the women had betrayed him one way or other. Indu had aborted his child without his knowledge. Sharon had cheated on him and robbed him of the right to be Dolly's father. Nimmi, Sofia, Fauzia had abandoned him for no apparent reason. He was no saint, but he had never sinned so greatly to be punished so badly.

Saturday afternoon they toured the new shopping arcades. Pepsi. Coke. Nike shoes. Adidas sportswear. Benetton. Lacoste. Levis. Sony Television. Bangalore was caught in the nascent throes of burgeoning consumerism. Thronging crowds populated the shops.

Why did this keep happening to him? Karan had always trusted his gift of colour to make decisions, understand people, build relationships. It had worked in his favour during his younger days; made him a star. Somewhere along the way it had all gone awry; reduced him to a wreck. A little bit after his parents' death. Mostly after he had moved to LA.

Love eluded him. Like a cat's tail. Go after it, and you can never catch it. Walk away and it will follow you. May be he should try that next time.

Why did he make the same mistake many times over? Why did he look to find love from the wrong people, all the time? Were his aspirations irrational? Did he hanker for unattainable goals? Unrealizable outcomes? Why did he secondarize his aspirations, bandwagon them to please his loved ones? To seek their approval?

Only questions. No answers. *I hope Indu's reporter will find Danny soon.*

****

Saturday evening, Arjun persuaded Karan and Aarti to go pub hopping in downtown Bangalore. They tried the Xenon Pub on M.G. Road first. It was crowded with college-going boys and girls, making them conscious of their thirty-plus status. Next, they tried the Yin-Yang Pub on the adjacent Brigade Road. Again, they left very soon -- the music was too loud and the air was thick with cigarette smoke to which they were all allergic.

They finally settled down at the Zen Pub-N-Disco, a small crowded pub shaped like a space shuttle with a revolving dance floor at the centre. They were assigned a table on the mezzanine overlooking the dance floor. Every other table at the Zen was taken. The crowds were yuppie. Gallons of Kingfisher beer were being imbibed on that night. No different from any other Saturday night. The dance floor was where the action was.

Arjun would not take his eyes off Aarti. He had soon whisked her off, trotting down the spiral staircase toward the dance floor, leaving Karan alone at the table, drinking.

"You can give those young girls a run for their money." Arjun whispered in Aarti's ears as she descended the stairs beside him on stiletto heels, her shapely legs peeping out of the slits of her burgundy pencil skirt, her bare ivory arms a sharp contrast to her multi-coloured blouse. Her short silky hair tickled his cheeks.

Aarti pressed her body closer to Arjun's as they jived away on the dance floor. Arjun felt a stirring in his loins every time Aarti's bare legs or arms brushed against him as they danced. Scent of a woman. It had been a long, long time. Arjun had been celibate for five and a half years; by choice; ever since Madhu had gone out of his life. His body had lost the desire for sex. His professional work as a psychiatrist, therapist, and counsellor, had helped him sublimate his sexual energy. Healing the hurt of his patients was the major mission of his life. Until this day.

Aarti's body was pressed close, very close to him. Her breasts lightly touched his chest with every movement of the dance. The stirring he felt would not go away.

Madhu had given him a lifetime's worth of love to cherish in the few months they had been together. Was he betraying her?

****

Aarti could sense Arjun's excitement every time she pressed her body closer to him. Each time, she moved away. His eyes exuded a peculiar mixture of awe and attraction every time he looked at her. Aarti was enthralled by his infectious smile; she marvelled at his easy confidence.

"*Kabhi main kahoon kabhi main sunu ke maine tumhe dil de diya* [Sometimes, I say it, sometimes I hear it, that I have given my heart to you . . .]" The DJ was playing a romantic song from *Lamhe*, the avant-garde movie in which the young heroine falls is in love with a man old enough to be her father.

The story of her life. Aarti stopped dancing. Her thoughts turned to Doctor Siddhartha. The Protector she had sought all her life. He had been so dependable, so approachable. Was it only a week since she had found out that he did not love her?

The psychedelic lights on the dance floor turned from violet to indigo to blue to green to yellow to orange to red to pink and back to violet. Aarti looked up at the mezzanine. Karan continued to sit at their table alone, drinking and watching them intently. She waved at him; he waved back.

Why did Karan have that peculiar look in his eyes? Aarti wondered. Was he falling for her too? Stop it. She told herself. Stop psychoanalyzing your friends. The world does not revolve around you.

When the dance floor got even more crowded, Arjun and Aarti returned to their table. The three friends sat watching other couples dance away like there was no tomorrow. Each lost in thoughts their own.

"No marriage plans for you?" The inevitable question. From Arjun.

"The beautiful girl married at twenty to a successful man six or seven years her senior. Mother of two kids -- a son and a daughter, by the time she is thirty. Dutiful wife, loving mother, obedient daughter-in-law. Isn't that the societal norm?" Aarti said slowly.

Karan was listening intently. Did she detect kindness in the way he looked at her? Aarti's mind meandered desultorily.

"Not for me." She shook her head gently in disdain.

"What happened?" Arjun caressed her bare upper arm.

"Love transcends all barriers. Age, Gender, Caste et al are the diktats of society to thwart love, promote strait jacketed family life . . ." Aarti was in the mood to express her innermost feelings.

15. Still Waters Run Deep

Aarti had always been scared. Of what? Nothing in particular. Her fears were largely indefinable. That day her fears had come true. The same day that she had learnt that her thesis *How Gene Variations Affect Drug Responses* had been accepted and the university had decided to award her the Ph.D. Aarti had dedicated the past five years of her life doing research in the field of biogenetics at the Jambu Dweep University located some thirty miles outside Delhi.

The day had started as usual. Aarti was at her desk reviewing the results of genetic research on the computerized systems and making reports, when she had received a brown paper package addressed to her -- the label was laser-printed; there was no return address.

She was not expecting a gift from anybody. Nor had she requested her mother to send her anything. What could it be?

She ripped open the package with a mixture of apprehension and curiosity. The package contained a piece of deliberately soiled new lingerie.

Was somebody trying to stalk her? Who could it be? What message did the gift contain? Who had sent it? Aarti had the strongest premonition that something was about to go drastically wrong with her life that day.

She closed her eyes and inhaled deeply. Was there anyone to protect her?

The kind and classically handsome face of Dr Siddhartha

materialized in the eye of her mind. His forehead etched with well-defined lines, each line probably with a story to tell, twinkling eyes, an aquiline nose, rosy lips that appeared to be in a perpetual smile contoured by his salt-and-pepper moustache, the deep cleft in his chin, all proclaimed his aristocratic bearings.

"Congratulations on your PhD. And I hear that you have unravelled more secrets of the DNA helix that causes ...."

On hearing his deep baritone voice, she opened her eyes. He stood framing her doorway in his Friday casuals -- Dockers khakis and a crisp blue shirt with the top button open, revealing a peek at his silvery chest. He looked majestic, almost regal -- his right leg was crossed over his left, as he leaned on the doorframe holding a mug of freshly brewed coffee in his left hand -- the pink manicured fingers and the delicate silver ring on his little finger paradoxically complementing his strong hairy hands.

" . . . Proving that nothing is impossible in this possible world." He raised his left eyebrow.

"Good morning Dr Siddhartha . . ." her voice trailed off when she noticed that his left eyebrow remained raised, a taciturn gesture of asking what was the matter.

"You can surely tell me what is bothering you." Siddhartha walked over and sat down in a chair across from her. He looked her straight in the eye. "You look battered."

Aarti stared at him. Bewitched. How did he even know she was upset? Uncanny. He was a mind reader.

"Only if you want to." He added hastily.

With quivering hands, Aarti held out the opened package toward him.

"Hmmm . . . anonymous mail." He dialled an extension on the telephone. "Let me take care of your safety for you."

Soon the university security officer materialized. He had a volley of questions for Aarti. Had anyone asked her out in the past few weeks? Did she have a boyfriend? Did any of the students hate her?

Aarti was exasperated -- she had absolutely no idea who it could be. She was visibly embarrassed and wished the whole thing would end. The security officer made her fill out a questionnaire. Siddhartha requested him to get police protection for Aarti. The security officer promised to have the matter investigated.

Aarti could not concentrate on her work that morning. She busied herself with routine tasks like running reports, updating spreadsheets, and filing papers.

"Relax. The security officer will take care of the harrowing matter." At a quarter past noon, Siddhartha reappeared. "Why don't I take you out to lunch to make you feel better?"

Aarti had gone out to lunch with him on several occasions in the past. The mentor and his protégée. They usually went to one of the vegetarian restaurants in the university neighbourhood. In the initial days, they had mostly discussed work. Lately, Aarti had begun to open up, giving him glimpses of her not-so-eventful life.

Aarti, however, knew very little about Siddhartha's personal life. He never talked about his family. At work, there were no photographs on his desk. There were no rumours about him on campus.

****

Siddhartha's gray Maruti Zen was soon speeding out of the lush green university campus toward the city. The day was sunny and hot. Aarti was dressed in a pastel blue skirt and a key lime blouse. In the ladies room, she had taken a moment to apply pale pink lipstick and brush her loose hair.

Aarti had never been surer of her feelings for Siddhartha. She was mustering the courage to reveal them to him at lunch. She had fallen in love with him the very first time she met him. Her feelings retained the same intensity she had felt that first day. Initially she had thought it was awe. Then she had believed it was infatuation. Later she had suspected it was imagination. With passage of time, she was convinced this was It. Love. She shared a deep emotional bond with him. The more she knew him, stronger were her feelings for him.

The Zen finally stopped at a modern two-tier house. This was no restaurant. A middle-aged man in a butler's uniform opened the door. Siddhartha simply introduced him as his man Jeeves. The dining table was set for two. Jeeves served them an elaborate meal from soup to dessert.

"This is the best antidote for homesickness," Aarti complimented Jeeves's cooking.

Ensconced in his own lair, Siddhartha appeared more relaxed and friendly than she had ever seen him. Soft sitar music played in the background -- Pandit Ravi Shankar. Yaman Kalyani *raag*. The upbeat version.

"When was the last time you saw your family?" Siddhartha enquired.

"More than a year now. I always used to go home in May. This year I missed being with mummy on Mother's Day." Aarti was enjoying the last spoonful of the rich cream-based dessert.

"That was last month. Do you know the significance of Mother's Day?" He wiped his hands on the napkin. "In the seventeenth century, many of England's poor worked as servants to the wealthy and lived at their employers' houses. Once a year they would have the day off to spend the day with their mothers."

Aarti was intrigued by his ability to store these nuggets of trivia. "Mummy will be retiring soon -- she is turning fifty-five." She said. "I have been pestering mummy to come stay with me for a few months."

"I turned fifty-two last month . . ." Siddhartha reminisced the halcyon days of a bygone era, his youth.

Aarti had not heard beyond the first three words. She had known he was several years her senior. Nevertheless, the articulate revelation that he was almost the same age as her mother hit her very hard. She knew what people would say -- that he was old enough to be her father. She did not care. He did not look a day older than forty.

Jeeves brought in the coffee tray. The room fell silent. Siddhartha was never uncomfortable in silence. Aarti needed the silence to assimilate the courage for what she was planning to say.

"You have a bright future. Now that you have your PhD," Siddhartha looked at her with a hint of silent expectation. I know you will do me proud; his eyes seemed to be saying.

"What about your personal life?" Siddhartha's voice was as soothing as the soft strains of the sitar in the background. "Your mother must be coaxing you to get married."

Aarti looked up at him and nervously ran a hand over her silken hair. She had blow-dried it that morning. "I have something to tell you." She held her breath.

"That whole thing about being above the marriageable age by Indian standards. I do know from your resume that you are thirty five . . . ." Siddhartha stopped talking mid-sentence.

Of course. He would have known from her resume that she was thirty-five. Now or never. She had to say it; she had to know for sure what life had in store for her. "I want to spend the rest of my life with you." She felt like a teenage girl confessing her puppy love. If Siddhartha was taken aback, he did not show it. If he had expected it, he did not show that either. His handsome face remained impassive. Siddhartha got up from the dining table, walked over to the entertainment centre, brought back a photograph and handed it to her.

Aarti studied the photograph, a family portrait -- a younger Siddhartha standing next to a preteen boy with a long mop of dark hair covering his forehead and a smart young woman in a sleek pantsuit. Siddhartha had never talked about his children before. Her guess had been right. He was a widower. She got up from the dining table.

"This does not change anything. I will make friends with them." Aarti stood before Siddhartha who was now seated on the living room recliner.

Siddhartha's eyes were moist. "That is not possible." He looked up at her.

"Nothing is impossible in this very possible world." Aarti kneeled down on the carpet so her eyes were level with his.

"I am responsible for his death." Siddhartha dropped his face into his hands.

That may have explained his silence and reclusiveness. "The Bhagvad Gita says that the sorrow of losing one's child is the greatest sorrow in this world." Aarti said the words with great gravity.

"Ironical. Avinash means invincible." Siddhartha said softly.

"What about your daughter?" Aarti asked.

"I have no daughter." He lowered his raised eyebrow. Exhaled deeply. His sorrow was too deep for the tears to flow freely. Perhaps.

The sitar strains continued to play in the background -- the soulful Bhairavi *raag*.

Siddhartha seemed deeply perturbed despite his attempts to maintain composure. "You have to know the whole truth." He led Aarti by the hand through the house into a large bedroom, the master suite. "I have loved only one woman and I will always love her." He pointed at the middle-aged woman lying on the king-sized bed, dressed in a nightgown, her scraggly gray hair tied in an untidy bun. She was immobile, her eyes vacant. Her face registered no reaction on seeing them.

It was a while before Aarti slowly deciphered that the face of the pretty woman in the photograph had aged into that of the invalid who lay before her.

Siddhartha relived the worst tragedy of his life. It had happened almost ten years back. Siddhartha, his wife Mrinalini, and their twelve-year-old son, Avinash, lived in Canada then. Calgary, Alberta. On their way to Banff, a skiing resort in the Canadian Rockies where Avinash was representing his school in a tournament, their SUV had met with a terrible accident. Avinash had died instantly. Mrinalini, who was still in her early thirties then, had suffered grave injuries of the brain and spinal cord and been rendered a vegetating vegetable.

"I still don't understand how I came out unscathed," he sat on the bed and took Mrinalini's unmoving hand in his.

"I moved here soon after. I was fleeing the ghosts from the past." He wiped the saliva that had dribbled out of Mrinalini's permanently open mouth.

"You will always remain my favourite student. My heir apparent at the university. And a dear friend." He looked at Aarti.

Aarti stood transfixed. To control the flow of emotions in her heart, she averted her gaze from his ever so kind eyes.

"I do not harbour any romantic feelings for you." Siddhartha added.

Aarti could feel Mrinalini's hollow piercing eyes burning a hole in her forehead. She reverted her gaze to Siddhartha.

"You are a very attractive woman. You will find somebody closer your age that will make you happy."

Aarti's world had come crashing down. She may have known the truth in some corner of her mind. She had let her dreams ride high on hope.

"If I have ever done or said something that gave you the wrong impression, please forgive me." He said.

Aarti had cruised the zenith of the tidal wave of euphoria. She was unprepared to sink to the depths of the nadir. How could she tell him that it was not his fault she found him irresistible? Or maybe it was. A serious scientist, highly intelligent, dashingly handsome in a very refined way. Silent yet understanding. She had worked with him for over two years. Was she wrong in nurturing these feelings for him?

"I have dedicated my life unflinchingly to two things -- my work and my wife. I possess neither the energy nor the desire to enmesh myself in any other bonds." Siddhartha covered Mrinalini's unmoving body with a satin quilt.

Soft strains of Beethoven's Fifth Symphony wafted out of the small audio player. There was a sense of doom permeating the maestro's piano composition. Beethoven was rumoured to have said of the opening bars: "Thus Fate knocks at the door."

Aarti was fighting her tears. Fate had indeed knocked at her door, knocked her off. Aarti's mind felt like a kaleidoscope that was being shaken. The package she had received that morning had proved to be ominous. It was indeed a portent of the disappointing outcome of her love for Siddhartha. She felt herself collapsing . . . .

When Aarti opened her eyes, she found herself lying on the couch in a corner of Mrinalini's bedroom. Siddhartha had draped a shawl over her and lowered the venetian blinds to make the room darker. Beethoven's Fifth Symphony had ended. Siddhartha's palm was on her forehead. His touch was soothing to her burning skin. His eyes were kind, his manner protective, paternal almost. The association bothered her. She had to get out of there.

****

A de-energized Aarti returned to her bachelorette pad. In moments of distress, Aarti always thought of her mother. Anupama meant unequalled. Her mother had unequivocally lived up to her name. Always.

Anupama was eighteen going on nineteen when one fine day in the idyllic town of Mysore, she had returned from college to find her home brimming with guests. Her parents had found her an alliance -- a mechanical engineer working at Bangalore's prestigious Hindustan Aeronautics Limited. Anand had liked her photograph and was coming to meet her.

Bhavna was born ten months after the wedding. Around the same time, Anand got his first promotion at work. Their idyllic bliss was too good to be true. Anand had bought himself a new Bullet motorbike to celebrate -- despite Anupama begging him to wait until the month of *Aashaad* had passed -- superstition had it that *Aashaad* was the most inauspicious time of the year.

August 1, 1962. It was raining heavily. Anand had not returned home well after midnight. Anupama was waiting to tell Anand that she was pregnant again. Telephones were rare contraptions. None of their neighbours possessed one. It was well after midnight when Anupama heard the doorbell. A motley crowd of strangers accompanied by a police constable in dangling khaki shorts was at the door. Fate had rendered her a widow at the prime age of twenty.

Resuming her studies from home, by the time Aarti was a toddler, Anupama had earned her BA in English literature and secured a job as a schoolteacher at a British-style missionary convent.

Aarti loved reading fairy tales. They were an escape from the yearnings of life that would never be consummated. Happy endings only happened in books. Never in real life. She was probably five years old or six when she arrived at this grand conclusion.

At school, Aarti was the classical good girl. Anupama took great pride in signing her report cards. No matter how dearly she loved her mother, it made Aarti sad that she was the only girl in their class whose report card did not bear a father's signature.

"I want a daddy." Bhavna often pestered her mother. "Marry again."

Aarti was the sensitive one. *God, let mummy say no. God, please give me back my Appa.*

"Appa lives in my heart. I am mummy. I am daddy too." Anupama had a standard response.

Anupama would take her daughters out every week. Clad in their Sunday best they would leave at eleven in the morning after a home-cooked brunch and be back before four o'clock in the afternoon no matter where they went. To Bangalore's beautiful gardens -- Cubbon Park and Lal Bagh. The Science Museum. Black-and-white Laurel and Hardy movies. The temples. Aarti dreaded these excursions. The red buses were overcrowded. If only her father were alive, he would have taken them out on his Bullet motorcycle.

When they were teenagers Bhavna often argued with Anupama. "Mummy why didn't you remarry? Because of what will the people say?"

"No. Because I did not want to," Anupama replied.

Sacrilege. To even think of someone else in the role of Appa or mummy's husband. Aarti never joined in these discussions.

"People are so old-fashioned. Hypocrites. One rule for women. Another rule for men. When my friend Uma's mother died last year, her father remarried within six months."

"Bhavna, No gossip."

"Thank God, we have made some progress. Thirty years back, the same Uma's great aunt had her head shaved when she became a widow -- she was only fifteen or sixteen then."

"That is sad," Anupama said.

Thank You God that mummy did not have to go through that ordeal.

When she was fourteen, Aarti participated in an inter-school essay contest on immortal characters from Indian mythology and won the second prize. Anupama and Bhavna accompanied her to the prize ceremony held at the Town Hall. The master of ceremonies read aloud a paragraph from Aarti's prize-winning essay.

> What a paradox. In contemporary times, the term Sati Savitri is used derogatorily to connote traditionally dressed, conservative and meek women. On a deeper analysis, Savitri is one of the most audacious women in Hindu mythology.
>
> Savitri was the bold and beautiful daughter of an old and wise king. She fell in love with a penniless prince and despite an eminent seer's warning that Satyavan, the fatal recipient of a doomed curse, would die within a year after their marriage, determinedly went ahead and married him. On the prescribed day, as Satyavan lay down resting his head on Savitri's lap, his soul left his body. Savitri trailed after Yama, the God of Death, pleading with him to take her with him to the land of death or restore Satyavan's life. The God of Death explained to her, how he could not take her there, since her time of death was far, far away, and he offered to grant her any boon except Satyavan's life. In a show of exemplary wit and courage, Savitri asked that she have wonderful sons. However, how could she have sons without her husband? Trapped by this unambiguous paradox, the God of Death relented.
>
> Savitri is one character that all modern girls should emulate, so they learn to be the masters of their own destiny . . . .

Anupama and Bhavna had clapped until their hands had worn out. The event photographer had clicked a colour photograph, a rarity in those days, as a relic to posterity. Looking at the instantaneously developed Polaroid, Aarti had wistfully thought of the fourth person who was absent from their family photograph of three -- her father whom she had never seen. Aarti was unable to rejoice in the cherished moments of her academic victory.

The same night, in the tiny bedroom she shared with Bhavna, Aarti had glued a small black-and-white picture of her father, Anand Rao, to the prized colour Polaroid at the exact spot where he should have been. "God, my life has no meaning. If only you had not taken away Appa . . . ." She was staring at her handiwork when

Anupama had walked in.

"Mummy, you are even more courageous than Sati Savitri. Had we lived in those mythological times, you would have brought Appa back, wouldn't you?" Aarti had hugged her mother tightly.

****

Aarti had not wanted to get out of bed the next morning -- everything seemed meaningless.

Love can handle betrayal -- but when the object of love reciprocates respect and affection, to cope with such unrequited love is nigh impossible. Even in rejection, Siddhartha had been the epitome of what every woman wants. The man she loved was even worthier than she thought -- but she had to learn to live without him. Would she ever get to learn it well?"

She could not bear to see Siddhartha anymore. Day in and day out. He would be a reminder of the dreams she had dreamt, the life she would never have. Happy endings happened only in fairy tales. Never in real life. Had she not learned that lesson early in life? Thank God for that.

Aarti looked at the colour Polaroid of her family from her school days, like she had done every morning, for the past twenty years. Frightfully shocking. The little black and white photograph that stared back at her was no longer that of her dead father Anand Rao. The face belonged to Siddhartha. Yes. Professor Siddhartha.

How had that happened? The power of the subconscious? Had she done that in her sleep? Aarti had no answer. Yet, she had found the answer to her life's problems.

First, she visited the university admissions office and requested that her application for postdoctoral research be withdrawn. The dean of admissions was unhappy with her decision. Yes, she had changed her mind. No, she would not reconsider her decision.

Next, she called up her travel agent and requested she be booked on a flight to Bangalore. The next day. Sunday.

She had one mission to accomplish before Sunday. Aarti spent the next few hours in the library doing research on the origins and significance of Father's Day. Her last stop was the university bookstore . . . .

****

A black-and-yellow taxicab sped out of the lush green university campus toward the city weaving its way through the narrow roads of Delhi filled with buses, trucks, mopeds, rickshaws, hand-pulled trolleys, bullock carts, and the ubiquitous Maruti cars. The cab trudged through old Delhi's ancient bazaars filled with open-fronted restaurants and spice shops from which drifted aromatic smells, going past Hindu temples and domed Muslim mosques that warrened amidst clustered houses and sprawling *havelis*, all buzzing with commotion.

The taxi cab passed through the imposing India Gate, a high arch memorial built in commemoration of the thousands of Indian soldiers killed during World War I that bore a striking resemblance to France's Arc de Triomphe, and entered the broad tree-lined avenues of a posh locality, stopping at a modern two-tier mansion in South Delhi -- the residence of Professor Siddhartha.

Aarti, the cab's lone occupant, smartly dressed in a gray-and-pink ethnic ensemble, disembarked from the cab and walked through the gate, toward the front door, her Ray-Ban glasses raised over her hair like a barrette. The cab waited outside the gate for her to return. Siddhartha's man Jeeves opened the door and led her inside.

Waiting for Siddhartha, Aarti gazed out of the huge bay windows of the lifeless sitting room, at the magnificent view outside. The blazing sun. Green trees. The River Jamuna. India Gate. She had been here only two days back though it seemed like such a long time ago.

"A penny for your thoughts!" On hearing Siddhartha's deep

baritone voice behind her, Aarti turned around and faced him. Her guru. The deep cleft in his chin appeared deeper . . . .

"Happy Father's Day." She pulled out a square envelope from the Guess leather bag slung over her left shoulder and held it out to him.

Siddhartha raised his left eyebrow quizzically; his limpid eyes twinkled merrily as he read the card, aloud.

Thank you for always being there for me

With you I feel protected

You are the reason why God made fathers

Happy Father's day June 21 1998

 - Love and regards

"I can tell you the significance of Father's Day." Almost by rote, Aarti recited, "It was first celebrated in the early 1900s by a grateful daughter to honour her father who had raised his six children single-handedly. She wanted the world to honour good fathers the same way as mothers . . . ."

"You obviously did your homework." Siddhartha looked at her with a proud smile on his rosy lips contoured by the salt-and-pepper moustache. "You will always remain my favourite student," his voice was laced with a trace of morning huskiness.

Maatru devobhava. Pitru devobhava. Acharya devobhava. Aarti bent down and bowed at his feet with reverence. On an impulse. The ultimate sublimation of divine love. Mother is God. Father is God. Teacher is God.

"*Deerghayushman Bhava.*" Siddhartha placed his palm gently on her head and blessed her. May you live long.

When Aarti got up, the Ray-Ban sunglasses were covering her eyes. She did not want Siddhartha to see her tears. The mentor and protégée stood looking at each other for a while. Silence, the most effective means of communication, was comforting.

"Adieu!" She walked briskly toward the black-and-yellow taxicab parked outside, without looking back.

New Delhi Airport. The Jet Airways flight was ready for takeoff -- it awaited the last laggard passenger. "*Kripaya dhyaan dhijiye.* Please pay attention. Last call for Ms Aarti Rao bound for Bangalore on Jet Airways flight 512 . . . ." The ground attendant was making the final announcement as Aarti, having just cleared security, came rushing toward the gate, dragging her cabin luggage behind her. She zoomed through the narrow aisle of the aircraft toward the lone vacant aisle seat.

Who was it who had said that home is where the heart is? A truer statement than that Aarti could not think of. Four hours later, she would be home in Bangalore with her newly earned PhD. She would no longer be alone and miserable. She would be with her mother, the only constant in her life.

16. Natty Nineties: Confabulation

June 28 1998

Sunday Morning. Aarti joined Karan and Arjun in downtown Bangalore. Indu was at work once again -- the annual edition of *GLITZ* was being released that day. For old time's sake, Aarti had insisted they watch a movie together. She had chosen *As Good As It Gets* starring Jack Nicholson.

"Remember the time Karan dragged us along to see *One Flew Over the Cuckoo's Nest* at a morning show?" Arjun reminisced as they stood in line to buy their tickets.

"Academy award winner. Great movie. Jack Nicholson is a great actor. You should all watch something better than mushy Hindi movies." Aarti imitated the Karan of yore, playfully hitting him with her purse.

Karan looked at her briefly, then away. He was still assimilating Aarti's unrequited love story from the previous night. Aarti had definitely shown great restraint in dealing with her disappointment. She had always come across as the sensitive one. She seemed to be made of sterner stuff though.

"What a snob you were." Aarti said in her normal voice.

"Three tickets please." Arjun offered his credit card to the clerk at the counter.

Despite having balcony tickets at a premier theatre, they did not enjoy the movie-going experience. Neither did the fans function nor was the air conditioning turned on; broken chairs, sticky floors, scurrying rats trying to eat the food crumbs strewn around, the theatre was in a horrifying state. They left the theatre a few minutes before the movie ended, so it would be easier to exit.

"I am disappointed we missed the climax," Aarti said as they descended the steps out to the overcrowded parking lot.

"Let me make up for it," Arjun said. "How about Pizza Hut?"

"I wish Indu's reporter would hurry up and find Danny," Karan said as they got into the car.

"Problem." Aarti tightened her seat belt. "Indu says that particular reporter is on extended leave."

"She should put someone else on the job," Karan said.

"I will talk to her." Aarti assured him.

The red Maruti Esteem arrived at their destination on Cunningham Road in a matter of minutes. The traffic was light -- laid back Bangaloreans still loved to laze at home on Sundays. In contrast, Pizza Hut, inundated by young workative techies from neighbouring software companies working over the weekend, was bustling.

Arjun ordered veggie pizzas with local toppings -- mango chutney and *paneer* -- especially for Karan.

Togetherness was comforting. The late afternoon sun streamed through the glass walls of Pizza Hut and dispersed into a spectrum of colours around them.

"You are such a prominent psychiatrist." Aarti turned to Arjun. "I wonder why you are still single."

For a moment, Arjun looked uncharacteristically morose.

Karan and Aarti looked at each other. What was his story?

Arjun pulled out a small album from the depths of his *kurta* pocket. "Pictures of my life."

17. Rhyme Nor Reason

May 21 1991. "Rajeev Gandhi, former Indian Prime Minister was assassinated while campaigning for the Congress Party in a small town near Madras. A powerful bomb hidden in a basket of flowers exploded, killing him instantly. The murder is being blamed on his arch enemy the Liberation Tigers of Tamil Eelam (LTTE), a violent guerrilla group fighting for a separate homeland for Tamils on the island of Sri Lanka. Rajeev Gandhi's death has shocked not just our nation, but also the entire world. It marks the end of an era, the rule of the Nehru dynasty that led India for all but five years since independence from Britain. He was so young, only forty-six years old . . . ."

Dammit. Arjun turned the television off. He had seen the same newscast a dozen times in the last twenty-four hours, cooped up in his tiny flat on the twenty-fourth floor of a Bombay skyscraper. The bustling city of Bombay was under curfew.

The whirring noise of the ceiling fan was driving him crazy. Bombay was unbearably hot in May. Even in the early hours of the evening. He could not afford air conditioning. For the umpteenth time, Arjun rummaged through the array of magazines that cluttered the floor, hoping to find an antidote for his advanced state of ennui. *I need a shrink myself. Maybe I should indulge in some self-therapy.*

That is when he heard the door buzzer. Cannot be. Who would dare to be out during curfew? Sporadic bouts of violence had already been reported in several parts of the city. He heard the buzzer again. Louder. Nonstop. He looked down at himself. An old pair of tracks and a bare torso. He went into the bedroom in search of a T-shirt before opening the door.

"Arre *maami*, why did it take you sooo long . . . ," A voluptuous woman -- dressed in a white-and-pink silk sari and a doctor's coat, a huge pink *bindi* on her forehead -- stood at the door. "Who . . . who are you?" she asked.

Arjun detected a hint of fear in her voice. "The resident of this flat," he said. "I have lived here for the past two years."

"Where did Saro *maami* go?" The woman patted her top knot.

"My father lives alone in Mangalore, refuses to come live here in Bombay, and says he is scared of the traffic here . . . ," Arjun kept talking.

"That too without telling me?"

"Is this some kind of a joke?"

"Did I choose the wrong floor?" She pouted her luscious lips.

They were pink. Rosy pink. Arjun noticed she wore no lipstick.

She tapped the number plate on the wall with a well-manicured finger. "2401. Saro *maami* has lived in this flat for the past thirteen years."

"Saro *maami* -- who again? I have never heard of her."

"My aunt. My father's sister."

"Wait a minute."

"Are you a relative from her husband's side?"

"What apartment complex does she live in?" Arjun stepped out.

"This apartment complex, of course." The woman knitted her brows.

"Chitrakoot?" Arjun asked.

"No. Sheesh Mahal . . . ." The brass nameplate affixed to the open front door with peeling paint had finally caught her eye. DR. ARJUN RAO. CONSULTING PSYCHIATRIST. She remained silent for a while and then burst out laughing.

Arjun stared at her pearly teeth. "You mean you entered the wrong building? Happens. The two buildings are identical though they are located a block apart. Confusing? I am not surprised . . . ."

"I received a call that Saro *maami* was feeling faint."

"I admire your guts. I was watching the newscast. There has been a lot of rioting and violence everywhere. Though not here. However, you never know. You should not be taking that kind of risk . . . ."

"Gosh. I have to take the stairs again." She said. "Your lift is out of order."

"And climb up another twenty-four floors in the other building. I am sure their lift is out of order too. Same management. Funny, huh? Considering that, the power rarely goes out in Bombay, I do not know what it is with these two building complexes. Power outages are so common in Bangalore. By the way, that is where I come from . . . ."

"Can I call Saro *maami*?"

"Sure. Come in. I can get you a glass of water. A cup of tea if you will. I am not that good at making coffee."

"Water sounds good." The woman stepped in gingerly and looked around. "Dr Madhumati Shankar. Ophthalmologist. Jaslok Hospital." She introduced herself and proceeded toward the telephone.

She knew everything about Arjun by the time he walked her over to Saro *maami*'s flat. She insisted that he call her Madhu. "All my friends call me that."

"I forbid you to leave Saro *maami*'s flat until the curfew is lifted. Promise?" He held out his hand.

"Promise." She smiled at him mockingly.

Back home, unable to watch any more TV, Arjun switched on some music. *"Dil tadap tadap* [The heart flutters] . . ."* wafted the melody from the fifties. One of his father's favourite tunes. From an old movie called *Madhumati.* Arjun played the same song all night. Madhumati. Had she started haunting him?

****

A week later Arjun received a call from Madhu. She was having a small get together to celebrate her thirty-fifth birthday. Most of the people she had invited were doctors. Could he make it?

Of course, he would. He had waited for this call all week.

Madhu's flat was spacious by Bombay standards with three bedrooms, their doors covered with thick cotton drapes in true middle-class tradition. Classical Carnatic music wafted from an audio player strategically hidden in one of the rooms. M.S. Subbulakshmi. His father's favourite singer, thought Arjun. Appetizing aromas wafted in from the kitchen. A beaming Madhu dressed in a brand-new Kanjeevaram sari welcomed him in. An elderly couple bustled around the dining table laden with aromatic South Indian food -- Madhu's parents.

Most of the other guests had already arrived and seated themselves on the fabric-covered sofas. Small talk centred on the medical profession. Of cantankerous patients and hypochondriacs. Of emergencies and medical miracles. Of the latest medical breakthroughs and the lack of amenities in Bombay hospitals. Arjun had an opinion on every one of these matters. He enjoyed the opportunity to express them.

Madhu kept thrusting plates refilled with food into his hands intermittently. *Idlis* and *dosas* and *vadas* accompanied by piping hot onion *sambar,* pistachio-green coconut chutney, and thick creamy yogurt. She kept filling his cup with steaming Madras coffee. Tucking away the food shamelessly, Arjun had a sudden yearning for his father's cooking.

The other guests had brought small gifts for Madhu. Flowers. Chocolate. Books. Music. Arjun was embarrassed as hell for coming empty-handed. Thoughtless. He needed to cultivate social etiquette meticulously. Brain wave! He would ask her out to dinner.

Disappointment. Madhu was going out of Bombay for a whole month, participating in boot camps for treating the poorer sections of society. Predominantly in the rural areas of the state of Maharashtra and the adjacent Karnataka. She would call him once she was back.

The next month was the longest period of Arjun's life. Time was relative -- he recollected Alvin Toffler's *Future Shock*, a book he had read long back. How, for a three-year-old, a month can seem very long, it being a significant portion of the child's lifetime, one out of some twenty months of memory and consciousness. Whereas for a thirty-year-old adult, it is a small fraction. Something like one out of a three hundred and fifty.

Nevertheless, for a thirty-year-old man who has fallen in love for the first time in his life, a month is a long, long time. Some forty thousand odd minutes. A minute before he was about to call her, Madhu called him to say she was back.

He asked her out to dinner but settled for lunch -- she did not like going out on Sunday evenings and none of her other evenings were free. They lunched under a bright blue-and-yellow canopy at a restaurant overlooking the Arabian Sea and walked on the sands of Juhu all afternoon.

"I haven't felt this carefree since I left college!" Arjun was ebullient.

"Leaving our footprints on the sands of time," Madhu said.

"Dreamy and poetic."

"I am only quoting Longfellow!" Madhu laughed.

****

The next few months were a paradox of togetherness and separation. Madhu would go away on her boot camps for weeks at a stretch. When she was back in Bombay, they would spend the weekends together.

Every week Arjun called his father -- his only friend -- and gave him a minute-by-minute account of his moments with Madhu.

"Madhu loves South Indian classical music. You know I have never in my life been to a music concert before. I have attended three in the last month. Halfway through the concert I doze off but believe it or not, Madhu does not nag me. She treats me to delicious home-cooked dinners instead . . . ."

"She makes the most delicious *masala dosas*. Crispier than even you can make. She is so straight out of the sixties . . . ."

"Yet, she is a very bold woman. You know, she had this long line of patients yesterday. All with appointments. Then this hotshot movie hero Ramitin Diaz arrives. Thinks he is dying because he has a minor cut under his eye from a fall he had during one of those stunt scenes. He tries to make use of his star status to get in immediately, even brings pressure from the hospital management. My Madhu would not budge. She told the management clearly that she would see her patients in the order of their appointments . . . ."

"Believe it or not, Ramitin agreed to wait his turn -- he was so impressed with her boldness. She has now won a celebrity fan. For life."

"Yesterday, I had this bad cold. Guess what Madhu gave me? Brandy and water. Just the way you used to when I was a kid."

One week when Arjun called his father as usual, his father had news for him. "Madhu's parents called me yesterday. They asked me if you would marry her."

"What did you say?" Arjun sounded anxious.

"I said yes."

"How can you do that, Appa? Why don't you wait for me to make my own decisions?" Arjun was annoyed.

"I was teasing you. That is what I said."

Arjun consented to marry Madhu soon after.

"Appa, you think I am doing the right thing? She is six years older than me." Arjun anxiously called his father.

"Mutual understanding is what really matters," his father said.

"All the guys I know have married girls six or seven years younger than them," Arjun confided.

"Have you asked Madhu what she thinks?" His father's wheezing was audible over the phone lines.

"She said age is but a mere detail or something like that. I told you she has a very poetic style."

"Girls are generally believed to mature faster than boys -- emotionally and biologically." His father answered, clearing his throat several times.

"Appa! You know I am very mature for my age."

"Conventionally the girl was always a few years younger than the boy because girls were married off in their early teens."

"Male chauvinism. Marrying a younger girl tilted the balance of power even more in favour of the male." Arjun reasoned.

****

December 13 1991. *Dharmecha Arthecha Kaamecha naati charami* [In my duty, financial commitments, in my needs, I consult you, take your consent and act upon; I shall not violate those]. *Saat Phere* -- Arjun and Madhu were taking their marriage vows going round the holy fire seven times -- so that they remain united for seven lives. Sa Re Ga Ma Pa Da Ni Sa. Sa Ni Da Pa Ma Ga Re Sa -- traditional *nadaswaram* music trumpeted the seven notes.

The wedding, held at the Indus Tree Club premises in Bombay was a simple affair, attended by a handful of Madhu's friends and relatives apart from her parents, Arjun's father, and, of course, Saro *maami*.

Madhu was dressed in a maroon Kanjeevaram sari with intricate gold embroidery and decked with chunky temple style jewellery -- she carried the traditional outfit very well. Arjun was very uncomfortable in the ethnic silk *dhoti-vastram* ensemble he was wearing. Despite the belt tied over it, he was bogged by insecurity that his *dhoti* would come undone at any moment. He had resisted wearing it in favour of a more modern suit, but Madhu had insisted he wear the traditional South Indian garb.

Give some. Take some. Was that not the secret to a successful marriage? When he had announced they would have to forego a typical honeymoon because of work pressures, Madhu had taken the news very well. She had agreed that his career as a consulting psychiatrist at one of Bombay's top hospitals was nascent and budding and that he could not afford the luxury of taking time away from work.

Madhu's friends seemed to be more bothered by the news.

"You should go to Maldives." The maudlin Malti said.

"Or Lakshadweep. Everyone goes there these days." From the lethargic Lata.

"How about Goa then? Not very far from Bombay." The garish Gita.

"The whole point is to get used to each other. Home is as good a place as any." Madhu and Arjun exchanged knowing smiles.

"How can you not go anywhere?" Gaudy Gayatri looked at the

others, and they nodded their heads in collective disapproval.

"Khandala or Panchgani at least?" Malti gave it one last try.

"Okay girls. Keep thinking I am unromantic and old-fashioned. I am being practical." Madhu looked around at her friends.

"Who is the shrink now? You or him?" They exclaimed to cover up their collective embarrassment.

"This is the best way to end the discussion," Madhu whispered to Arjun. "I know they think I am anachronistic. Most of them got married early and subscribe to the Mills & Boon style of love and romance."

Arjun diplomatically kept out of the discussion since he did not know Madhu's friends well enough. When talk veered to the intricate designs of *mehndi* on Madhu's hands -- girl talk -- Arjun took the opportunity to move away and join his father at the other end of the room.

"It is a very personal decision -- to go or not go on a honeymoon. I don't understand why all these women and their mothers insist on sending us on one." He grumbled in a low tone that only his father could hear.

His father started coughing. "Did you go out in the rain? Did you go to bed without wearing a sweater? How many times have I told you to keep yourself warm? You never listen to me."

His father's cough would not stop. "Appa. Enough of living alone. Now that I am married, come live with us."

His father had not consented to live with the newly-married couple in Bombay. He had insisted he would continue to live in Mangalore, his hometown.

****

Honey. In the initial days of their marriage Madhu had not liked Arjun calling her that. She found it too western.

"I have always fantasized about calling my wife, honey. Look at it this way. Madhu literally means honey in English. You can't object to that!" Arjun argued.

"What's in a name after all? A rose by any other name or whatever that poetic thing you like to quote . . . ," he burst out laughing. "I know, I know, I have taken away the words out of your mouth."

"I am not talking to you. Anyway you talk enough for both of us." She had not spoken to him for a whole hour. As always she had given in eventually.

In the initial months of their marriage, Madhu's gynaecologist had advised her against having a baby. Her vaginal tract was surprisingly too small though Madhu was amply rounded and chubby. In addition, she was above thirty-five.

"You can channel your motherliness toward me. Your own overgrown child." Arjun had made light of the situation as they drove back from the hospital in their little red Maruti car.

"I could not have had you when I was six," Madhu quipped.

"In a way you have given me motherly love. One thing I have not known in life." Arjun braked the car abruptly as the traffic light had turned red.

"Stop it!" Madhu screamed. "Sounds incestuous!"

"My father has always been a father and mother to me. He has done an exemplary job. Yet, he is a man. Not a woman." Arjun pressed the accelerator as soon as the light turned green.

"Is this some kind of auto-psycho analysis or what? The Oedipus complex?"

"The Oedipus complex refers to the child's attraction toward the parent of the opposite gender and rivalry toward the parent of the same gender. This is believed to happen when the child is between three and five years old -- termed the phallic stage in the psychosexual development of the child . . . " Arjun elucidated Freudian theory until the car had reached its destination.

"Once a shrink, always a shrink," Madhu said.

The sounds of the sea could be heard. The Arabian Sea. The setting sun was fast disappearing in the distant horizon. A breeze of cold air swept into the car. Madhu rolled up the car window as fast as she could.

****

If their pre-marital courtship was a dream come true their post-marital romance had turned the dream into reality. Harmonious and peaceful.

"I can't believe it. A whole year has gone by." Madhu turned to Arjun, as they were getting ready to go to bed. Their first wedding anniversary was fast approaching.

"How do you want to celebrate the big day?" he asked.

"Let's have a belated honeymoon." Madhu peeled off the quilt.

"Your wish is my command. Pick a place and I will make the arrangements. I have not seen any place other than Bangalore, Mangalore, and Bombay. So you have a wide choice!" Arjun got into his side of the bed.

"Let's visit your father in Mangalore." Madhu sat at the dressing table pampering her skin for her nightly beauty routine.

Arjun looked at her with renewed respect. She knew how much he missed his father. Despite their best collective attempts, they had not succeeded in convincing the ailing man to come live with them in Bombay.

"That is the best gift you can give me," his heart brimmed with affection.

Madhu turned off the lamp and stood up. She shook off the thick cotton housecoat. Underneath, she was wearing the flimsy lacy negligee he had bought her for their wedding night. She had been too shy to wear it then. Madhu sashayed toward Arjun seductively, grabbed his hair, and cupped his face in her hands. . . .

Later, when they were both spent and satiated, Madhu had fallen asleep immediately. Arjun spent the night looking at her peaceful visage and listening to her mellifluous breathing. God! Thank You. Thank You. Thank You. For giving me the most wonderful woman in the whole world! Without the asking! *Somebody up there indeed loves me.*

****

December 6 1992. A week before Arjun and Madhu's first wedding anniversary. It was mid-morning. Burning news first broke out on BBC.

"The ongoing conflict between the Hindus and Muslims over the contentious Babri Masjid at Ayodhya reached new heights when a mob of Hindu extremists tore down the mosque and annihilated it to nothingness. Ayodhya is the birthplace of Lord Rama according to Hindu mythology. The same Ayodhya where stood the Babri Masjid. Hindu extremists had been campaigning to demolish the behemoth and build a Hindu temple in its place for the past few years. This day more than two lakh people decided to take the bull by the horns . . . ."

Arjun panicked. Madhu was still at the Jaslok Hospital. She had been summoned to the hospital for an emergency in the wee hours of the morning. He called her immediately.

"I am coming home now. I forbid you to leave the house today," she put the phone down without giving him a chance to reply.

She had read his mind. Arjun had desperately wanted to drive to the hospital and escort her back. What if something happened to her on the way? He could not risk that.

"In retaliation to the attack, inter-communal Hindu Muslim riots have broken out across the country. Mobs are mercilessly attacking every innocent individual they are encountering . . . ," The newscast continued. Arjun switched off the television when he could take it no more. Hindus. Muslims. What difference did it make? Why could they not coexist in harmony? Why did they insist on jumping at each other's throats all the time? Where had humanitarianism gone?

The next few hours were the longest and most torturous hours of his life. Tick tock tick tock . . . the ticking clock resonated within the confines of the small flat. Fear gnawed at the pit of his stomach. He paced to the window and back every few minutes. He flushed glasses of cold water down his throat.

He switched on the new CD player. "*Aaja re main to tumse khadi is paar ke ankhiyan* [Please come. I am standing on the other side today] . . . ," from the movie *Madhumati*. How appropriate the words were in this moment of separation.

Arjun dozed off. He dreamt that Madhu was pregnant. With twins. A girl and a boy. They would be the quintessential Indian family. *Ham do hamaare do.* The popular family planning slogan of the seventies propagating a two-child family. They would be the cynosure of all eyes. Their kids would inherit Madhu's beauty and his brains. What if they turned out to be the other way round? His beauty and her brains? An old George Bernard Shaw joke. In their case, that would work too. Arjun may not have been a Brad Pitt, but he was not bad looking, and Madhu was very intelligent.

Arjun was awakened by the ringing telephone. He had wanted to relish the dream. Reality was so different. Madhu would never bear him a child.

Arjun picked up the receiver. "I was exploding with worry. Where are you? I kept shouting not to leave the hospital, but you put the phone down in a hurry . . . what do you mean you entered the wrong building? How could you do this again, honey? I was crapping bricks . . . " Arjun chided Madhu incessantly in total exasperation.

****

Having seen the breaking news on BBC, Madhu had gotten into her car and gingerly started driving toward home. There was chaos everywhere. Her car was stopped twice by the police. Each time, her bag was checked. Each time, looking at the huge pink *bindi* adorning her forehead, unequivocally proclaiming her Hindu status, the police officer beseeched her in worried tones to get home as soon as possible.

Many of the roads were deserted. All commercial establishments had downed their shutters. Some roads had been blocked by the police. She heard gunfire go off in some distant zone. Her bones were cold. Her forehead was simmering hot. Sweat poured out of her body drenching her white-and-pink silk sari. She kept reciting the Hanuman chalisa verses for courage. "*Jai Hanuman Gnaana Guna Saagara, Jai Kapeesha Tihu Loka Vujagara . . . .*" Her chants reverberated inside the small red Maruti car.

Madhu drove the car as fast as she dared in the narrow alleys of Bombay and managed to reach Jallianwallah -- she only had another two or three kilometres to go before she was home safe and sound in Arjun's arms -- when she saw the billowing smoke, burning flames ahead. She saw that several vehicles had been set ablaze.

She had two options. One, hope for the best and continue toward the blaze. Surely, there would be other people there. She could seek protection in somebody's house. Would anybody really be able to protect her?

Alternatively, veer away from the alley, on to the main road, and take the longer route back home. God knows what the situation was on that road. Which was worse? Known devil or the unknown evil?

At that moment, Madhu saw two men hurling themselves toward her car. Strong hefty men. In their twenties perhaps. One of them held a bulky tote bag in his hands. They were gesticulating wildly to stop the car and waving the tote bag toward the car even as they came running toward her.

"God! Take care of my Arjun after I am gone." Madhu did not fear losing her life. Having born a mere mortal was death not every man's inevitable destiny? As she screeched her car to a halt, the two men hit the bonnet. The bigger of the two got into the front seat and the other man got onto the back seat with the tote bag.

"Turn around or we will all be dead," the big man growled. He leaned across and turned the steering wheel to the right in the direction of the main road. Madhu did as she was told. The sacred thread on his left shoulder, peeping out of his shirt collar, proclaimed he was a Hindu. No way would these men kill her. What if they raped her? It was one thing to die, another thing to live in shame. Now she was frightened.

Silently, she drove to the main road. The man at the back kept asking her to go faster and kept waving the bag at Madhu. God alone knew what they were carrying in it. Madhu did as she was told.

Surprisingly the main road was deserted. Madhu drove as fast as she could, the speedometer needle hitting sixty kilometres. Intuitively she drove toward Jallianwallah. Fear still gripped her body. She could not even remember the lines of Hanuman chalisa correctly any more. Like a stuck record, she chanted the first line repeatedly in her mind. *"Jai Hanuman Gnana Guna Saagara Jai Kapeesha Thihu Loka Vujagara . . . ."*

As she turned off the Jallianwallah main road, the big man spoke to her for the first time, thanking her for stopping the car and saving their lives.

They were nearing her apartment complex when they heard more gunshots going off. Two more cars were burning on the road. A mob was beating a middle-aged couple to pulp. A body was strewn on the ground. A bullet from the gunshot grazed one of the car's tires. The two men jumped out of the car along with the tote bag, dragging Madhu out with them. The driver-less red car veered off on its three wheels and hit the curb stone.

"I live here. Come in. Come in." Madhu whispered hoarsely. In a way, the two men had been her saviours even if they had only postponed her death by a few minutes. She felt a gush of gratitude amidst the fear. God had answered her prayers. He had sent them to protect her. She owed them one.

The mob had started running toward the threesome.

The two men beseeched Madhu to hide. Before she knew what was happening they had pushed her roughly into the compound of her apartment complex. Crouched under a bush, inside the compound of the apartment complex, her breathing heavy, she could hear the thud of several pairs of running feet. Had the mob spotted the two men? She hoped not.

The sound of gunshots going off filled the air. She covered her ears and lay prone on the mud, under the prickly bush. She could feel the distant thud of bodies hitting the ground. Had her saviours been vanquished? Minutes after they had thanked her for saving their lives? One of those ironies of fate.

Scared, Madhu waited for the marauders to come in through the gate, find her, and kill her. God. Please make sure Arjun does not come out now. Protect him. She prayed. For yet another last time. She looked around. The tote bag lay near her, its contents strewn in mud -- idols and photographs of every conceivable Hindu God -- that is what the men had been carrying! Madhu hastily stuffed them back in the bag.

Five minutes. Ten minutes. An hour. Nothing happened. The roads were silent. Madhu finally took the courage to peer out hesitantly from under the bush and then made a quick dash for the stairs, the tote bag in tow. Nobody had seen her. She was home! Safe and sound. The lift was out of order yet again. She climbed up the twenty-four flights as fast as she could until she reached the safe haven of their apartment. 2401.

Exhausted, she rang the bell with urgency uncharacteristic of her. Looking at her reflection in the glass window, she was horrified. Her hair had come undone. The pink powder *bindi* was smeared all across her forehead. Her hands had scratches from the prickly bush. Her white sari was covered with mud stains. Yet she was alive. After a series of ordeals.

The door did not open. She panicked. Had something happened to Arjun? She continued to ring the bell incessantly finally collapsing in the arms of whoever opened the door. Arjun. No. It was not Arjun. The hands that held her were soft. She opened her eyes to see the worried face of Saro *maami*.

"*Raam. Raam.*" Saro *maami* muttered as she wiped Madhu's face clean with the *pallu* end of her sari and then shouted out to the servant maid to fetch some strong coffee.

Madhu had called Arjun immediately thereafter.

****

"Will the insurance pay for the lost car?"

"We'll worry about that after things calm down. I am glad you are alive after all that you went through." Arjun replied. "I am coming over. Now . . . ."

"I forbid you to leave our flat until the violence subsides." Madhu ordered.

Her words brought back memories of another day when they had met for the first time.

"So near, yet so far." Madhu whispered.

"Honey, I love you." Arjun put the phone back on the cradle. Madhu was back safe, though she had entered the wrong apartment complex. He was not afraid to die himself. He was afraid of losing those he loved. Madhu, for one. His father, for another. He could not imagine a life without either of them.

He had to find a way to go over to Sheesh Mahal. Arjun looked out of the window. Not a soul on the street. There was a gunman posted at the gate of every apartment complex. Sheesh Mahal was a good two thousand feet from Chitrakoot Apartments. He looked at the living room clock. It had stopped.

He heard a deafening sound. Was it thunder? More gunfire. Why was the CD player silent? He pressed the Play button. No luck. He ejected the oft-used CD out, blew on it to remove any dust, and reinserted it. The Madhumati CD refused to make any more music. It was corrupted.

He picked up the cordless and dialled Saro *maami*'s number. No dial tone. The telephone lines were out. What a tragedy! He switched on the TV.

". . . There has been a shoot-out at Jallianwallah. Twenty people are feared dead when attackers forcibly invaded several apartments, set off crude hand grenades and opened fire indiscriminately. There is blood everywhere. Glass, furniture, and bodies have been flung into the road by the force of the blasts . . . ."

Arjun rushed to the bedroom, his heart was in his mouth. He could see Sheesh Mahal from the window. Glass, furniture and bodies lay on the road outside Sheesh Mahal. The gunshots he heard minutes ago were from the shootout at Jallianwallah. Arjun rushed out into the road. "Madhu! Never leave me!" He kept screaming until he had reached the debris outside Sheesh Mahal.

Madhu's body was a mangled mess of flesh and blood -- it no longer had a face. Arjun recognized it from the white and pink sari she had worn to the hospital in the middle of the night. There would be no first anniversary. Madhu's life had run out when their life together had just begun.

If only Madhu had not made the mistake of going into the wrong building -- the same mistake because of which he had met her -- he would not have lost her.

Life changes in a moment. For no rhyme or reason.

Yet everything happens for a purpose.

Except one never knows that purpose until later. Sometimes never.

God Almighty has a predetermined blueprint for each one of our lives.

Arjun had returned to Bangalore soon after. His father -- the only constant in his life -- had come down from Mangalore to live with him.

18. Natty Nineties: Moments

June 28 1998

The mild afternoon sun had vanished. Gloom had descended in the late afternoon sky. Lashing rain washed the glass walls and roof of the Pizza Hut. None of them had eaten the ice cream the waiter had placed at their table. It had melted completely.

Karan's eyes were moist. Ever since his return, Karan had wished he could be like Arjun, marvelling at the confidence he radiated and the restraint he maintained. There was an aura of quiet poise about him. Arjun's life had seemed picture perfect. Karan had not suspected that a tale so tragic lay buried beneath that joyous demeanour. Indeed Arjun had transcended the vicissitudes of life, found his own equilibrium, learnt to live life with equanimity.

Aarti had quietly slipped her hand into Arjun's. She had taken the album from Arjun and continued to pore over the pictures.

Arjun excused himself to go to the bathroom. Aarti sat watching Arjun as he weaved his way through the crowd. Her eyes exuded a mixture of awe and attraction, Karan noticed. Aarti and Karan kept up a mild banter until Arjun returned.

Arjun and Aarti expressed an eagerness to leave immediately. Karan did not want the weekend to end. He dreaded the thought of going home to his lonely existence. He called up Indu from Arjun's cell phone and asked her if she would meet him.

"Haul your ass over to my office," Indu's raucous laughter

followed. "I will take you wherever you want to go, and do whatever you want me to do."

Karan walked out of Pizza Hut, hailed an auto, deposited a one hundred-rupee note in the driver's hand, climbed in, and announced his destination. The ploy worked; the driver did not try any tricks. In a while, the auto had deposited Karan at the doorstep of the *GLITZ* office on Benson Avenue in Old Bangalore.

Karan was asked to wait in the plush lobby -- granite floors, track lights, imported furniture, postmodern art, a glamorous secretary. Karan settled down on the black leather settee. Radio station FM 92.7 played an inane song.

Ivory and Ebony
Ecstasy and Agony
If hate be the other side of love
The heart knows not how not to love
Love is pain, pain is love.
How I wish I could cease to love
Lock my heart in a velvet glove
Send it off with a homing dove.
Why live life when there is no love
Love is truth, truth is love
Can time reawaken the dream of love?

Not the Paul McCartney classic . . . most likely a local band.

"Sweetheart let's get out of here." Karan soon heard a familiar voice. The next minute, he was being dragged by Indu out of the door, toward a sleek Mercedes-Benz parked in the office compound.

****

Sunday evening. Topkapi, the Turkish restaurant located on the twenty-fourth floor of Bangalore's only skyscraper on M.G. Road, was full. Indu and Karan were immediately assigned a cosy little table in the far corner nevertheless. Indu happened to know the restaurant manager.

"They serve the best liquor." She grinned lasciviously and placed their order without even a cursory glance at the menu. Two large vodkas for herself. Bacardi and coke for Karan. A plate of Turkish appetizers.

A pregnant silence descended between the two ex-lovers.

Was this the same girl he had lost his virginity to? Karan looked at her sadly. Her face was barely discernible under the ambient lighting.

Que sera sera. Indu started singing in a low voice, inserting fake lyrics to the tune of the Doris Day song.

When I was just a little girl
My mother asked me What will you be?
Will you be pretty? Will you be rich?
Here's what I said to me:

"Sh sh sh." Karan looked around them.

"Don't you Sh sh sh me."

Que sera sera
Whatever will be will be.
I will become pretty I will become rich.
Never a good girl I will be a witch.
The future is here to see.

The waiter arrived with the order. Indu took large gulps of vodka.

When I was a big girl in school
My teacher asked me What will you try?
Will you paint pictures? Will you sing songs?
This was my wise reply:

What had he seen in her? Karan picked up his glass. For all her bizarre behaviour, she had remembered correctly, what his favourite drink was.

Que sera sera
Whatever will be will be.
I will paint pictures I will sing songs
Always a bad girl I will only do wrongs
The future is here to see.

A good-looking guy that satisfied her lust. That is all he had meant to her. Correction. One of the guys. Karan's disappointment suddenly morphed into impotent rage. Indu had robbed him of the opportunity of being a father without giving him a chance. Having his own child would have given a new direction to his loveless life.

When I grew up and fell in love,
My lovers asked me, "What lies ahead?
Will we have rainbows day after day?"
Here's what I said to me:
Que sera sera
Whatever will be will be.
There will be no rainbows day after day
Only pain and suffering everyday
The future is here to see.

"You are off your rocker." Karan said brusquely.

Indu stopped singing. She had drained one glass of vodka by then and picked up the other. "I am glad I left you."

"How could you stoop so low?" His hurt, cached all those years, had risen to the fore. "How could you abort my child without telling me?"

"I had big ambitions. You would have tried to stop me."

"You ruined my life."

"I saved you from a fate worse than death."

"Cut the drama."

"You are such a loser. I could tell. Even then." Her laugh was vicious.

Indu had done it wilfully. It was unfair. The child could not have been created without his involvement; yet it had been destroyed without his knowledge.

"I did not want to deal with your emotions." She drained the second glass of vodka and snapped her fingers at the waiter to order another.

19. Ecstasy and Agony

August 1983. Indu started as a copywriter for *GLITZ*, a glamorous high society magazine publication in Bombay, soon after disappearing from Karan's life without so much as a goodbye. Karan was studying in the Bangalore College of Engineering at the time; the two of them had cohabited for two years. On completing her BA, Indu had found the job with *GLITZ* without Karan's knowledge.

Indu zoomed up the echelons of the *GLITZ* corporate ladder fairly quickly -- it helped that she intermittently slept with the big boss, an aristocratic old man probably older than her father.

Her love life was in full bloom. Regularly, she cruised the local colleges, seeking good-looking young studs to embellish her nights. She dated an upcoming model, Ramitin Diaz -- a Persian guy with a smooth, toned body and copper red hair and green eyes, who, unknown to her, granted sexual favours to powerful men and women in high places in a bid to propel his modelling career. At the same time, she also dated a small-time cricketer who was desperate to revive his careening cricketing career, Sunny Suri -- a hairy hunk with bedroom eyes. Her boss was now the chairman of *GLITZ*. How could she say no to him?

Was she a nympho? Possibly. She had read that men had sex on their mind all the time, that a man could have had sex five minutes back but the minute he saw an attractive woman he would start thinking about sex again. She was no different. She craved male attention. Her body craved sex. All the time. Sex was biological.

Indu had risen to be the chief editor of *GLITZ* by the time she was thirty. She had made a place for herself as a high-profile celebrity interviewer. Her subjects? Baby doll Alisha Chinai -- India's first pop singer who was crooning her way to the top with "Made in India." Parmeshwar Godrej, empress of the Godrej empire and numero uno amongst Bombay socialites. Ex-captain of the Indian cricket team -- Ravi Shastri -- who had turned commentator post-retirement. Superstar, Amitabh Bachchan, who, after a series of flops, was on a comeback trail with the chartbusting song "*Jumma chumma de de . . . Jumma chumma de de chumma . . .*" Indu had been poised to interview Prime Minister Rajeev Gandhi before he succumbed to an untimely and tragic death from a human bomb, a woman named Subbulakshmi, planted by the Liberation Tigers of Tamil Eelam (LTTE).

Life is a paradox. Never optimal. Too much or too little. Drought or deluge. Sunny Suri found out about her affair with Ramitin; he dumped her and married a traditional girl that his cloistered family had chosen for him. Close on the heels of that event, Ramitin bagged his first starring role in a Hindi movie and decided he had no time for Indu. Around the same time, her boss, the grand old man of *GLITZ*, retired.

Old habits die hard. Occasionally, she continued to cruise the local college scene. The college boys no longer considered her attractive -- she had crossed thirty, the magical age that meant over-the-hill for the young and foolish twenty-somethings. Besides, the boys had more choice -- urban girls of the nineties were a lot less prudish than their previous generation. They were open to putting out, willing to cohabit, and they were much younger.

Finally, Indu decided it was time she anchored herself for life. Indu's parents had long given up on her. Her father had never been able to exercise any control over her. Her mother was riddled with remorse and blamed herself for not being strict enough with her daughter and getting her married when she was still in her twenties

-- the magic marriageable age for Indian girls from good families. Once Indu applied her mind to something, she knew exactly how to go about getting it.

****

A rich husband was not that difficult to find. Indu met him at a socialite gathering at the Oberoi Sheraton, Bombay's most opulent hotel. Sheetal Singh, the host -- one of Indu's bosom pals -- had chosen to seat her next to Bharat Agarwal, the scion of an illustrious business family. Thirty-five years of age, balding and rotund, he needed a total makeover. Bharat was dressed in a maroon silk shirt tucked into a pair of shiny black pleated pants, pointed brown shoes with tassels and white nylon socks. The top three buttons of his shimmering shirt were open, revealing a chest so hairy it would have put a grizzly bear to shame. His neck was adorned with several gold chains, all buried in the forest on his chest. His teeth were stained red from chewing *paan*. There were at least five gem-studded rings on his fingers.

Right through dinner Indu's tenacious efforts to strike up a conversation with Bharat were somewhat thwarted by his monosyllabic responses, throwing her into the throes of frustration, the fear of failure. The seven-course dinner was reaching its end; dessert and wine were being served. A very good-looking Kashmiri waiter approached their table and started pouring rich red wine into crystal glasses. Indu could feel his electrifying presence behind her. The waiter leaned to place the wine glass in front of Bharat. His hot legs pressed against her bare back. Indu pressed her tingling thighs together lustfully.

Oops! An entire bottle of the ruby red wine had toppled down from the waiter's tray onto Indu's lap, patterning the front of her champagne-coloured georgette dress with a maroon octopus, the spreading tentacles reaching out to the most intimate details of her body. The Kashmiri waiter became profusely apologetic, offering her a clean table napkin.

Her face fraught with tears, Indu looked imploringly at Bharat. The wine had soaked through her dress to impart a glistening glow to her moist skin. Her ravishing body begged to be protected from the ravaging eyes around them.

She could feel Bharat's eyes piercing the curvaceous mounds and orbs in the clinging wet dress as he pushed his chair back and got up, motioning her to follow him. Indu almost clung onto him from behind as they made a quick exit into the hallway, onto the elevator, down to the parking lot. Once they were in the car, she maintained the flow of one-sided conversation. His responses degenerated from monosyllabic to nonverbal as his eyes darted surreptitiously toward the front of her wet dress, to the huge stain on her belly.

On arriving at her apartment building off Juhu, Indu invited him up to her tenth-floor flat. She seated him in the tiny sitting room, arming him with a copy of the latest edition of *India Today*, and pouring a glass of whiskey on the rocks, before disappearing into the bedroom.

When she emerged a half hour later, showered and scrubbed, clad in a satin housecoat, Bharat was thumbing through the pages of the latest edition of *GLITZ*. A whole array of *GLITZ* magazines were strewn around him.

Indu refilled his drink, poured a glass of Chardonnay for herself, and switched on her brand-new five-track Panasonic CD player. Jazz music filled the room.

"Sorry for making you miss the dance."

"I don't dance. Two left feet." He said.

Indu made herself comfortable on the settee. "That stupid waiter. If he weren't so gorgeous, I would have gotten him fired."

The whiskey had probably loosened Bharat up -- he seemed to be suffering a serious bout of verbal diarrhoea. Indu sipped her Chardonnay and listened.

The Agarwals had wanted him to get married at the ripe young age of twenty-one. Fifteen years later, the quest for the right girl was far from over. His parents did not fully fathom his requirements. He did not have the time to fall in love or for romance -- he was too busy building successful businesses. His elder brother had a son who was twenty. Both his younger brothers had been married ages ago to wealthy girls chosen by his parents.

When Bharat had finished his fifth whiskey, he asked Indu to dance with him. She smiled indulgently -- trying to ignite him with a languorous press of her body. Sixty seconds. Bharat had passed out in her arms. She arranged his fat body on the couch with great difficulty and retreated to her bedroom.

****

Indu was a late riser -- by the time she came out of her bedroom the next morning, Bharat was gone. So was the entire stack of *GLITZ* magazines. That was a good sign. When she opened the front door to collect the milk sachets she found a bouquet of red roses on the door step. With a card.

"I have never gotten drunk in my life before. Nor have I passed out in the arms of a girl as beautiful as you. As they say, there is always a first time. Will you have dinner with me this evening? I hope you don't disappoint me." -Bharat

She was getting somewhere. Indu dressed for dinner in emerald green, a colour that complemented her dusky complexion to perfection. The effect of the sheer chiffon sari draped over a tight satin underskirt with knee high slits was tantalizing, especially when she walked; her hips swayed within the confines of the tight skirt, her bare legs visible through the sheer chiffon and the slits, complementing the bare arms, neck, and back left uncovered by the silk halter blouse.

Wining and dining. Dance and music. Psychedelic lights. A gala evening. When Bharat dropped her home that night, she thanked him, bid a hurried good bye, and rushed in without looking back.

Like the old-fashioned, middle-class girl that she was not. She actually liked the part. For the novelty.

Their next date was a music concert by tabla maestro Zakir Hussain at Bombay's famed Shanmukhananda Hall. Indu allowed Bharat to give her a good night kiss when he dropped her off at eleven o' clock.

The day after, he proposed with a ring from De Beers, a diamond solitaire surrounded by tiny sapphires.

Indu accepted without much ado. Immediately, she called Sheetal to give her the good news.

"*Mubarak*, darling," Sheetal congratulated Indu. "He is a multi-millionaire -- worth well over a hundred and fifty crore rupees."

"*Shukriya* sweetheart," Indu thanked Sheetal.

They could not stop laughing as they relived the moment when the bribed waiter had deliberately allowed the whole bottle of wine to topple onto Indu's dress and pretended it was an accident.

"All it took was a crisp five-hundred rupee note," Sheetal boasted.

"He was so good-looking." Indu faked an orgasmic groan. "He had me soaking wet."

"You bitch," Sheetal cackled.

"Where did you find him?"

"You want him? Five thousand rupees a night should cover it," said Sheetal, the eternal businesswoman.

"No. no. I am saving myself for the *patidev*. *Mera pati mera parameshwar hain* . . . my husband is my God."

"*Suno. Suno. Billi sau choohe khaa kar Haj par chalee gayi* [Hear. Hear. The cat is going on a pilgrimage after eating a hundred rats] . . . ."

"I crossed the hundredth man mark a long time ago," Indu giggled.

"*Randi kahin ki* . . . you slut." Sheetal bid goodbye.

****

Indu and Bharat were married in traditional Punjabi style with a whole week of festivities. Indu hated the elaborate wedding ceremonies but preferred concentrating on the positives. A wedding trousseau from the most upscale fashion houses and designers. Traditional Indian dresses designed by Ritu Berry and Tarun Tahliani. Guess and Gucci accessories. Chunky Indian jewellery from Surajmal. A grand reception at the Oberoi Sheraton. *GLITZ* even featured the event in their "Marriage of the Month" section. A honeymoon in Australia and Singapore. Indu discovered to her amusement that Bharat was a virgin. He did not ask, and she did not tell, that she was not one.

Bharat had made it clear to Indu that breaking away from the joint family was anathema. Indu deigned to relocate to Bangalore and live with Bharat's parents, his brothers, their wives and children -- a large, conventional joint family under a single roof.

The plush family mansion in suburban Bangalore was humungous, with fourteen bedrooms, fifteen bathrooms, but a single kitchen. It was staffed by a horde of servants. The Agarwal household possessed a fleet of Maruti cars and three imported cars for its members' collective convenience. Indu sought a transfer to Bangalore and continued to work for *GLITZ* as Regional Editor, South India, a position she loved for the power, the partying, and the perennial limelight.

The first few years of their marriage were a roller-coaster ride that survived all odds. Indu did not get along with any of the members of her husband's family. She set her own boundaries and abided by her own rules. Bharat also abided by her rules. Like all thirty-something business tycoons of his time, Bharat was on a money-minting spree; she was the trophy wife.

A makeover for Bharat was Indu's first post-marital activity. "You are fat, honey. You dress garishly."

Indu made him shed twenty-two pounds in two months. Gym workouts and liposuction; a diet of fruits, vegetables, water, buttermilk, and dry *rotis*. More significantly, nothing whatsoever cooked in his mother's kitchen -- no meat, no butter, no oil, no sweets. Her mother-in-law silently cursed Indu calling her the modern avatar of some wicked witch from the bygone era.

Indu replaced his shimmering silk shirts and shiny pleated pants with cotton button-down shirts from Arrow and Allen Solly and custom fit trousers in blended wool. "Brown shoes with black pants! It will ruin *my* image." She coached him on the nuances of mixing and matching shoes with trousers and socks with shoes. She made him remove all his chains and rings. Small mercies -- he was allowed to wear a single piece of jewellery at any point in time. Above all, "No *paan* for you," was her super commandment.

Zack, their son, arrived as planned on their second wedding anniversary. He grew up in the care of servants and grandparents -- Indu was caught up in the whirlwind of career advancement. She had helped *GLITZ* grow into a national hotshot magazine.

Like most second-born children in modern families, daughter Tina was an accident. Indu did not have time for another child. Nor the inclination. The pregnancy made Indu depressed. Bharat was worried. The gynaecologist assured them that Indu would turn the corner once she saw the baby.

Indu refused to feed her baby. A nurse was appointed to nurture Tina. Indu would burst into tears at the sight and sound of Bharat -- blaming him for premeditating a second child and pushing her into this pitiable plight. She was prescribed Prozac, the latest wonder drug, the panacea for clinical depression.

Indu grew gradually disinterested in life. On maternity leave, she never left home, staying in bed for days together, crying intermittently, and eating no food. Prozac did not work its wonders because she stopped taking it.

One day Indu announced that she needed a vacation. She would visit her parents in Calcutta. She did not want Bharat or the kids to go with her. "I need time for myself. My own space."

****

A glowing Indu returned to Bangalore a month later. She had gained ten pounds. Unknown to Bharat, she had started drinking. A peg or two at night. Never more.

Indu had always frenzied over how the joint family was dysfunctional and pleaded with Bharat that they should nuclearize. Homeboundness exacerbated her frustrations. She threw a temper tantrum on just about anyone who tried to talk to her. None had the courage to oppose her.

One afternoon, on seeing her mother-in-law engrossed in a soap opera that eulogized the soap's mother-in-law and penalized the daughter-in-law, Indu was piqued; she picked up an expensive blown-glass urn from the coffee table and hurled it at the monitor -- shattering the picture tube. Shards of glass were embedded in the cheeks and eyebrows of the young servant maid who was also watching the soap -- she would require plastic surgery to repair her damaged face.

The maid's father had created a public scene, threatening dire consequences on the Agarwal family since his daughter's looks were permanently marred and her chances of a decent marriage drastically reduced. He had cursed Indu with the most vicious words in his putrid vocabulary. It had taken a lot of pleading from the Agarwal family and a bit of money to calm him down, in addition to footing the bill for the maid's plastic surgery expenses and making promises to find the maid a decent match and finance her dowry. Indu found the whole episode very funny; she would not stop laughing about it. "I can't stay at home anymore."

The Agarwal family must have heaved the proverbial sigh of relief when Indu decided to go back to work with *GLITZ*. Her life was soon an endless chain of parties and late nights. The kids were again relegated to the servants. A peg or two no longer satiated her. She needed a whole bottle of vodka or gin to see her through the day. Every day.

****

One Sunday afternoon, wandering around in the small garden, dressed in a flimsy lace negligee, Indu discovered two huge rattan baskets of ripe alphonso mangoes on their compound. She picked up her mother-in-law's walking stick, walked over to the baskets and gave them a sturdy knock, sending all the mangoes flying into the neighbouring drains and sewage. When the fruit vendor discovered his entire livelihood had been destroyed he went raving mad, showering choice abuses at Indu and attracting a huge crowd of passersby to gather in front of the mansion.

Indu found the incident so funny she could not control her laughter. This must have enraged the fruit vendor even more. He collapsed in the middle of the road making the crowd go berserk. The Agarwals had to call the police to save their house from being vandalized and pay off the fruit vendor handsomely.

The same night, Bharat suggested to Indu that they see a therapist.

"How dare you?" Indu stood at the entrance of the dressing room, a clay mask on her face. "You are jealous. I am the smart wife. I make you appear ordinary."

"I want us to be happy." Bharat walked toward the closet, unbuckling his belt.

"Then you should see a therapist." The dry green clay mask was cracking in several places.

"You are always angry, always upset." Bharat unbuttoned his shirt. "I can't bear to see you like that."

"Counselling will do *you* good for your self-confidence. It will make *you* a smarter husband." Indu laughed devilishly and poured herself a large vodka.

"I want you to stop drinking." Bharat stood in front of the open closet in his underpants.

"Fat bastard." Indu cackled condescendingly and noisily sipped her drink. "How many times have I told you to stop eating oily food? After all the trouble I took . . ." Indu reached out for the empty bottles under her dresser and started pelting them at him one after the other. Bharat ducked each time, letting the bottle hit the granite floor -- the glass breaking into minute particles.

"Stop using that awful hair dye." Indu's torrent of words died when she could find no more objects to throw at him. She poured the last drops of vodka in the glass down her throat.

Bharat advanced toward her, twisted her hand and brought his face close to hers. "Listen to me or else . . ." His voice was menacing.

"Phew! *Paan* again." Indu turned her face away with repulsion. "Hick." She hit him with the empty vodka glass in her free hand, ran into the bathroom and closed the door.

In the days that followed, Indu drank round the clock. Compulsively and incessantly. At work. At home. At every Page 3 party she attended. Bharat seemed to have chosen the path of least resistance -- a visit to the therapist had not cropped up again.

20. Natty Nineties: Que Sera Sera

June 28 1998

"I would not wish this on my worst enemy . . . ." Indu looked at the expensive Movado watch on her right wrist.

Topkapi was still crowded. The waiter was taking good care of them -- Indu was indeed a favourite customer of the restaurant as she had claimed.

"A bad girl like me deserves this fate."

"Nobody deserves this."

"Are you still in love with me?" Indu asked.

"I will always love you as a friend."

"I can't take it anymore." Indu pushed away her empty glass. "Bharat still loves me to death."

"Did you ever cheat on him?"

"Never." Indu burst into tears. "That is what is killing me."

"Is that why you drink so much?"

"I don't want to be this one-man woman." Indu extracted an array of vials from her purse and repaired her makeup with the help of a hand mirror. "I don't know how long I can go on."

You need professional help. Karan felt like screaming. How could he suggest something like that without incurring her wrath? They had been two of the smartest and most outgoing students of Xavier

Junior College. Why had they both ended up like this?

"Bad karma." Indu was finally ready to go.

"Nothing is bad or good. It is all in the mind." Karan escorted her out of the restaurant.

"You were right about why I drink." Indu rested her head on Karan's shoulder as they waited for the elevator to take them down. "You can still read my mind." Her lips nuzzled the nape of his neck. "Like an open book."

****

Seated in the chauffeur-driven Mercedes-Benz, Indu's mind plotted the next course of action. Karan's return had reignited the passion she had once felt for him. It made her feel even more smothered with her situation. She had to break away from the joint family -- the palatial Agarwal bungalow in suburban Bangalore. That called for some drastic orchestration.

"I will only wear *khadi*." Indu declared at the breakfast table the next morning. Minutes later, she stood in the centre of the master bedroom doling out her expensive silks and chiffons to the servants. As expected, her mother-in-law called up Bharat and ordered him home immediately, 'to knock some sense into the head of that of wife of his'.

"I will no longer wear any jewellery." Indu unlocked one of her jewellery cases. As expected, her mother-in-law intervened -- forcibly taking custody of the jewellery -- to be sent away for deposit in the bank locker.

Indu called the Shanti Helpline in retaliation. Shanti was a popular NGO that helped underprivileged women in distress -- Indu had once interviewed the founder. "Shanti Shanti Shanti." Indu gasped, when a volunteer answered the phone. "I am a prisoner in my in-laws house. They have confiscated my jewellery. They may set me on fire. Cooking gas. Help . . . help . . . ."

Within minutes the house was swarming with Shanti volunteers. Even some neighbours had arrived -- despite the high-profile community they lived in and the relatively large distance between adjacent plots -- everyone loved free drama. The volunteers offered to call the police.

"I was only rehearsing for an interview. I am Indumati Agarwal, the chief editor of *GLITZ*." Indu did a quick *volte-face*. Apologizing profusely, she ordered the servants to serve *pakoras* and tea, all the while smiling triumphantly at her mother-in-law who was seething visibly at the avoidable disgrace.

The volunteers had left by the time Bharat arrived. The mother-in-law begged Bharat to break away from the joint family and live separately, so that Indu would stop humiliating them in public.

In a matter of days, Bharat and Indu had moved into the plush new bungalow that the family owned on the outskirts of West Bangalore; with their two children, a retinue of servants, and a new fleet of cars. What Indu wanted had been proffered on a silver platter. Liberation at last.

21. Natty Nineties: Discovery

July 18 1998

A whole month had passed by since his return. A peculiar restlessness continued to engulf Karan -- he was impatient to find Danny. Indu's reporter had not been successful. Karan had been checking with Indu every day. He would call her later in the afternoon -- she never woke up before noon -- she partied every night.

Karan drove his old Fiat in the direction of Aarti's house -- she had invited her friends over for lunch. Karan barely recognized the streets; there had been a major revamp during the years he was away. Houses had been replaced by multi-storeyed apartment buildings everywhere. The address numbers were even more erratic than before. Often, road names were missing. The roads were mostly deserted. *Janta* was probably watching television. The latest movies. Indian and foreign. The choice of channels was unlimited. Sony. MTV. STAR. Zee. Doordarshan.

When he had effortlessly succeeded in getting lost in the maze of roads, Karan reluctantly stopped the car in front of a roadside shop. He had to repeat his question three times in quick succession before the shop owner unglued his eyes from the mini-television monitor. Karan was relieved to find out that he was only a block away.

Aarti and Anupama lived in a luxurious penthouse in Anand Apartments, a tall multi-storey building that now occupied the plot where Aarti's whitewashed house had once stood. In the wake of India's liberalization, like all middle-class families in the neighbourhood, Anupama must have sold out to the apartment builders for a huge profit that included the penthouse apartment and a contract clause that the complex be named after her late husband, Anand Rao.

Karan and Arjun arrived at almost the same time. Aarti was seated at her computer in the cosy niche attached to the drawing room. Sunlight streamed in through the skylight and the open French windows. The living room was done up in bright ethnic colours. Karan and Arjun touched Anupama's feet in reverence.

"God bless you." Anupama beamed at them. "The last time I saw you both was at Bhavna's wedding."

"To think that was the first wedding Arjun ever attended!" Aarti's eyes twinkled.

Anupama excused herself to go into the kitchen and give finishing touches to the quintessential Mysorean meal she had prepared.

"Why is Indu not here?" Karan asked Aarti.

"She is attending one of her Page 3 parties. Hotel Leela Penta."

Aarti and Arjun kept up an intense conversation during the course of lunch. Karan remained characteristically silent. They were in the midst of enjoying Anupama's homemade dessert when the phone rang. Indu was on the line. Aarti switched on the speakerphone.

"Good news. My reporter has located Danny's address." Indu's voice sounded slightly slurred. At two in the afternoon. "He says the place is full of movers and packers."

Redemption at last. Danny was not dead. "Danny may be going away." Karan looked at Arjun. "Better hurry."

Arjun looked at Aarti.

"I feel a migraine coming," Aarti said. "I need to rest a bit."

****

The red Maruti Esteem speeding down the quiet tree-lined Benson Avenue in Old Bangalore came to a halt in front of an old-fashioned bungalow with a sloping roof, an anachronism in modern times, apparently an architectural relic from the bygone British era. Karan and Arjun got out of the car, opened the heavy wrought iron gates, and ambled up the driveway to the central portico. They had arrived at the address supplied to them by Indu's reporter -- Danny's residence. They looked at each other victoriously.

An elderly man in shirtsleeves and a spotless white *dhoti* stood in the veranda shouting out instructions to domestic help in the vernacular. Leading Karan and Arjun inside, he introduced himself as Gopi -- a supervisor of the staff.

Danny's house was beautiful -- large open spaces, natural lighting, straight lines, minimalist décor, muted colours, innovative themes, antique wood furniture . . . cardboard boxes were stacked everywhere.

"Where is Danny going?" Karan asked.

"Sir, coffee?" Gopi tried to play the gracious host.

Neither Karan nor Arjun belied any inclination to imbibe the coffee that had been offered. "We want to see Danny. We are his friends." Arjun said in chaste Kannada, the same vernacular language that Gopi had used.

Gopi warmed up. "This should not have happened to Danny-Sir." He looked around as if to make sure no one could hear what he said.

"What happened? Did Danny have an accident? Is he sick?"

Gopi motioned to Karan and Arjun to follow him, leading them into the uninhabited precincts of the master bedroom.

Danny's bedroom was elegant -- brightly-coloured abstracts on the wall, a lavender satin comforter on the queen-sized poster bed, plush multicoloured area rug with geometric patterns, fabric-covered venetian blinds, black and rust leather cubes carelessly strewn across the room . . . yet no photos of anyone anywhere.

"Fate played a cruel trick on Danny-Sir . . ." Gopi looked up toward the ceiling and made a fatalistic gesture with his hands.

Karan and Arjun looked at each other. Seeta Murthy had been correct then. Danny was dead.

"Danny-Sir committed suicide." Gopi whispered conspiratorially to them, intent on filling them the gory details on how he had discovered Danny's body in that same bedroom three weeks back.

Karan felt cheated. By Fate. He would never be able to ask Danny for his forgiveness. For letting him down, the one time, he had needed his support. He wanted to flee.

Arjun appeared more stoical. As a doctor, he was probably trained to secondarize his own emotion and remain clinical under such circumstances. "Danny never opened up with us, ever. God only knows what he was hiding." He sleuthed around the bedroom.

Karan stood at the bay window and stared ahead. He could feel Danny's presence in every object around him. Danny had been a different colour at different times. What colour would he have been now? *Orange -- the colour of pain?*

"Was Danny married? Can we meet his family?" Arjun asked Gopi.

"Danny-Sir lived alone ever since I came to work for him." Gopi pulled a wooden chair over to the wall-to-wall cupboard and climbed on it. He took out a bunch of keys from his shirt pocket, unlocked the door to the topmost shelf, brought out a plastic sack, patiently untied the cord that knotted its mouth, and pulled out a large leather-bound book. After wiping it clean with the edge of his *dhoti*, he held it out toward Karan and Arjun.

"Danny-Sir wrote in this black book all the time." Gopi made an overtly subliminal suggestion that they should read it.

"Looks like a diary," Arjun whispered to Karan. "I hope it throws some light on his death . . . ."

"I can only read Kannada." Gopi diplomatically relayed to them that he had not broken the code of honour and read the contents.

Karan winced inwardly. Deep down, his gut may have been aware of the sordid contents of the black book.

"Gentlemen, you have relieved me of my burden." Gopi folded his hands Namaste-style. "I can go back to my native place without any worry."

****

Arjun's red Maruti Esteem was soon retracing its route on the tree-lined Benson Avenue, making its arduous journey back to South Bangalore, in the hot afternoon sun and arrived at Karan's house. Aarti and Indu arrived soon after. They had no words to express their shock as Karan and Arjun undertook the painful task of relaying the disturbing news.

"Danny *bachaoed* me a couple of times." Indu took out a steel flask from her purse and took a quick shot of the contents. "Good boy. Always helpful."

"I feel so selfish. I used to reach out to him only when I needed him to solve *my* problems . . ." Aarti was sobbing.

"I have always been a bad girl." Indu took another shot of vodka. "Is it my turn next?"

The Star TV channel was beaming the 1970's movie *Anand,* the ultimate ode of friendship between a terminally ill but eternally cheerful patient Anand and the sullen faced doctor Babu Moshoi, who treats him. Even as the tearjerker-movie unfolded on the TV screen, the four friends sat huddled on the living room couch reading from the black book magnanimously given to them by Gopi.

Some Day, Some Place. . . . Turned out to be a touching memoir of Danny's life. Danny had seen every colour of the rainbow. He had even found the pot of gold. Sadly, he was not destined to enjoy it. His despondency and helplessness were inherently palpable in the writing.

22. Some Day, Some Place

October 25 1996. The call was a little intriguing to say the least. "I want to meet you. It is important." The caller identified himself as a recent college graduate.

"Do I know you? How did you get my number?" I was baffled. At work, the morning had been unusually busy for a Friday.

His reply was crisp. "From a friend."

The best thing, I decided, was to check him out. "Where do we meet?"

His reply was quick. "Six o'clock this evening at the Holiday Inn, if it suits you."

He had it all planned out. "How do I recognize you?" I kept my voice flat and emotion-free despite the surge of adrenalin for which I knew not the cause.

"I will recognize you." His tone was teasing.

I was a trifle perturbed that a perfect stranger knew so much about me.

"My name is Tony. Bye." He had disconnected.

Why did he want to meet me? I had no clue. Why had I agreed to meet him? On an impulse, perhaps.

"Honey, do you have any plans for the evening?" I called my wife, Priyanka, a leading interior decorator, whose clientele boasted several big names, a virtual who's-who menu. Caught in the vortices of our whirlwind careers, we were used to having lesser and lesser time for each other.

"Mom will be dropping by. She wants me to take her to see the hit movie. *Dilwale Dulhaniya Le Jaayenge* . . . ," Priyanka replied.

"I have to attend a business dinner. After my promotion last month, things are moving." Partly true. I was managing three to four projects and heading a team of over thirty professionals at work.

"Don't worry about me. I know how hard you worked for that promotion." Did I sense a trace of relief in her voice the way she said this?

"What would I do without you? You are so understanding." There was definitely a trace of relief in my voice.

****

At a quarter to six I was lounging in the hotel lobby in Friday clothes -- Dockers khakis, an open-necked turquoise blue shirt, and tan loafers. Looking tensely at my watch every few seconds, I felt like a starry-eyed teenager waiting for his first date. Dammit, it is my first date, at least with a man! Date? Fat hope! Good fantasy! I knew not what God had in store for me.

I had realized my attraction for members of my own sex when I was sixteen or seventeen. I had been scared at first. After that, ashamed sometimes, guilty at other times. Rapacious for information all the time.

Gay rights, alternative lifestyles -- these were western concepts I read about from time to time as I grew older. I identified with them, but how could I have liberated myself in the claustrophobic social milieu? I had never even met one other person who was gay-identified. In fact, I never even had the opportunity to air my opinions on the subject. In the protectionist milieu of the conservative seventies and the cloistered eighties, western lifestyles could not have influenced the average household.

Pre-liberalized India had been insulated from the developed western world. Society was regressively repressive. Marriage to a person of the opposite gender was the societal norm. Rather, a fact of life. Family supposedly took precedence over the individual.

Exactly at a quarter past six, a good-looking young guy, fair and slim like a model, of average height, materialized at the entrance of Holiday Inn. He was stylishly dressed in tight Levi jeans and an electric blue T-shirt, a small gold stud in his right ear. His long flowing hair was silken and well-groomed. I instinctively knew this was Tony. At the same time, I was overcome by a bout of insecurity that he may not be. I fervently began wishing he were.

He looked around nervously; his hands kept smoothing his well-coiffeured hair; he bit his nails one or two times. On spotting me, his face broke out into a relieved grin. His eyes twinkled mischievously as he walked toward me.

By the time I stood up and offered my hand to the slightly self-conscious Tony, I had lost my heart to him. I had fallen in love with yet another man, for the umpteenth time in my life. To fall in love and not be loved, to lose the man before he even realized I was in love with him, had been the oft-repeated story of my life. I could very well write a treatise on all the men who had coloured my life in the fertile imagination of my mind.

****

My first serious crush had happened in junior college -- Raaj, my lecturer. Tall, dark, and handsome, he was barely older than most senior students were -- this was his first job. His vibrant personality, lively dialogue delivery, and charming jokes ensured high attendance in his classes.

Day after day, week after week, I sat in the front row, watching his every movement, savouring his every word. Night after night, I fantasized about him. Olive complexion, muscular pecs, hairy hands, bushy moustache. The few times he had pointed in my general direction or asked me to answer a question, I revelled in the attention; I also wished to turn invisible, lest I make a fool of myself.

I was taking baby steps in garnering courage to talk to him outside class, with little success, when, one day, I ran into him near a movie theatre. A conservatively-dressed, nondescript girl accompanied him. When he introduced her as his wife, I was distraught. It took me months to recover, to overcome the dejection.

This was only the beginning; my life became a continual series of unilateral emotional attachments thereafter.

Then, there was Bobby, one of my classmates. We travelled by the same bus every day -- the college campus was located in the outskirts, away from the hustle and bustle. I felt protected by his warm and assuring presence. I loved the physical proximity of sitting next to him in a crowded bus -- the warmth of his strong thighs pressed against mine, the silken, prickly feeling of his hairy hands brushing against me with every swerve of the bus. He possessed a joie de vivre that was infectious, succeeding occasionally in drawing me out of my introverted shell. I can still get aroused by the memory of the aroma of his strong sweat comingled with Mysore sandalwood soap.

****

It was with Kay-Kay that my emotions crossed the thin line separating love and friendship. He possessed an air of bravado that alternated with a peculiar vulnerability. I still remember the feel of his prickly cheeks on my neck, the wetness of his tear-stained face, as we walked down the road in the middle of the night, the day his girlfriend left him. The more time we spent together, the more hopelessly I fell in love with him. In the college library; the campus deli; hanging out at the pubs . . . The protector and the protected. The sensible and the sensitive. The odd couple as we came to be called on campus. After several bouts of vacillation, I made up my mind to confess my true feelings for him.

I was nervous. I kept looking at my watch every few seconds. Kay-Kay and I were seated in the open-air terrace garden of one of Bangalore's pubs. The small black-and-white TV was beaming the evening news. Something about the attack on the Golden Temple of Amritsar. The good-looking hunk, Tejinder Singh was reading the news.

"I have something to tell you . . . ," I finally mustered the courage to look him in the eye. "I admire you. Immensely. I adore you. Profusely. I worship you. Fervently. I love you. With all my heart." Out it all tumbled.

"You are not drunk are you?" There was a look of disbelief on his face.

"*Kaash.*" I said in a low voice. In the realms of my mind, I kept thinking, I wish I were drunk, that would give me the courage to *show* my feelings for you.

"It is a phase. You will get over it," Kay-Kay said.

I do not want to get over it. I would rather die once and forever . . . I continued to talk in my mind.

"My feelings for you have always been normal," he said.

Normal. Paranormal. Sub-normal. Abnormal. All one and the same to me. My mind continued to race on its own track. I said nothing.

"That of a friend. Nothing more. Nothing less," he said.

More is less. More is not enough. More is meagre. Love unlimited. My thoughts meandered. You are so handsome. So vulnerable. I had the strongest urge to get up and touch him. I stared at him soundlessly.

"Don't look at me like that," he was saying.

I sat immobilized, blissfully unaware of my surroundings, immersed in my own internal monologue. I do not need to look at you. Your image is etched in my memory.

He shuffled his legs under the table; they accidentally brushed against mine.

"You perverted bastard," Kay-Kay exploded and rushed out.

The Evening News had ended. Tejinder Singh, the good-looking newsreader was bidding good-bye. I had no idea how long I sat there after Kay-Kay left.

I went into a deep depression following this incident. By making the mistake of crossing the line, I had lost a good friend. The only real friend I had ever made in my life. I vowed never to lose my heart to a straight man ever again. Was I in control of this?

****

I stayed faithful to myself until I met Sid a few years later. Sid was a junior co-worker at my first workplace, an electronics firm near Delhi. I developed a massive crush on him. The nature of our work demanded we spend extended hours cooped up in my cubbyhole cubicle. Our constant togetherness at work exacerbated my feelings.

Sid looked up to me with adulation; I mistakenly thought he reciprocated my arduous feelings. One day, I tried to seduce him in his bachelor pad.

"I like you as a person. I respect you as a colleague. You are a role model for my professional life, but I cannot sleep with you. Or any man for that matter. Not my cup of tea. I can promise that this secret will remain between us." Sid's cool, understanding response not only doused my passion but also reiterated my fallibility.

Luckily, this was the era before workplace sexual harassment policies were formulated, or I might have lost my job. I moved back to Bangalore after that, opting for a more high-profiled job at a high-tech multi-national firm.

A few years later, Dev had left me devastated. Dev's wife and I were good friends. I hung out with the two very often. My admiration for Dev was probably mirrored in my eyes, reflected in my behaviour; I was an open book when I was in love. He was no doubt flattered by the attention. He flirted with me outrageously -- constant body contact, double entendres, a familiarity that transcended the heterosexual norm. The undercurrents were unmistakably erotic. I did not have the courage to make the first move; I hoped he would make one. He never did. I never expressed my true feelings for fear of losing a friend.

Did he reciprocate my feelings? I had no way of ascertaining this. Dev and his wife eventually moved out of Bangalore, drawing the curtain on the disconcerting vibes we had experienced.

I wished I could meet a gay man who would reciprocate my attraction. If wishes were horses then beggars would ride and whatever else from that verse from *Alice in Wonderland*, until pigs would fly. You got it. They never did.

****

Around this time, I met Priyanka, a professionally trained interior decorator. I wanted to redo the old-fashioned house I had inherited from my grandfather, located on the calm and peaceful tree-lined Benson Avenue in old Bangalore. Large open spaces, natural lighting, minimalist décor, muted colours. That was my kind of a house. With her creative yet pragmatic approach, Priyanka translated my dream to reality. Apart from having similar tastes, we enjoyed each other's company. We became good friends.

The day after I moved in, Priyanka proposed to me. We were seated across from each other around the low coffee table -- glass and mahogany. "*Nazar ke saamne jigar ke paas . . . koi rahta hai* [The one who lives nearby . . . in the line of sight] . . . ." The super hit song from the movie *Aashiqui* played in the background.

Priyanka took my hand in hers. "You have such slender fingers -- so artistic. I love the way you talk, the way you dress, the way you conduct yourself. You have great taste." She continued to stroke my hand.

I looked at her delicate ivory fingers, the nails painted a warm coral. "*Tu meri aashiqui hain . . . tu meri zindagi hain* [You are my love, you are my life] . . ." Another *Aashiqui* song now played in the background.

"Will you marry me?" she asked me softly, her brown eyes sincere. "I have been thinking about this for some time."

I was taken aback. The evening sun had set -- the orange-pink twilight was giving way to dark ghastly shadows on the walls. I could hardly see her face in the darkness. I needed to switch on the lamp.

She must have mistaken my confused silence for reluctance, maybe even indifference. "I know this is not the norm -- me proposing instead of you. I thought it would not matter. I don't think you are that conventional."

The clock began to strike. I closed my eyes in rumination. She waited patiently for the chimes to stop. "Does it mean no?" Her voice was low with a hint of anxiety.

I needed time. "This is so sudden, let me think about it," I said.

"Whatever you decide, you will always be my friend." Priyanka got up to leave, brushing her lips against my cheeks.

Watching her walk away, her black hair flowing down to her waist, I rubbed the lipstick marks off my cheek. Should I accept her proposal? My head battled with my heart.

She was pretty no doubt; a trim figure; good taste; well dressed; sweet temperament -- most men would kill to have a wife like her.

I was wary of the numerous unfulfilled emotional attachments I developed for men. They had no future. They happened only in my mind. Apart from the times I had fallen in love -- Raaj, Bobby, Kay-Kay, Sid, Dev, there had been innumerable instantaneous infatuations that fizzled out within days. I was past thirty. How long would I wallow in this self-destructive cycle?

I craved to be loved. My family had never been close to me emotionally. My mother had never understood me. She lived in a world all her own, dotted by my more conventional brother, his wife, and their kids. My brother who was a good twelve years older had never bonded with me. My father had never been there when I needed him. Our relationship had never transcended beyond the cordial.

I had never been the son my father wanted. I had done well in my studies, but he had found nothing spectacular to say or show off before his associates -- I was a sissy, I was taciturn, and I hated sports. My brother was the chosen one -- outgoing, dashing, loquacious, the cynosure. Besides, he was a famous and successful surgeon who had bestowed my parents with two grandchildren.

I worshipped beauty in all its forms. I enjoyed the company of beautiful women. But was I physically attracted enough to marry one? Priyanka or any other?

****

Two weeks later, I accepted Priyanka's proposal. A shrink I went to for therapy convinced me that everything would be fine if I married.

Marriage is never a solution to life's problems. Alas, it was too late by the time I learned this truism. I constantly yearned for a different life and continued to fantasize about men making love to me. With my career zooming northward in management circles, I had neither the time nor the courage to pursue any sort of relationships with men. Not that I had any opportunity either. In addition, I worried about my moral commitments to Priyanka. I was trapped in a marriage where I had little to offer.

In the next few years, Priyanka and I gradually drifted apart. Sex was never a staple ingredient of our marital life even in the initial years; it was a perfunctory ordeal, a major sham, a torturous put-on. Fortunately or unfortunately, the marriage had not borne any children.

My one-sided crushes continued unabated. But my dreams always died a premature death. There would be no togetherness with any man. I felt desperate. Often, I needed all the control I could muster -- to smile, converse, respond and operate in the corporate world, and show no inkling of my enormous pain. My heart heavy, mind in a daze, afraid to dream, apprehensive of being happy, I still had to wear the mask. Control over one's senses and the ability to hold off gratification, were supposedly the signs of maturity.

****

The Holiday Inn lobby was deserted. It was too late for the lunch and business crowds and too early for the party and dinner crowds. I gripped Tony's hand in a warm handshake. His hands were soft and cold. His arms were rosy pink and hairy. As I escorted him toward the fireplace in the lobby, his thigh brushed innocuously against mine. The vibes were electric.

Surprise! I did not hear the voice of warning this time. In the past, every time I lost my heart, a little voice had always warned me of the futility of the pursuit -- a signal of caution that I religiously ignored. Hopefully, with Tony, things would be different. Though I felt a flutter of excitement, there was an accompanying element of nonchalance -- whether Tony would reciprocate, was not in my control. I was willing to accept whatever outcome God had in store for me.

I sank into the velvety comfort of the cushioned chair, trying to contain my excitement. I had to stop deceiving myself. I would live life the way God had intended it to be. I would break out of the shackles I was bound to . . . I would liberate my soul, realize the truth.

Tony sat across from me, our legs touching, his shining black eyes fixed on mine. Having ordered coffee, I looked on, expecting Tony to make the first move; he was the one who had called me. Deep down, my mind battled to prevent an imminent onslaught of depression-inducing disappointment.

Tony filled in the details. He had first seen me at the same Holiday Inn where we were now meeting. I had been a public speaker at a NASSCOM seminar. Tony had not been at the seminar. He had been at the salon and then at the swimming pool.

"You are a very attractive man, sir. I am falling in love with you," he said.

I was ecstatic. My intuition was right. In life, there is always a first time. This was mine! Nodding my head in acquiescence I said, "Please stop sir-ring me. Call me by name." How much did he know about me? I wondered.

"I know you are married. I know you are a senior manager at Texas Instruments. I know you socialize at the Cantonment Club." Tony continued to look at me.

Uncanny. I hoped he was not reading my mind. "Aren't I too old for you?" I prayed he would say no.

"I am not exactly a teenager. I will soon be twenty-two. And you can't be very much older?" He smiled seductively.

I was much older than him, thirty-five. I was glad I had maintained myself well. I admired his uninhibited outspokenness.

We had dinner and cocktails at the Chinese restaurant in Holiday Inn. We talked and how. Soon I knew everything there was to know about him, or so I thought.

He loved western classical music, tolerated jazz, abhorred rock music. He was a vegetarian by choice. Black was his favourite colour. He had started smoking at twelve. Now, at twenty-two, he was allergic to cigarette smoke. Bacardi and coke was his favourite drink. He had briefly done drugs in college. He had given up after a horrific accident in which one of his friends had died while he had miraculously survived unscathed. Tony had no siblings; he had been hopelessly spoilt by his doting grandfather. Tony's best friend had been a girl who had married a total stranger at eighteen and broken all contact with Tony. He missed talking to her; she had been his only confidante. He had no other friends. He yearned for intimacy.

It was well past midnight when we finally got up to go. Tony hugged me tight and kissed me passionately on the lips, on the steps of Holiday Inn.

I looked around with fear. What if somebody saw us? I could not savour the ecstasy of the moment uninhibitedly.

Tony wanted me to go home with him. I reminded him I had to go home to Priyanka. We went our separate ways.

****

We met at Holiday Inn again the next morning. Tony was dressed in cut-off jeans and a white tee. He gave me a warm hug and kissed me on both my cheeks. In the parking lot this time. I looked around, petrified. What if somebody saw us?

We lolled around having a lazy continental breakfast and chatted. I learned more about Tony. He fantasized about being a model and walking the ramp. His father, a well-known film producer, had taken Tony to the US for a holiday when he was ten. Tony had become enamoured by the way of life in the US and aspired to immigrate there.

I could not keep my eyes off him. Every time he lifted his arms, I had a bewitching glimpse of the twin bushes of silky hair in his ivory armpits, his hairy navel above the band of Calvin Klein underwear. I desired him madly. "You smell nice," I told him.

"Polo Sport." He replied, caressing my thighs -- he found them irresistible. He could not keep his hands off me.

We were both in an advanced state of sexual tension as we rode toward his apartment -- that was to be our rendezvous, the first time and ever after. Seated on the pillion of his motorbike, the wind flapping pleasantly at my face, I gripped Tony's waist as tightly as I could and closed my eyes shut. What if somebody saw us? I was beyond caring, finally.

When I opened my eyes, the motorbike was approaching a skyscraper near downtown Bangalore. Tony's long silky hair was all mussed up. "The wind has made love to your hair," I joked, smoothing it back, as we entered his chic apartment.

The ambiance transported me into a faraway world. Peacock blue walls. A cobalt blue area rug. Low couches upholstered in turquoise blue and indigo. Afternoon sunlight streaming in through sheer violet-coloured curtains. Citrus-scented candles. Lilting piano music. I felt exhilarated -- I was on the threshold of a new life.

Tony had opened doors to new vistas, initiating me into a completely new experience -- he was the more experienced of the two. As I stood gazing out of the window at the tall buildings in steel and glass, all around, Tony drew my head to his chest and parted my lips with his tongue. In a euphoric blur, I could make out his face lingering above mine.

Priyanka's attractive face haunted me for a while, but disappeared soon. I did not choose to fall for men; I was made that way, by God himself, who I was sure, was male. That assuaged my guilt.

Tony's hands caressed my chin, slid down to unbutton my shirt. My taut nipples were electrified by his soothing touch. His fingers travelled down, massaged my belly, and continued their journey southward to unzip my jeans. I closed my eyes to let the serenity sink in.

The music stopped. I opened my eyes. Tony was naked save for a white thong that contrasted with the thick black carpet of matted hair across his flat, fair belly. His tumescence was silhouetted against the sheer fabric. Mesmerized, I buckled to my knees. Exactly as I had dreamt a trillion times, in the twenty-five years following my pubescence, I explored every magic nook and crevice, feeling the silken smoothness of his body fur, pleasuring him -- I lost all concept of time until he let out exquisite squeals of delight and collapsed in blissful ecstasy.

I would like to believe I attained *Nirvana* that day.

****

The next few months flew by. Tony and I saw each other every day. Our togetherness was an end in itself. Sometimes, we met for lunch, other times for dinner. Frequently, we browsed shopping arcades and bookstores -- we had similar tastes in clothes and books. Often, we spent time at his apartment -- talking, listening to music, drinking. Always, we made love.

Every time we made love, I marvelled at the deep sensuality he exuded, the profound sensitiveness he displayed in fulfilling my innermost needs. He made me feel the novice I was, despite my age. He had discovered the joys as a young teenager, at a residential school. His yen for men was an addiction. He liked pretty women too he said; he had dated a couple of them.

The irony of it all struck me. All of thirty-five, I had always known I was gay. Growing up in the suppressive seventies, I almost never had the opportunity to admit it. Societal taboos and my own unresolved conflicts had made me a prisoner, trapping me in a marriage to a beautiful person, no doubt, but the wrong gender. And here was Tony, barely out of his teens, cocksure of who he was and what he wanted, the best of both worlds obviously. A product of the permissive nineties in post-liberalization India, he was not a victim of fate but the master of his own destiny.

I was no longer merely in love with Tony; I had begun to love him unconditionally. I lived for the moments of togetherness with Tony. I found pleasure in giving love and more love. It gave me a new purpose. How long would it all last?

For the first time in my career, work became a drag. I could hardly wait for the clock to strike five. Evenings spent at work, weekends lost in the office, were outdated. My nine-to-five routine made me susceptible to the Machiavellian machinations of colleagues looking to make trouble for me at the office. My boss and I were now constantly at loggerheads. I was becoming a nervous wreck. I began popping tranquilizers to soothe my frayed nerves -- my blue dolls -- as I lovingly called them.

Priyanka and I had even less time for each other. My workaholic ways and the occasional travel had always kept me busy before. I now spent that time with Tony instead. Priyanka rarely sought any explanations about my absence. Did she presume it was work? Was she too trusting? Did she not care? I would soon find out.

Given the nature of her clientele, Priyanka had become a permanent member of the A-grade party circuit in Bangalore. Sometimes it bothered me that she never invited me to escort her anywhere. Even when we were at home together, Priyanka spent a lot of time on the phone. In the recent past, a mysterious male voice had asked for her on several occasions. A new client, she had said. I had not pressed too far. People living in glass houses should not throw stones.

It had to happen one day; I finally garnered courage to bring Tony home one afternoon. I had talked to him so much about my home décor that he had wanted to see it. We lazed around the house drinking beer; we watched a movie in the guest bedroom -- *My Beautiful Launderette* -- my first gay movie; then the inevitable happened. Throwing caution to the winds, we ripped each other's clothes off and hungrily made love on the queen-sized bed. Satiated, Tony left soon after while I lounged around languorously until nightfall.

****

A day later, I found a pair of black socks under the bed. When I tried returning them to Tony, he said they were not his; he had been wearing sandals that day.

When I returned home, I found Priyanka smoothing the comforter in the guest bedroom, a peculiar look on her face, as if she was missing something. She said something about tidying up and left abruptly. I was puzzled. I swallowed a blue doll to soothe my nerves. Had she found out about Tony and me?

"We need to talk, honey," Priyanka told me later in the evening. I had a huge foreboding that we were on the verge of a massive showdown. Definitely, she had found out. I popped a second blue doll.

I called Tony. "Do you have any plans for the evening? I am having dinner with my wife." I sounded apologetic.

"I need to do some shopping," Tony sounded casual. "Don't worry about me."

Did I detect relief in his tone? It bothered me. "You are so understanding, Tony."

Recently, I had sensed an element of restlessness in Tony. Was it another man? I hoped not. An intense, meaningful relationship with a mature man might have seemed a novelty after a string of brief encounters with boys; was the lustre fading with time? On the other hand, it could just be the wait to visit the land of milk and honey that beckoned him -- his father had promised to send him abroad for some course in filmmaking. Was it a matter of time before he left me? I swallowed a third blue doll to appease my agitation.

Priyanka ordered pizzas from the Pizza Hut. We dined together for the first time in several months. The beers I consumed with the pizza made me nauseous. I lay flat on the couch staring at the revolving ceiling fan, waiting for Priyanka to speak first.

"You have been kind," she said, daintily sipping sweet red wine. "Life with you has been peaceful, but, honey, you know something is missing."

I was aware that she was sitting on the ivory leather sofa opposite me. My eyes remained closed. I had always felt suffocated by our marriage.

"I have met a really wonderful man." Priyanka, I am sure, was looking in my direction as she said this.

There were times when I had indulged in wishful thinking. What if she wanted out? Wouldn't I be free to live with Tony? If he left me too, would there be others?

"He proposed to me this evening," Priyanka walked toward me. "I am sorry to do this to you."

Now, liberation at last? No, somehow there was no elation at the thought. I felt sad instead. She had been good to me. We were friends, had few conflicts, almost no fights. My sexual-orientation, I had never externalized to her. If she had sensed it, she had said nothing.

Hearing no response, she leaned over me, our faces almost touching. "Forgive me." Her voice was soft and her eyes misty.

I had betrayed her too. I had to tell her, now or never. I could not live with the guilt if I didn't. "I have fallen in love too." I finally opened my eyes.

She winced and moved her face away from mine. "Moral retribution." She kept switching the lamp off and on.

I had to get this out of me. "With a man, a very beautiful man." I got up from the supine position. "I was born gay." Out tumbled the details.

"Please forgive me for what I have done to you." My remorse was genuine. I tried to hold her hand, but she brushed it away brusquely . . . .

****

I heard Priyanka start her car and drive away. This was the first big row of our marital life. And the last. Woman's intuition? Had she realized at some point in time that I was gay? Had she waited it out until she had found herself another man? I would never know the answers to these questions.

I went into the bathroom and reached for the box of blue dolls I kept hidden in the wicker basket underneath the sink. First came the sobs. Then the tears. Sorrow? Relief? Guilt? I could not fathom. A bit of all perhaps. Exhausted by emotion, I fell asleep in the bathroom, the cool marble floor soothing my burning cheeks.

It was well past noon when I woke up next morning. My body was cramped from its awkward position. Three cups of coffee later while I was in the shower, I got a call. I prayed it was from Priyanka.

It was Tony. He had called from the airport. He was leaving for Delhi to be with his family -- his father was having an emergency operation. "Au revoir. I will be back soon." He blew me a kiss through the phone.

The next few days were a blur. Priyanka moved back with her parents who lived in north Bangalore. I sought deeper solace in my tranquilizers. We would soon apply for divorce on mutual consent. "When something is over it is over for good. Let's make it as painless for each other as possible." We both agreed.

She came over intermittently to pack her clothes and belongings. I let her take whatever she wanted. Antique furniture pieces; a collector's choice of carpets, accent rugs and lamps; several objets d'art; traditional paintings; modern sculptures; a personal computer; the piano; a whole bunch of discs, tapes, curios . . . . She only took what belonged to her. She did not want my money.

On her last visit, she hugged me tight and kissed me on both cheeks. Her eyes shone with unshed tears. The parting was brief. "Adieu."

There was a deep vacuum inside me. We realize the real value of what we have only after losing it. Such is life.

****

Much against my wishes, I called my family and gave them the news. I had to get over with this. As expected, my mother blamed Priyanka and went on to curse her own luck. I felt obligated to hear her out. Facing friends and relatives bothered mother. She agonized about the repercussions on dad's health -- he had not been keeping too well lately. She pleaded that Priyanka and I reconcile, remain husband and wife in the eyes of society, whatever our personal differences.

My explanations proved futile. She kept insisting I tell her why we split so she could patch things up. I kept telling her in vain that the reasons for our split were too personal. My father refused to speak to me. I could hear my brother's abusive voice ranting in the background. Thankfully, my mother did not allow him on the phone.

Once the call ended, I pressed my throbbing forehead against the cool marble wall in the bathroom. It felt good. Instinctively, my hand reached under the sink for the blue dolls.

Tony did not call me in the days that followed. My calls to him went unanswered. I was going berserk not knowing what to do. Everything seemed purposeless. Life without Tony was unthinkable. I cried endlessly through the nights that followed.

I had craved for life with a man without having tasted its joys; all I need is one brief affair -- the memories would be enough to take me through the rest of my life, I had thought then. I had the memories now; but they would not suffice -- I wanted Tony to be with me for the rest of my life. Tony was not just a part of my existence anymore; he was my whole existence.

My workplace had become hell. My performance became as erratic as my mood swings. I was denied my bonuses. Confrontation made things worse. I could not stop agonizing why my career had to go bad now. Eventually, I quit my job even before I found another. In the frame of mind I was in, I was not motivated to find another job. Had I made an effort, it would have been a matter of days. However, I was beyond caring. Money was not a major problem; I had some inheritances to live by comfortably, for a while at least.

I had to see Tony. He was all I had left. I caught the first available flight to Delhi.

****

It was late evening when I arrived at Tony's bungalow. The security guard subjected me to close scrutiny before letting me in. My mind was numb as a uniformed servant guided me through an opulent sitting room, up the stairs into Tony's master suite, and served me tea and samosas, which I did not touch -- swallowing a blue doll instead.

I tried to flip through the pages of a magazine, in vain. I was too nervous to do anything. Time stretched into eternity, I was engulfed by a strong wave of agitation. I swallowed two more blue dolls and immediately felt better.

My heart came to a standstill when Tony entered the room. Even before he could lock the door, I collapsed in his arms, kissing him repeatedly on his forehead, his cheeks, his lips, his nose, his ears, his neck, his chest . . . I did not want to let him go. I closed my eyes, rested my head on his shoulders. I felt protected. The tears came, in fits and bursts at first, then a continual flow. As I told him everything that had happened to my life in the last few days, Tony held me tight, without a word.

I looked into Tony's brimming eyes -- I could see it all -- the hurt, the dilemma, the anticipation. In that instant, I knew the truth that was going to ensue.

"Sweetheart, I am leaving for New York," he said. "Next week. To do that course in film-making."

"I am happy that your dreams have come true."

"I have been dreading this moment."

"I love you dearly." My words came out in a hoarse, broken-voiced whisper.

"There is no future in our relationship." Tony was crying like a baby.

I was too stunned to react. The full impact had yet to sink in. Perhaps he aspired to have a conventional family -- a pretty wife, cute kids, societal status.

Tony was reaching out for the Kleenex. "I would rather end this now than make it worse for you later."

Now or later it was all the same to me. "Never will I leave you" is what I wanted to hear. I was swept by a wave of futility. I had lost it all. The dream had ended. Like all good things. I could not deal with this any longer.

We spent the last night of our life in his bed clinging to each other. Neither of us slept a wink. The warmth of our bodies was a mild comfort to our agonized states but not sufficient to ignite a passion in either of us. Though we desired each other. As madly as ever.

Tony drove me to the airport the next morning. Dressed in cut-off Levi's and a tank top, his silky hair dishevelled, he stood in the aisle waving his hands vigorously, tears streaming down his cheeks, oblivious of the crowds around. The single gold stud no longer adorned his right ear; it was adorning my left ear.

Why had God done this to me? Why did he take away Tony now? Why had God made me one way and forced me to lead my life another way? There was no beginning, no end to the torrent of thoughts that inundated my mind.

****

In life, I had learned to cope with everything and usually succeeded. But this time my coping mechanism could not bear the burden of the events; I surrendered to God's own will; the trauma was indescribable.

Under duress, one depends on two things for solace -- work and loved ones. How ironical I had neither. I was bereft of a single soul that cared for me. Sad, but true -- I realized at that point in my life that I had no friends.

I did not call my parents anymore; I hated the reprimands and dreaded the advice they subjected me to. I was firmly addicted to my blue dolls. Getting up from the bed was a torture. Once up, I had no purpose for the day. When I looked in the mirror -- eyes sunken, skin ashen, face haggard, I saw a wrinkled old man who had no will to live.

I started losing track of time. How long since Priyanka left me? Six months or eight? How long since I last saw Tony. Last year? Yesterday?

One night, my brother called me. "*Pitaji* had a heart attack. He may not make it. It is all your fault." Agony pierced through my heart as my brother's rant continued unabated. "What a bad reputation you gave us. No job. On top of it the divorce. *Pitaji* could not face the humiliation, attend any social gathering and now . . . ."

If I was a disappointment before, I was a disgrace, now. I would never be able to look Dad in the eye again even if he lived. Any chance of gaining his acceptance was completely snuffed to death.

My brother made good use of this opportunity to vent his bitterness, contempt, and fury. "People will not stop gossiping about your affair. They think it is another woman. God knows where they heard it . . . I have always known about your homosexual tendencies. You . . . ." I banged the phone down before he uttered the dreaded word he reserved for such occasions. *Gaandu.* The barbarically derogatory word for homosexuals.

I had nothing to live for, nothing to look forward to in life anymore. It seemed like an eternity ago when I had been happy and successful -- great job, amiable wife, passionate lover -- everything going for me. Except, I had been living out a blatant lie.

The blue dolls, my blue dolls, they were all that I needed. I reached for the tall bottle that proudly stood on the headboard, housing my blue dolls. Uncorking it, I swallowed one, two, three, four, five, downing them with mugs of cold water. Then a thought struck me -- why not, why not -- the best way out of the imbroglio that my life had become.

Wrapping a purple robe over my soiled tracksuit, I walked out of the house. The tree-lined avenue appeared quiet and peaceful in the moonlit night. My old-fashioned white bungalow with the sloping roof seemed dwarfed amongst the high-rise apartments surrounding it. I entered the sky-scraping apartment complex down the road, riding the elevator all the way to the terrace.

I hesitantly put one leg across the parapet; somehow, looking down, my courage failed me. What if I survived the fall? Worse, maimed for life?

At that moment, I heard footsteps approaching. I felt the presence of the security guard. He must have come to lock the terrace door. Heart beating fast, I pulled my leg back.

****

In a daze, I somnambulated back to the house, my own haven that would ensconce me in its creases and protect me from the traumas of my mind.

Priyanka. She had indeed translated my dream into reality, transforming the old-fashioned house into this dazzling sanctuary. Despite the daze that made me dizzy, I journeyed from room to room, visiting every nook and corner, imbibing the familiar ambience -- straight lines, innovative themes, antique wood furniture . . . There were no photos of anyone anywhere. The journey ended when I arrived at the master bedroom -- my final destination.

I looked around the bedroom with admiration yet another time -- one last time. We had both shared such wonderful taste.

An obscure song played in the background.
Some Day Some Place
I'll be waiting for you in Solitude
Some One Some Where
Will be looking for me with Fortitude
Some Day Some Place
We'll be meeting together with Latitude
Some One Some Where
Will be blessing us with Gratitude
One Day One Place
We'll be leading our life in Lassitude
Some Day Some Place
I'll be waiting for you in Solitude

I removed the robe and lay down on the queen-sized bed, my head popped up against the mountain of pillows mounded against the headboard and opened the black leather book -- my own personal journal -- for the zillionth time. The story of my life. Incomplete. Now I knew how to complete it . . . .

I reach for the tall bottle of blue pills standing faithfully on the headboard, uncork it and swallow every single one of the blue pills, washing them down my gullet with tall glasses of cold water. I close my eyes, lie sideways and curl up my knees, drawing them close toward my stomach. I cover myself fully with the comforter.

Patiently, I wait for death to engulf me. Some day, some place . . . Tony . . . I cannot forget you . . . I cannot live without you . . . Priyanka . . . I won't betray you . . . Please don't leave me honey . . . Father I will be an ideal son to you -- dashing, debonair, outgoing . . . Tony where are you? . . . I only feel pain . . . Some day, some place we shall all be one again. Until then . . . All I ever wanted in life was . . . God please make up your mind next time -- allow me to lead my life the way you make me . . . .

The synergistically soporific blue pills cast their terminal spell -- taking me deeper and deeper into a phantasmagorical oblivion. The black leather book lies on the bed orphaned, its pages fluttering indiscriminately as they engage in a mad swirling dance with the cold gush of air blowing from the briskly rotating ceiling fan above . . . .

23. Natty Nineties: Apocalypse

July 18 1998

On Star TV, *Anand* had ended. *Babu Moshoi.* The dead Anand's soulful endearment for his doctor friend echoed silently across Karan's house. Karan had finished reading the black book aloud to his friends.

The mood was melancholic. Aarti and Indu could not contain their tears.

Karan had been fingering a flat, semi-hard object between the book's hardcover and the leather jacket. He had instinctively known what it was; he was deferring the moment of confronting it.

"Is this really a memoir? Danny may have been delusional," Arjun said.

"No matter what, the pain is real." Karan extricated the flat object from the black book's leather jacket -- a faded red confetti star.

Life indeed was ephemeral.

Aarti took the star from Karan's hand and walked out of the main house toward the Five Star Café. The others followed solemnly. Aarti opened the windows of the Five Star Café, switched on the lamps and hung the faded red confetti star from the ceiling -- all five stars were now back in their place.

Arjun and Aarti stood staring at the stars silently. Indu continued her love affair with the flask of vodka. Karan rummaged through the shelves of the bookcase until he found an old photograph of Danny from the Xavier Junior College days. He placed it over Danny's black transistor radio on the top shelf of the bookcase, to form a sort of shrine in Danny's memory.

"Danny was a victim of time and place. Young men and women of today are no longer shy of coming out, expressing their sexuality. It is a recent phenomenon. Some change is in the air. At least in the metros. If only Danny could have claimed that kind of freedom earlier in his life." Arjun would not stop discussing Danny's situation.

"Unfortunate, we all moved away. Had we been there . . ." Aarti dabbed her eyes with Kleenex. "We may have helped."

"Bullshit." Indu sat down on the divan and switched on the table fan.

"We were young then. Even had we known, we may not have had the maturity to deal with such a sensitive topic." Arjun said. "We may have just made fun of him. There is no telling how a bunch of youngsters will react. No matter how close someone is. At that age all that matters is to fit in."

"People must have seen Danny and Tony together. No gossip?" Karan looked at Arjun.

"You have lived away too long dude. This is India. It is not unusual for two guys to hang out together all the time. Tongues wag only when a man is seen with a woman, even if she is his mother, sister, friend -- whoever. Two men together, nobody cares . . ." Arjun placed Danny's black book in front of the shrine.

"I wonder why Danny's wife didn't confront him earlier," Karan said.

"Danny was a good guy. Sensitive. Kind." Arjun said.

"Not all women married to straight guys are necessarily happy," Aarti nodded her head in a show of concurrence. "Believe me. Men can be loud and boorish, insensitive and silly . . . ." Aarti picked up Danny's black book.

Karan closed his eyes tightly shut. *You perverted bastard.* The shameful words he had uttered reverberated in Karan's mind. Karan had borne the burden of guilt of an unsolicited apology from that day onward. Now he would carry it to his grave. Once again, he had been cheated by Fate. He could never ask Danny for forgiveness.

"Danny was always there for me." Aarti clutched the black book to her bosom. "The last time I called him, if only I had asked him, at least once, how his life was going . . ."

"I should have attempted to connect with him. I could have helped him -- as a friend, as a counsellor." Arjun joined her on the path of self-reproach.

Karan stood transfixed on the carpet in the centre of the Five Star Café entrenched in his own memories. If love could transcend all barriers, why not that of gender as well? Danny had probably loved him deeply. Yet, there was no way Karan could have reciprocated that love; at least not in the way Danny had wanted.

"If only I had asked, he may have disclosed something . . ." Aarti turned the pages of the black book disoriented.

"May be we would have averted his death," Arjun let out a deep sigh. "I feel very ineffective."

If only. Should have. Would have. Could have. Words of a loser.

The more they talked about Danny, the more it agitated Karan. He was reading through the eye of his mind what was written in his memory. With inerasable ink that leaked pain.

"If only I had been supportive . . . I wish I had not shunned him." Karan said aloud.

"What did you do?" Aarti and Indu asked in unison. Aarti's tone was mildly inquisitive; Indu's strongly accusative.

Karan knelt in front of the little shrine he had made for Danny in the Five Star Café, as if trying to commune with Danny's spirit in a bid to beg for forgiveness.

"*I* am the Kay-Kay in Danny's diary . . ." The load was finally off his chest.

****

"How the fuck could you call him such a terrible name?" Indu shook Karan by the shoulders with great force. "He was your friend!"

Karan had assumed the role of a penitent in confessional mode hopeful of assuaging his guilt. He was taken aback by the sudden assault. "My intention was not . . . ." Karan roughly brushed Indu's hands off from his shoulders.

"Shut the fuck up." Indu's eyes flashed with unbridled anger. "You have never cared for anyone but yourself."

"Let me explain . . . I did not mean to . . ." He got up and turned around to face her.

"You have no compassion you fucking bastard." Indu was yelling.

Aarti watched the sparring duo with a look of helplessness. Arjun tried to intervene; Indu ordered him to keep out of it.

"Look who's talking." Karan said. "You were the one who killed my unborn child. Without telling me." The back of his neck was throbbing.

"You were not good enough to be the father of my child." Indu pulled him toward her by the collar of his shirt.

Karan was losing his cool by now. "Yeah, I was only good enough for . . ." he muttered under his breath as he brushed her hands off yet another time.

"Yes. You were only good for a fuck." Indu was relentless.

"Thanks for the compliments." Karan's tone brimmed with sarcasm. "If only you had not aborted our child I would have brought up that child single-handedly."

"No you wouldn't." Indu wiggled her index finger in Karan's eye, almost touching his dark pupils with the edges of her sharp manicured nails. "You would have somehow lost that child. Very easily."

"Dolly!" Karan's pained scream was involuntary. Nothing hurts more than the bitter truth.

"Fuck you." Indu pushed him aside and stormed out of the Five Star Café.

Karan refrained from swearing back at Indu for fear of offending Aarti. He picked up the small table fan Indu had donated to the Café and flung it out through the open garage door, instead. The metal crashed on the small rocks outside with a clang.

"Indu is fully drunk. She needs help." Aarti ran after her friend.

Karan sank back on the divan. Arjun came over and sat next to Karan, placing his cool fingers on Karan's forehead. The power of touch worked like magic on burnished nerves; as the bond of friendship gave them the liberty for uninhibited ingenuousness, both men were aware of their true feelings; they had triumphed where most men fail. Yet another time.

****

The interminable proceedings of the day had been exhausting. The Five Star Café wore a deserted look.

"Indu's driver has assured me he will drive her home safely." Aarti joined them back several minutes later. "Karan, who is Dolly?"

"My daughter. The little angel who was taken away from me."

Karan was in the mood to deplete the torments of his mind. The tumultuous relationship with Sharon, the birth of Dolly and the parting he was being forced to endure because of Troy, Dolly's natural birth father. . . "God not only took Dolly away from me but also my gift of colour." He concluded looking from Aarti to Arjun who sat flanking him on the divan in the semi-darkness of the early evening.

Unburdened. Karan's mind was light.

Enlightened. Arjun's eyes appeared kind. Sadness? Empathy? Solace?

"I could never have imagined that you were such a doting and devoted dad." Aarti stared at Karan wide-eyed.

Did Karan detect admiration there?

"I had no idea that all those years, you could see with colour." Arjun said.

"I always wanted to tell you that you were the most brilliant shade of blue. I used to refrain out of fear that I would not be understood."

"Sounds exotic. I wish I could see people in colour." Aarti interjected.

"The trait is genetic. The scientific word for people, who experience sensations of colour, is synaesthetes. Some can perceive names and even emotions with an associated colour . . ." Arjun sounded like an expert excerpt from a medical journal.

Relief. The semblance of a smile descended on Karan's face.

"The experience may vary from person to person. Different people do not necessarily associate the same colours with the same objects. It is a special ability -- viewing the world in multimedia all the time. The syndrome is very real, not imaginary; it is attributed to complex feedback mechanisms in the human brain. I always wished I could meet somebody who had experienced it . . . ." Arjun would not stop talking.

The words were music to Karan's ears. He felt exonerated from the prophecies of doom that sometimes haunted the inner precincts of his mind. "I wish I get my gift back," he said.

"Synaesthesia was the subject of the conference I attended in New York last month. Research in the area is very limited still . . . ."

What colour am I? Karan wondered, for the first time. *Orange, the colour of pain? Violet, the colour of compassion?*

"You are a renowned psychiatrist. Can't you restore Karan's ability?" Aarti's question halted Arjun's volley of words.

Aarti and Karan looked at him expectantly.

"Medical science has its limitations." Arjun said slowly. "Only recently have we begun to understand this mysterious syndrome. There is no known cure for temporary loss. In fact there are no documented cases of anyone who has abruptly stopped experiencing the colours. Maybe someday in the not so distant future we will find the answer."

Part Four

24. Natty Nineties: Debacle

July 19 1998

Sunday afternoon. In the solitary confines of his living room, Karan watched Indu interview Booker Prize winner Saloni Sinha on The Zee TV show *Celebrity Circus.*

The television interview -- a live telecast -- turned out to be a disaster from the word go. Indu was visibly drunk; her speech slurred; every once in a while, her hands shivered unsteadily. When Saloni Sinha began talking about her dead husband and became emotional, Indu reacted with vile laughter. When Saloni Sinha narrated a funny incident, Indu responded with steely silence. The worst gaffe happened toward the end of the interview.

Saloni Sinha finished recounting her experience in London where she had received the Prize, and smilingly offered an autographed copy of her book *The Mother of All Mistakes* to Indu.

"I don't read this rubbish," Indu said cattily. "Only good for the awards." She tossed aside the book callously.

At that point, Zee TV had taken the program off the air.

You lack compassion, you fucking bastard. The memory of Indu's slivery tongue sliced through Karan's mind as he switched off the television. The words had not stopped torturing him for the past twenty-four hours.

An hour later, he received a call from Indu. "Karan, I have to see you. Come now. Come now. Come now." She begged him.

Don't Go. Don't Go. Don't Go. The voice inside Karan's head told him.

"Can you give me your address?" Karan's voice asked Indu. How could he say No? Poor thing. Indu had made a debacle of herself on the TV show. She had probably taken Danny's death to heart. He would give her solace.

Karan's rickety Fiat wound its way westward toward the outskirts of Bangalore. The roads were freshly asphalted. Sunlight accentuated the new chrome and glass buildings, contrasting heavily with the dull brick walls of the old. Karan was relieved when he arrived at his destination, a plush bungalow surrounded by a manicured lawn and an artificial pool, without getting lost. *AGARWALS* stated the nameplate outside the gate.

"I can't take this pain anymore." Indu's screams reached Karan's ears even as a member of the household staff led him in, per her orders.

Indu was staring at herself in the mirror on the bedroom wall. "Give me mercy killing," she was begging her own image.

"Man should not play God," Karan said to pacify her.

"How do you know that?" Indu was excited.

"Killing is a sin," Karan remained standing near the bedroom door.

"Tell me how you know that," Indu sounded frightened. "You can read my mind." She pointed an accusatory finger at him.

Karan was puzzled. He wished someone would come into the room.

"Karan, please, please don't read my thoughts," Indu pleaded with him. "Man should not play God. Killing is a sin. I had used those exact sentences at a college debate. How naive I was then," Indu was speaking to herself.

Karan walked over toward the bedroom window in a bid to be as far away from her as possible.

"You can't read my mind. You were there when I said it!" Indu was laughing villainously. "I just remembered this other girl at that same debate. She came prepared with a long speech on youth in Asia." Indu rambled along. Her laugh was louder. "Euthanasia. Youth-in-Asia. Euthanasia. Ha ha ha . . ."

Karan looked in the direction of the bedroom door hoping to spot one of the servants.

"I have sent the ayah to the drug store. The others are attending to their chores." Indu volunteered information. "*I* can read your thoughts," she said triumphantly.

Karan stared out of the bedroom window. Smoke billowed from the nearby slums; half-naked, malnourished children played in the dirt as their emaciated mothers went about their housework.

Abruptly Indu sat down on the bed and spoke to Karan in a soft voice. The top management at *GLITZ* had not viewed her catastrophic performance on television kindly, instantly forcing her to go on indefinite leave. "Sabbatical, my foot. The fuckers fired me and recalled the grand old man, my old fuck buddy."

Karan did not understand the dichotomy of Indu's thought process. Partly logical, partly illogical. In a matter of minutes, Indu had traversed a wide gamut of thoughts and emotions. Some random. Some rational. Was that how the term method in madness originated? Did this mean Indu was mad?

"I still love you Karan." He felt a cold hand at the nape of his neck. He turned around.

She ripped the buttons off her *kameez* with one swift move of her left hand. "I never stopped loving you," she moaned and lunged toward him. In her right hand, she held a bowl of vanilla ice cream with a cherry on top.

He caught her hand roughly in midair. The vanilla ice cream splashed all over Karan's crotch.

"I want to recreate your twentieth birthday." Indu stuck out her tongue and bent down to lick the ice cream off the front of his pants.

On his twentieth birthday, she had covered his crotch with vanilla ice cream and treated him to a blowjob. His first. Definitely not her first. The memory heightened his anguish.

Karan kicked Indu with such brutality that she thudded toward the farther side of the room. He pulled at the window curtain with such force that the curtain rod thumped to the ground. Crudely draping the coarse dusty curtain over her semi-naked body, he rushed out of the bedroom. Indu was as vile as ever.

Karan got into his Fiat and sped away as fast as he could. Was this his bad karma coming back to him for shunning Danny?

****

"Indu has a drinking problem," Aarti was telling her mother, as the two sat watching Indu interview Booker Prize-winning author Saloni Sinha on Zee TV in the privacy of their plush penthouse.

"In her own words, she cannot function if she does not consume a whole bottle of vodka every day."

"Why don't you send her to Alcoholics Anonymous?" Anupama switched off the television. The program was being taken off the air following Indu's misdemeanour.

Aarti continued to sit and stare at the TV screen. Her fingers kept playing with the remote. They had already lost Danny. They could not afford to lose Indu.

It was almost three hours later that Aarti arrived at Indu's garish bungalow in West Bangalore. The front door was open. "Don't melt my bones. Go away you witch. *Saasuma* -- my mother-in-law -- has sent you. Don't try to save me . . ." Aarti could hear Indu's screams from the portico. She walked in the direction of the room from where the screams emanated.

"My bones are melting. I cannot walk. I cannot sit. I cannot stand." A howling Indu lay on the cold granite floor, a coarse curtain draped over her. An ayah was bathing Indu's left wrist with warm water; another ayah was cleaning the shredded mess created by a broken bottle.

Aarti was horrified. Indu had unsuccessfully tried to slash her wrists.

"I can't take this pain any more. Give me mercy killing."

Aarti had no way of knowing that mercy killing had been Indu's latest manic mantra. Drastic measures were needed. Aarti arrogated the liberty of telephoning the Xavier Hospital for an ambulance.

"That TV-watching girl, I marred her looks. Nobody will marry her now. She is cursing me. Nobody will marry me . . . ." Indu was inconsolable in her manic state.

Aarti placed the palm of her hand on Indu's burning forehead hoping to calm her. She had no clue what Indu was agonizing about.

"That fruitwallah had a heart attack. I destroyed his mangoes. His curse is on me . . . I am having a heart attack." Indu's screams were eventually drowned out by the sound of the approaching sirens. The ambulance had arrived. "I am a witch. A bitch-witch . . . ." The medicos placed the wailing Indu on a stretcher and wheeled her away.

Riding in the ambulance, Aarti looked sadly at the sedated Indu -- mouth open, saliva dribbling down her multiple chins, a funny expression on her bloated face framed by the horrid hennaed hair. Was this the same girl once referred to as the queen bee during their college days?

When the ambulance reached St. Xavier Hospital, it was late evening. Arjun's team was waiting; Aarti had called him from her new Nokia 5190 and apprised him of the situation. Indu was whisked away for diagnosis and treatment.

Aarti exited from the hospital and hailed a cab. She had contained her anger long enough; it was now time to give someone a piece of her mind.

****

After leaving Indu's house Karan had driven his old Fiat to the Cantonment Club where he spent the rest of the evening drinking a steady stream of solitary aperitifs. Bacardi and Coke. His favourite drink when he was sad or elated. Or both. Night had fallen when Karan returned home.

Aarti was pacing the length of the huge living room with a brisk rhythm. The cup of tea Maharaj had placed for her on the dining table had gone cold.

Karan's heart filled with joy. He rushed toward her, his arms outstretched to give her a friendly hug.

For a split second, his world suddenly went dark. When it had passed, his cheek tingled from the slap bestowed by Aarti in lieu of a hug. His reflexes had never been sharp.

"Where were you when we needed you? I have been calling your house by the minute?" Aarti held out her cell phone.

Karan had not yet recovered from the blow. "I can't afford a cell phone." He walked toward the bathroom so he could splash some cold water on his reddened face.

"Have you ever thought beyond yourself?" Aarti intercepted him. "Where were you?"

"You are not my mother."

"Look at you. Fully drunk." Aarti's eyes spewed fire.

Karan had never seen Aarti this livid before.

"You are no longer twenty. You can't let your testosterone run your life . . . ."

"I have no idea what you are saying," Karan stated with great dignity.

"You almost killed Indu today. Who is next? Me?"

"I did not kill anyone."

"I found Indu half-naked in the bedroom, her wrists slashed. She told me what you had done to her . . ." Aarti moved back a step.

"Lies. Indu was lying." Karan intervened in own his defence.

"Why don't you get yourself a personal slut?"

"Stop screaming. Let me tell you what really happened." Karan kept his voice low.

"A friend. Another's wife. Whoever." Aarti whirl winded out of the house, the forceful flow of her fury unabated. "Sex maniac. *Hawas ka aadmi*," she rushed toward the Five Star Café.

Gone in sixty seconds. The Five Star Café had been destroyed by the time Karan reached there. The posters on the door had been torn down. The red confetti stars were charred -- Aarti must have struck a match to them. *THE CAFÉ IS CLOSED FOREVER. MEMBERS ARE GONE.* She had written with a black marker on the walls of the garage.

Karan stood staring at the havoc Aarti had unleashed. Indu had unabashedly converted his innocence to guilt. Aarti had proclaimed her verdict without giving him a hearing. Karan felt like the proverbial book that people judged by the cover. If only they had the patience to read the book?

25. Natty Nineties: An August Month

August 1 1998

Karan and Arjun both turned thirty-six. Arjun invited Aarti and Karan for dinner at the Taj Residency Hotel. *Memories of China* was Arjun's favourite restaurant. Ebullient in wishing Arjun, Aarti remained distant with Karan. She had not spoken to him since their skirmish.

The evening did not seem like a celebration of their birthdays. The three were still grieving the death of Danny in their own private way. They were also worried about the mental condition of Indu, who was still at St. Xavier Hospital.

"Indu will remain in the hospital for several weeks," Arjun said. "She has been subjected to all kinds of intensive tests, including radiological tests for cancer possibilities. She was diagnosed as schizophrenic. That explains the bizarre behaviour, the violent mood swings -- manic highs to suicidal lows, the rage and the depression, not to forget her delusions of grandeur."

The waiter arrived to take their orders. None of the other tables in the restaurant was occupied.

"Indu never had a reason for conflict or sorrow ever in her life. Wonder why she was hit with such a malady?" Aarti asked Arjun.

"Destiny?" Arjun swept his long boyish mop of hair away from his left eyebrow where it had descended.

"Did Danny's death do this to her?" Karan asked Arjun.

"It may have only been one of the triggers." Arjun gave a slow nod of the head. "Her condition is pathological; it is caused by a chemical imbalance; the root cause is genetic though environment may play a pivotal role in the degree and extent of its manifestation."

Their wine orders arrived. With the Manchurian appetizers.

"From what Bharat, her husband told me, she has suffered extreme mood swings ever since the birth of their second child, almost two years ago. It seems that she was wrongly treated for depression. Her schizophrenia has reached an advanced state. She is strongly suicidal. I was forced to recommend a bout of electroconvulsive therapy." Arjun briefed his friends.

"You mean shock therapy?" Aarti stopped sipping her wine.

"Much against my wishes." Arjun said.

"Indu a conductor for electricity?" Karan beckoned the waiter and asked him to turn on the fan.

"The last resort," Arjun nodded his head ruefully.

"Surely there is a less painful way of treating her." Aarti placed her glass of wine on the table.

"We had no other option."

"Cruel." Aarti had tears in her eyes. "I can't take it."

"She is heavily medicated. Recuperation will be slow." Arjun finished talking about his patient.

The waiter had brought in the food orders. Hot and sour soup; American Chopsuey; Schezwan fried rice. Chinese dishes cooked the Indian way. A comfortable silence descended over the table as the three friends focused their attention on the food. It gave them an opportunity to internalize the intensity of their emotions.

None of them had much of an appetite for the food. They all refused any dessert. Unanimously.

Aarti took a small sip of green tea. "I should not have destroyed the Five Star Café that day." She said softly as if speaking to herself.

"You destroyed the Five Star Café?" Arjun's voice betrayed his indignance. "How could you?"

"Forgive me for saying all those hurtful things to you," Aarti looked Karan in the eye. "I was wrong to blame you for what was Indu's destiny."

"No one has a right to be nasty to anyone else." Arjun sounded unusually stern. "Respect for the individual is paramount. Basic human dignity."

"I should not have been so judgmental," Aarti raised her fingers in a sign of peace.

"All is fair amongst friends." Karan accepted her apology with grace.

Aarti signalled the waiter to bring them the check. "I am the only one not celebrating a birthday. Today, the treat is on me." She proffered her credit card.

****

If only I did not have to deal with my mind! If only I could switch it off, suspend all thinking, blot out the unpleasant memories? The ghost of the dead Danny continued to haunt Karan, turning his idle mind into the proverbial devil's workshop.

What was happiness? Bliss? He had never experienced it. Ever. Was such a life worth living? Death was the only certainty in this uncertain world. He was willing to embrace that certainty; but the timing was not in his hands.

Aarti and Karan met on and off, for lunch or coffee. Aarti was considering a job offer from the prestigious Indian Institute of Science. "I love teaching. But the pay is peanuts." She sounded unsure.

A US-based biotechnology company that had recently set foot in

Bangalore had made her an offer as well. For the position of research scientist in the field of Pharmacogenomics. "How gene variations affect drug responses -- that is what my research was all about. And now I will have a chance to use my findings in developing drugs and medications that may turn out to be revolutionary in saving human life." Aarti was as excited as the proverbial kid in a candy store.

"Erudite professor or hotshot globe-trotter?" Karan teased her.

"They are offering an obscene sum of money, great perks and travel abroad." Aarti joked.

"The winds of change brought about by India's liberalization."

"Seriously. What should I do?"

"Go with your gut."

"I have spent sleepless nights trying to decide. I convince myself for hours that I should take the MNC job, that such a wonderful offer may not come my way again and again, that it would be fun to travel around the world . . . while it has always been my dream to teach I am tired of living from pay check to pay check. I am pushing thirty-five . . ."

"Analysis-paralysis. If you have to convince yourself so strongly, that may not be the right option." Karan said.

Eventually Aarti rejected both offers. She needed more time to decide what she wanted to do with the rest of her life, she told Karan.

Karan revelled in this new role, that of Aarti's confidante. Her nearness was precious to him. He wanted to savour every moment, hoping to create an oasis of pleasant memories for the future.

****

August 29 1998

The month of August trudged along at a lethargic pace. Saturday morning. Karan woke up with a start when the blazing sun streamed in through the bedroom window. Maharaj had drawn the drapes apart. Ribbons of sooty dust particles floated in. The squalid odour from outside was a strange mix of petrol fumes, burning leaves and overripe mangoes fallen from the trees. The roads were unusually silent, dotted by the occasional bark of a dog, moo of a cow, honking horn of an auto.

Come to me son. Vikramaditya's son. The mysterious voice settled into a jingle inside his head. Ever since he had visited the second floor room, the jingle had become an everyday occurrence, a part of his regular routine, accompanied by an apparition that beckoned him -- the slim and tall woman in a silver taffeta ball gown with thin pink lips that met in a straight line. Having recognized the face and the dress from the white album, Karan had come to associate the voice in his head as that of Lila.

If he had not lost his gift, what colour would Lila have been? *Brown maybe? Or dirty yellow?* Two colours he abhorred the most. Was God punishing him for what had happened in the second-floor room that fateful day when Anita and Vikramaditya were both killed? He was engulfed by a sense of claustrophobic paranoia. He could take it no longer. He had to get out of the house. He wished the spectre of Lila would stop haunting him.

Minutes later Karan got into his old Fiat and backed it out of the garage, rapidly. There was a scrunching noise; he stopped the car and looked back. He had banged the car into the gate. He got out of the car and assessed the damage. The car's bumper had rusty brown scratches from the gate. The right fender light had shattered. *Fuck!* He was not used to these damned gates! Karan kicked the rusty gate open with his leg and got back into the car, racing past *ANAATHA RAKSHAKA -- THE ORPHANAGE* and *PARADE -- THE DEPARTMENT STORE* as he continued to drive in the direction of Arjun's house.

The old Fiat thudded over potholes, struggling to avoid pedestrians and bicycles, even a stray cow and a dog. Panic gripped Karan. *Bloody hell, people had no road sense over here.* He swerved the car to the middle of the narrow street a couple of times to avoid the onslaught of the oncoming scooterists and auto drivers until he had an Oops! moment. He was the one driving on the wrong side of the road. In India, right was wrong for driving. Karan veered the car toward the left edge of the road.

Soon Karan had succeeded in getting lost in the maze of roads yet another time. Déjà vu. He cursed himself. He never learned from his past mistakes. The story of his life. Exasperated, Karan stopped the car in front of a new bungalow that stood in the midst of a landscaped lawn and got out. He had to ask for directions -- as much as he hated it.

ARJUN RAO. CONSULTING PSYCHIATRIST. ST. XAVIER HOSPITAL. The name plate proclaimed that the new bungalow was Arjun's house. Karan had been looking for the old gray house of yore that had stood in one corner of the huge plot; no wonder he had not found it before though the neighbourhood had looked familiar.

A Nepali Gurkha in a khaki uniform sat perched on a stool outside the gate guarding the bungalow. There was a look of suspicion in his eyes.

Karan knew he was a mess. Soiled track pants. An old T-shirt with toothpaste and coffee stains. Bathroom slippers. Unshaven face and uncombed hair. Was the Gurkha wondering if he was one of Arjun's patients?

"Is Arjun Saab home?" Though Karan spoke in the vernacular, his western accent may have eradicated that suspicion. The Gurkha opened the gate and led him in.

The marble-floored lobby was strewn with several pairs of men's slippers. Karan walked across the lobby and stopped transfixed at the double-glass doors leading into the living room.

"*Om bhoor bhuva suvaha. Tatsa vitar varenyam bhargoho devasya deemahi . . . .*" Rows of Brahmins clad in white *dhoti*s sat on brightly coloured durries chanting Sanskrit mantras.

Arjun and his father, both clad in white *dhoti*s, their foreheads smeared with ash, sat amongst the multitude of Brahmin priests, eyes closed, chanting the mantras in perfect unison. The sunlight from the windows captured the serenity on their faces. They were so alike -- peas in a pod. Karan looked at them with wistful envy.

A huge black-and-white photograph of a young woman in her twenties whom Karan recognized as Arjun's dead mother had been placed on a low-lying table facing the white-clad men. The flickering flames of dozens of *diyas* created a halo around the face in the photograph. The air was thick with the aroma of sandalwood from the burning incense. The low table was strewn with flowers of every conceivable colour and fragrance.

It was a memorial service for Arjun's dead mother, the *Shraadh* ceremony rites performed according to the Hindu calendar, Karan realized. Then, it was his mother Lila's death anniversary too. No. Lila would never be his mother. So what if she had given birth to him? Only Anita could be his mother.

The mantras ended. The head priest began explaining the significance of the mantras in the vernacular language. "When a person dies only the body perishes. The indestructible soul leaves the dead body and joins the mass of souls. That is the meaning of becoming one with God. Birth and death are for the body. The soul can neither be born nor can it die. That is the essence of the Hindu philosophy."

Growing up, Karan had never been religious. Just like his father, Anita used to say. Unlike her. Anita would spend hours every day in the small temple, her own private *mandir*. Cleaning her favourite gods. Applying vermilion, turmeric and sandal paste. Chanting Sanskrit *shlokas* and singing soulful hymns. Doing *aarti*, the orange-red water staining the silver plates. Lighting lamps and burning camphor and incense. Offering *Prasad* -- almonds, raisins and cashew.

Karan had never acquired the knowledge to carry out the Hindu traditions. Anita and Vikramaditya were his gods. Memories and nostalgia were the prayers he offered them.

"The soul is energy," the head priest continued the discourse. "You educated people know that energy can neither be created nor destroyed. The same principle applies to the soul. The soul from a dead person becomes a part of the big pool and another portion leaves the pool to enter the body of a new born. Thus the transmigration of the soul continues."

Sound rationale. Karan turned his head to his left, catching sight of his own reflection in the full-length mirror affixed in the lobby; a grumpy old bedraggled man in an un-bathed state donning filthy clothes. How horrible. He moved away from the door and stood against the lobby wall; he did not want to be seen by the Brahmin priests clad in spotless white.

Karan could hear the continuing discourse. "What is the significance of the *Shraadh* ceremony? When a person dies not all her desires and aspirations will have been appeased. The soul will be unstable; it will try to satisfy its unfulfilled desires through the body of the person it enters. This is not good. On the day commemorating death we should chant mantras that meet the soul's desires and offer food to the poor to prevent this . . . ."

The discourse would soon be ending. Food would be served to the Brahmin priests. Karan beat a hasty retreat before he was spotted, speeding back home at breakneck speed.

****

It was a miracle Karan reached home without having an accident. He headed directly to the Five Star Café, sat square legged on the carpet and closed his eyes. The sun's rays filtered into the Café through the two small windows.

Lila had died the same day as Arjun's mother. Yet no one had ever conducted Lila's *Shraadh* ceremony. Is that why his life was such a mess? What if he sent for their family priest and have Lila's overdue *Shraadh* ceremony performed? Would Lila's hunger, thirst, and lust be sated?

Why had he not thought of this before? Karan opened his eyes and looked around. May be the magical powers just started working.

Karan immediately dispatched Maharaj to fetch Vishnu Sastry, their one time priest. In the meantime, he prepared himself to perform the rituals -- taking a hot shower, having a quick shave, donning a spotless white pajama *kurta*, applying lots of gel to hold his unruly locks in place and even trimming his grubby nails.

That day, with the assistance of Vishnu Sastry, Karan performed enough Vedic rites to make up for whatever had been denied to Lila's soul in the past thirty-six years. Vishnu Sastry's chants got louder and louder as his purse grew heavier and heavier.

Lila would no longer ruin *his* life by *her* wanderlust. Karan was convinced. He decided to top off the evening by footing the bill for a month's worth of groceries to *ANAATHA RAKSHAKA -- THE ORPHANAGE*.

Mr and Mrs Iyer, a childless couple, were the founders of the orphanage. Mr Iyer, after working for over twenty years for a public sector bank had sought voluntary retirement, applied for a government grant, and started the orphanage a few months back. The orphanage, home to a dozen or so children, was housed on rented premises, the dilapidated twin houses in the corner of the street painted bright green, yellow, and orange. The owner had recently sold out to commercial builders and demanded they vacate the house in six months' time.

"Sir, if you can rent your house to us, it will be a big favour. I know you live in the US; otherwise, I would not have asked." Mr Iyer, his face writ large with apprehension, made his plea.

Karan's mind sought a decision. His gut prompted him to agree. His head intervened. He would soon get a job. What if he proposed to Aarti? Where had that come from? Was he secretly falling in love with Aarti? Probably. What if she accepted his proposal? Possibly. Now that Lila's soul had abandoned him, nothing was impossible.

They would then have children together. Definitely. He needed the house for his family.

"I am not going back. I am here for good." Karan apologized.

"Please let me know if you ever change your mind." Mr Iyer clasped Karan's hand with clammy fingers.

Watching Mr and Mrs Iyer looking at each other dejectedly, Karan felt a trifle of shame. One day in the not so distant future, when he was well-settled in life, he would help them and make up for this lapse. His intentions were honourable; his circumstances were not permitting.

26. The More Things Change

Life goes on. One of the great realizations of adulthood is that life is pretty much monotonous and events of significance are relatively few and far between.

Karan's quest for a corporate career in India was not fruitful. He had sent his resume to several companies but no job offers were forthcoming. His trust funds were dwindling; he had started eating into the capital. All he was looking for was a fucking manager's job. With any one of those goddamn IT companies of which there was a surfeit. Hewlett-Packard. Sun Microsystems. Infosys. Wipro. Oracle. And head-hunters were a dime a dozen.

Wow! What an excellent resume!

Were they interested?

Definitely.

When would he interview?

Soon. They would get back to him when a suitable position came up.

He never heard back after that. A few days, one week, two weeks. He would try calling the head-hunter.

Oh, they took someone else. Other openings were soon going to come up. Would he be interested? With other multinational companies expected to make their foray in India.

Sure why not? And so it went.

Was there no correlation, however weak, between process and outcome? He was twice as capable as the average person by any standard. He put twice the effort needed for the average outcome. What did he get? A fraction of the average outcome if he was lucky. The negative equivalent most of the time!

Karan had intensified his job search, changed his strategy, applied to non-IT companies. Levi Strauss. GE Capital. Ogilvy and Mather. In a couple of instances he made it to an interview. From his perspective the interviews went well. He had left with his self-image intact and his confidence reinforced. Except he never heard back. Finally, he called the Head-hunters.

Yes, his interviews had gone well. One of the interviewers had liked him. They were considering others as well. They would get back to him as soon as they had made a decision. Nothing really happened after that.

Karan could never quite fathom what was missing. He had it all. Education. Confidence. Capability. Charm. Was he just not likeable? Did everyone develop a pathological aversion for him at sight?

He would never learn the untold truth. He was not part of the classic old school boy's network. He had been away from India too long for that.

His pursuits died a natural death in the course of time. *Karmanye Vaadhika Raste Maa Phaleshu Kadaachana* [Thy right is to the effort only. Not to the fruit thereof]. Karan consoled himself, quoting from *The Bhagvad Gita*. One day in the not-so-distant future, he would get what he deserved. Would that include Aarti?

****

Deepavali, the festival of lights that venerated the victory of good over evil, was fast approaching. Anita, as long as she had been alive, had celebrated the festival with characteristic élan -- an elaborate Lakshmi *pooja*, a grand feast, an open house filled with relatives and friends. The children burst crackers the whole day in their brand-new clothes, the men played cards and bet real money, the womenfolk sang *bhajan*s and performed *aarti*s to Goddess

Lakshmi -- the provider of wealth and fortune. In the evening, the house was decorated with a lakh *diyas*, adults joining the children for a scintillating display of fireworks in the garden and the revelry would continue late into the night.

Now that he was back in Bangalore, Karan desired to revive the tradition of Deepavali. His efforts to rebuild contacts, however, had met with limited success. Not all his relatives were pleased to hear from him after all those years of being out of touch -- their replies to Karan's invitation were evasive if not downright offensive. Implied but unstated, Karan was somehow responsible for the death of his parents -- his relatives had not forgotten the nasty rumours that had circulated after Anita and Vikramaditya had lost their lives in the spooky shootout. Only a handful of them accepted the invitation, though with caveats of their own.

Karan traced a few classmates from his engineering college days -- not all of them accepted unequivocally. Arjun intended to bring his father along; Aarti promised to bring her mother along. Lawyer Iyengar and Doctor Ganapati, and Karan's invitee list was complete. There would be no more than fifty people for Deepavali. Very different from the hundreds of visitors that thronged the house in the days of glory.

****

October 21 1998

Deepavali day. Six o'clock in the evening. The strings of electric lights wound around the house for the festival of lights were turned on -- there were no *diyas* to be lit. Clad in an old silk *kurta*-pajama, Karan stood at the gate waiting for his guests. The whole neighbourhood was ablaze with multitudinous firework displays. "*Diya jale diya jale . . . jaan jale . . .* [The light burns . . . the heart burns . . .]" Film music blared from loudspeakers on the road while a close-circuit TV monitor showed superstar Shahrukh Khan gyrating rustically with a bubbly girl whose dimples were deeper than his.

All kinds of marketing wars were going on in the commercial

establishments on the South Bangalore main road. Raffles. Discounts. Free gifts. Competition was fierce, marketing tactics aggressive. People of all strata of society dressed in brand-new clothes thronged the shops. To buy consumer durables and electronics -- brand-new washing machines, coloured refrigerators, Sony television sets twenty-seven inches wide. To take delight in the gifts -- stainless steel utensils, synthetic saris, brightly coloured baubles, and twinkling trinkets. The evil spell of consumerism was upward bound.

The relatives arrived sporadically. Some were genuinely pleased to see Karan; others sounded furtively gleeful that he had not reached the pinnacles of prosperity that had been predicted for him. They had all been curious to see how Karan had weathered the times. The friends he had invited arrived with their families; all had successful careers; all were married with two kids each.

Why was Karan not married yet? The universal question. Karan tried bearing its brunt with stoicism.

Adults and kids alike attacked the mounds of fireworks Karan had stacked in the veranda with great gusto. Strings of crackers went off, cracking away ceaselessly accompanied by dazzling showers of light -- the ubiquitous flowerpots -- followed by loud ear-splitting atom bombs and zooming rockets.

Eight o'clock. Karan's face lit up when Arjun arrived with Aarti and her mother Anupama. In the last three months, Karan had seen very little of Arjun, whose life was dedicated to treating his patients.

Aarti looked lovely in an indigo silk sari with multi coloured motifs, augmented by elegant jewellery -- an intricately carved gold bangle at her right wrist, delicate chandelier ear-rings that dangled amidst the short dark hair framing her triangular face, a matching choker that clasped her slender throat, a ring on every finger; a glittering *bindi* on her forehead.

Vishnu Sastry performed the Lakshmi *pooja*. Anupama and Aarti sang the customary *bhajans*. The festive dinner was catered from

Kamat Café, the popular restaurant chain in Bangalore. Karan's friends and relatives were soon caught up amongst themselves in conversations of their own, centring on their careers, material acquisitions and their children's achievements.

Watching Aarti, feeling her presence in his house, hearing the echo of her energetic voice, Karan thanked God for momentarily bringing light into his house.

Aarti was enjoying herself immensely -- gorging away on the sweets buffet -- talking and laughing animatedly with Arjun -- her twinkling eyes competing with the sparkle of her eye shadow every time she looked at Arjun. There was unmistakable chemistry there.

Eleven o'clock. All the guests had departed. Maharaj had put out all the lights. Everything went silent outside; everyone had retreated. Karan switched on the television. *Hum Saath Saath Hain*. Song and dance sequences from the latest movie on family togetherness flooded the screen.

Would Aarti ever reciprocate his love? Highly unlikely. Apparently, she was very much in love with Arjun. *Hum Saath Saath Hain*. The joint family continued to eat sweets and make merry, the members of the huge cast prancing around the expensive Film City set clad in colourful costumes. How could anyone be that happy? Karan was beset by a huge vacuum. He switched off the television.

He had not succeeded in recreating the magic of old times. The Deepavali celebration he had organized for the first time might as well be the last. He had failed in this endeavour too, like everything else in life. He would always remain an outsider here. Just like Danny. Just like Indu. None of them was designed for life within the formulaic parameters of the Indian society.

27. The More They Remain The Same

October 22 1998

The autumn morning was pleasant and breezy. Karan parked his battered old Fiat in the portico of the Agarwals' bungalow, next to the elegant Mercedes-Benz. Karan had procrastinated against the dreaded visit; he had not seen Indu after the fateful day when she was hospitalized almost three months back. Now that Indu was home -- she had been discharged a few days back -- Karan had decided to get over with it.

A fat balding man with a bulging paunch came over and gripped Karan's hand in a sweaty handshake.

"Indu has told me all about you," Bharat's demeanour was calm.

Even about our affair? Had Indu really told her husband all? About the long list of men in her life? Sunny Suri, ex-cricketer; Ramitin Diaz, ex-film star; the old stooge, her ex-boss at *GLITZ*; countless college boys; Karan Khanna, the loser.

"That you were friends at Xavier's and that you have been in the US . . . ," Bharat said.

Indu barely recognized Karan. She held his arm silently for a long time. Bharat patiently coaxed the drowsy Indu to swallow an array of coloured pills. She soon fell asleep.

Bharat and Karan sat in the drawing room watching a rerun of the French Open semi-finals on a twenty-seven inch wide screen TV. India's dynamic duo in tennis -- Mahesh Bhupathi and Leander Paes -- was playing.

The house was very quiet; the children were both in the midst of their afternoon siesta. There were pictures of them everywhere. They had both inherited Indu's once-stunning looks.

Bharat turned out to be a friendly soul. "I only hope that Zack and Tina have not inherited Indu's disorder. I do not want them to go through the same pain. My only prayers to God -- spare them and give me the pain if you have to." Bharat's bottled up emotions had found an outlet.

Karan, desperate for a dedicated distraction to forget the perennial turmoil in mind, listened with full attention.

"There are bad days and there are worse days." Bharat went on to give Karan panoramic glimpses into the world of pain that Indu inhabited.

Indu had returned home from the St. Xavier Hospital after two months of treatment. Despite the glut of prescription medicine, her mind traversed a volatile trajectory of agonizing emotions. Only the details differed from day to day.

"Pain. Pain. Pain. My sins have come back to bite me," she would shout. "Everybody in the whole world is cursing me," she would bawl. "God take me away. I cannot bear this pain. I am a witch. A bitch-witch," she would curse herself to exhaustion.

Frequently she would sing a disjointed medley of unrelated songs at the top of her voice. Tunelessly. "Pain, pain, go away. All the boys can come out and play . . . *Yeh karma hain mere karma hain . . . Kya karo Ram yeh mere karma hain . . . Itni shakti hamein dena daata . . . maa tujko mere salaam . . .* All things bright and beautiful the good God made them all."

Bharat had initially blamed himself for Indu's disorder. Arjun had invested the time and effort to explain the intricacies of paranoia schizophrenia. While this had not absolved Bharat of the guilt he was grappling with, it helped reduce the intensity. He had become very protective of Indu after witnessing her pitiable state in the aftermath of the shock treatment. He had mastered the art of handling her myriad moods and manic bouts. Lithium was helping her attain a state of nonchalance. Her life may gradually settle into an enforced monotony.

Leander Paes and Mahesh Bhupathi were on the verge of winning the French Open semi-finals. Bharat's transference was complete.

Karan's mind sunk it all in. Bharat really loved Indu; he would do anything for her. In the end, that is what mattered. A loving husband. Two lovely children. Modulated Ecstasy. Extenuated agony. Indu's life was lovely despite seeming de-lovely.

****

The same afternoon, Aarti was meeting Karan at the Atlas Centre, a thirteen-story building in downtown Bangalore. Shopping arcades populated the lower floors of Atlas Centre. A multi-cuisine restaurant had sprouted in the penthouse. The remaining floors held office spaces, mostly ten-foot square in size, all of them new and vacant.

Aarti veered Karan toward one such vacant office space on the fifth floor. She had finally decided on the future course of her career, after much deliberation in the last three months. The fateful turn of events in their friends' lives had been apocalyptic.

"Dysfunctional families are not just a western phenomenon. They are even more marginalized in a suppressive society as ours."

Aarti was to be the founder member of her own philanthropic foundation. She was negotiating for angel funding and embarking on efforts to get contributions from high profile citizens of Bangalore. Her vision spanned multiple programs based on the target population segments. Mental Health Management for working women and homemakers. Clinical counselling for students and corporate sector employees. Helpline and support groups for the GLBT community. Financial aid and social support services for single mothers.

"Noble. Ambitious." Karan said as the two of them looked

around the office space that would soon get an identity of its own.

"I have decided to give back to the world and make it a more beautiful place," Aarti concluded.

"May I propose a name?" Karan encircled Aarti in a bear hug.

Aarti disentangled herself with a smile. Karan was so predictable. Vulnerable, yet protective. Like a doting father. The epiphany had hit Aarti that morning. On waking up, when she had looked at her favourite colour Polaroid picture with her family, as she did every morning, something had changed. The little black-and-white photograph that she had glued to make the family of three complete was no longer Anand Rao, nor Siddhartha. It was Karan. She had no memory of doing it -- just like the last time when Siddhartha's photo had replaced that of her father Anand Rao. Subliminal slips.

Aha! She had found the solution to her life's problems. She had finally learned to resolve her feelings in her relationships -- lover, father, and friend. In Siddhartha, she had tried to find all of this in one man. That is why she had been hurt.

This time round she would not make the same mistake. Karan would always be one of her closest friends. Arjun was the man she loved. Confident and sexy. Strong yet sensitive. With an aura of quiet poise. Tender and alluring.

"The Clemency Foundation. Do you like the name of your new organization?" Karan was asking her as they stood in front of her to-be office.

"Arjun proposed to me yesterday -- after going back from your house." Aarti almost screamed with excitement. "I accepted."

****

The same evening. Karan and Arjun were in the poolroom of the Cantonment Club. Karan was racking the billiard balls inside the triangle.

"I have some news to share," Arjun said.

"Dude. Were you thrown out of your profession for cradle-snatching?" Karan focused his cue to strike the first striped ball.

"I got lucky. It turned out she was thirty-five claiming to be sixteen." Arjun was the perfect foil for Karan's wit.

"Did she get a sentence for masquerading?" Karan laughed.

Arjun did not join in the laughter. "I have something important to tell you."

Karan's cue stick sent the billiard balls flying into the pockets. One after the other. Effortlessly.

Arjun took a step forward and stood next to Karan. Life with Madhu had been a dream come true. She had given him a lifetime's worth of love in those few months. After her death, he had not yearned for another woman. Until Aarti had come into his life and changed his involuntary resolve. The consummate woman. The oscillation of their souls was synchronistic. Inner harmony.

"You are dying of cancer and have willed away everything you own to me, your only buddy . . . ." Karan looked up at Arjun.

"Keep fantasizing."

"Aarti and you have decided to get married."

"How do you know?" Arjun was bewildered.

"You are a lucky man. Aarti has chosen you." Karan talked rapidly. Too rapidly. He stooped back down and concentrated his attention back on the last striped ball.

It was then that Arjun had his epiphany. "You are in love with Aarti. Aren't you?" He stooped down so his eyes were level with Karan.

"Love is a beautiful experience." Karan missed his strike. "Aarti is my friend. You are my friend. I love you both."

"Tell me the truth."

"Love does not mean I have to possess her, marry her, and be with her all my life. I want her to be happy." Karan handed over the cue to Arjun and stood up straight.

Arjun felt the pangs of Karan's sorrow tear through his own body as he held the cue vertically in his hand. Life had always betrayed Karan. He wished he could make up for it somehow.

"I know she will be happy with you -- she has chosen you." Karan's eyes were shining.

"Today you have really lived up to your namesake. *Daana Veera Shoora Karna.*" Arjun dropped the cue onto the pool table, scattering the remaining balls.

"The more things change, the more they remain the same." Karan engulfed Arjun in a tight hug.

Arjun wiped a tear from his eye. Karan's nobility had touched his soul. Always the giver. Never the receiver.

Karan walked over to the bar, grabbed a bottle of champagne, and popped it open. "Hear! Hear! Hear! Dr Arjun Rao, the most eligible bachelor in town, is relinquishing that title today . . . ." His voice was drowned out by the applause that emanated from the crowd.

All around, people were congratulating him. Arjun accepted their wishes with grace and sipped his champagne.

****

The night was clear. The moon was in full bloom. Karan drove home from the club his mind clouded in gloom.

His heart had dropped to the depths of an abyss. Did he have to go through it again? He had no choice. Why o why did this happen to him? Love, pain and disappointment? Was he not destined to get love?

The car slowly moved along the broad boulevards of South Bangalore with the rose garden dividers.

If he stopped chasing love, would love find him then? What if nothing changed? A blur of bleak monotonous days for the rest of his life.

Karan took the last turn into his neighbourhood and braked the car; he had remembered that he needed to pay Maharaj his weekly allowance. He parked the Fiat on the left side of the road and approached the Citibank ATM near the entrance of *PARADE -- THE DEPARTMENT STORE.*

Some people get what they want in life. Others have to make do with what they get. What had he really gotten out of life? Was there a meaning to this farcical existence? This meandering journey from one torment to another? Maybe there was. In God's scheme of things. He would have to find out what it was.

Waiting for the ATM to dispense crisp notes, a fluorescent banner caught Karan's eye. *24-Hour Surfing.* An Internet café had opened shop on the second floor of *PARADE.* Karan pocketed the cash and slowly walked back toward the car.

He always secondarized his own interests to that of others and consequently did not take the right action. Aarti, Arjun, Indu . . . they had all gone after what *they* wanted. They had been prepared to pay the price demanded of them. Even Danny.

Karan stood looking at the gaudily painted twin tenements opposite the department store as he fingered his pockets for the car key. *ANAATHA RAKSHAKA -- THE ORPHANAGE.* The obsequious faces of Mr and Mrs Iyer came to his mind. He had met them on the day he had performed Lila's *Shraadh* ceremony and ordered groceries for feeding the orphanage kids.

Danny. Dolly. The two people in the world who had offered him unconditional love. He had failed them both badly. In different ways. It was too late to make amends for what had happened with

Danny; but he still stood a chance with Dolly. Years down the line, he did not want to face a fresh bout of regret that he had irrevocably lost Dolly. If he did not set right his folly somehow -- the series of mishaps in his life may never end.

One of the windows of the orphanage was open. Karan thought he saw the face of a little boy peering at him. Soon a little girl had joined him. Was it not past their bedtime? Karan looked at his watch. Half past nine. When he looked up again the faces were gone. The room was in darkness.

Wait a minute; was that a flash of orange? It would be nine in the morning in LA. He wondered what Dolly would be doing. Would she have been enrolled in day care? He had to ensure she was safe with Troy. Or find a way to get her back. He had made it easy, very easy, for Troy to walk away with Dolly.

Karan crossed the street, opened the gate to the orphanage, walked up the few steps, and knocked on the green door illuminated by a single naked bulb hanging from the awning above.

Mr Iyer opened the door and switched on a bright fluorescent light in the veranda. "I knew you would come." Pointing to a fake brown leather sofa, he invited Karan to sit down.

Mrs Iyer stood near the curtained door that connected the veranda to the rest of the house.

Karan remained standing. "You can use my house for your orphanage." He hoped that the one noble gesture he was making this day would have the power to influence the future course of his life in some positive way. What goes around comes around.

"You are a good man." Mr Iyer adjusted his falling *dhoti*. "Thank you. Thank you. Thank you."

"You can move in by the first of December."

"We are poor people. How much rent should we pay, Sir?" Mr Iyer, the eternal accountant, folded up the ends of his *dhoti* in an act of fortification against future slips.

"You don't have to pay me any rent."

"Free! Such a big house! Market rent will be . . ." Mr Iyer's mathematical mind went into calculation mode.

"My lawyer will draw up a lease agreement for a nominal sum of one rupee per month."

"I was getting worried, Sir. We have to vacate this place by the end of the year. We have not found another place." Mr Iyer continued to unburden.

Mrs Iyer disappeared into the house.

"You will be responsible for paying utilities and maintenance bills." Karan said with a hint of impatience. "I expect you to keep the house clean and not damage it in any way."

"Going back to your country, Sir?" Mr Iyer flashed his entire set of yellowing teeth.

"*This* is my country." Karan shook his head in a subtle gesture of reprimand.

"You have come like God." Mrs Iyer reappeared in the veranda holding a large silver plate filled with vermilion-stained water.

Nothing in his life had prepared Karan for what happened next. Mr and Mrs Iyer vigorously rotated the vermilion water-filled plate in front of his face -- they were performing an *aarti*. By the time, Karan held up his hand to object, the brief ritual was over.

Mrs Iyer dipped her right thumb in the plate and put a wet vermilion *tilak* prominently on Karan's forehead.

"You are *Daana Veera Shoora Karna* Sir." Declared Mr Iyer as both husband and wife knelt at Karan's feet -- their hands folded, their heads bowed down with reverence.

"You should not have done this," Karan stepped back. "I am a mere mortal."

Daana Veera Shoora Karna. Twice in one day. He was not noble. He did not deserve such a lofty epithet. Karan bid them a hasty goodbye and walked back into the moonlit night.

What did the US law say on adoption practices? He had papers signed by Sharon's parents. Why had he not thought of that before? He had to find the answers to his questions. He had to find a lawyer, understand his rights, and if necessary, fight his case and regain custody of Dolly. He had to act quickly, find a way to protect her.

A fleeting dash of orange. Or was that violet? He walked past his parked car, through the open door of *PARADE,* and climbed up the flight of stairs leading to the Internet café.

Nothing was forever. Not even failure. One day in the not so distant future, he would find success.

Karan spent the rest of the night surfing the Internet, researching what the US laws said on adoption and short-listing LA-based lawyers he could approach. He had taken the first big step in his quest for self-redemption.

28. Full Circle

November 16 1998

In life, one gets what one deserves, not what one negotiates. Thirty-six is an age when a lot people have either made it in life or know where they are headed and working toward making it. Is it the age to start all over again?

The Cathay-Pacific flight was ready to take off from the Indian soil in the wee hours of the morning. Karan sat at a window seat near the middle of the aircraft. He was on his way to Los Angeles via Hong Kong.

Karan's mind caught fleeting snapshots of things that could have been, things that would never be. Aarti would never learn of his true feelings for her. He felt no regret. Memories of those few days would live with him forever. Nobody could take that away.

The flight attendants were giving safety instructions, demonstrating the use of oxygen masks.

Arjun and Aarti had been engaged the previous evening. A simple Hindu ceremony and a banquet style dinner. It made Karan happy to see Aarti happy, to see Arjun happy . . . The same happiness caused his heart to ache too. He wanted to be with them, share their happiness. He wanted to disappear, stop hurting himself. The heart knows no reason, just the rhyme.

The flight was taking off, gaining in altitude. Karan looked at the glittering city lights as they started to reduce in size to tinier and tinier specks.

The clouds stretched out infinitely through the window. Aarti was waving from a cloud, glittering diamonds swinging delicately from her ears, ethereal in a peacock blue sari and adorned with an assortment of necklaces and bracelets studded with gems of every colour -- pearl, onyx, ruby, coral, topaz, opal, emerald, sapphire, amethyst. *Aarti was green. A pleasant aquamarine green. Soothing and serene.* Her glowing eyes were shiny with unshed tears. If Karan tried extending his hand out of the window, he would have touched her.

The ascent was over. "Electronic devices may be used as soon as the seat belt sign is switched off . . ." The flight attendant was making the announcement.

Arjun had joined Aarti on the cloud. He was waving at Karan. *Arjun was blue. Cobalt blue. A rich Prussian blue.* On and off -- *teal and turquoise. Green and Blue. Arjun and Aarti were aquamarine.* Tranquil and thrilling.

Good God! Nothing was colourless anymore. His gift had been restored! Karan closed the window and reclined the seat back.

Amongst the ashes of despair glimmered embers of hope.

Afterword: Daana Veera Shoora Karna

Karna is a key character from the great Hindu epic Mahabharata who is known for his extreme benevolence. The story of Karna is the supreme paradox. Of Victory in Defeat. (The name Karan is a regional variation of Karna.)

Karna's destiny was sealed at birth -- when he was born to an unwed mother. Princess Kunti had chosen to test the veracity of the boon she had been granted, chanted the mantra that had evoked her union with Surya, The Sun God and given birth to Karna -- the Sun's son. Fearing societal stigma she set the cherub afloat on a lotus leaf. All his life Karna had to withstand the worst of this impulsive misdemeanour.

Karna was blessed at birth. He was born with the divine armour and ear studs that made him invincible -- *Kavacha* and *Kundala* -- as long as they remained on his body.

Karna was cursed in boyhood. By his revered Guru, the sage Parashurama, that despite being the best archer of his times his bravery would not save him from defeat at the most crucial hour of his life. Root Cause? His endurance power. His faux pas? Lies. Deceit. In his eagerness to master the scriptures -- the Vedas and the Upanishads -- Karna had joined Parashurama's ashram by pretending to be a devout Brahmin boy. Once when his Guru was asleep with his head on Karna's lap, an insect started to bite his thigh. Not intending to wake him, Karna had clenched his teeth and endured the intolerable pain, unaware that the oozing blood would grow from a slow trickle to a warm stream, awaken his Guru and unwittingly reveal his secret -- no Brahmin boy could have tolerated such intense physical pain for such a long time.

Karna was humiliated in his youth. In public. By the great sage

Dronacharya, the Master Archer. For wanting to show his skills in an archery contest for the most valiant princes. Despite the blue Kshatriya blood that flowed through his veins, he was a pariah amongst other kings and princes, the true *Kshatriyas* -- the valiant warrior class -- for not possessing recognizable credentials. He was recognized as the *soota putra* -- the son a of the low caste charioteer couple that had found him on the floating leaf, adopted him and brought him up as their own son.

Karna was a born loser. Unlucky in love. He was not allowed to be a contender at Draupadi's *Swayamvara*. Else, Arjuna would not have won Draupadi's hand in marriage by his show of skills and then shared her with his four brothers in reverence to Kunti's inadvertent advice. Karna never became aware that he was the only man Draupadi had lusted after even if only for a moment.

Karna was the epitome of nobility and valour -- *Daana Veera Shoora* -- that was exploited even by Indra, the king of Gods, at the most crucial hour of his life, by asking him for the *Kavacha* and *Kundala* that made him invincible, leaving him susceptible to defeat and death.

His sin? Undeniable loyalty. To his friend Duryodhana, the epitome of wickedness -- the one and only Kshatriya King who deigned to redeem Karna's humiliation. In public. By bestowing the gift of the kingdom of Anga, elevating his status from *Soota Putra* to *Anga Raja* in an instant. Always treating him as an equal.

Karna was the master of his own fate, forever making hard choices. Like refusing his mother Kunti's offer to make him the King of Hastinapura, his undeniable birthright. Reason? The price he had to pay -- of having to fight the war against his only friend -- the wicked Duryodhana.

Eventually Karna succumbed to death and defeat at the hands of Arjuna, his own brother. Only because of his earlier act of magnanimity -- giving away his *Kavacha* and *Kundala* -- which would have otherwise maintained him invincible.

Had Karna not died the world would have ended. The Bhagvad Gita is testament to this fact.

Glossary

Aarti. An auspicious ritual

Abba Jaan. Father

Abhi isi waqt. Now, at this very moment

Adda. Favorite hangout place

Aloo paratha. Bread stuffed with potato

Antakshari. A song based game

Appa. Father

Arrey! Oh!

Bachaoed. Saved

Badam. Almond

Bakra. Literally, lamb. Colloquially, Gullible fool

Behanji. Literally, sister. Pejoratively, a dowdy-looking girl

Beta. son

Bhairavi Raag. Set of notes in Hindustani classical music, with sombre overtones

Bidaai. Farewell

Bindi. Forehead decoration worn by Indian women

Bisi bele bath. A rice and lentil dish garnished with curry spices

By-two coffee. A single order of coffee shared by two people

Carrom. Table top game sometimes known as Indian finger billiards

Carrot *halwa.* Indian pudding

Cassata. Similar to Neapolitan ice cream

Chaddis. Old-fashioned underwear

Crore. Equals 10 million

Dahi vada. Lentil based snack dipped in yogurt

Deewana. Mad person

Desi(s). Colloquial for person(s) from India living in the US

Dhoti-vastram. Ethnic dress worn by men in South India

Divan. Sofa without back and without arms

Diya(s). Small lamp(s) used for auspicious occasions

Dramebaaz. A melodramatic person (colloquial)

Dum maaro dum. Popular hippie song from the seventies on the euphoric spell of smoking pot

Dum. Courage. Can also mean "puff of smoke" when used colloquially

Dusshera.Ten-day long festival during October

Funda. Short for fundamental

Gayatri mantra, a highly revered Sanskrit hymn for Hindus, found in the Vedas

Ghagra-choli. Long flowing North Indian skirt and blouse ensemble

Goras. Colloquial for white people

Gulab jamoon. Flour-based Indian dessert immersed in sugar syrup

Gulal. Colored water

Gurkha. Security guard

Hanuman Chalisa. A set of hymns evoking Lord Hanuman; prayer chanted for courage

Havan. Sacred fire

Havelis. Old-fashioned palatial houses

Idli. Vada. Sambar. Lentil puffs, lentil doughnuts, and a spicy liquid curry

Janta. Colloquial for general public

Jodi. Pair or Couple

Kaash. If Only

Kashmiri pulao. Rice dish garnished with vegetables and exotic spices

Kheer. Milk-based dessert

Lakh. Equals one hundred thousand

Lamhe. Moments

Lassi. Yogurt-based shake

Ludo. Board game based on the roll of dice

Lungi. Ethnic garment worn by men at the torso to cover the lower half of their body

Maami. Aunt

Malai kofta. Cheese and vegetables in gravy

Mandir. Temple

Masala dosa. Lentil pancake with spicy vegetable stuffing

Masala Papad. Lentil wafer topped with nuts, crunchy vegetables and spices

MCP. Popular acronym of the times standing for Male Chauvinist Pig

Mehndi. A temporary ethnic tattoo -- part of a popular ritual at weddings

Mera puraana hero. My dear old hero

Mills & Boon. Popular romance novels

Mishti doi. Yogurt-based dessert

MNC. Multi-national company

Moda. Ethnic stool

Mubarak. Congratulations

Mysorean. Belonging to Mysore

Naan. Bread baked on a clay oven

Nada. Drawstring

Nadaswaram. Trumpet

Nimbu paani. Lemonade

NRI. Non-resident Indian

Paagal. Mad person

Paan. Betel leaf

Page 3. A-list events with celebrities that get featured on the third page of the local newspapers

Pakoras. Savory snack

Pallu. Loose end of the sari

Pathan suit. Ethnic suit worn by men

Patidev. Husband (archaic)

Pitaji. Father: respectful way of addressing

Pooja room. Prayer room

Prasad. Sacred offering

Puri-saagu. Fried Indian bread and exotic curry combination

Raam. Raam. Oh God

Rasam. Spicy lentil based soup

Roomali roti. Thinly rolled bread

Rosogollas. Dessert made of cottage cheese

RTO. Regional Transport Office, the government agency that issues driver licenses

Saab. Hindi term for Sir

Saali. Slang term of address

Saasuma. Mother-in-law (colloquial)

Saat Phere. The seven steps

Shanti. Peace

Shlokas. Sacred verses

Shukriya. Thank you

Sindoor. Vermilion powder

Tabla. Indian version of the drums

Tamasha. Dramatic scene

Thali. Plate

Tilak. An auspicious mark on the forehead

VIP. A premium brand of men's underwear

Yaman Kalyani Raag. Set of notes in Hindustani classical music

Zari. Gold thread embroidery

About the Author

Born and bred in idyllic Bangalore, Jayant lives in scenic Seattle. He holds an MBA from The Indian Institute of Management-Bangalore and has donned different professional hats over the past twenty years -- Corporate Trainer, Management Consultant, Technology Manager, Financial Planner, and Faculty at Business Schools.

An avid reader since childhood, Jayant was always enamoured by the power of the written word and the intricacies of the English language. While he had several stories going on in his head and penned some of them partially on paper, the real impetus to heed his calling and practice his passion came in the form of Vikram Seth's *A Suitable Boy*, which he happened to read while immigrating to the US. That is how *Colours in the Spectrum* was born. Thereafter, Jayant completed the Certificate Program in Literary Fiction at the University of Washington.

Jayant has compiled and edited two non-fiction publications -- anthologies of true incidents from the life of a gifted humanitarian, ever since. An inveterate film fan, he has written the script for a full-length feature film and is optimistic of finding serious takers. He has also begun work on his next novel, tentatively titled *Family Secrets*.

In his free time, Jayant volunteers with several professional organizations in the Seattle area. He is a member of the Board of Directors of IIM Americas -- an alumni association of premier B-schools. His wife Vidhya is a Human Resources professional and a dilettante marathon runner.